BURNING STATE

ROB SINCLAIR

Boldwood

First published in Great Britain in 2025 by Boldwood Books Ltd.

Copyright © Rob Sinclair, 2025

Cover Design by Head Design Ltd

Cover Images: Colin Thomas and iStock

A CIP catalogue record for this book is available from the British Library.

Paperback ISBN 978-1-83703-203-7

Large Print ISBN 978-1-83703-202-0

Hardback ISBN 978-1-83703-201-3

Trade Paperback ISBN 978-1-80656-129-2

Ebook ISBN 978-1-83703-204-4

Kindle ISBN 978-1-83703-205-1

Audio CD ISBN 978-1-83703-196-2

MP3 CD ISBN 978-1-83703-197-9

Digital audio download ISBN 978-1-83703-199-3

This book is printed on certified sustainable paper. Boldwood Books is dedicated to putting sustainability at the heart of our business. For more information please visit https://www.boldwoodbooks.com/about-us/sustainability/

Boldwood Books Ltd, 23 Bowerdean Street, London, SW6 3TN

www.boldwoodbooks.com

PROLOGUE

THE MIDDLE EAST – SEVERAL YEARS AGO

The heavy gunfire and explosions continued outside on the ground five stories below. He stooped low by the blown-out window in what would have been a living area of a modest family apartment. Thick dust now covered what remained of identifiable belongings and furniture, this whole area having been caught up in the fierce and deadly fighting several weeks ago. Several weeks of bombardment, from the air, from the ground, from inside the damn building itself, judging by the lines of bullet holes he'd seen on interior walls.

Several weeks of bloodshed and a mounting death toll, of mainly civilians.

Given the barrage, it surprised him that the building remained standing at all. That any building around here still stood. That any people around here – non-combatants in particular – were still alive.

But they were.

He turned his head to look at the group of four huddled in the corner, on their haunches. Man. Woman. Girl. Boy. Their petrified faces, their messy clothing, spatters of blood – most of it not theirs – told a lot of their story.

'For Christ's sake, can anyone hear me!' he shouted into the mic on his lapel. 'I have Echo. He's still alive. I need an extraction. Rooftop.' He rattled off the coordinates. Again. 'And tell those goddamn idiots to stop firing on us!'

As the words left his lips a momentary pause came in the fighting outside, an eerie hush hanging in the smoke- and debris-filled air. He locked eyes with the girl. Her fear bore into him, as though trying to tell him, to warn him, to cry out to him...

He slowly, silently lifted his body up a few inches to look over the windowsill, down below...

Thwack.

The bullet sank into his shoulder and he threw himself back and to the floor, grimacing in pain. The four in the corner shouted in panic.

'Arghh!' he roared, pulling himself back up. 'Will somebody fucking—'

The explosion cut short whatever expletive-laden demand he'd been about to make to what was left of his team. He had no clue from which direction the blast had originated, or if it'd been a projectile, a bomb-drop or even just some IED in their vicinity.

What he did know: he was falling, crashing down amid concrete and broken wood and twisted metal. Thud. Fall. Thud. Fall. His body was batted around, tumbling over and over, until he came to a stop on a crumpled heap of rubble. He coughed out blood and grit. The dust and smoke around him slowly cleared as he fought to stay in the world of the living.

Shooting. Shouting. Heightened again now.

Screams too.

He tried to lift his body. Couldn't. He did nothing but squeeze his eyes shut pathetically as a beam of concrete thudded down onto his right foot.

He yelled in pain again. Tried once more to move. Again failed.

Shooting. Screaming.

He looked up. The building still stood around him. Kind of. The floors had given out. One. Two. Three.

He barely even reacted at another explosion nearby and his eyes and mouth and nose filled with charred debris once more. He coughed, spluttered, rubbed at his face with his one free hand, tried to battle through disorientation.

Shooting. Screaming.

Screaming. Louder than the shooting now.

He twisted his head. Not far, really. As much as he could. Couldn't even figure if his body was pinned or numb or... just not entirely connected.

He found a pair of eyes. The girl's. Not even two feet from him. It was her screaming that filled his head. A bed of concrete sat on top of her, only her head and left shoulder sticking out from underneath, her face streaked with black grit and blood and horrifying fear.

'Papa!' she screamed.

Papa. Her papa. Echo.

His gaze moved across to her right. No eyes staring back at him there. Just a mangled, lifeless body.

Screaming. Screaming.

Not just the little girl, he realized, but a woman too.

He couldn't see her. Just hear her. Hear them both. Their calls of anguish becoming more panicked, more pained if that were even possible.

No. Not just their screams. Something else too was taking over...

Hissing.

Crackling.

Fire.

Within seconds the flames were leaping around him, licking closer and closer. Initially the woman's screams became louder still, but mere seconds later and they'd been drowned out by the roar of the flames.

He found the girl's eyes again. No screams from her now. Just a dejected pleading, pain-filled, as the flames engulfed her tiny, trapped body.

He roared with effort as he tried to pull his leg free.

He finally managed it. But not before the fire had surrounded him too. He thought he was yelling but he really couldn't tell anymore. He tried to breathe but only sucked in the supercharged air, feeling like his insides were burning out.

Unimaginable pain swept over his body, every inch of him alight, clothes disintegrated, skin bubbling and sizzling.

Nothing at all he could do to stop it.

Nothing at all he could do except to close his eyes and will for it to end.

1

ATLANTA, GEORGIA – PRESENT DAY

I'd parked the van on the corner of Piedmont Avenue and Ellis Street. About half a mile from the building I didn't need to go into today. How times had changed for a mission like this.

I didn't need to go into the building. Although I did still need to access it.

Which explained why I was sitting in the back of the van at my homemade computer rig – two machines, three screens total that I used to control and watch my little army at work. Drones. Six of them. Five were set to automated routes, traveling back and forth right underneath me. Most of the multi-mile sewer network beneath Atlanta's downtown was inaccessible to people, the pipes being too narrow. Unlike the gargantuan brick-walled tunnels seen in movies, like the nest where the Penguin famously hid with his minions and led his destruction in Gotham City, the majority of real city sewer networks were simple pipes, put through the ground beneath buildings using boring techniques. Eight inches, twelve inches... Some of the larger connections could be up to thirty-six inches in diameter.

Definitely too small for a person, unless they literally

wanted to crawl through shit, although even then the risk of drowning in the flow would be stupidly high.

Well, unless you understood the system properly.

Like the three-foot diameter pipe that led right underneath the van, heading west underneath Ellis Street. Right now, with virtually zero rainfall over the Atlanta area for the best part of five weeks, the stormwater run-off was a trickle rather than a surge. Barely three inches of water steadily moving along. Plenty of space above it to run the five drones.

Back and forth. Back and forth. Four trips, four pick-ups and drop-offs for each unit.

And soon enough that task was complete.

But not before I'd already made progress with drone number six. Errol. A little different to the other five. A little more advanced, despite his smaller size. I didn't give all the machines a pet name, but Errol deserved his personification given his more prominent role. Stupid, perhaps, but the sad truth was these machines were more reliable, more loyal than people, and it felt like a little reward for Errol, in a strange way. An acknowledgment of his value to me.

Errol was already inside the building. He'd initially traveled through the sewers too but had then been able to move from below ground to above ground because of the opened hatch.

OK, so that opened hatch, and one opened door, and one removed grille vent had been a key part to this whole setup, and had to be performed by an actual human being.

That actual human being was Dominic Von Hausen, a disgruntled maintenance employee who'd only recently overcome a frivolous sexual assault allegation from a female office worker, and, knowing he was getting back at his employer, had happily taken $2000 from me, few questions asked, for performing those three simple tasks.

Perhaps he'd come to regret his part, if he or anyone else connected the dots.

Or perhaps Dominic would suffer a terrible accident in the not-too-distant future...

I watched the left screen intently as I worked the joystick. Errol climbed and climbed, moving up through the air duct system.

It was true that most big city sewer systems were unlike those seen in the movies. In contrast, big office building air heating and cooling systems were often exactly like they were portrayed in movies. Intertwining networks of metals shafts ran between walls, between floors. Big enough for a human? Yeah, probably. But why the hell bother crawling around when Errol was so much more adept than me or anyone else at moving through these tight spaces?

Twenty-third floor. East side.

I brought Errol to a stop on the floor of the shaft, the camera looking out through the space where the grille had been removed and into the room beyond. Not a particularly big room. A functional room with several hefty server towers, fans whirring, lights twinkling, wires crisscrossed all over the place.

Not the only server room in this huge building. The main one sat on the lower ground level. This one, high up, had a more specific use.

I turned on Errol's thermal camera. The screen turned almost entirely ice-blue. Cold. Just the way the servers liked it. No sign of any orange, red. No people.

I pushed the joystick up a little and Errol took off once more, into the room, along the line of servers. I hit the keyboard to engage the command to keep Errol hovering on the spot and worked the little arm under his belly. Out it came, the 'hand' my view on the screen. I moved it forward tentatively, carefully, toward the port on the server. It reminded me of sci-fi movies I'd seen where spacecraft were docking against much larger space stations. Except this was all on a much more miniature scale, even if it filled the screen I was looking at.

The ports connected and I could almost feel the whir of the hard drive on my computer suddenly engage as the software spun at whirlwind speed, hacking through the security measures to gain access...

Green light.

It'd taken all of thirty seconds.

The time bar appeared on the middle screen as the data dump started, not into Errol but wirelessly into secure cloud storage. The modern way.

Five minutes to go.

At two minutes twelve seconds I heard a siren close by outside and tensed just a little. It wasn't really unusual to hear such activity in a big city like this, though. Not least in this part of the city where this morning, just like several mornings over the past few weeks, there was yet another 'protest' taking place, orchestrated by one of several far-right factions that had grown in power and significance recently.

But that protest was two blocks away, and even if the event had turned ugly, like many did, the siren shouldn't have been passing right by here...

Except the noise was growing louder, coming closer.

I left the terminal and moved to the back of the van and opened the door ever so slowly to see a police cruiser parked right behind me, lights flashing, the officer out of his car and glaring.

'No parking here – you're blocking the intersection.'

I pushed the door open a little further to reveal myself, although I kept my cap pulled low over my forehead so he could see little of my face. Well, not my face, but the latex mask I was wearing.

'My guy's down below,' I said, indicating the open manhole cover. 'You want me to move the van and have him decapitated the moment he steps up?'

The officer said nothing to that but kind of squinted and cocked his head a little as though trying to figure what he was looking at. He took a step forward, fingers hovering toward his sidearm.

But the guy had no point to make here. The van was legit. Kind of. I'd stolen it and I knew it hadn't been reported yet because the two men I'd stolen it from were a little tied up right now. And I'd properly marked out the area around the van with cones and a sign.

'We'll be done in a few minutes,' I said.

Except the officer didn't look convinced. Maybe he hadn't just stopped on the off chance.

Had someone tipped him off?

But who the hell could have done?

The officer took another step forward.

Beep... Beep... Beep...

The final countdown sounded out from behind me.

Only seconds to go.

The main reason why I was perfectly relaxed, even with the dubious-faced lawman in front of me. The officer's head cocked even further at the sound from my van, like a confused dog, as though the tilting of his head would help him to understand the situation better.

Whether it did or it didn't, time was up.

The explosion a half mile behind me caused the ground to shudder and rumble. The roar of the explosion got louder and louder for a few seconds before the blast wave swept over us.

'Holy shit,' the officer shouted out, cowering as he held his hat to his head.

Then the guy rushed back to his car and sped off, just like that.

The immediate calmness after the explosion, as people's brains scrambled for an explanation, didn't last long. Panic soon took over. Cars revved, people rushed about shouting and screaming. Sirens blared. Alarms too.

I closed the van doors and sat back down at the terminal. Errol was done, but I'd wanted to have him out of there before the explosion. I just had to hope the vents were intact enough to retrieve him in the... ninety-six seconds I had left before the second explosion.

'Come on!' I willed as Errol whizzed back through the air ducts, fighting through smoke and dust, which thickened as he descended.

Crap. A blockage. The duct had caved in. No way around it. I swung the little device out through a hole in the vent wall and into... an office. I spun Errol around and around. People were there. Some on their feet, panicking; others dazed, looking bewildered, some unmoving.

One of them, a suited man, fixed his gaze on Errol. Then cowered as Errol sped toward him. But it wasn't the man I was aiming Errol for but the blown-out window.

Out into the open. Not the intention. But the only way now. With the homing set I left the terminal and pushed open the doors and jumped down to the chaos outside. I pulled on the manhole cover to clank it back into place. Then I grabbed the cones and the sign and slung them into the back of the van.

I was about to jump up inside when I realized a woman was standing right there on the sidewalk, staring at me.

I held her eye a moment. Noted the disturbed look on her

face as she tried to figure out what she was looking at. A look I received all too often. It didn't bother me anymore. In some ways I relished it.

I simply shrugged at her. Because I knew what was coming. And she didn't.

Boom.

The second explosion was bigger than the first. More devastating. I was inside the van already before the blast wave hit. I'd slid into the driver's seat seconds later while the street sat in that same lull as before. The calm before the sheer panic.

Through the calm I heard Errol's gentle whir. I wound down the window and looked up, and reached out and plucked my little friend from the sky.

I smiled as I put the star of the show onto the passenger seat next to me. Then I fired up the engine and glanced into the side mirror. No sign of that woman now. That police officer was long gone too. Whatever suspicions those two had held, seeing me would hardly be the first thing they remembered about this morning.

And if at some point they did...

It didn't even matter that much.

This mission was completed. A success.

'Sorry about your brothers,' I said to Errol. Thanks to the little interlude with the policeman, I hadn't sent them on their return trip. The explosions would have torn them apart. 'They died a good death.'

Like so many of my team members had over the years.

I swung the van around and headed away.

2

BARCELONA, SPAIN

Another beautifully sunny spring day in the Catalan capital, with not a wisp of white in the sky. The sunglasses and cap James Ryker wore helped shield him from the intense rays from his position facing south toward the monolithic Camp Nou stadium, home of FC Barcelona. The recently renovated stadium could hold 105,000 people. Right now it was packed out, the non-stop chorus of chants and cheers and boos reverberating around Ryker 200 yards away.

He checked his watch. Not that he needed to, really. He had a good read of the time.

Late. Definitely late.

'Is this guy ever going to show?' came Xavi's voice through Ryker's earpiece.

Ryker simply kept his eyes on the entrance to the eight-story apartment block across the road.

A lull in the crowd noise from the stadium... then thunderous uproar.

'They scored again,' Xavi said.

Ryker checked his watch once more. Nothing but habit now.

'And there's only a few minutes of the game left,' he said.

'Which means pretty soon you'll have a hundred thousand people battling around you.'

'At least they'll be in a good mood,' Ryker said.

'Yeah, well I'm not. I hate Barcelona.'

'The place or the team?'

'Both, actually.'

'Spoken like a true Madrileño,' Ryker said, smiling, but a moment later he stiffened when he saw the man coming out of the apartment block. Not just any man: their mark, Rafael Ospina.

'I see him,' Ryker said. Xavi wouldn't be able to – he was two miles away at their mark's intended rendezvous spot.

'Carrying anything?'

'He's wearing a Barça shirt.'

'But is he carrying anything?'

'Yeah. Backpack.'

'OK. He must have it in there. Is he going north?'

Which would be directly toward Ryker, initially, and on to the bus stop for the route that would take him exactly where he needed to be.

If he was taking public transport, at least. If he had a vehicle, then Ryker would hop on to the moped he'd brought here earlier. Not a powerful machine by any stretch, but about the best way to travel through a congested city.

'No,' Ryker said. 'He's going south. On foot.'

Which was about the least expected route. And it also gave Ryker a dilemma as to whether to follow on foot too.

A satisfied roar filled the air around Ryker.

'And the game's just finished.'

'He planned this. And with his Barça shirt? He's gonna be lost in a sea of blue and red.'

Which was exactly what Ryker thought too as he peeled away from his spot – no choice now but to head after Ospina on foot.

'Did he make you?' Xavi asked.

'No,' Ryker said, about as sure as he could be.

'Then why is he heading south?'

Ryker didn't answer. He had no answer.

'Stay on him,' Xavi said. 'Do not spook him.'

Ryker said nothing to that either. As if he needed to be schooled on such things, especially by a man some fifteen years his junior. But while Ryker was in this city on this assignment, he was working with Xavi, an agent for Spain's CNI – the Centro Nacional de Inteligencia – which handled both foreign and domestic intelligence. Ryker preferred to work alone – always – because when things went off-plan, as they very often did one way or another in his world, he needed to know the other people around him were on his wavelength.

So far he didn't know enough about Xavi and what he'd do if their plan here turned to shit.

Perhaps he'd find out sooner, rather than later, Ryker mused.

Within a few yards the crowds were already building, the first to leave the stadium moving quickly to escape the masses and be first to wherever they were going. Not even thirty seconds later and the street around him was packed as tens of thousands of jubilant fans poured out, singing, bouncing, waving flags and setting off flares. And all moving in different directions, which only added to the congestion as several waves butted up against one another creating bottlenecks all around.

Ryker, trying to outpace the flow moving south, pushed and shoved and did his best to keep on top of Ospina, but his mark was several inches shorter, slighter, and perhaps wearing the fan-gear really did help Ospina too, because after a few accidental shoulder barges Ryker could sense a rise in disgruntlement in the people around him, as though they knew he didn't belong.

He bobbed up on his toes, trying to keep Ospina in sight but the guy had pulled away some, now close to fifty yards in front of Ryker as they approached a huge bottleneck where the crowd intersected a major road. The masses slowed almost to a stop. Ryker continued to push his way through, as carefully as he could.

Not carefully enough.

Someone shouted out at him, shoved him in the back. Straight into the path of the man in front who spun around, angry glare on his face. Two men, shouting and gesticulating at him.

'Lo siento. Lo siento,' Ryker said to each of them in turn.

'Bet you wish you had the Barca shirt now,' Xavi said joyfully.

Ryker only grunted in response before he took another heavy shoulder from a man to his right. A shouted expletive followed and Ryker was about to turn to offer another apology before he realized he'd lost sight of Ospina beyond a row of parked police vans.

He bobbed on his feet again as though the added height would give him a better view. It barely did.

'I've lost him. I think he took the left onto Avenida de Madrid.'

A much wider street, with several lanes of traffic which

hadn't been taken over by the herd of pedestrians, even if the traffic was pretty much backed up.

'Another bus route?' Xavi said.

'Possibly.'

Ryker reached the corner, headed left. Past the bottleneck, the crowd became thinner, and Ryker picked up his pace as he scanned.

'Bus stop,' Ryker said. 'I see him. Shit. And the bus is there.'

Ryker wanted to break into a jog, but doing so would only alert Ospina. The guy was on edge, searching. Only when he'd boarded the bus did Ryker start to run.

'It's heading to Montjuïc,' he said.

'Montjuïc? But that's not the—'

'It's not where we thought he was going. But it's where he's going now.'

The last of the waiting passengers stepped on board. The driver looked out to the road. Ryker waved at him. The driver seemed to be caught in two minds as to whether he could be bothered to wait or not, but Ryker stepped into the road to make the decision a little more straightforward.

'Gracias,' he said as he stepped on board, placing his card against the reader. He kept his gaze down, not wanting to make eye contact with Ospina. 'I'm on,' he whispered into the mic.

'I don't know about this, Ryker. Should I stay here? Or head to Montjuïc?'

'Stay there. Just in case.'

Xavi grumbled. Ryker said nothing more.

The journey didn't take long. Ospina was at the door as the bus came to a stop at the base of Montjuïc, a prominent hill in the center of the otherwise pretty damn flat city. Up top lay gardens, a castle, a palace, and the Olympic stadium, among other monuments. It was an area favored by tourists but was also sprawling and far less crammed than the tightly packed grid-like streets of the city below it.

'I'm getting off,' Ryker said, jumping up at the last moment and apologizing to the driver as he darted through the already closing doors. 'He's heading up.'

And Ryker really didn't know if that was a good thing or not.

He held back a little as Ospina started up the twisting stone steps.

'OK,' Xavi said. 'I'm not waiting here. It's already more than an hour past the rendezvous. We got the wrong time, the wrong place.'

'Maybe,' Ryker said. 'But it is happening. I'm sure of it.'

Xavi grumbled again and a moment later Ryker heard the noise of Xavi's dirt bike revving up. And Xavi wasn't that far away, really – he'd likely be able to get to Montjuïc in ten or fifteen minutes. Ryker understood his frustration though. The intel they had came directly from Ospina himself – off of a dark web messaging site where they'd hacked Ospina's account to gain access. They didn't know exactly what stolen intel Ospina was delivering today, and they didn't know to whom. They'd not been able to hack the account of the person he'd been in contact with – the username a meaningless jumble of letters and numbers – and they had no clue as to the person's real identity. They knew only that Rafael Ospina, an asset with ties both to the CNI and the UK's SIS, was delivering intelligence he shouldn't be delivering. They had a time and a place for the meet. Except both time and place were, apparently, wrong.

Which meant Ospina and his contact had made alternative arrangements through a different channel.

Which perhaps meant one or both of the parties knew they were under surveillance.

And yet it looked like the meet was happening still...

'Where are you?' Xavi said a few minutes later as the Olympic stadium came into view, its distinctive columned facade making it look like a Roman amphitheater.

'The stadium.'

'OK. I'm nearly there.'

Ryker continued past the stadium toward Plaça d'Europa, a huge open-plan square with the Torre Calatrava needle-like tower in one corner.

'We're at the square,' Ryker said. 'He's stopping here.' At one of the many obelisks that ran through the square.

Tourists were dotted here and there, posing for photos and sitting on benches to enjoy the sunshine and the views. Ryker tried his best to fit in, initially moving beyond Ospina, around his back to a secluded spot by the road, between two thickets.

He heard the whine of a dirt bike approaching. Spotted Xavi coming to the top of the hill off to his left, over by the stadium. He slowed and passed by Ryker and Ospina a few moments later, Xavi giving no acknowledgment to Ryker.

'I see someone,' Ryker said, noting the lone figure approaching from by the tower. A slight figure, possibly a woman, with dark jeans and dark jacket. She wore a baseball cap, low, like Ryker's still was, so he couldn't see anything of her face above her mouth. 'This is definitely it.'

He could tell by the increased nervousness in Ospina's demeanor.

Ryker pulled back a little bit more into the shaded bushes, crouched down.

He spotted Xavi on foot now, hovering a hundred yards away as he pretended to take pictures of the area with his phone.

Ryker took his phone out too.

The woman was about ten yards from Ospina when he slipped the backpack from his shoulders. No talking. No signals.

The woman walked up to him, took the backpack from his grip and continued on.

Ryker clicked away on his phone's camera the whole time.

'She's coming your way,' Ryker said to Xavi.

'I've got her.'

Ospina was already heading away in the opposite direction. They wouldn't follow him. No point now. They had the evidence of the handover. Now they just needed to know what had been handed over, and to whom.

Xavi did a poor job of being inconspicuous as the woman neared him.

Yes, the idea was to find out who she was. But not to accost her in such an open, public place. And for all they knew she was just an intermediary, about to drop the package with the actual party of interest.

'Remember, follow first,' Ryker said, sensing that Xavi was about to jump the gun...

No. Perhaps he wasn't, after all. But the jitters still got the better of him and the woman knew it.

She whipped out a handgun. Xavi wasn't ready, still caught between two minds.

The woman fired and hit Xavi in the leg. He fell to the ground, yelling in pain, as bystanders jolted and cowered and then shouted in panic. Ryker and the woman began sprinting at the same time. She took the road on the right, to head back down the hill and was temporarily out of his sight.

'You OK?' Ryker shouted to Xavi, who was writhing on the floor.

'Don't let her get away!' Xavi shouted back.

Ryker heard an engine fire up. A gritty sounding engine. Motorbike.

'Here!' Xavi said, tossing the key to his dirt bike at Ryker as he passed over him.

Ryker grabbed the keys and raced to the bike. He turned it on, pulled the throttle and shot away. He skidded around the corner. Spotted the woman a hundred yards ahead on a much more powerful bike than his. Certainly more suited to open roads. Which meant Ryker had to keep her off open roads.

She saw him. Had to slow her speed a little to turn and fire off her gun in his direction. The bullet whizzed past. She followed the road around a sharp left, heading on down below Ryker.

Follow directly or...

Use the dirt bike for what it was intended.

Ryker tugged on the handlebars and took the bike off the asphalt and onto the grassy, dirt shoulder. He stood off the seat as the bike bounced and jolted over the uneven ground.

Below him the woman picked up speed again on the straight, another tight corner up ahead of her. Ryker pulled the throttle even more and the bike wobbled and he fought to keep control.

She spotted him, gunning for her. Turned the weapon toward him.

She didn't get a chance to fire.

She hadn't noticed the truck approaching and riding one-handed she veered toward its path. Its horn filled Ryker's ears and as she righted her direction at the last second only narrowly missed a head-on collision.

Her bike momentarily disappeared behind the truck as she passed it. Ryker continued down. Adjusted his aim just a little to anticipate where he'd intercept her.

The truck moved on past.

There she was.

Smack-bang where he expected her to be.

And smack-bang was exactly what came a moment later as his front tire caught the back end of her bike, sending them both flying. Ryker bounced once on the asphalt, his shoulder taking the brunt of that painful hit before he tumbled onto the next shoulder beyond. He tried to anchor his arms, flip-flopping a couple of times before coming to a stop.

He groaned in pain.

'Ryker, what the hell is going on?'

He didn't answer. Had Xavi seen?

Ryker pulled himself to his feet. The woman lay in a heap ten yards from him, the broken, twisted, hissing bikes between them.

Her gun lay just out of reach.

Which she seemed to realize a moment later as she leaped up and went for it.

Ryker went to head her off and lashed out with his foot, kicking the gun from her grip. It bounced away and clanged into her bike. Ryker launched his foot into her chest and jumped onto her to try and pin her, but she fought back and caught him in the groin with a knee, an elbow to the face. They grappled and she spun around and to the top, pulling him into an arm bar.

She shouldn't have hesitated. She should have just broken the limb. Ryker moved his body with the resistance, then grabbed her arm with his free hand and twisted them both around, and soon the roles were reversed.

'Wait, wait, wait!'

Despite his intentions, Ryker did.

'We're on the same team!' she yelled, grimacing from the pain in her arm which remained at bursting point.

'You have no idea what—'

'I'm CIA!' she shouted. 'Please. I'm CIA.'

He hadn't had time to process that before she lashed out with a hidden knife. The blade sliced across his forearm and Ryker let go of her and rolled away. But not before pulling on the strap of the backpack to take it from her. He rolled over again, aiming for the gun. Except as he reached out for it...

Feet.

Xavi. He scooped the gun up.

'No!' Ryker shouted.

Too late. Xavi fired. Ryker rose. Spun around. The bullet had hit the woman. Shoulder. But it hadn't stopped her from turning and sprinting.

Sprinting for the edge...

'No!' Ryker said again, both to Xavi and the woman. Neither listened. Xavi fired. The woman jumped as the bullet hit her back.

She dropped out of sight.

Ryker raced to the edge. The woman's body bounced and clattered across shoulders, across rocks and to the sidewalk right at the bottom of the hill.

She lay there unmoving, her body broken and bleeding.

'What the hell?' Ryker said to Xavi.

'I just saved you, didn't I? And you got the package.'

Ryker looked down at the bag. Opened it up.

'Except we didn't, did we?' he said, showing Xavi the empty interior.

The guy's face dropped and he stumbled to Ryker's side to stare down below.

Down below, where seconds later a motorbike raced up to the woman. Two people on the back. The passenger jumped off and went up to her. Checked her neck as if there was any chance she'd survived the bullets and the fall.

No. Clearly she hadn't. The passenger opened the woman's jacket and took out the tablet computer. They momentarily glanced up at Ryker and Xavi's position as if in acknowledgment, or mocking or something...

Seconds later they were back on the bike which sped away, out of sight, the prize in their possession, the dead woman left sprawled, no further use for her.

3

The top floor of the modern glass-fronted office building, a couple of streets away from La Rambla, had a fabulous view of the city, ironically Montjuïc dominating the horizon. Ryker gazed out of the window, eyes focused on that area. He could make out the palace, the castle, the stadium. He watched the cable cars slowly trudging along their lines from the top of the hill and down to the marina. He couldn't make out people on the hill from such distance, yet as he stared he replayed the earlier moments in his mind repeatedly, imagined the woman banging and clattering down the hill as he looked to that very spot from across the city.

The door opened behind him. He turned to see Xavi emerging from the meeting room, head down, sulking. He came up to Ryker.

'Everything OK?' Ryker asked.

'Just so you know... I told them everything that happened. I backed you. I hope you'll do the same for me.'

An odd thing to say, really.

'Everything? So... about how you gave the mark the jitters,

which got you shot?' Ryker said. 'And then when I had her pretty much subdued, you decided to shoot her. Twice. And now she's dead and we've no idea where the stolen intel is, even what it is, or who's got it?'

Xavi pretty much snarled at him, and maybe Ryker could have been a bit more mellow. The guy had been shot, after all. But mainly because of his own poor judgment, Ryker had decided. And in the hours since the incident... he'd mulled whether Xavi's actions really were down to incompetence or something else.

The something else being that he knew more about the whole situation than Ryker did. Perhaps knew who that woman was. Perhaps had made a clear decision to kill her, rather than a knee-jerk reaction.

The two men stared at each other in silence before Peter Winter stuck his head around the door and beckoned Ryker inside.

One other person was in the room with Winter – Irene Nevado.

Winter was Ryker's long-time ally and at one time Ryker's boss, though it was many years since Ryker had been an official employee of any government agency. If official was even the right word to describe the clandestine role Ryker had held back then. Now his ties to SIS were even more tenuous, though that was more through his own desires. The best way to describe his role now was 'consultant', if security agencies had such things.

Irene Nevado was Xavi's boss. Ryker had only met her once before. She was a typical stuffy bureaucrat as far as Ryker could tell. She'd need to appease whoever her boss was for what went wrong today, which meant either Ryker or Xavi – or both – would need to be made scapegoats.

Except Ryker was many, many years and many, many assignments on from caring about being blamed for ops gone wrong, whether it was his fault or not. If they wanted to put today's mistakes on him and kick him off this assignment, kick him out of this country... so be it. He was here to help, so if they didn't want him to help, he'd leave.

He took a seat at the large glass meeting table, the other two in front of him, that view of Montjuïc behind them. Ryker tried not to dwell.

'Do you have anything to say?' Nevado asked, her tone as cold as the look on her face.

'What do you want to know?' Ryker responded.

'Why a simple surveillance operation ended up with a woman being shot and killed on the streets of Barcelona. With many witnesses.'

'Who is she?' Ryker asked.

Nevada's face soured further, but she didn't answer.

'Do you know?' Ryker asked.

Still no answer.

'And what about Ospina? Has he been brought in now the exchange has taken place?'

Nevado shuffled in her chair.

'OK,' Ryker said. 'Let me take a guess. Ospina is missing?'

'We haven't been able to locate him.'

'Do you know what data he was selling?'

'Excuse me, Mr. Ryker, but I'm the one who'll be asking the questions here.'

Ryker sighed. 'And this is one reason why simple ops like this go wrong. Because you keep your main assets in the dark.'

'Why don't you just start by telling me what happened today. From your perspective.'

Except before Ryker could even attempt to respond, Winter held up his hand to stop the conversation.

'Sorry, Irene, but I think we heard enough from Xavi about what happened.'

'Excuse me?' she said, anger taking over now, her face creased over. 'Both of you are here as guests of the CNI, and this is a formal debrief requested by the—'

'Again, sorry for interrupting, but the debrief is done,' Winter said. 'You got what you needed from your man.'

'You can just write down that I agree with Xavi's statement,' Ryker added.

'All of it?' Irene asked him.

Ryker shrugged.

'You're sure about that?'

The question was asked in such a way to suggest that Xavi probably hadn't been too kind about Ryker's role earlier. But... he really didn't care.

'Verbatim. What he said is what happened.'

She looked incredulous but packed up her papers. 'OK. Then I'll be recommending to the director that this... arrangement with SIS is brought to an immediate end. And frankly? I'm glad for it.'

She said that as though it was a big win of some sort, a stinger to hurt both Winter and Ryker.

Neither of them said anything and moments later she stomped out of the room.

'I mean, you could have played along with her box checking a bit more,' Ryker said to Winter once they were alone. After all, Winter was still tied to the government machine and he had to toe the line a lot more than Ryker did.

'It doesn't matter,' Winter said. 'Because whatever you'd said to her, you're done here. I'm sorry.'

'Is that your decision, or—'

'It's my decision, but it's not quite as—'

He stopped when a knock came on the door. Winter checked his watch.

'And this is why I needed her gone sooner rather than later.'

Winter rose and opened the door to reveal a suited man on the other side – a little podgy, with a round and heavily lined face, white hair. Ryker didn't recognize him.

'You must be James Ryker,' the man said. 'I'm Warren Klein.' American accent.

Ryker got to his feet and shook the guy's hand. Klein gave a bone-crushing shake.

'Let me guess,' Ryker said, retaking his seat as Winter did the same. Klein took a seat at the head of the table. 'You're from Langley?'

Klein smiled.

'And let me further guess,' Ryker continued, connecting some of the dots, 'you haven't flown here from there in the few hours since that woman was scooped up off the sidewalk at Montjuïc.' Klein winced at Ryker's cold words. 'Not unless you have a supersonic jet. Which means you were already in the city. The country, at least.'

Klein simply responded to Ryker's deductions with a few nods.

'So who was she?' Ryker asked. 'She told me she was CIA. Was trying to tell me more perhaps, before Xavi shot her.'

'Yes. She was CIA,' Klein said. 'Although she wasn't my agent, and I'm not party to what her objectives were in this city.'

'So you don't know why a CIA agent was in Barcelona to procure stolen intel from an SIS asset?'

'You'll just have to accept that what she was doing here was... sanctioned,' Klein said.

'Did you know?' Ryker asked Winter. 'That the CIA were on the other end of this... what, exactly? A trap for Ospina?'

'Not exactly,' Winter replied.

'Then what?'

'The thing is, Ryker,' Klein said, 'your role has been explained to me by Peter and... it's unfortunate in many ways that a man of your experience finds himself in this position. But you are on the outside, looking in. And I can't put things anymore bluntly than that.'

'I don't need to know. Got it. I guess I'll be going then.'

Ryker went to get up.

'Ryker, just... hear him out,' Winter said.

The way he said it caused Ryker to pause.

'You don't remember me, do you?' Klein said.

Ryker searched his brain. He was generally pretty damn good at remembering faces, if not always names, but he really didn't think he knew Klein.

'Should I?' he asked, retaking his seat.

'You weren't James Ryker back then,' Klein said. 'You were Carl Logan.'

Ryker clenched his fists under the table.

'A long time ago, huh?' Klein said.

'Yeah.'

'And a lot's happened since then. For you, me, the world.'

He paused. Was Ryker supposed to say something to that?

'You probably don't remember me because I was only a junior analyst back then, but I worked for the JIA, like you did. For a while, I worked with Mackie. Winter too.'

Ryker clenched his fists harder still as the memories of that old – often painful – life surfaced in his mind.

Three names Klein had brought up. Three dead names.

The JIA. The Joint Intelligence Agency. An off the books outfit run jointly by the UK and the US, formed as part of the Global War on Terror in the early 2000s. Ryker had been a field agent for them, carrying out black ops for nearly two decades – his whole adult life to that point. But the JIA was long since disbanded following an implosion after years of infighting and power struggles and too much public exposure – not in the least because of the fallout from some of Ryker's missions.

Mackie. He'd been Ryker's original boss there. His mentor. A father-like figure, really. Except Mackie was long dead too following an assassination in Russia.

And Carl Logan. Ryker's real name. An identity long since declared dead to keep him safe from authorities and enemies from that past life.

He wouldn't admit it, but it made Ryker feel vulnerable that this man knew about any of that. Other than Peter Winter, very few people in the world did.

'I'm not saying this to rattle you, Ryker,' Klein said. 'I'm saying it to try to get you on the same page as me. I know a lot about your past, but most importantly, I know about your skills. I know about your strengths. I know you're dependable. An asset the likes of which we just don't see often enough anymore.'

'OK,' Ryker said. 'Thanks for the flattery. But now's the time to start talking. What's happening here?'

Winter and Klein shared a look.

'I'll say what I can,' Klein said. 'Which isn't a lot. The dead woman was Silvia Gabarro. Puerto Rican. We picked her up out of UCLA and she's been working in Spain for the last four years. She was a good—'

'Why is the CIA working against SIS?' Ryker asked, looking at both men.

Klein sighed. Winter didn't react at all.

'You did know, didn't you?' Ryker asked Winter.

'It's not relevant now,' Klein said.

'It is to me. Because it feels like maybe I was set up. Used. There are only two scenarios here. One is that SIS knew about Gabarro, that she was the one who'd be taking that intel from Ospina, and that means me being here at all was pointless, bogus. And that poor woman lost her life needlessly today. The other is that SIS didn't know about her. In which case... why the hell not? Why would the CIA be working against their biggest ally?'

Winter squirmed a little in his seat, suggesting his discomfort at whichever answer was the truth, although neither he nor Klein made any attempt to clarify which scenario was the correct one.

'I was never told what intel Ospina was privy to, or what he would be selling,' Ryker said. 'And I never found out either. But something tells me at least one of you knows exactly what was on that tablet.'

Klein sighed.

'And do you know who now has possession? Is it the CIA or someone else?'

'I'm sorry, Ryker, but didn't I already say you're finished on this op?' Klein said. 'Your help isn't needed here. So you don't need to know anything more.'

'You came all this way to tell me that?'

'No,' Klein said. 'But when I found out you were involved here... I came to convince you to work with me. Something else. Something bigger.'

A curveball.

'Something else connected to what Gabarro was working on?'

'Now there's a good question,' Klein said, smiling at his own comment. No one else did. 'OK. I can see I'm not winning you over, so I'll give you this. We know that tablet is now in the hands of a group with close connections to people previously involved in Terra Lliure.'

He paused, as though testing whether Ryker knew the reference. He didn't.

'Terra Lliure were a Catalan nationalist paramilitary group,' Klein said.

'Terrorists.'

'Some would say so. They were disbanded decades ago, but their principles, the beliefs and aims, weren't erased. Catalan nationalism is on the rise again.'

'And the CIA cares because...?'

'Because this isn't an isolated incident. There's a wave of ultra-right wing and other nationalistic groups gathering backing across Europe, and across North America too. We know it's not all through coincidence that it's happening now.'

'You think these groups are planning... what? Coordinated attacks?'

'These groups already have attacked,' Klein said. 'Covert attacks. Stealing intel through hacking and other means, cyber-attacks, election meddling. But also overt attacks, bombs, shootings. You heard about Atlanta?'

'The bombing?'

Klein nodded.

'I read twenty-six people died,' Ryker said. 'And an unidentified lone wolf is the suspect.'

'Correct. And the CIA would like you to help find him.'

Another curveball. Ryker looked from Klein to Winter. Neither man was giving him anything.

'Me?'

'The situation is... complicated,' Klein said. 'But you can see from what happened here today that cross-border agencies aren't necessarily as aligned as they should be. That within the biggest agencies, not everyone understands what everyone else is doing, which means different parties often working at cross purposes without them even knowing.'

'So... you want me to ride under it all. An unofficial investigation.'

Klein smiled. 'You got it. Like I said earlier, I know what your skillset is, Ryker. And you're far enough removed in this situation to mean you're entirely untainted.' Which basically meant he could be trusted more, even if Klein hadn't explicitly said that. 'You'd have no official jurisdiction in the US. You'd be working alone, no oversight from the CIA or anyone else. But you need to find out who was really responsible for that attack. What their motives are. And do what you can to make sure there aren't more attacks on US soil.'

A pretty broad remit.

'You don't think the FBI, the police, are capable of figuring it out?'

'I didn't say that. What I'm saying is that I want you there too.'

'But I'll have no official access to any investigation into the bombing? Or anything else?'

'No,' Klein said.

'Then where the hell would you expect me to start?'

'A man of your talents, experience? I thought you'd be able to figure that out.'

And Ryker was sure he could too. But something about the way Klein said it suggested he was only being facetious.

'Or you could start here, if you wanted.' Klein opened the folder in front of him and scooted a piece of paper across the desk to Ryker. A profile.

'Adam Hannigan?' Ryker said. 'Governor of Georgia.'

'Governor of Georgia now. Formerly the National Security Adviser under the last president.'

'And where does he fit in?'

'Great question. You may have heard about this, you may have not, but his eldest daughter, Abby, has been missing for nearly six months.'

'And you think that's linked to the bombing?'

'Is it?' Klein said. 'Again, this is what I need you to tell me. What we do know is that there were rumors of her being targeted by an underground right-wing group.'

'Targeted, as in...?'

'As in her affiliation to that group may explain her disappearance. We also have this.' He pulled out his phone and tapped at it before holding the phone out toward Ryker.

A voice recording played. A woman's voice.

'There's... a bomb. It's gonna be bad... It's the KDD Tech office. This isn't a hoax... You have to help those people.'

Silence for a few moments.

'You think that's her?' Ryker asked.

Klein nodded. 'Yes, we believe it's Abby Hannigan, although we can't be certain.'

'And this warning was—'

'Received by the local FBI office three minutes and twenty-eight seconds before the first of two explosions at KDD Tech. Not enough time for them to do anything about it.'

Although the way he said it suggested he believed more could have been done. Had the call been taken seriously at all?

'Whether or not she's working with the culprit, or culprits, whether she's with them of her own free will, or under duress... we don't know. But I suggest you finding her is a good goal. And speaking to her family is your best starting point in America.

This gives you basic cover to go on from there. A private investigator hired by the family.'

'Will Hannigan know the truth? About who I am?'

'Yes. At least as far as you were sent over there by me, and that you're there to help find Abby, and help find whoever was behind those explosions. But he won't know anything much about you other than what you choose to tell him. And no one else, no other agency or authority will know anything at all.'

The room went silent. Ryker's brain churned. He didn't like a lot of what had been said in the meeting, even if he would be lying if he said he wasn't massively intrigued.

And helping to stop further terror attacks? He wouldn't be true to himself if he refused.

'Of course, you'll be remunerated for your assistance,' Klein said.

Ryker didn't bother to ask how much. His work had never been about the money. The only thing holding him back now was the niggling doubt about why he was being asked to do this.

'Will you do it?' Klein asked.

'Yeah,' Ryker said. 'I will.'

'You're exactly the man I remember,' Klein said, rising to his feet with a wide smile. Handshakes all around before Klein headed for the door.

'Oh, and Ryker... Perhaps this goes without saying, but there's a lot going on out there that I, and others, don't understand. So use your wits. Don't. Trust. Anyone.'

Klein left the room. Ryker and Winter were both silent for a while.

'Anything else to say?' Ryker asked.

'Not from me. You good?'

'Not really.'

'You'll be fine.'

Winter got to his feet.

'But you did know about all this, right?' Ryker asked. 'Klein. The CIA's involvement here.'

'I think we've gone over that enough already.'

Had they? Because Ryker really didn't think he knew any more now than when he'd first stepped into the room.

Winter was at the door.

'Let me know when you're done out there,' Winter said. 'You'll be missed.'

'Yeah.'

'And Ryker? Just remember what Klein said.'

'About me not trusting anyone?'

Winter didn't say anything. The answer was pretty obvious.

'Klein, you mean?'

Again no answer.

'And what about you?' Ryker asked. 'Should I still trust you?'

Funnily enough, Winter still said nothing before he opened the door and headed out.

4

ATLANTA, GEORGIA

Ryker took the bridge over the Chattahoochee River, heading into the East Cobb area of Metro Atlanta. A left on Paper Mill Road and the concrete jungle of the city twenty miles south seemed a world away as he wound the car along a twisting, undulating road, thick-canopied trees in full bloom dominating the view to either side. Fences and walls further helped to hide the properties that lined the road from view. They did a good job but didn't offer complete seclusion as Ryker still caught glimpses of the multimillion dollar mansions every now and then. An eclectic mix of styles, really. Many were classic brick-fronted family homes, but some were space-age-looking glass and metal boxes, others were stone-built monoliths with classical columns as though they'd been planted here in Georgia straight from ancient Rome. Another with a stone facade had turrets on either corner evoking the look of a medieval castle from Northern Europe.

The home Ryker stopped at was unique in this mishmash of often tasteless wealth. The white-painted house was built in an antebellum style with a columned veranda running across the front. The wrought iron gates at the front of the property were open so Ryker drove on through and up the driveway past the manicured gardens to the house.

He parked and stepped out into the sunshine. The sky here was as clear as it had been in Barcelona three days ago, although the temperature was much warmer, even if it remained far from the stifling summer highs that he knew gripped this area in a months-long chokehold.

Altogether pretty damn pleasant, really, the scent of the nearby rose bushes tickling his nose as he walked up to the front door.

He didn't need to knock. The door was opened by a smartly dressed middle-aged woman. She greeted him with a not so friendly smile. Not suspicious, as such, just a little put out by him being there.

'I saw your car coming up the driveway,' she said. 'I'm guessing you're James Ryker.'

'Yes,' he said, holding out his hand. 'Pleased to meet you.'

She reluctantly took his hand and gave a limp shake. 'I'm Brenda. My husband is in the office. I'll take you there.'

Ryker moved inside behind her, noting the lingering smell of varnish, perhaps from the remarkably pristine flooring which looked to be original to the house.

'You have a beautiful home,' Ryker said as he scanned around. High ceilings, large rooms, obviously expensive albeit a little bit gaudy furniture. No expense spared.

She kind of squirmed at his comment. 'This way.'

She led him toward the back of the house, Ryker glancing into the rooms they passed, peeking at ornaments and pictures as he went. They passed a large family room with a huge stone fireplace, an even larger family portrait above the mantle. Five people in the picture. Mom, dad, daughter, two sons. From the little Ryker knew, all of the kids were grown and had left the roost now. Brenda led them to a partially closed door. She knocked and poked her head around, and Ryker caught a glimpse of Adam Hannigan sitting at his large dark-wood desk, phone pressed to his ear. He motioned to his wife to give him a moment and she spun back to Ryker looking even less comfortable than before.

'He's just finishing up. Can I get you anything?'

'Just some water, please.'

'Of course.'

She left Ryker standing there like a bit of a chump. He looked around the hallway behind him again, taking in the array of picture frames on a sideboard nearby. A lot of happy smiling faces there, although not many included Abby, he noted. At least not of her as a teen or adult.

'James Ryker?'

He spun around to see Adam there at the door, a satisfied grin on his face as though he'd just caught Ryker out.

'Yeah,' Ryker said, holding his hand out. A much firmer handshake from Hannigan than from his wife. He wasn't the tallest guy, under six feet, but he had a presence about him, an aura – arrogance mostly – that a lot of politicians had, probably needed, to get themselves to where they were in life.

'Come and take a seat.'

The office was huge. More than a little flashy, in an old-world way. Wood-paneled walls took up the spaces that the floor-to-ceiling bookshelves didn't. Two huge chandeliers hung from the beamed roof: one over the desk, the other over the two leather sofas in front of another stone fireplace.

They ended up on the sofas. Hard, uncomfortable sofas. Style over function.

'You came straight here from the airport?' Hannigan asked.

'Yeah,' Ryker said.

'You're probably tired then.'

'I slept on the plane.'

'Warren explained to me... the basics here.'

'Yeah? Which is what?'

The guy shifted in his seat a little, as though not liking the question or Ryker's tone perhaps. Not that Ryker had intended to be in any way awkward, but the fact was, even if he'd traveled all this way for good reasons, there was still a lot about the setup he either didn't like or didn't fully understand.

'Given who Warren is, what I know his job is,' Hannigan mused, as though struggling to get the right words out, 'gives me a pretty good indication of who, or rather what you are. If you know what I mean.'

'I guess so.'

Brenda returned with a tray containing two glasses and a jug of iced water. She placed it on the coffee table between Ryker and Hannigan.

'You sure I can't get you anything else?' she asked Ryker. 'You're not hungry?'

'I'm good. Thank you.'

She made to move off.

'But don't you think you should stay?' Ryker suggested. 'You do know why I'm here, right?'

She looked at her husband rather than answer.

'Yes,' he said. 'Brenda understands why you're here.'

'To help you both find out what happened to your daughter.'

Brenda looked from Ryker to Hannigan. 'I... I... er—'

'Take a seat, darling,' Hannigan said, patting the spot next to him.

Brenda did so. She looked like she'd rather be anywhere else in the world.

'So what do you want to know?' Hannigan asked Ryker.

'Everything,' Ryker said. 'Assume I know nothing at all about your daughter, your family. Because basically, I don't.'

Hannigan snorted as though he didn't really believe Ryker.

'Just give me the basics to start,' Ryker suggested. 'You have three kids, right?'

'Joe is our eldest,' Brenda said. 'Then Kyle. Abby is our youngest.'

'She's twenty-four,' Hannigan added.

'And you're all close?' Ryker asked.

Hannigan was looking more and more agitated, though Ryker really couldn't understand why.

'Obviously not as close as we'd like, Mr. Ryker, otherwise you'd most likely not be sitting there right now.'

Ryker nodded in response. 'Do your sons still live nearby?'

'Joe lives in New York,' Brenda said. 'He's an attorney. Married. He has a young boy himself now. Kyle lives in the area still. An accountant for a big firm in the city.'

'And... Abby? What did she do? Before... you know.'

'Abby never lived far from home,' Brenda said. 'She went to college here, in Georgia. She came back to live with us after she graduated. But she... struggled more than her brothers did to find what she wanted to be.'

'So she never worked?'

'She did, but...'

'She had several jobs,' Hannigan said. 'She could have been anything she wanted to be, but she never really found her feet.'

'When did you last see her?'

They shared a look. 'More than six months ago,' Hannigan said. 'We haven't seen or spoken to her since then.'

'Do you—'

Hannigan raised his hand to prevent Ryker's follow-up question.

'Sorry, Mr. Ryker, but wherever this conversation goes from here, whatever it is you think your scope of work is here in this country, my wife does not need to be party to it. And please, don't think it's because I'm some dinosaur who doesn't believe in my wife's worth. It's because I'm trying to protect her.'

'Protect her from what?' Ryker asked.

He got no answer.

Brenda couldn't have left the room anymore quickly. She closed the door behind her.

Hannigan rose to his feet and moved over to the dresser where a tray of decanters sat on a silver platter.

'Would you like one?' he asked.

'I'm good.'

He poured himself a large measure and sat down again before taking a big sip.

'You think I'm obnoxious,' Hannigan said.

'It's too early for me to make that call.'

Hannigan laughed.

'Liar. But I meant what I said. There're a lot of things happening in my family, and you don't need to know about them all. You're here for a reason—'

'To help find your daughter.'

'But we both know that's really only a small part of your remit, and even if I'm privy to a lot of very confidential information still, about all sorts of different matters – including some of the background to you coming here – my wife is not. So I'd appreciate it if you keep any conversations about this matter away from her from now on.'

Ryker didn't say anything. He could see the man's point. Kind of. Even if he didn't like it.

'What do you know about me?' Hannigan asked.

'Until a couple of days ago? Very little. I knew your name.'

'From my time in Washington?'

'Yes.'

'I spent more than two years as the last president's National Security Adviser.'

'I heard that.'

'I probably would have stayed in that position had he been up for re-election, but you probably know the story on that.'

Ryker kind of did. The last president initially wanted to stand for a second term, but infighting – a coup, of sorts – saw him leave quite acrimoniously in the end and his successor rose to the top of contention with barely a challenge. But his promises of radical change hadn't yet been put into action, leading to growing discontent on both sides of the political divide.

'Seems like you've done OK since then, though,' Ryker said.

Hannigan kind of snorted at that. 'The point I'm making is that from my previous role, I know a lot about the shadowy world people like you operate in. A lot more than the vast majority of the public do. My wife included.'

'I believe you.'

'But that role doesn't define me. Who I am. Where I came from. What I stand for.'

'Which is?'

'This, Georgia, is my home. As you alluded, I'm governor now, and being in this position is my proudest achievement. Every day I get to stand up for the people of this great state. Striving to make the life of every citizen here better than it's ever been before.'

Spoken like a true politician. It sounded like he was getting ready to film a campaign ad.

'And don't let the nice house fool you. I'm a man of the people. For the people.'

Ryker nodded but didn't respond, just looked around the room as though taking in the opulence. Even if the general public swallowed Hannigan's words, Ryker wasn't sure he did.

'You lived here long?' Ryker asked.

Hannigan's eyes narrowed as though he didn't like the question.

'More than twenty years. Both before and after my time in Washington. All my children spent most of their childhoods right here in this home.'

'I saw the sign on the way in,' Ryker said, referring to the metal sign on the roadside which gave a brief history of the old house. He'd seen several others nearby on other similarly old properties. His comment drew a more animated look on Hannigan's face.

'This part of Georgia has a rich history,' Hannigan said. 'Many of the towns around here go way back to before the Civil War. There aren't many homes remaining from back then, but this is one of them.'

'A former plantation?' Ryker suggested.

'Yes, actually,' Hannigan responded, a little snottily.

'The sign said Theodore Otton was the original owner. Was he a relation of yours?'

'No, he was not. No Ottons in my lineage.' Hannigan had gone all sullen for some reason, but after a brief silence he became a bit more animated again. 'Grand old Theodore Otton. Georgia's king of cotton,' he said, kind of singing the words. At least that's what Ryker thought he was doing. 'It's an old rhyme. There's a full verse to it, but I don't remember the rest.'

He waved that thought away.

'Had a heart attack when they freed his slaves, his soul was oh-so rotten, is how it ends. I think.'

Hannigan clenched his jaw tightly shut as he studied Ryker a few moments. 'So you already read up on this place then,' he said.

'Wouldn't you expect me to?'

'Slavery is an unfortunate part of this region's history—'

'And racial tensions an unfortunate part of its present.'

'Yes, it is. I guess you're alluding to the recent protests we've been having here. Across much of the south.'

'The growing voice of discontent from the far right. Yes. In part I was referring to that.'

'The far right. I hate that term. Far right, the radical left, wokists, all these tags are designed to separate us. It's why the current president won out because people are clamoring for change. The simple point I come back to is that a lot of ordinary folk feel like their voices aren't heard anymore. That's what we really need to understand and figure out.'

'I'd agree with you on that.'

'But back to your first point... The cotton trade was one of the reasons why this state, this country, prospered at all. We can't wash our hands of our past mistakes, but we also shouldn't pretend it didn't happen or that it didn't shape where we are today. I'm not ashamed to live in a house like this.'

'I never said you should be.'

'But I wonder why you even brought that up.'

'I'm just trying to get a read of you. The situation here.'

'You think because I'm a wealthy conservative politician, living in the former home of a plantation owner, that I'm an inbred racist who harks for days past?'

'I never said anything like that. But from what I understand, your daughter did potentially get mixed up with an extreme far-right group.'

'Here we go again, far right this, far right that. If you knew anything about me, you'd know that's not what I represent at all. An outsider like you might think our slave-owning past defines this area. Segregation too. But what about the more recent past? Personally, I think the civil rights movement and the era since then have shaped cities like this even more. For the better. And like I said to you before, I work for the benefit of this state and all of its people.'

'I get it,' Ryker said. 'I'm not suggesting otherwise. But tell me about Abby. What happened with her.'

Hannigan paused and took two sips of his drink as though composing himself.

'I don't even know how relevant this is to whatever Klein wants you out here for.'

'He wants me to find your daughter.'

'No. I want my daughter found. Klein figures doing so will help him in his mission too.'

'His mission being to stop terror attacks.'

'Maybe. But don't try to pretend that the two things are directly correlated, or that you're really here solely for my benefit.'

'OK. Fair enough. Tell me about Abby.'

'Abby is my youngest. My only daughter. She was a sweet girl.'

'Was?'

'Do you have any kids of your own?'

'No.'

He shook his head despondently. 'Then maybe you won't understand. But they all change. However nice and sweet and polite they are, every teenager turns rebel in some shape or form. She was never a bad kid, but she did come under some bad influences.'

'Such as?'

Hannigan sighed. 'A boy. If you can believe it?'

'And this boy is called?'

'Craig Boswell.'

'They were together?'

'On and off for a couple of years. And Brenda and I were never happy about it. With a strong-willed teenage girl, you can imagine how that went.'

'But it ended?'

'Yes. Years ago. She was only just eighteen. This was before she even went to college.'

'What happened?'

'What happened? Craig impaled his truck on a streetlight after traveling at more than ninety miles an hour under the influence of who knows what.'

Ryker said nothing as he worked that over in his head. Not quite the answer he'd expected.

'I take it from your lack of reaction that I'm telling you something you didn't already know from Klein or your own research,' Hannigan said.

'Correct.'

'Craig was an idiot. A thug. His parents were and still are assholes.'

'Noted. But how does all this fit into the—'

'White supremacy?'

'Not exactly what I was going to say. But carry on.'

'Craig and his friends formed this stupid little group that they called the White Lions. You can guess why they chose the color. They were dumbass racists, nothing more, nothing less, but my daughter, God only knows why, took an interest in some of their... beliefs. Even though she had more of a brain than the rest of that group put together.'

'So you think she was feeding their beliefs really, rather than the other way around?'

'I'm pretty sure that's not what I said. She was still an impressionable young girl at that point.'

'An adult, when Craig died.'

'A very immature and easily led young adult.'

'OK. And what happened to the White Lions after Craig died?'

'Not a lot. Most of them went off to college or got jobs here and there. The group fizzled out, and after Craig died, Abby had nothing to do with it.'

'You're sure about that or is that just what you—'

'I'm sure of it. Abby moved on. Went off to college.'

'And that was the end of her interest in—'

'Yes. That was the end of her involvement in anything like that. Call it a teenage blip, whatever. We never had any other problems with her. She went to college, got her degree. She came back home while she tried to figure out what was next.'

'And then... what? One day she disappeared out of the blue?'

'Yes.'

'No more boyfriends? No more affiliations to far-right groups leading up to that?'

Hannigan winced, perhaps at Ryker's continued use of the phrase far right. But what else was he supposed to say?

'No.'

'And this was when?'

'We last saw her October 29. A Saturday. She took her car to the mall. Gave me a hug and her mom a kiss before she left. We never heard from her again. The car was still there, key, phone, purse inside. No signs of a struggle.'

'What did the police say?'

'That there was no evidence of foul play. And we never received any kind of a ransom, so kidnapping seemed unlikely.'

'And what do you believe happened to her?'

Hannigan sighed. 'Honestly? We feared the worst. And as time wore on... You've no idea the torment it's caused us as parents, the pain of not knowing. But the longer it went on, the more I had to believe that she was dead. Either through her own hand or someone else's.'

'Did you ever worry about her taking her own life before she—'

'No. Never,' Hannigan said, once again interrupting Ryker. It was as though every time Ryker tried to say something uncomfortable he felt compelled to cut him off, to save him from pain or perhaps just embarrassment. 'But no one ever really knows what goes on in other people's minds. I think what I'm trying to say is that her death became the most obvious explanation. Until...'

'Until the voice note?'

Hannigan nodded, clenched his fists.

'Does your wife know about it?'

Another nod.

'Anyone else in the family?'

'Our sons. We couldn't keep that away from them.'

'So you believe the voice is hers?'

'One hundred percent. It's her.'

Klein hadn't been quite so conclusive.

'And what do you think it means?'

'It means she's alive.'

'It means she had prior knowledge of a terrorist attack not even thirty miles from here that left more than two dozen people dead.'

Hannigan clenched his jaw closed again. More tightly this time, and Ryker noticed a vein at the side of his head throbbing.

'I'm not saying that to annoy you,' Ryker said. 'I'm saying it because it's a fact.'

'Perhaps it is.'

'Do you have any information as to who carried out the attack or why?'

Hannigan chewed on that one for a few moments.

'All I know is what's been reported to the press. What I've reported myself to the public.'

'A lone wolf. White male suspect. Early thirties.'

'If you want more details you'd have to speak to the police or the GBI, FBI, whoever.'

'But what do you believe is happening here?'

'If I knew that... there'd have been no point in me agreeing with Klein for you to come here, looking for my daughter. That bomb attack was a tragedy. An atrocity. I know that law enforcement is doing everything to find the perpetrator and we will have justice. But for me, personally, Abby is my focus. I want to know where she is. I want her back with her family.'

'Understood. And the White Lions—'

'Mr. Ryker, I think I've told you everything I need to about that. That ridiculous bunch of misfits was from a long time ago. If you're as good at what you do as you should be, given a man of Klein's experience sent you here, then you've more than enough information to start turning over a lot of stones around here.'

'And that's what you want me to do? Because turning a lot of stones sometimes... causes a scene or two.'

Hannigan seemed to mull that over for a few moments. Ryker wondered whether that meant the guy was aware of some of Ryker's past 'exploits'. It was certainly possible, given his previous role in government and his links to people like Klein. Or maybe he was just chewing on the warning from Ryker. That this job could get messy. And that mess could, inevitably, come back to Hannigan one way or another.

'You have no official jurisdiction here,' Hannigan said. 'You're a private investigator, following the same laws and rules as every other member of the public.'

'So if I get caught out doing something I shouldn't be, trying to find the answers to help you... neither you nor Klein are going to stick your neck out for me?'

'No, Mr. Ryker, I'll be a little bit blunter than that. If you bring any problems to my door, I'll end you. That's a promise. I don't like this setup, but I see... that it might work.'

'This setup? You mean the fact Klein has delegated this task to me, an outsider, under the noses of law enforcement. Why do you think he did that?'

'You'd have to ask him. I just want my daughter found. That is my one and only priority here. I've made myself clear, right?'

'Pretty much,' Ryker said.

'Then I think we're done,' Hannigan said, standing as if to solidify the statement.

Another handshake before the host showed Ryker to the door, although they hadn't made it there before Hannigan's phone rang in his pocket. He fished it out, answered and kind of waved Ryker on his way out. The door was closed behind him before he'd moved to the porch steps.

Altogether a frustrating first meeting, Ryker felt, and he hadn't warmed to Hannigan at all, particularly as he knew the guy eyed Ryker with more than a little suspicion. But why? Ryker was there to help find Abby. To help understand how she'd become involved in – or at least had knowledge of – a recent terror attack.

Perhaps Hannigan was only nervous about what the truth would reveal.

Ignorance is bliss, or something like that.

And no doubt Ryker would be made a fall guy somehow if the truth had any potential to jump out and bite Hannigan on his ass publicly. Yeah, he wanted his daughter found. But the man was also a lifelong and now very senior politician.

Ryker paused by his car, deep in thought as he looked back at the pristine-looking home. He heard a car behind him, engine rumbling as the vehicle pulled off the road and headed toward the house. A big Ford truck. Ryker had never met the man driving it before but recognized his face from the pictures in the house.

Kyle Hannigan. The second born. Accountant in the city.

He stepped out of his car. He was taller, leaner, more athletic than his dad, although he had the same confidence in his eyes. He had a square jaw that made him look like an action movie hero.

'You must be Kyle,' Ryker said.

'Yeah. Let me guess – you're this new PI my mom and dad were expecting.'

Interesting that they'd told their son about Ryker. Not such a secret mission, apparently.

'That's me.'

'The way I heard it, they didn't ask for you to be here. But you were sent anyway. From England?'

'Yeah. The accent's a bit of a giveaway, huh?'

'Everything about you is a giveaway.'

He looked Ryker up and down with disdain as he said that. Ryker didn't bother to ask exactly what he meant by the obvious attempt at an insult.

'I came here expecting a bit more warmth,' Ryker said. 'It's almost as if you and your family don't really want Abby found.'

'If that's what you think, then you really don't know anything.'

'Yeah? So tell me something.'

'Whatever you think is happening here...'

'Honey, you're here!' came the call from behind Ryker. Brenda was standing there at the door, wide smile on her face as she stared at her son. 'Come on inside now.'

Kyle said nothing more to Ryker before he brushed past him and up to the house.

5

The twenty-something miles from the Hannigan residence in East Cobb to the heart of Atlanta took more than an hour, the mega-highway – a dozen or more lanes across in places – was snarled up nearly the whole way. A regular sight, Ryker had heard on the radio.

It gave Ryker plenty of time to think about what he'd learned, even if he really hadn't found out much new from Hannigan and his family. Except for the names Craig Boswell and the White Lions. Both of those were new to Ryker. Hannigan had suggested both were from Abby's distant past. Problems from a rebel teenage stage that she'd long moved on from.

Recent events suggested otherwise. Was Hannigan's judgment clouded by his subconscious desire to still see his daughter as his sweet little girl? Or was he simply not giving Ryker the full truth?

Finding Abby was her family's number one priority. But Ryker's number one priority was understanding who had laid a deadly bomb in an inner-city office building. Hopefully before the perpetrator, or perpetrators, struck again.

Ryker found a parking lot a couple of hundred yards from the office of KDD Tech and walked over to the building. The final passage into the city had been made even more difficult by the closure of several roads around the area by yet another angry protest, which, according to the news, had grown in size and prominence since the bombing. The day before police had been forced into action when a counter-protest had clashed with the several hundred-strong crowd. More than forty arrests had been made, several police officers injured, and big voices from both sides of the political divide had blamed the other for rising tensions, for the violence, and for the apparent use of excessive force by police. Impossible to really know the rights and wrongs in the situation from the heavily politicized press coverage.

Chanting drifted over as he made his way to KDD Tech. A few sirens here and there too. Nothing too rowdy or raucous yet today, he didn't think.

He got to within half a block of the office building before the police cordon halted his progress. A line of tape ran across the road, blocking access, and Ryker stopped to look at the still chaotic scene beyond. Three days after the bomb had ripped the building apart, the authorities had now fenced off the immediate area around the office to block from view whatever was happening on the ground – both the last desperate efforts to recover missing people buried under rubble, but also the investigation and analysis into what had happened.

Still, even with the privacy fence in place, there was nothing that could be done to hide the fact that activity beyond the fence remained heightened, with myriad vehicles overspilling from the fenced area, from police cars to ambulances to construction equipment. Various huddles of people were there too, from uniformed officers to workers in hi-vis gear with hard hats to others in casual clothing, some in formal business clothing. Ryker watched them all for a few minutes, trying to figure the different dynamics.

Finally his gaze rested on the office itself. The ground level fence couldn't hide the sheer devastation to the building. The high-rise structure looked like a birthday cake that a hungry dog had been left alone with for a few seconds, one side of it haphazardly chopped away, the insides crumbling and caving in on what remained. Office furniture was strewn around and in places hanging over the edge of the abyss. Framed pictures were in place on walls. The forlorn furniture and fittings somehow made the destruction all the more real and gut-wrenching.

Ryker had seen the wreckage caused by bombs in all sorts of situations. Roadside IEDs, suicide vests, car bombs. Even just standing from his vantage point gave him a few clues. The fact the building was standing at all meant the explosives most likely had been concentrated at one side of the building. Yet the public reports of the blast revealed that the explosives had detonated under the building. The office block had an underground parking lot, so a vehicle left down there was an obvious possibility. But then, for maximum destruction, wouldn't the bomber have placed the vehicle directly in the center of the building?

To Ryker's eye the damage leaned more to a suicide bomber on foot, or even to a vehicle either being left on the outside or driven into the side of the building.

So why the report of the explosives coming from underground?

'Can I help you, sir?'

Ryker looked over to the uniformed policeman who'd wandered up to him.

'Terrible, isn't it?' Ryker said. The officer's eyes narrowed a little, perhaps because of the accent.

'It is,' he said.

'The crime scene experts are still on site?' Ryker asked.

'Will be for days. It's a pretty big deal, don'tcha think?'

He said that as though he thought Ryker were an idiot.

'They figure out where the bomb was yet?'

Even more suspicious looks from the officer now.

'You should move on,' the officer said. 'People're kinda jittery around here right now. Around the whole city, really.'

Ryker's eyes fell on two people beyond the officer who'd taken notice of the exchange. A man, a woman. Both were plain-clothed but they had the stoic look of FBI or something similar.

Ryker moved away.

The authorities would be working around the clock at the scene for days to come. No way Ryker was getting on to that site anytime soon. Not unless he found someone to get him inside.

He headed away along the main road, high rises all around him, this area being the heart of the city's big-business orientated midtown. Even at this short distance from the bomb site there were plenty of pedestrians about, vehicles too. People going about their normal daily business. Though the atmosphere certainly felt edgy – jittery, as the officer had suggested – which Ryker felt was likely not just because of the bombing but the ongoing nearby protests too.

Ryker stopped outside a convenience store. He'd seen a woman being interviewed on TV standing outside there. An eyewitness, apparently. As far as Ryker could tell from the information in the public domain, she was the main reason why the police had settled on a lone white male suspect. Early thirties.

She'd seen a man acting suspiciously at the time of the

bombing. A man in a utility van. He'd sped away from the scene. No explanation had been given as to how the woman, a half mile away from the explosion, had decided that man was the culprit, but apparently the police seemed to agree given the information that had been shared with the public.

So what were the police not sharing?

Ryker stood on the sidewalk and looked along the street in both directions, his brain churning. His gaze rested on the convenience store. It was open but all quiet in there. Then his eyes fell to the ground. The road. The manhole cover.

'You lose something down there?' came a female voice from behind him.

He turned to the woman. She was a few years younger than him, perhaps late twenties, with long reddish hair, jeans, brown leather jacket. He recognized her. He'd seen the same woman minutes before, beyond the police tape at the bomb site.

So, whoever she was, whoever she worked for, his plan had worked, in a way. He'd got her attention by loitering just a little too long. Had then made his way to this spot – a spot directly related to the bombing – knowing that perhaps eyes would follow him here.

Like the officer said, people were jittery right now. Suspicious.

'No. Nothing lost,' Ryker said. 'But I am looking for something.'

'Is that why you were over by KDD? So what're you looking for?'

'Answers. And you?'

She smiled, her green eyes lighting up. 'Ha, so you saw me over there?'

'I did. And then you followed me over here,' Ryker said.

'So what's your story?'

'Same question to you.'

'I was on the other side of the tape, so feels like I have more... reason to be hanging around out here than you do.'

'And that reason is?'

'I was speaking to an acquaintance. You were just standing around there looking suspicious as hell. Which, given the state of alert here right now, either means you're a dumbass or... something else.'

'Something else?'

She didn't say anything to that.

'So what are you?' Ryker said. 'FBI or something?'

She laughed. 'No, mister. Not even the wrong end of the stick. Completely the wrong stick, I think.'

Ryker raised an eyebrow.

'I'm a journalist.'

Ryker frowned.

'What? You don't like journalists.'

'I've had some... experiences.'

'You have better experiences with law enforcement?'

'Actually... not at all.'

She laughed again. 'This is getting real interesting. You'll have to tell me about that.'

'Reveal my secrets to a journalist? Highly unlikely.'

'You're a Brit too. So what's the deal, you being here?'

'Just a tourist enjoying some sights.'

'Yeah. You like that manhole cover?'

'I mean, it's not my favorite.'

'I like it.'

'OK?'

'It's pretty interesting though, right? Half a mile from where a bomb attack tore through an office block. Straight line from here to there under the ground. And this being the exact same spot where an eyewitness saw... something.'

Ryker looked around, making sure no one else was paying them attention. Because this conversation – as weird as it was – had taken quite the interesting turn.

'Yeah,' Ryker said. 'How about that?'

She didn't say anything in response but definitely looked more than a little smug about something or other.

'You must have some good inside contacts,' Ryker said. 'Given you were the other side of the tape back there.'

'I like to think so.'

'Are they telling you anything? Because what I've seen in the press so far is more sanitized than a plague house.'

'You'd know that from experience?'

'The plague house or stifling the truth?'

She smiled again though a head shake too suggested she wasn't quite on the same page as him.

'You're right,' she said, 'they're keeping everything pretty tight right now.'

'And why do you think that is?'

'I have theories.'

'You enjoy comparing notes with others?' Ryker asked.

She thought about that one for a few moments. 'If it helps my cause.'

'And that cause is?'

'Finding out what really happened here.'

'Then we should definitely compare notes,' Ryker said. He held out a business card to her. A hastily prepared business card printed for him by someone in Klein's orbit to show Ryker's credentials as an apparent PI.

'Private investigator? I'm pretty sure the FBI, the GBI didn't bring you in here. So who hired you and why?'

'We'll get to that. I show you mine, you show me yours.'

'I don't have a business card.'

'Not really what I meant.'

'Then I really don't think I like what I think you meant.'

They both tried to stop themselves sniggering at that but both failed.

'Childish,' she said. 'That's cute.'

'I've no idea what you're talking about,' he said.

'Sure you don't. But you want to compare notes? What's in it for me, because way I see it, I'm the one clued in here, not you.'

'I wouldn't be so sure about that.'

'Yeah? So give me something. Otherwise, as much of a shame as it'd be, I do have other places to be.'

'You know about the phone-in?'

The playful look on her face dropped.

'What phone-in?'

'Anonymous call. A warning. To the FBI. A little over three minutes before the first explosion.'

Her frozen features gave away the answer.

'A female,' Ryker said. 'Which itself blows apart the idea of this lone wolf male.'

She said nothing for a while, but Ryker knew he had her. Her natural investigative instincts, perhaps the dollar signs of a big scoop, had drawn her in.

'So how about that note swapping idea?' Ryker said.

'Yeah. OK. Let's get a drink. But you're buying.'

'You lead the way.'

* * *

Not quite the place Ryker had expected they'd end up in.

Perhaps a straightforward coffee shop, café, or even just a park bench somewhere.

The Rowdy Tiger was a whiskey bar deep in the business district with a ridiculously large selection of amber. Not many people there before lunchtime. Ryker wasn't even sure why they bothered opening so early on a weekday. But open it was, and he and his newfound ally settled into a booth in the large, open brick-walled tavern with a water and a whiskey each. Her choice.

'Kentucky straight bourbon,' she said. 'A good starter.'

'This is how you get people to talk to you? I'm more used to... alternative methods.'

She shifted a little uncomfortably as though unsure what he meant. Probably justified – even if he'd meant it to be light-hearted, the reality was that he'd gone to some pretty extreme lengths in his time to get people to talk.

'You haven't told me your name yet,' Ryker said.

'Megan Valentino. Meg.'

'Valentino. Italian?'

'On the paternal side. Great grandfather. Other than the name there's not much to it now. What about you, James Ryker?'

'Me?'

'A Brit over here, way down south.'

'We'll get to that. So you're a journalist? Who for?'

'Investigative journalist. I do my own pieces.'

'Sell to the highest bidder.'

'Often it's more like persuade someone to bid at all.'

'And what's your angle here? Because in my experience investigative journalists tend to see a bigger picture. More than just reporting simple facts after an event.'

She took a sip of her whiskey before answering, as though she needed the time to form the answer.

'No angle. This is local to me. The biggest event of this type here since '96.'

'The bombing at the Olympics?'

'Exactly. And I was only tiny then, so how could I not want to be involved here, now?'

He didn't push anymore. He didn't fully believe her, that she was only on this because it was a big local story. Time would reveal if she was telling the truth.

'You're from around here then?' he asked.

'Born and raised.'

'And you know this place?' He looked about the room as he took a sip of the whiskey. It tasted damn good. Smooth, rich.

'Yeah,' she said, laughing. 'But it's not like I'm an alcoholic.'

'Of course. You just enjoy whiskey before lunch. Who doesn't?'

She scoffed at that – playfully, he thought. 'You know what the name means?'

'Rowdy Tiger? Does it describe a patron who's sampled one too many?'

'No. It's from the Free and Rowdy Party.'

He pursed his lips to show he had no clue what that meant.

'It's not a recent thing. It goes back to the nineteenth century. They were a political group, opposed to the Moral Party. Perhaps you can guess what the two sides represented.'

'One was for prohibition; one was against.'

'Bingo. Everyone knows of prohibition in the twenties, but in Atlanta? We've had multiple periods. But every time alcohol was made illegal here, people just went around the rules. Moonshine was the go-to drink, still is in a lot of rural places. The illegal speakeasies where people headed to – the amoral people, I guess – were known as blind tigers.'

'Because the moonshine made them blind?'

She laughed. 'Maybe. But let's put that fun stuff to the side. I still want to know why you, a PI as you claim, are here in Atlanta at all.'

He didn't say anything.

'You said someone called the bomb in before it happened.'

'Yeah.'

'How do you know about that?'

'Your sources didn't tell you?'

'No. They didn't.' And she sounded pretty disappointed by that.

'The caller was female,' Ryker said.

'You said that already.'

'And it was only three minutes before the explosion.'

'The first or second. You know there were two, right?'

'Yes. And I mean before the first.'

'Three minutes. Not nearly enough to actually help anyone.'

'Not really. Which is an interesting fact in itself.'

'As is, why aren't the authorities publicly talking about this? About whoever this woman, this accomplice is?'

'Exactly.'

'Do you know?'

'I think so.'

Her eyes narrowed. 'Interesting. Because you didn't say which of the two questions you were answering. So now I'm thinking both. You know who she is, and you know why her existence hasn't been revealed.'

He hadn't explicitly answered both of those questions. But he decided not to argue, given she was actually right. The obvious reason why the caller hadn't been revealed to the public was because authority figures knew it was Abby Hannigan, and they were desperate to keep that quiet because of the political ramifications, particularly in a city already at boiling point.

Yet Ryker's knowledge of Abby being the caller was by far his biggest hand here.

'You're not going to tell me who she is?' Meg asked.

'Not yet. You first.'

She sighed and finished off her whiskey. 'You want another?'

'I'm good.'

She picked up his glass and finished that too. 'Don't mind me.'

She sucked in air between her gritted teeth, likely an attempt to ease the burn of the liquor.

'There were two explosions,' she said. 'No one yet knows why. Perhaps it was deliberate, to cause more chaos than just one blast, perhaps it was a mistake. A timer malfunctioning or something. Although I don't think that, because what I've heard is that this was really well-planned.'

'You know where the blasts came from?'

'Underground.'

'The parking garage?'

'No. The sewers.'

He nodded. 'The manhole cover,' he said, thinking out loud.

'The police have connected the dots there but aren't going to make it public yet because they don't fully understand what it means. Those sewers aren't big enough for someone to just walk around the city—'

'So it needs a more discreet method of delivery. RC vehicle? Drones?'

She stopped and stared at him, and he couldn't tell what had caused her to pause. 'You seem to know a lot about this kinda thing.'

'Just thinking logically.'

'They don't think it was an RC vehicle as those pipes contain standing water, which would mess with the transport and the payload.'

'Drones then. Which means someone skilled in flying them, perhaps someone skilled in modifying them with a carrying arm of some sort. And a lot of time and patience to go back and forth dropping enough explosives, in the right places, to cause that kind of damage.'

'C4, to be precise.'

Ryker hadn't known that, but it made sense. 'Which is another giveaway. It's not like you can make the stuff in a vat at home.'

'No. It's not. But you were there at the store earlier, so you've probably figured how that location plays into things.'

'The eyewitness. The man in the van. So that woman really did see the bomber? He never even had to get close to the building.'

'That's what it sounds like. He was most likely setting the explosives from there. But that brings us to one very big question.'

'Which is?'

'Why KDD Tech? No one's claimed responsibility for this attack.'

'Do you know the answer to that?'

'I know that in the history of bombings of this nature, targets are picked for a reason.'

'KDD Tech develops software for use in—'

'Manufacturing supply chain logistics, inventory data management, blah, blah, blah. That's what they like to tell people. But I know for a fact they have contracts with the DOJ, the Pentagon, the military.'

'And how do you know that?'

'Just accept that I know it.'

Fair enough. But she obviously had some very knowledgeable and very talkative sources.

'What's your theory then?' he asked. 'That this was politically motivated?'

'Without a doubt. Which side of our messed-up political situation would do this? I have no idea. And I also don't know if it's some faction from within the US that's attempting to disrupt... something. Or if this is a fight being encouraged from outside sources.'

'It could be both at the same time. An internal group being spurred on, politically or financially, from the outside.'

'Possibly the worst-case scenario.'

They both fell silent for a few moments. A group of three men walked in, business attire, smiles and laughs between them as they headed to the bar. Perhaps the onset of a lunchtime rush.

'Now would be a really good time for you to start telling me something,' Meg said. 'Are you really a PI?'

'It's not a bad way to describe what I do.'

'That's a strange answer.'

'It's the only one I'm giving.'

'Is James Ryker your real name?'

'Yes.'

'Maybe I'll look into that.'

'Go ahead.'

She sighed, and he knew his stalling wasn't winning her over. He had to give her something, unless he was content to just end this meet-up already.

Except he wasn't. Because she intrigued him, on a personal level, but mostly because she had sources. Sources, and therefore possible in-roads, that could become valuable to Ryker here.

'I was hired by Adam Hannigan,' he said.

That frozen look again. Then she reached for the whiskey glass, looked at it glumly as though she'd forgotten it was already empty.

'The governor?' she asked.

She looked far more wary now than before. Glanced at the three guys at the bar even though they were paying Ryker and her no attention.

'Yeah,' Ryker said. 'That one.'

'Because?'

'Because my job is to help find his missing daughter, Abby. Do you know about her?'

'Everyone knows about her. It's a big deal. Wait...' She leaned in and whispered the next words. 'You think Abby Hannigan had something to do with this?'

She said it as though the prospect was outrageous. Perhaps it was.

'The caller?' Meg asked, voice still low.

Ryker nodded.

She slumped back in her chair. 'That... makes no sense.'

'Perhaps it makes a lot of sense. From what I heard she's long had ties to a far-right faction. The White Lions. You know about them?'

Ryker was saying too much now. He knew that. But his gut told him to keep going.

'You said yourself you've lived in this area your whole life—'

'It doesn't mean I know about everything that goes on here,' she countered.

'But that name does mean something to you?'

If not to her, then maybe to her law enforcement sources.

'It does,' she admitted without any further pressure.

'Craig Boswell,' Ryker added. 'That's another name I have, someone who was involved with the White Lions. Someone who was very close to Abby.'

'You're talking about events from a long time ago.'

'Six years. Not that long. So you do know that name too.'

'It was a big story. Craig Boswell was dating Abby Hannigan.'

'Yeah. I heard that.'

'And you also heard about how he died?'

'A car crash.'

Meg scoffed. 'Yeah. A crash. Do you know who was chief suspect in that crash?'

'Suspect? Why was there a suspect?'

'Because eyewitnesses claimed his car was run off the road. The make and model were reported at the time. I don't remember the details, but I do remember who had a vehicle just like it back then. Who was questioned by the police more than once but never charged.'

'Yeah?'

'Kyle Hannigan.'

The buff, square-jawed brother.

Not surprising that Adam Hannigan had said nothing about that. Although he had given Boswell's name to Ryker, which was perhaps a surprise given what Meg had just told him.

'Tell me more about the White Lions,' he said. 'Are they still active?'

'I honestly don't know. I've not heard the name for a while.'

'Do you know who to ask to find out more? A name or a place that you could point me to?'

She didn't answer straightaway, just studied him as though searching his brain for further answers to unspoken questions.

'Something tells me that even if I say no, you're going to force your way to some answers soon enough. The hard way, if needed.'

Was he that obvious?

'It's what I do,' he said. 'So your choice is simple. Help me get some answers and be first in line to write it all up after, sell the story of your life. Or... not.'

Once again she didn't say anything.

'Do you know someone who can help us or not?' he asked.

'Yeah,' she said. 'Yeah. I think I probably do.'

6

The bar on one corner of a wide intersection a few miles outside the town of Canton was aptly – perhaps boringly – named the Roadhouse. Despite the vast swathes of asphalt, the road itself was quiet, even in the middle of rush hour. But Canton was a way further north than where the Hannigans lived in the suburbs of East Cobb, the city of Atlanta further afield to the south of there, and even if a lot of the area around Canton was still built up, it had an altogether more small-town, rural feel to it.

Meg had arrived before Ryker, and he found her hanging out by her big and rather battered Honda SUV. Not a new model, but still the type of car many suburban moms and dads drove. Perhaps she had kids; Ryker actually hadn't asked her anything about her personal life. Or perhaps, like many people around here, she just decided bigger was better, and safer. No point in being the only person driving around in a compact car if everyone else had tanks that would flatten you in a collision.

Ryker parked next to her and looked around the mostly quiet street and parking lot as he got out.

'Just in time,' she said, a quick glance at her watch.

Actually, she'd said to meet him at six, and he was ten minutes early. They'd gone their separate ways in Atlanta several hours ago as she waited for a return phone call from her 'contact'. Ryker had used the time in between to find a hotel, rest up, do some basic internet searches of the names he'd gained since arriving in the US earlier in the day. Craig Boswell. The White Lions. Megan Valentino. He hadn't found out much about the first two, but had now read several of Meg's pieces, most of which consisted of uncovering malpractices of powerful figures and companies in and around Georgia. Her last big scoop, from several months ago, was when she'd blown open a corruption scheme at a health insurance company. A good, thorough investigation, from what he could find, with a substantial amount of evidence gathered from various inside sources. He'd have to find out more about how she did that – at least as it related to his own investigations.

'You know this place?' he asked her.

'No. Never been. Not my style, really,' she said, glancing over at the bar.

Ryker wouldn't say it was rough-looking, exactly, but it was certainly of a different nature – and likely with a different audience – to the upscale bar they'd been to in midtown earlier.

Probably a lot easier on the wallet too though, which wasn't a bad thing.

'Who are we meeting here?' he asked, as she'd been pretty vague in her messages earlier.

'He's called Wayne Stanton. I don't know him, but I was told he was good friends with Craig Boswell and some of the others from the White Lions.'

'Told by who?'

She laughed, although it was more a condescending laugh

than one of amusement. 'You know the first rule of someone like me, surely?'

'Never reveal your sources?'

'Exactly. Otherwise I'd never get anyone to talk to me.'

'Anything else I should know about Stanton before he gets here?'

She thought about that and sighed.

'Expect him to be brash. A bit of a redneck. This isn't a bad area but we're a long way from midtown now. He's got a few misdemeanors in his past. Assault. DUI.'

Ryker nodded.

'You look like you can take care of yourself,' she said, looking Ryker up and down.

An obvious assumption given his six-foot-four height and hefty frame, though he liked to think he could handle himself well despite his size. In fact, experience had taught a hell of a lot of people exactly that.

'I guess so.'

'I hope so. Because I can't. Not my thing at all. But just remember, around here? A lot of guys are carrying. Either on them, or something in their vehicle.'

'Noted. What about you?'

'Do I have a gun?'

'Yeah.'

'Let's hope the answer to that never becomes relevant here. But if you could... look a bit tough. Or something.'

Ryker raised an eyebrow. Stood a little taller. He puffed his chest out. Rolled up the sleeves of his shirt. 'This help?'

The look she gave him – like he was an idiot – suggested not.

'Let's go get a drink.'

* * *

The bar's interior was everything Ryker had expected from the outside. Several large screens for sports, a huge bar with a multitude of beers on tap, wall of spirits behind. Various flags and framed photos and other memorabilia of sports teams – both pro and college, both local and from further afield – covered the walls.

They settled into a booth, sitting side by side. Meg had gone for a soda this time, and Ryker felt it was at least partly because she was increasingly nervous for what was to come. He went for a large, tantalizingly cold beer. A local brew he'd not heard of.

Pretty damn good, he thought, taking nearly a third of it in his first swig.

'Feel better now?' Meg asked him.

He didn't get a chance to answer, because no sooner had he swallowed the liquid than the doors opened and two men walked in. The fact Meg kept her wide-eyed attention on the arrivals told Ryker one of them was the man they were waiting for. He tensed a little as the two guys scanned the room. Both were mid-twenties, one short and stocky, the other tall and athletic. The shorter had a bushy beard, lumberjack-style shirt, big work boots. The taller had a heavily stubbled face but closely shaved hair on top, an array of tattoos on his thick arms.

After clocking Ryker and Meg, the taller nodded over before the men went to the bar. The barman knew them, Ryker thought. A minute later, both had a beer and the short guy propped himself against the bar, glaring over at Ryker and Meg as his friend headed across.

Meg got to her feet.

'You must be Wayne?'

He reluctantly shook her hand, eyeballed Ryker who remained rooted.

'Yeah. You Megan?'

'I am. This is James.'

A slight nod to Ryker before Wayne slumped down into the booth. He sat back against the leather, spread his arms out across the top.

'You're better looking than you sounded on the phone,' Wayne said. 'Not bad at all, actually.'

'Thanks,' Meg said.

'Girl like you... I could get you some good work around here.'

'I'm flattered, but I have a job.'

'Yeah? You know Missy's?'

'No.'

He stared at her a few seconds. Obviously trying to make her uncomfortable. Then he smacked his lips. 'It's my uncle's place. I can just imagine you up on the tables there. You'd make a tidy dollar. We'd have to open an over thirties section, but I mean... Yeah.' He shrugged. Perhaps at his own douchebaggery.

'I don't think that's gonna happen,' Meg said, and Ryker could tell she was offended. Not in the least because he knew she was only twenty-eight.

Stanton shrugged again before glaring at Ryker.

'What are you? Her dad or something?'

'If I was her dad I'd probably have taken offense already, and we'd have a problem.'

Wayne smacked his lips again. Perhaps it was supposed to be intimidating.

'He's my protection,' Meg said. Ryker would have preferred if she hadn't.

'Protection from what?'

'From scumbags,' Ryker said.

He stopped himself from saying like you at the end. No need to get things heated so soon.

'Doesn't look like he's gonna do much protectin'. What are you? Fifty? And that fucking accent? What? Are you gonna annoy me to death saying bottle of water?'

He said those last words in a ridiculously over-the-top English accent. Ryker almost smiled at it.

'I think that's probably enough for introductions, don't you?' Meg said.

'Yeah. So what do you want from me?'

'You knew Craig Boswell.'

No answer as Wayne held her eye. The fact he was surprised by the question suggested he hadn't known exactly what he was there to talk about. Ryker had no idea how she'd otherwise sold the meet-up to him.

'I did.'

'And the White Lions. Were you part of that?'

'That was all a long time ago.'

'But you were part of the group?'

'Was I?'

'I was told you were. You're not in trouble about anything. It's just... I'm doing some research on them. I heard there's something of a resurgence. If not in name, then at least the cause. You've heard about all the protests going on, right? Maybe that's linked too.'

Stanton shrugged.

'I'm trying to find out more about the White Lions. Who's involved now. You know anything?'

'No. I don't.'

'So it's not something you're involved in?'

'No. It ain't.'

'But you did know Craig—'

'I already said I did.'

'And what do you think happened to him? Really.'

Stanton sipped his beer. He looked like he was about to answer but then a guttural thrum of an engine outside stole everyone's attention. Bright headlights pulsed through the grimy windows as the approaching vehicle slowed and parked. Stanton and his friend exchanged a glance. Ryker and Meg too.

Moments later the door opened and three men stormed in, each a little older than Wayne and his friend. The oldest and shortest of them strode straight over and slipped into the booth next to Wayne, budging him over without either saying a word. The other, more meaty-looking two, hovered.

'You know who I am?' the guy next to Wayne asked, looking from Meg to Ryker.

He got two nos in response.

'I'm the guy you should have come to. Instead of this little prick.' He slapped Stanton across the ear. The young guy looked all sulky now, his bravado on the wane.

'I'm Megan Valentino,' Meg said, holding her hand out to the newcomer.

'I don't give a fuck what your name is. What I want to know is why you're around this part of town, asking questions about things, people, you shouldn't be.'

'I... er... I'm a journalist.'

'Course you are. Well I'm here now. So ask away.'

Meg had lost her stride. All of her confidence. She hemmed and hawed, looking to Ryker as if for support.

'I want to know more about the White Lions. It's... for a piece I'm writing... You've heard of all the protests down in the city, right? I'm trying to figure out if the White Lions are back. If they're involved in any of that.'

'What the fuck are you talking about?'

'That's just a part of it. The main theme... is about how the government, its policies, are alienating, marginalizing young white men across the country.'

Smart play at the end, because the guy looked like he was considering her answer. Looked like he maybe wasn't so angry about the intrusion into his world after all if Meg was on his side.

But then his natural anger, suspiciousness returned.

'Show me your phone,' he said to Meg. 'You too, big man.'

'I'm not doing that,' Meg said, as Ryker took his phone out of his pocket.

'Unlock it.'

Ryker did, turned it so the guy could see. He'd already figured what was happening. The guy wanted to know if this conversation was being recorded.

'Now you,' he said to Meg.

'No.'

The guy sighed then looked over at his friends. One of them smashed a beer bottle against a pillar, sending glass and sticky liquid all over.

'Hey!' the barman shouted, but then backed down when he received a death glare.

'Show me your damn phone or your friend gets it in the neck. And I'm not playing.'

'Do it, Meg,' Ryker said.

'Thanks, big guy, for the encouragement, but who the fuck told you to speak?'

Meg finally reached down and dug in her purse. Ryker saw her try to quickly mess with the device but the guy jumped up from his seat, reached across and grabbed the phone from her. He stared at the screen as Meg reeled in shock.

'Just what I thought.'

He stood up, dropped the phone and stomped on it a few

times. Meg jolted with each strike. The guy remained on his feet once satisfied that the phone was destroyed.

'Both of you, get out. And I don't wanna see either of your ugly faces around here again.'

'Come on,' Ryker said, pulling on Meg's arm.

She seemed reluctant, as though there was a way for her to talk these people around. But then she relented and got up. Ryker could tell she was upset, not just because of the phone but the confrontation. Her legs were shaking. Her eyes bleary.

'Don't forget what I said about Missy's!' Wayne called over from his seat. 'We'd all love to see what you got!'

'Ignore them,' Ryker said, again gently pulling on Meg's arm. Best just to get out of there now.

But they hadn't made it to the door when two women walked in from the street.

They were all laughs and giggles but then one – dyed black hair, dark clothing, thick black eyeliner – locked on to Meg.

'You?'

Ryker pulled harder on Meg's arm now, determined to get to the door and out.

'Hey, Jay! I know her! She's with that GBI bitch!'

Ryker sensed the movement behind. He let go of Meg, spun, and prepared to take on whichever of the guys had burst forward.

Except before he could do anything, Meg had spun too, reached into her purse, pulled out the pepper spray and unleashed it into the bearded man's face.

He screeched and reeled back.

And everyone else descended.

'Get to the car!' Ryker shouted at Meg, moving in front of her as the guy with the broken glass came forward. He swooshed it through the air. Ryker crisscrossed his wrists to block the strike. Used his heel – into the man's chest – to push him away.

His friend was already lunging forward too. An attempted haymaker. Ryker dodged, grabbed his arm, flung him forward and his head smacked off one of the beams.

Glass-guy was back on his feet. He darted forward again. Ryker sidestepped, grabbed his wrist with one hand, grabbed two fingers with the other and yanked back.

Snap.

The man screamed. He released his grip on the broken glass. Ryker took the shard in his hand, wrapped one arm around the man's neck as he went up behind him for cover. He placed the tip of the glass against the man's skin, right below his left ear.

'Keep back!' Ryker shouted at the circling crowd.

Stanton and his friend looked poised to attack. The two women who'd come in seethed but looked like they just wanted to see blood rather than spill it.

The boss-guy? He just stood, arms folded, looking really, really angry.

'No one else needs to get hurt,' Ryker said.

'He broke my fingers!'

'I'm gonna back-step out of here,' Ryker said. 'I'll let him go. Then we're out of here, and this is over.'

'You think this is over?' Boss-guy said.

Ryker didn't respond to that. Just took two more steps back until his foot brushed the door.

He was about to lower his hand, the one with the glass, to open the door when he saw Stanton reaching to his side.

Gun.

Ryker released the man and kicked him forward, before hunkering down as the gun blasted. Wood splinters splatted into him as he wrenched the door open and dashed outside. He ducked even further down as bullets pinged into the cars by him.

'Go, go, go!' Ryker shouted at Meg, who was already in the driver's seat of her car.

Ryker went for the handle of the passenger door but Stanton – or one of the others, who was now armed too – was already outside and another bullet smashed into the window, spraying glass everywhere. Ryker rushed around the front of the vehicle and slid down behind the wheel the other side.

He heard the footsteps across the hood. Muted voices. Then laughter.

'We know you're there!' Stanton shouted. 'Come on out. We only wanna talk.'

He got a whole lot of laughter to that comment for some reason. Ryker didn't see the joke.

Ryker leaned further down, looking under Meg's car. Several sets of feet the other side.

'Get out of the car, Meg,' Stanton said.

Ryker couldn't see her from his position, but he willed her not to. Would they really just execute her – him? – there in the parking lot? He highly doubted it.

'You don't got a choice, Meg. Get out the car.'

The door right by Ryker opened and she stepped into the open, glancing down to Ryker momentarily as though asking what the hell else she – they – could do.

At least, that's what he thought she was doing. But then her hand slipped out from her jacket pocket, ever so slyly.

Gun. A compact little handgun. Not much to it at all. Probably fired little more than ball bearings.

A lot better than nothing.

She dropped it and Ryker reached out and scooped it up

and lay down on the ground and pointed it out underneath the car.

Bang, bang, bang, bang.

At least two hits from the four shots. A lot of screaming and shouting. Ryker leaped up over the hood of Meg's car. Shot at whatever moved. He raced up to Stanton who was cradling a bleeding shoulder as he tried in vain to re-aim. No chance. Ryker smashed into him, his elbow crunching into the guy's chin and sending him flying.

Ryker didn't see the strike from behind him coming. A blow to the head. A big, hefty blow. Baseball bat? Metal pole? He lurched forward. The gun spilled from his grip. He took another hit to his legs and went down to one knee.

Rough hands grabbed him from behind. Tried to pin his hand behind his back. An arm snaked around his neck.

Boss-guy stepped into view.

'You stupid fu—'

He didn't finish. Or maybe he did but Ryker just didn't hear as he snapped his arm free and sank his teeth into the flesh right by his mouth. Then he jumped to his feet and reached back and grabbed the man there and dropped down again, tossing the guy over his shoulder and into a heap on the floor.

He spun and swiped the feet of the second man behind him.

Saw the gun on the ground only a few feet away. Not Meg's. A much better one.

He went to get it but one of the women kicked it away and he dove across the ground for it.

He heard an engine firing up. The boss-guy's truck. A huge thing on meaty, off-road tires. The brake lights flicked off and the vehicle shot back, and Ryker rolled out of the way just in time before being crushed. He looked across. Meg was still by the car.

'Get in!' he shouted.

The truck swung around, headlights blinding.

And then it gunned for him, the raucous engine making the ground shake. The looming beast was too big, too close. Ryker fired the gun in desperation before he dove to his right. Would have still been pulverized by the monster machine had the driver not tugged on the wheel at the last moment. Perhaps a mistake. Perhaps intentional. Ryker had no idea.

Smash.

He jolted from the huge impact – metal on metal – but then jumped back to his feet.

Froze.

Steam hissed out of the front of the truck, clouding the view, but no mistaking what the truck had hit.

Meg's car.

But not just her car. Meg was sandwiched between, her whole body up to her shoulders crushed between the two vehicles.

Her startled eyes stared into space as her head quivered, blood dripping from her mouth.

An eerie silence took over for a second or two before shouting and screaming once more.

'Go! Everyone! Get outta here!'

He wasn't even sure if it was the same person shouting all those things but within seconds everyone was fleeing, jumping into vehicles here and there. The truck reversed and Meg's body – now freed – slumped down and Ryker dashed forward and didn't quite catch her before she smacked into the ground.

He slid down to her, pulled her crumpled body onto his lap.

'Meg.'

Pathetic that that was all he could think to say.

'You caused this,' Boss-guy said, looking down at Ryker from his open window, no hint of regret from him before his truck sped away.

Meg gargled and coughed blood and locked eyes with Ryker.

'You'll be OK,' he said, knowing exactly how weak that sounded.

He reached for his phone. Hit 911.

'You're gonna be OK,' he repeated.

Her eyes didn't leave his.

'This... is... quite... the scoop... huh?' she choked out.

A moment later her eyes slid back and her head flopped, and after that she didn't move at all.

7

The drive north was long but otherwise straightforward enough and I arrived in the town of Greensboro, North Carolina before nightfall. I'd been here before. Several times, actually. I'd sat outside the gates to this very house, watching, analyzing. Planning. Not that this particular plan needed much elaboration. Often simplicity was supreme.

The leafy street in this part of the town was quiet, with no traffic at all. Each of the homes here was a multimillion-dollar mansion, not for the seriously wealthy, but people who'd certainly made it into the top 1 percent. I didn't begrudge people who lived like this. Not anymore. My purpose, my outlook on the world, on humanity was on a much bigger scale these days.

A car turned into the street a couple of hundred yards in front of me. It slowed as it approached and I knew this was the vehicle – the person – I'd been waiting for.

The car pulled to a stop at the gates which slowly swung open. Moments later and the car rolled forward and I opened my door and stepped out into the darkness. I scurried in through the open gates, keeping to the dark spots, my black clothing only helping me to further blend into the night as I followed the car to its next stop at the side of the house. The engine shut down and I heard the click as the doors unlocked.

I raced to the passenger door, flung it open, and sank into the seat. I pressed the barrel of the handgun to the cheek of the man behind the steering wheel.

'Move. I dare you.'

He didn't. Almost a disappointment, really.

'Who the fuck are you?' he asked, his eyes fixed ahead of him. He had one hand frozen on his door handle. His other was on his thigh, his fingers spread out as though he was thinking about reaching for something off to his right, between us. Gun in the center console perhaps. Or in the glove compartment which he had absolutely zero chance of reaching now.

'Put your hands on the steering wheel. Ten and two.'

'I asked you who the fuck you are?'

'Just do what I say.'

'You want money? Is that it?'

'Move your hands now.' I pushed the gun further into his cheek, causing his head to bend to the side. His face was all twisted in a scowl – anger consuming him and winning out over fear. It was the reaction I'd expected from this man. But I knew it wouldn't last.

He moved his hands slowly onto the wheel.

'Keep them there.'

'You want the car?' he said. 'Take it.'

'No. I don't want your car.'

'Money? How much do you want? We can do it right here. I'll transfer it from my phone. Then you can fuck off and leave me and my family alone.'

'Your family?'

He gritted his teeth, perhaps regretting his words, as though he'd just revealed something he shouldn't have. But he hadn't. I knew so much more about this man than he'd ever know.

'You mean your wife and daughter?' I said. 'They're inside, aren't they?'

He said nothing.

'You're worried I'm going to go inside?'

'You have no need to. Whatever you want, I'll get it for you.'

I laughed. A petty reaction, really, and I knew he didn't understand it. Not yet.

But I was done with his negotiating already. He didn't notice me slip the syringe out of my pocket with my right hand and his only reaction as I plunged it into his neck was a surprised jolt as his brain battled to figure out what I was doing, and what he should do.

Nothing. With the barrel of the gun pressed to his face, he did nothing as the tranquilizer coursed through his blood.

'Please...' was all he said.

One hand slipped from the wheel. Then the other. I opened the center console. Yeah. Handgun.

He should have gone for it. It would have been his one and only chance.

The keys to his house were there too. I lifted those out and dangled them in front of his barely open eyes.

'Look what I found,' I said. 'I hope your family is more welcoming than you.'

He moaned something unintelligible, though the panic in his eyes was clear before they closed and his head lolled.

I stepped out into the darkness once again and made my way to the front door.

* * *

The family home was quiet all around me as I headed back down the stairs, and I stopped in the hallway a moment to look over the wall of family photos. Dad, Mom and daughter. Vacations to the beach, skiing, hiking. The typical life of a wealthy American family.

Happy times.

Not so much anymore.

I opened the front door and moved outside and over to the car. The man of the house was still out cold. And he was hefty. In his mid-fifties, it had clearly been many years since he'd been at his best fitness-wise, his once muscular frame now overly pudgy. Probably to the tune of 250 pounds. A dead weight with him unconscious, and it took me several minutes to drag him out of the car and to my minivan which I'd brought closer to the house.

Not long after and we were on the road.

Not long after and we arrived at our next destination.

Nothing special about this place. Just an empty warehouse, quiet enough that the noise wouldn't disturb anyone.

A bit of effort to get him inside and prepared and then it was time to wake him up. I could have let that happen naturally, but I wanted to be back in Georgia from this detour – of sorts – sooner rather than later.

The shot of adrenaline roused him almost instantaneously, his eyes springing open, his body flexing and shuddering. The confusion on his face as his brain calibrated was a real picture.

'Welcome back,' I said, as I rested on my haunches in front of him.

He fought against the restraints on the chair to which he was tied, wide-open eyes bouncing around the room.

'What are you doing!' he shouted. 'My... my family?'

A hopeful question, if anything. I said nothing in return.

Just watched the confusion, the turmoil, ebb and flow on his face as conflicting emotions surged and wrestled for control. He was such a mess already. If the world could only see him like this.

'If you hurt them...'

I still said nothing.

'What do you want from me?' he shrieked, desperation winning over in that moment. 'Money? You want money?'

'This isn't about money. That should be obvious by now.'

'Then what? Please... just tell me my family—'

'I'm sorry.'

He stopped talking, and even though I knew he wanted to be mad, he started to sob.

'You should have been there to protect them,' I said.

Now he was shaking, almost uncontrollably.

'You want me to tell you what I did to them?'

No words. Just sobs.

'While you were unconscious I let myself inside. I think your wife thought it was you coming home. She met me at the door, all smiles. Until I rushed her and smashed her in the face with my fist. I tied her up then found your daughter in her room, headphones in her ears, so she hadn't heard me coming. I tied her up too. Took them both to your bedroom.' He squirmed and pleaded but I wasn't really listening, only intent on telling him the story. 'Then your girl watched as I ravaged your wife. Gloria? Wow. And she fought. She really did. Right until the end. I'm sorry to say, it got ugly. Real ugly. I'm talking blood and guts and who knows what else all over.' I brushed my clothes down. A little dramatically, really. 'It's why I had to change. And it wasn't my intent to go that far with her, but she... made me do that. She shouldn't have fought so hard.'

'You bastard! I'll kill you!'

'No. You won't. I promise you, I was a lot quicker with your girl. I'm not sick like that. I wouldn't touch a girl that young. This wasn't about that. Not about sex. Not about control. This is about you. Punishing you. The bullet to the head was the kindest thing I could do for your daughter. I hope you agree.'

I'm not really sure what his words were that followed, such was the uncontrolled nature of his screams. A lot of swearing, a lot of promising me he would hurt me, and the like. I let him get it all out, until he was spent. His voice hoarse. His face bright red and dripping with sweat, just as his mouth dripped with spittle.

He finished with a pathetic, 'Why?'

'The first sensible thing you've said.'

And I was about to answer him but his anger won out again.

'Take that mask off, you piece of shit! I wanna see your face! I wanna see your face! I wanna look you in the eyes and for you to tell me what the hell I did for you to hurt two innocent—'

'Innocent,' I said. Not forcefully. Quite quietly. But the word, my interjection, stopped his tirade and caused him to pause. 'Innocent is an interesting choice of word. What does it mean to you?'

'What are you talking about? I don't know who you are or why you're doing this!'

'You will. And just to be clear, your wife and daughter were innocent. Innocent of your wrongs as a man. But does that mean they didn't deserve to suffer? Because I had to cause you pain. And through them I could.'

Sobbing again. Until I laughed.

'OK. Shit.' I held my hands up. 'I'm sorry. I take it all back. I might have told... a little fib just then. Several, actually.' He looked so goddamn confused. It was glorious! 'Peter. I never touched your wife or your daughter, you dumb fuck.'

Confusion. Relief. Confusion. Hatred. Solace. The roller-coaster of emotions was really something to behold.

'That is the truth,' I said, hand to my heart. 'They weren't in the house. And I knew that before I went inside.'

I'd never intended to hurt them. Not directly, anyway. Of course, their lives would be forever changed after tonight, but that was something different.

'Why are you—'

'Doing this?'

I moved my fingers up to my face, to the mask. Not the usual prosthetic I wore, but a simple hockey mask, like that psycho in the horror movies used to wear. It seemed more apt here. More in keeping with what I was doing. The thick plastic had muffled my voice some, which perhaps explained why he'd had no clue yet who I was, even though he definitely knew me.

It was time now for the reveal.

'You wanted to see my face?' I said.

I pulled off the mask and ran my fingers over my lumpy, bumpy, shriveled, contorted skin.

His mouth was open, his eyes wide again, but he said nothing for a few seconds.

'You,' he said. 'You're—'

'Don't say my name. Neither my real name nor that disgusting moniker.'

'You're dead.'

'The person I was... died a long time ago. The lump of flesh that barely resembled a human being... the lump that they brought back here... me... it's not the same person.'

'I'm...'

'What? Sorry?'

'It wasn't my fault!'

He shouted the words with such conviction that perhaps he really did believe them.

'Shall I tell you why I went into your home?'

He didn't answer the question. Although I didn't really give him much time before I pulled the handful of military medals from my pocket.

I opened my palm to show them to him. He shook his head, as though not yet understanding.

'You got these, while I got this!' I yelled, pointing to my destroyed face before I lurched forward, my eyes an inch from his, for the first time struggling to contain myself. He didn't move. Held his breath as though unsure what I was about to do or perhaps just because he was so disgusted by me being so close to him. And he was right to be. I knew what I looked like. The face was only the start. He was lucky he didn't have to look at everything else.

I grabbed his chin with one hand. Dropped all but one of the medals and I forced the little piece of metal between his gums and into his mouth. I shoved another in as he bucked on the chair. Another. Another. The next one I had to really hammer home as he tried his best to clamp his jaw shut. I'm pretty sure at least one of his teeth shattered in the process and blood dribbled from his lips.

The fifth medal... It took some effort. And I was angry. I thought I could do it and stay calm and in control, but it was becoming a struggle. As he fought against me I used so much power, pushed so hard, that I ripped out the bolts holding the chair to the ground and it – and him – fell backward, me landing on top, crushing down on his ribs. His mouth opened just enough from the blow, and I shoved that last medal inside, finding more space than I'd imagined.

I soon realized why.

The fall had caused the medals to fall to the back of his throat. He coughed and wheezed, his bloodshot eyes panicked.

'How many men died for you to get your rewards?' I said quietly, almost a whisper with my cheek against his, my mouth right by his ear.

Of course he couldn't answer.

'How many lives were destroyed?'

Nothing but the last gargles of a dying man in response.

'It seems right to me that those medals are now the cause of your end.'

I lifted off of him to look into his defeated eyes.

'But... have you truly suffered yet, like I've suffered? Don't you think you should have to feel what I felt?'

I yanked open his jaw and fished the medals out one by one. The last was wedged deep and I had to force pretty much my whole hand in there, the sides of his mouth splitting a little for me to do so.

But I saved him. He choked and spluttered, his face all contorted and purple.

'Please,' he mumbled. 'Please.'

As though he finally understood.

'Can you imagine the pain I endured?'

He shook his head. 'Please!'

But there was nothing he could say to change a thing now.

I took out the lighter and flicked the flame on and held it out toward him, watching the little flicker of light, reliving something in my mind that no human should have to live through.

'I hope after this you'll understand.'

I lit the end of his pants leg. A slow start. Nearly twenty seconds passed as he moaned and writhed with the flames not moving more than a couple of inches. Perhaps he still thought this could end some other way...

No. Only one way now.

Soon his whole leg was alight. Then his jacket sleeve lit up, next his chest, and pretty soon his screams really ratcheted when his head was finally engulfed, the skin and flesh across his whole body now cooking.

I watched, barely moving. The noise didn't last much longer. The noise from him, at least. Pretty soon the only sound I could hear was the raspy breaths from my nose – the way I always sounded now – and the roar of the flames that had consumed the man in front of me.

He hadn't endured for long, but in his last moments he'd finally understood some of the pain I'd suffered because of his mistakes. Mistakes? Perhaps a kind way to describe it. Actions. Simply his actions. Selfish, careless actions over many years, as though he'd only been playing chess with an old friend and not with the lives of countless real men and women.

And yet it wasn't just his actions that he'd had to atone for here, but the years of lies that had followed. Possibly that had preceded my torment too. Men like him... that's just who they were, how they lived.

What he would never know, or feel, was the pain I'd suffered in the months and years that had followed. First as I'd clung desperately to life, and then subsequently as I'd tried to rebuild something. That pain was true torture, both mentally and physically, far worse than his last short moments.

But he simply didn't deserve the second chance that I'd fought so hard for.

So I'd let him burn. Burn right through until all the fuel was consumed.

And once the fire was out, I'd move on to the next.

He wasn't the first and he wouldn't be the last to face their reckoning.

8

Disposing of the General's body had taken longer than expected and I decided against going straight back to Georgia. Instead, I made a detour west from North Carolina and into my native Tennessee. It'd been too long since I'd driven these roads, and perhaps I should never have left, or perhaps I should never have returned. Both of those outcomes carried solid arguments for and against.

As for going back like this, on a whim?

I couldn't explain it, even to myself.

I parked on the road outside 10835 Parkview Terrace. A modest house in a modest neighborhood on the south side of Knoxville. This wasn't my home. It never had been, yet this could and really should have been my life. My intended life.

The time was already past 10 p.m. and everything was quiet. I sat there in the dark for more than half an hour but saw nothing and no one before I gave up and retreated. No point in attracting unwanted attention. I found a shitty motel and paid fifty bucks for a single room for the night and got a surprisingly restful sleep. Perhaps some of my demons were finally vanquished. Although really I knew that wasn't the case, and in fact it couldn't be the case; I wouldn't allow for that, for any kind of comfort or pleasure in what I was doing because that was so far from the point, and there was still so much work to be done.

In the morning I skipped breakfast and headed straight back to Parkview Terrace, but this time parked a little away from 10835, although the house was still within view.

I didn't have to wait long before the garage door lifted up and the Hyundai Palisade rolled off the drive and headed away from me. Greg was behind the wheel. Claire's new husband. I didn't hate her for having remarried. She thought I was dead. No, the man she knew really was dead. Of course she should move on.

The school bus came around the corner ahead of me. A moment later and the front door of 10835 opened and Claire and Emily stepped out. The morning was chilly and Emily had a hoodie on, the hood pulled up so I couldn't see her face fully, nor her usually flowing hair. She was taller than when I'd last seen her. At ten years old she was growing so quickly now. She'd been so small, sweet, innocent when I'd last held her, talked to her.

Talked to her properly, I mean. Before.

I'll never forget those first days after waking up in the hospital. By waking up, I mean when my mind was finally lucid enough for me to remember things clearly, logically, as apparently I'd been physically awake for several weeks by that point. My body was still a mess – I couldn't move, couldn't breathe fully on my own, couldn't eat. Could barely speak. But I could say enough. I could say my wife's name. Say my daughter's name. At least clear enough for the nurses to hear, to understand.

It's hard to describe that moment of awakening. Because I

knew I'd been gone. That I was alive, that something real bad had happened, but that I wasn't in the room, so to speak. The severe trauma my body had suffered, the pain I'd endured to the point of getting the medical attention so desperately needed to keep me alive soon led to a coma, then awake but absent for a much longer time. But opening my eyes that morning, I somehow knew what it all meant, and I really, really so desperately wanted the first face I saw to be that of one of my girls. Claire or Emily. It didn't matter which one, I loved them both so much.

I didn't see either of them, although there's no doubt that the faces I did see were kind, welcoming. It helped ease my torment. Perhaps blindsided me a bit too, though.

I was back on US soil at that point, but nowhere near home. I was told Claire had already been by my side before I'd awoken but it was two more days before she returned, and she didn't bring Emily. I was so relieved to see my wife, but I already knew then that... things would never be the same. That something had been lost.

Claire couldn't look at me. Not like she once did. I was still covered in bandages then, so the worst of what I'd become was hidden, but it was as though she knew, just sensed what was underneath.

She wouldn't bring Emily. She didn't want to upset our daughter. That was fine too. Emily was so young and was dealing with her own trauma of having nearly lost her dad and not understanding why, if he was alive, he hadn't just come home. I didn't get to see her for another six weeks. Four days after the bandages on my face were off for good.

I'd not slept all night, I was almost giddy with anticipation. I was still mostly bedridden so I knew I wouldn't be able to jump out of bed and pick her up and swing her in my arms like I used to, like I wanted to so badly, but in my head I still expected it to be a huge moment of reconciliation. I just really wanted to see her face and her smile and for her to look me in the eyes and hold my hand, and for me to tell her I loved her and for her to say she loved me too.

Stupid, I know.

She barely even made it into the room before she froze dead in horror, holding on to her mom's hand so tight that Claire grimaced in pain.

Or perhaps just grimaced at her daughter's reaction to seeing her father. The monster.

The Burning Man.

Emily couldn't take it. No amount of gentle persuasion from her mother would calm her down. She was upset, scared, didn't want to be there. Didn't want to be anywhere near me.

And I didn't blame her one bit.

I shook the painful memories away. Claire and Emily reached the end of the driveway and for a brief moment Emily turned and glanced toward my car. But she just as quickly looked away again as she and Claire moved along the road toward the bus stop fifty yards away.

I sighed as I watched Emily step onto the bus, Claire by then deep in morning chit-chat with the other happy-looking parents at the bus stop.

I stayed in my car until everyone had dispersed, more than a couple of wary glances in my direction by then.

Doubts filled my head.

Why had I come here today? It hadn't been my intention yesterday as I headed into North Carolina.

But by the time the bus had left I'd figured why.

It was because of the General's family. Wife and daughter, just like mine. Perhaps they wouldn't yet know the man of the house would never return home, but when it did eventually become fact to them, their whole world would change forever. Perhaps they'd never know the truth of the man, why he'd deserved his end. It didn't matter to me one way or another. They'd suffer. Much like my family had suffered because of what had happened to me. Suffering. But not like he had. Not like I had.

No doubt though, my family were better off without me. Less pain for them this way.

I wondered if, in time, the same would be said for the General's family?

The hole in my heart growing larger, pulling, dragging on me, I started the engine and headed away.

* * *

The office block in Newnan, a city about forty miles southwest of Atlanta, wasn't particularly old. Perhaps twenty years or so. Yet it'd been styled as an old Victorian-era factory building with a redbrick exterior, tall black-painted lead-effect windows. From the outside it looked like a quite classy renovation. The inside had never received quite so much attention. Perhaps because the developer had never found enough clients to fill out the property. The result was that only the top two floors of the six-story block had ever been occupied, by a firm called BTC Capital – a local wealth management firm. BTC being Bryan Tucker Crawford. Although 'occupied' was quite a loose term as I'd been to this place many, many times now and my impression was that no more than four people worked up there.

Bryan Tucker Crawford. I'd heard others call him Bryan Fucking Clawface, and I kind of saw why as the guy was hardly movie-star handsome, but given my own position I was hardly one to use a jibe like that. To many of his closest allies he was known only by his initials. BTC – the man – was the owner of BTC Capital, and also behind the property developer that had originally built the office block. BTC had his fingers in so many pies around the state and beyond, was often lauded as one of the richest men in Georgia. I'd met him a few times, because he wasn't just letting us use this space rent free, he was also a close and long-time friend of Terrence Kielder – the man I was working with now. Kielder was the man everyone answered to, but BTC was the man whose millions were helping fund what we were doing. Helped fund so much of the growing discontent around the region and beyond, from the big-city protests – which were so often deliberately turned into violent melees – to the fierce and unrelenting social media smear campaigns and rallying calls. And he did all that without ever having his name associated with any of it. The way it had to be for him to eventually reap the rewards of our plans.

I parked my car in the near-empty lot and headed on into the expansive lower floor space. Bare concrete floors, walls, ceiling. Steel props were placed here and there as though to add to the industrial feel. A cluster of small, largely unfinished offices sat on the far side of the floor, and I heard voices that way and headed over.

I paused in the corridor and listened. What might have been a boardroom, if this office space had ever been properly finished, was the usual hiding place for Kielder and his closest confidants. I wasn't one of them. In fact, I had no hesitation in saying I was an outsider to most here, even if my being part of this group was essential. For all parties.

I heard three voices from beyond the partly opened door: Kielder, his voice measured and authoritative and with a distinctive Southern twang, but not so much that anyone from outside the area would consider him a yokel. Next was Reed. In his mid-fifties, he was actually about the eldest of all of the guys in Kielder's crew. And the term yokel definitely befitted this man. He was gruff, rough, a loudmouth misogynist, racist, homophobe. Saying we didn't get on too well would be a mild way of putting things. The other voice was Danny Meyers. A bit of an unknown to me, really. He was younger, more unassuming, but from what I knew he was well-educated, quick-witted, and came from a wealthy family. I didn't understand fully how he fit in around here, but somehow he did and I often thought that perhaps Kielder saw him as something of a protégé.

'Where the fuck is Stanton now?' Kielder asked.

'Lying low. Obviously,' Reed said.

'I don't want him lying low, I want him over here so I can tear his fucking fingernails off!'

Interesting. Something had got Kielder riled up. No, not something. Someone. Stanton. Wayne Stanton. I knew the name but not much about the guy. A nobody, really, as far as I was aware. An acquaintance of Reed. Nephew, perhaps.

'We need to let things quieten down,' Reed said. 'We don't need the GBI breathing down our necks right now.'

'We wouldn't have the GBI or anyone else anywhere near us —' Meyers now '—if you hadn't ridden up to Canton and started a firefight with—'

'Who the fuck asked for your opinion?' Reed cut in.

'Maybe I did,' Kielder added. 'But why don't you just explain to me... what the hell you thought you'd achieve by going in there guns blazing.'

'I didn't, did I? That guy made the first move.'

'The mystery—'

'Hey there, Marshall,' came the soft voice from behind me, and I cut my attention from the other conversation – argument

– and turned to Hailey. I hadn't heard her approaching. Perhaps she'd snuck up on me deliberately. She liked to do things like that. Hailey – I was sure that wasn't her real name, but it was the one she went by here – was officially Kielder's girl, even though she was a good ten years younger than him. Due to her relationship with Kielder – or perhaps in spite of it – she saw herself as part of this group, a voice to be listened to, even if some of the men – Reed in particular – didn't like the idea of having to consider a woman's opinion on anything. Unlike most of the others, Hailey didn't seem to mind my presence. In fact, she'd stuck up for me more than once in the past. Although I wouldn't go anywhere near as far as to say we got along. We simply didn't know each other well enough for that to be the case.

'What's got them all uptight?' I asked.

'You could just go ahead and ask them, rather than lurking.'

OK, so maybe she'd stuck up for me at times, but she was still Kielder's girl, and her loyalty was to him and not me.

'I only just got here. And when I heard the shouting... I didn't want to blast in there and—'

'What the fuck are you two doing out here?' Reed said, swinging the door fully open before he poked his ugly bearded head out. 'Snooping again, Burning Man? You fucking freak.'

'Zip it, dipshit,' Hailey said as she strode up to Reed and bumped his shoulder to move into the room.

Reed held my eye a moment before he grunted something and went back inside. I followed in to see all eyes on me.

'I don't know how long he was standing out there for,' Reed said.

'Not long,' Hailey confirmed. 'He wasn't there when I went to the restroom.'

'Have I done something wrong?' I asked.

'No,' Kielder said. 'But everyone's a bit on edge today.'

'And you've been missing for the best part of two days,' Reed said. 'Where the fuck have you been? And where the hell is Christine?'

Christine being the other woman in this group. She and Hailey were both expert computer programers, hackers, and were the key to us cracking open the data we'd – I'd – stolen from KDD Tech.

'Which question should I answer first?' I asked.

'Where have you been?' Kielder said.

'Personal business,' I answered, and I knew no one would particularly like that answer. As far as any of them were concerned I had no life, nothing worth doing, nobody worth seeing. As Reed had already said, I was a freak to them. A loner freak.

'You want to tell us about that personal business?' Meyers asked.

'No.'

'And Christine?' Reed asked.

'I've had no contact with her,' I said. 'Have you?'

'No,' Kielder said. 'None of us has. But we've already lost two days of work. We never expected Hailey to have to trawl through that data on her own.'

'She's not on her own. I can help,' I said.

'Except you've been gone for two days as well.'

Reed stepped closer to me. 'Tell us again about the last time you saw her.'

I sighed. 'Right after KDD Tech I met up with her—'

'Where?'

'Outside a Dollar General near East Point. I handed the data to her, went on my way. Just as we planned.'

'And the data was already here when I arrived,' Hailey added. 'But no Christine.'

'And no one's seen her since,' Kielder added.

'Or, if they have, they're lying about it,' I clarified. I received a lot of scathing, accusatory looks for that comment.

'Do we need to consider that the police have her?' Meyers asked.

'We need to consider it,' Kielder said. 'But I just don't believe that's the answer. She made it back here with the data then just disappeared? It doesn't make sense. And why would the police target her? She was nowhere near KDD Tech.'

'No,' Reed said. 'The only person that was... was you.'

He pointed a finger at me, both literally and figuratively.

'You are correct, Brad. Because I did all the hard work on the ground myself. Alone. Thank you for the realization.'

I gave him a little nod. He kind of growled at me.

'Want to tell me why you're all so antsy anyway?' I asked.

At first nobody did. But then Hailey decided to speak. 'Last night Stanton and Reed had a bit of a run in, up in Canton. Some—'

Kielder slapped her around the face. Pretty hard. It sent her off balance and she cradled her cheek for a few seconds, and when she removed her hand there were neat, red imprints of Kielder's fingers across her skin.

'You weren't there,' he said to her. 'And neither was I. So Reed, you do the talking.'

'Why should we tell him anything?' Reed said.

'Because whether you like it or not, he's part of this group as much as you are. We need him. You know that.'

'I'm sure we could find ourselves another resident psychopath if we really wanted to.'

'I don't want to. That's why he's here, and not someone else.'

The deep scowl on Reed's face suggested he didn't agree. He

sighed and continued to glower at me as though it'd make a difference to anything.

'Last night Stanton got a call from a journalist,' Reed said. 'Meg Valentino. I don't know everything to it, but he agreed to meet her, the dickhead. Only I got wind of it and realized it was a setup, that she was poking her nose in, trying to get some intel on us.'

'How'd you figure that?' I asked.

'It doesn't matter. I went up there to stop it. I had no time to do anything else. And I did stop it. Until Stanton's dumbass bitch turned up and blew the whole situation to hell.'

'Who? Kylie?' Meyers asked.

'I don't fucking know her name. But she and her friend burst into the bar unannounced and started yapping about how this reporter was known to the GBI or something and after that... everyone was fighting and shooting.'

Reed shook his head and looked to the floor as though having a hard time explaining the detail on that last part. Probably because of embarrassment.

'I'm sensing that didn't end well,' I said.

'It ended with Stanton and three others being shot and Reed smashing his truck into Valentino before he and everyone else ran off,' Meyers said.

'Valentino was doing the shooting?' I asked.

'No. She had a bodyguard with her,' Reed said. 'Don't know anything about him, name or nothing.'

'Except that he was British, apparently,' Meyers added.

'Sure sounded it.'

'And Valentino's links to the GBI?' I asked.

'We know now her brother's married to an agent,' Kielder said. 'Or was married to her.'

'It could be nothing,' Meyers said.

'Doesn't sound like nothing to me,' I added.

'No one asked you,' Reed responded.

The room fell silent and after a few more glares and the like were exchanged, eyes slowly turned to Kielder as though awaiting his verdict.

'You need to bring Stanton and anyone else who was there to me,' he said. 'Every one of them has to sit and look me in the eyes and convince me why I shouldn't bury them.'

'You can't just...' Reed started, but then obviously thought better of whatever he was going to say.

'What?' Kielder challenged.

'Stanton's a good guy. And if you start offing good guys every time they make a mistake...'

'He's got a point,' Hailey added. 'We need less heat, not more.'

'Would you keep that goddamn mouth of yours shut!' Kielder said to her before returning his ire to Reed. 'Just bring the dumbasses to me.'

'What does this mean for our plans?' I asked.

Reed threw his hands in the air with over-the-top indignation. 'Here we go again. Our plans. Fucking hell. What, not enough bombing and maiming over the last forty-eight hours for your liking?'

'We continue on,' Kielder said to me. 'But we are rearranging. I've taken out two of your targets for now. We need to speed up the end process some.'

'Sorry, what targets are out?' I asked.

'We'll go through that another time. I've got a few calls to make but you all need to be ready to move when I say.'

'Move on what?' I asked.

'I'll let you know. For now... go and get laid or whatever it is you do in your down time.'

Reed snorted in delight at that comment.

'And Reed, bring those idiots here.'

Kielder indicated to Meyers and the two of them left the room together.

Reed came up to me.

'You gonna tell me where you been all this time?' he asked me, his face right up in mine.

I didn't say a word in return.

'You know, maybe I'd like you, trust you a bit more, if you didn't wear that horrible fucking mask all the time. You want people to know you're not hiding something? Start by not hiding your ugly face.'

He poked my cheek. Well, poked the rubber covering my cheek. He wanted a reaction, I knew that. So I gave him none.

'Freak,' he said again. He tutted and shook his head and walked out of the room.

Just me and Hailey remained.

'You know what he's like by now,' she said to me.

'Reed?'

'Ignore him. He's an idiot.'

'I know.'

'But he has got a point, in a way.' She moved up to me and I flinched a little as she reached forward and put her fingers to my cheek. The same spot where moments ago Reed had jabbed me. Except her touch was gentle, almost comforting, even if I sensed a certain disquiet in her demeanor. 'I know what happened to you, and I know it must be hard, but—'

I grabbed her hand and held tight.

'This mask is my choice,' I said.

I let go and pulled her hand back down to her side, and I could tell my hard edge had upset her.

'And what about you, anyway?' I said to her.

'Me?'

'You let Kielder treat you like dirt. He smacks you around in front of his guys, belittles you. And you stand there and take it.'

'You know nothing about it,' she said through gritted teeth. 'And actually? My relationship with him is none of your business.'

'None of my business. Exactly. Same here, right?' I said, tapping my cheek.

I brushed past her without another word.

9

Ryker had spent two nights in the holding cells in Canton. He'd seen all manner of people come and go in that time, from terrified young men and women who sat shaking through their ordeal, to more seasoned criminals who acted like they owned the place and took pleasure in intimidating the others around them.

Ryker kept his head down, didn't interact with anyone at all except for the officers, and only when spoken to first.

He'd been interviewed twice the day before, and he'd answered all of the police's questions honestly, although not entirely fully. Anything about the Roadhouse was fine, but questions about himself, his past, he'd kept a little more tight-lipped on. The reality was that Ryker really didn't believe he'd done anything wrong, or unlawful even, and unless something were amiss here, he was sure they wouldn't be able to charge him with anything other than perhaps a misdemeanor before the forty-eight-hour deadline expired the coming evening.

Not that that made Ryker feel any better about the position he found himself in. Firstly, because he was genuinely regretful about what had happened to Meg, and seriously worried about whether she'd pull through. She'd been unconscious but with a faint pulse when the police had arrived. Ryker had been pulled away from her at that point, had watched from the back of a cruiser as the paramedics saw to her and hauled her into an ambulance. He'd been told little about her state since then, other than that she was still alive.

Secondly, he hated how things had turned ugly so quickly. Five men, two women had been involved in the fight against him and Meg, one way or another, and every one of them had got away. At least, he hadn't seen any of them hauled into here, even though they were the aggressors.

Which created just the slightest doubt in his mind that perhaps something underhand was already at play with Ryker in this jail, and not any of them.

Time would tell. He still had cards he could play if he did end up in front of a judge rather than being released later today.

Perhaps he'd come to that point sooner rather than later, because he heard the telltale racket as one of the officers approached, smacking his baton against the bars of the cell as he moved along, as though the intimidation for the already apprehended prisoners was necessary.

'Ryker, you're up,' the guy said, staring over.

Ryker pulled himself to his feet as the guard unlocked the cell door, others in the room glancing sullenly as Ryker headed out. He followed the officer out of the holding area, along a corridor to an interview room. The same room Ryker had been to before, classic police station style with a small, barred window, a table and three chairs and not a lot else.

'Sit down. She'll be here shortly.'

Ryker did as he was told. Even though there was a metal loop on the tabletop so a prisoner could be cuffed in place,

Ryker remained free-handed. Just one of many signs that he wasn't seen as a big threat here.

The door opened not two minutes later and a woman walked in alone. He'd not seen her before. She was short, a little over five feet, probably early thirties with a rounded face, dark hair in a plain ponytail to match her functional pants and jacket combo.

'James Ryker?' she asked as she took a seat. She'd brought a satchel with her, which she placed by her side, but didn't have any papers or anything else in her hands.

'Yeah.'

'I'm with the GBI,' she said, pulling out a badge which she briefly flashed in front of Ryker.

'OK.'

'Want to tell me about what went down at the Roadhouse the other night?'

'I think I did that already with the police.'

'Well, you can do it again for me, can't you? Or do you have something better to do with your time?'

Ryker sighed. 'No. I guess not. GBI, right?'

'Yeah.'

'Why are the GBI involved with a bar fight?'

'That's for me to know.'

'Don't you guys normally work with a partner?'

'Who said I'm here alone?' she responded, her eyes flitting to the camera up in the corner of the room. 'Please, just give me the run-through.'

So Ryker did. Mostly the truth. At least about what had happened in the bar, if not everything about why he and Meg were there in the first place.

He finished with the part about how he'd held Meg as he awaited the first responders. How he'd done that rather than run off like the others. How that in itself surely showed he was only ever acting in self-defense and wasn't out to hurt or kill anyone.

The woman nodded here and there, though the most telling reaction was how her eyes became more nervy, almost teary as he talked about Meg and the state she'd been in.

'How is she?' Ryker asked. 'How's Meg?'

The woman swallowed hard. 'Last I heard, she's still in a coma, but she's alive.'

'What did you say your name was?' Ryker asked.

The woman paused, lips tight.

'You didn't, did you?'

'No.'

'So what is it?'

She didn't answer but instead took out her wallet again and this time opened it fully and laid it out on the table in front of Ryker.

'Cindy Valentino,' Ryker said.

Cindy said nothing as she put the wallet away again.

'I'm guessing Valentino's not a very common name in these parts.'

'Probably not.'

'But you don't look much like Meg.'

'My ex-husband is her brother. I probably shoulda changed my name back but I'm kinda used to it now. Still part of the family.'

Ryker chewed on that for a moment. Not just the fact that Cindy was related to Meg, or had been, but about what it meant for the bigger picture of his role in Georgia in the first place.

'I'm sorry for what happened to her,' Ryker said.

'Easy to say now.'

'You know I did nothing wrong, don't you? That I was working with her?'

'Work. Interesting word. What is your work? Because I've had a good dig around and I can find next to nothing other than your age and the fact you're a British citizen.'

'I'm a private investigator.'

'Yeah? What kind of visa do you have to work here?'

Ryker didn't bother to answer that.

'And what is it you're investigating, exactly?'

'Maybe you know about that already,' Ryker said. 'Given I'm pretty sure you're one of Meg's best sources of information. Maybe you're even the source who pointed her toward Wayne Stanton in the first place.'

He noticed a flicker of anger in her face, which kind of answered his point.

'I'll tell you what I know,' she said. 'I know that two days ago there was a shootout at Roadhouse bar. A woman – my ex-sister-in-law – was very nearly killed. May never recover. More than one witness who was passing at the time has corroborated that much of the shooting was by one man. A man on a rampage, as someone put it. Charging at a group of others. A madman who was only stopped when people fleeing the scene to escape nearly ran him over. That man you, by any chance?'

Ryker said nothing.

'Seems to me that the best place for a crazy asshole like that would be behind bars.'

'True. Except it didn't really happen like that.'

'No?'

'You know that. Either that witness is lying, or they just read it all wrong. Probably they were just in a panic that they were so close to the incident at all.'

She didn't confirm or deny her opinion on that.

'What do you know about Wayne Stanton?' Ryker asked.

Cindy didn't answer.

'And the man who turned up in that big truck?' Ryker added. 'I didn't get his name, but he was in charge. Called the shots over Stanton at least. And a vehicle as distinctive as the one I've described to you can't be too hard to track down. I'm sure plenty of neighbors have complained of the noise if nothing else.'

'Except you didn't get the license. And neither did anybody else.'

Ryker clenched his teeth. No, he hadn't got the license. He'd been too consumed cradling Meg.

'But you do know about Stan—'

'Mr. Ryker, this is me asking you questions, not the other way around.'

Ryker looked up at the camera again.

'There isn't anyone else here with you, is there?' he said. 'The GBI aren't actually investigating anything here. Officially.'

She took a moment to think about that before answering. 'You want to know why I'm here?'

'Yes.'

'For Meg. No, there's no official GBI investigation, but that doesn't mean I have no power here. What I say and do when I leave this room will help decide whether you're allowed to go free or not. But the choice is really down to you. Tell me what you're doing here in Georgia. The truth.'

'I was hired by Adam Hannigan to help find his daughter, Abby.'

The surprise on Cindy's face, her silence, suggested that that was the first she'd known about it.

'Governor Hannigan?'

'The same. I was investigating a link between Abby and a

group of white supremacists called the White Lions. You probably know about them?'

She gave no indication either way, but he could tell she was deep in thought.

'I only met Meg a few days ago but she said she'd help me.'

'She wasn't working on... anything like that.'

'She was always straight up with you about what she was doing?'

'Of course.'

Ryker shrugged. 'She was an investigative journalist. In my experience people like that often only give you what they need to get you to help them.'

He hadn't meant that in an offensive way, but Cindy's look soured further, as though Ryker were talking ill of Meg.

'Anyway, she told me a source had given her Stanton's name. That he was a good person to find out more about the White Lions from. About what's happened to them and the people involved with them over the last few years.'

Cindy still said nothing.

'Except we never really got the chance to do that because the boss turned up and shut everything down. And then that fight started when one of the women with them recognized Meg. Recognized her as being with that GBI bitch.'

No response.

'Maybe she was referring to you.'

Cindy swallowed hard again. She looked shocked. A little scared.

'How would they know that?' Ryker asked. 'Meg hadn't met Stanton before.'

Cindy didn't answer.

'Do you know who the man is? The one in charge?'

'Like I told you before, I'm the one doing the asking here.'

But she looked and sounded flummoxed. Ryker gave her the time, but despite the statement, she didn't come back at him with anything more. Not until she sighed and sat back in her chair.

'You see the quandary I'm in here,' she said.

'Not really.'

'No? On the one hand, I believe it when you say you were working with my sister-in-law. And I trust her. Always.'

'Ex-sister-in-law, technically.'

She shook her head as though irritated by the comment. 'On the other hand, you've got quite the list of potential charges from the other night, some of them very serious. And frankly, after speaking with you... I don't trust you at all. And I like you even less.'

Ryker decided not to respond to that. Clearly he'd not done a great job of winning her over. But he didn't really care so much about whether she liked him. He just wanted to get out of jail so he could move on.

Cindy said nothing more either before she picked up her satchel and moved to the door.

'So what's your decision?' Ryker asked.

She turned to look down on him and held his gaze but didn't answer before she moved on out.

And no one else came for him so Ryker sat there. And sat there. Half an hour, at least, until the door clunked open.

'Your lucky day,' the burly officer said with a snide grin.

It didn't take long for Ryker to clear past the front desk and collect his things. And as he stepped out into the warm afternoon sunshine he wasn't particularly surprised to see Cindy Valentino leaning against a black Ford Explorer, waiting for him.

'I suppose I have you to thank?' Ryker said as he approached her.

She shrugged. 'I guess we'll never know what would have happened if I hadn't showed.'

'Are you bending any rules coming here on your own like this?'

'Not relevant to you.'

'So what now? The fact you're still here suggests you're not finished with me yet.'

'It's not that deep. Just a few things I'd rather say to you out here than in there.'

'Yeah?'

'Like when I said I don't trust you.'

'And you like me even less. Yeah, I remember. That stung.'

She looked like she didn't believe him. 'What I don't like is that I don't know you. That there seems to be nothing to know. And yet here you are in Georgia, working for a pretty powerful man on something pretty damn big.'

Ryker stayed silent.

'I know there's a lot of reasons why that might be the case, but I'm leaning toward a couple options in particular.'

'Which are?'

'I'm not gonna stand here and stroke your ego by going over it. But let's just say I'm not new to this sort of thing.'

Similar to something Hannigan had said to him, wasn't it?

'I'll ask you this one time,' she said. 'Are you really here looking for Abby Hannigan?'

'Yes.'

'Is that all there is to you being here?'

'That's more complicated to answer.'

'Are you gonna expand on that?'

'Not really.'

She sighed. 'I remember when she went missing. It hit the news. Was talked about for a few days. It was a big deal, the idea that the governor's daughter had been kidnapped or killed.'

'I can imagine.'

'I never had any involvement with any of it, but I do remember thinking how it was strange that it all went away so quickly.'

'In what way?'

'I already said. It was big in the news to start with. Then... poof. I've not heard about it for months.'

'Probably because there's been no developments. And there's been plenty of new news since.'

'Or maybe because the developments happened pretty quickly, but nobody wanted to make them public.'

Ryker thought he knew what she meant by that. 'Developments as in... the Hannigans, or the investigators figured out what happened to her?'

The flick of her eyebrows suggested he'd hit on her thought exactly.

'They realized she hadn't been kidnapped,' Ryker said, thinking out loud. 'She'd just run away. That's what you think?'

'More than that, I think they probably even found out exactly where she went. And it didn't look good on them, or Adam Hannigan specifically, so the story died. As stories often do when powerful people can control them.'

'If Adam Hannigan knows where his daughter is, why would he be paying me to look for her?'

She reached forward and patted him on the shoulder. A real show of mocking. 'Got it in one, big guy. And I'm judging by the bemused look that you don't know the answer. You don't like the idea of being used?'

No, Ryker didn't. Not at all.

'If you do find out the answers, though, I'd be pretty interested in knowing myself,' she said.

They stood in silence a few moments as Ryker's mind churned. He fished for one of his business cards and handed it over to Cindy.

'Probably best for us to stay in touch while I'm here,' Ryker said. 'Even if it's just keeping tabs on Meg.'

She didn't respond but took the card and put it away.

'You really don't know who was driving that truck?' Ryker asked. 'Just a name is all I need.'

'No. I don't.'

'And the woman who recognized Meg? The GBI reference was because of you, surely.'

'Yeah. I think so.'

'So who was she? Because Meg wasn't expecting anyone to know her there.'

'Most likely it was Gabriella Stricken. Her man ran a series of meth labs up in the mountains. He's doing a long stretch now.'

'You busted him?'

'Not just me. But yeah, it was the GBI. And Meg did a story on it.'

Ryker hadn't seen that one.

'You go chasing after Stricken and the people she hangs with, you can probably expect the same frosty reception you got at Roadhouse.'

'I think I can handle people like that.'

'And that worries me. I don't wanna get called out to a bloodbath anytime soon. Whether it's yours or other people's blood. If you have a discreet mode in your repertoire, now'd be a good time to activate it. For your and Meg's and my sakes.'

Ryker pushed his fingers behind his ear and twisted as

though turning a small knob. 'Activated. Sometimes it gets a bit stuck though.'

He winked at her. She tried to stay sullen but ended up cracking the slightest smile.

'I hope we don't see each other again soon.'

She opened her door and was about to close it when Ryker put his hand out to stop her.

'But if I did want to see you again? You know, swapping information and the like, over a coffee or whatever.'

'Is this how you did it with Meg too?'

'Did what?' he said, trying to act all innocent.

She said nothing but shook her head and grasped the door and pulled it out of his grip... but didn't quite close it.

'I've got your info. See you around.'

Now it closed. Moments later the engine roared to life and she was off down the street.

10

Of course he was glad to be out of jail, to have not been charged with any crimes and not have the prospect of his ongoing incarceration or deportation from the country looming over him.

But Ryker was far from happy. For starters, the woman he'd been teamed up with for barely five minutes was in a coma, perhaps would never recover. He didn't blame himself for what had happened to her; in fact, he'd tried really hard to get out of that bar without confrontation. Yet she was hurt, and it was because of her association with him.

He wouldn't let that lie.

He'd track down the people responsible.

But he also now felt a lingering anger toward Adam Hannigan. Cindy's parting comments had really stirred something in Ryker's mind. The official search for Abby had more or less halted within weeks of her disappearance. At least, it had dropped out of the main news. Cindy had been pretty clear in her suggestion that she thought the fall-off in interest in Abby was because the Hannigans had found where she'd gone. Had found that she'd not been kidnapped.

Given other events that had taken place, it suggested to Ryker that Hannigan had known months ago that Abby was OK, but that she had, one way or another, become embroiled in whatever offshoot of the White Lions was now in existence and he'd decided to simply move on instead, abandon her. Perhaps he hadn't known anything about what they were plotting, but it still irked that Hannigan had played things so tight-lipped with him.

More than anything, it made it feel as though Hannigan – but perhaps more so Klein – was using Ryker. That they both knew more about the situation than they'd told him and were withholding. For their benefit, most likely. And most likely because some of the truth was damaging to them, one way or another.

Ryker would park those theories for now though. He was a long way off going back to Hannigan and tying him up and making him talk. But it'd be an option further down the line if Ryker felt that he needed to do so for answers, if the danger to him – from not knowing the whole story – was becoming too great.

He had another lead to follow for now. And potentially another ally in Cindy Valentino.

His number one priority was in identifying the leader of that crew who'd turned up at Roadhouse, and he now had two names to start with in finding out that man's identity. Wayne Stanton and Gabriella Stricken.

He was pretty sure he'd shot Stanton. And one other. Ryker's first port of call was therefore a quick call around the area's hospitals, posing as a journalist from the local news, asking about the gunshot victims. Pretty basic stuff and it'd only confirmed that none of the hospitals had taken gunshot victims that night. Possibly true, or possibly they just weren't falling for Ryker's scam.

Not to worry. Ryker had plenty of contacts from his old life who could do a lot with nothing but a name. Old life. After all this time, he still thought of being part of the JIA as his old life. Yeah, the reality was that it was many years since he'd been an official part of one of the most unofficial intelligence agencies on the planet. Yet even after all this time he was still living and moving in the same circles. Old life. No, this was the same damn life just under a different brand, both for him and the agency itself.

Although it turned out Ryker didn't even need to use any of those contacts this time. Not for Gabriella Stricken. Like a lot of young people she shared way too much of her life on social media. Not that she directly gave away her home address or anything as dumb as that, but her profile and her pictures did give away her high school, which she graduated from five years ago. And it also showed that she worked at... Missy's. Yeah, that one. The 'gentlemen's' bar, as it described itself on its website. The one Wayne Stanton had taunted Meg about.

Not Ryker's typical hangout, but his next stop-off point. At least once he'd picked up his rental which he'd left outside Roadhouse two days ago.

And which remained pretty much alone in the parking lot when he arrived not long before 4 p.m. The only other vehicle was a bashed-up Ford F-150. The barman's, perhaps.

OK, so Missy's was Ryker's intended next stop, but perhaps a quick layover could work too.

Ryker headed over to the entrance. Locked. But he could hear faint music beyond. Probably the barman prepping for the evening. Ryker pounded the door. No response. He checked the street then pounded again and this time the music stopped.

He waited right by the wooden door. Noted the security camera a few yards from him up on the roofline. He looked straight into it. Gave a little wave.

'You recognize me?' Ryker shouted out.

No answer.

'I know you're there.'

'What do you want?' came the reply a few seconds later.

'To talk.'

'I've nothing to say to you. Please leave.'

'Like I said, I just want to talk.'

'And if you don't leave, I'll call the police.'

'Yeah? So you can tell them some more bullshit about me, like last time?'

No response to that.

'You know it's a crime to provide false information.'

'I never said nothin' wrong.'

'So why'd I spend two days in jail? And no one else?'

No answer.

'You saw what happened to my friend,' Ryker said. 'Meg was her name. You know, she might never pull through. All because of those assholes. They tried to kill us both.'

Still no answer.

'You know them. You know all of them.'

'No, I don't. Not all of them.'

'I've got two names already. Stanton and Stricken. I'm not sure on the others.'

'Mister, this ain't nothin' to do with me.'

'It doesn't have be. Tell me what you know about them. An address, a hangout, anything like that.' A hangout? This bar was probably the hangout, given how they'd all congregated.

'You've got ten seconds to get back in your car, then I call the cops.'

'I'd prefer it if you just called your friends. Get them all down here again.'

He was sure he heard a sigh to that, but the fact the guy hadn't already called someone told Ryker one thing: he probably wasn't part of the crew. And Ryker sensed he was scared. Of them, perhaps more than Ryker.

'An address for Stanton or Stricken or any of them, and I'm gone. You won't see me again.'

Ryker glanced over his shoulder. He'd sensed the vehicle behind him. Passing by a little too slowly. Sure enough, he spotted a police cruiser there. Like most vehicles around here it was big. A Chevy Tahoe, bull bar on the front, all blacked out except for the silver insignia. Pretty intimidating compared to the brightly colored little compacts seen in a lot of European cities.

The vehicle rolled to a stop right by the entrance to the parking lot. Ryker didn't think the barman had actually made the call. Most likely this was just a passing cruiser. The Roadhouse would be watched carefully for a while after the gunfight the other night. No one got out of the car though.

'Looks like you should get outta here,' the barman said.

'Yeah. But nothing stopping me coming back again, is there? And next time I won't be content to stand outside talking like this. We can make it a lot more personal if you like?'

Nothing.

'Last chance,' Ryker said. 'I can go and come back later. Or I can go and never come back.'

'I don't have an address, but I know about what happened to Stricken's man.'

'And that would be?'

'Haden. Earl Haden.'

'The meth cooker?'

The guy kind of snorted. Ryker didn't know what that meant. 'Yeah. Something like that. There's a place some miles north of here. Peltworth.'

'A town?'

'Not much of a town. But that's where they were. Probably where she still stays. At least when she's not taking her clothes off for tips.'

'This is all you got?'

'If you really wanna track them down, should be all you need. But if it were me... I'd not be going up that way.'

'Yeah. Looks like we're very different people then. Thanks.'

'Just don't come back here.'

Ryker wouldn't, if he didn't have to.

He moved away from the door and to his car, keeping his eyes on the cruiser the whole time. Still no one got out. He fired up the engine of his rental and hit the road, heading north. The cruiser tailed him. One mile. Two miles. Right until they hit the city limit. Then it stopped. Ryker carried on and a few seconds later watched in his mirror as the cruiser swung around and headed back into town.

A warning, perhaps, but nothing more.

It didn't matter much. Ryker might not need to head back that way now anyhow.

He quickly plugged Peltworth in to his GPS. The route took him almost directly north, into the Blue Ridge mountains. Cherokee country, many years ago, the Native tribal past still recognized in many place names. The original Cherokee had been forcibly removed from these lands during the Trail of Tears – a land grab orchestrated by powerful Whites as they sought to gain control of various resources, gold, cotton among the main ones in Georgia. But even if that exploitation of the land here had led to many riches, had seen urban centers like

Atlanta boom in more recent times, the mountains remained largely wild, rugged, and often unforgiving. And the communities that survived, rather than thrived, in the poor rural areas here were often the same.

Peltworth. Ryker had never come across the name, but it certainly conjured an image in his mind of days gone by. Of first settlers making a living in these wilds any which way. As he zeroed in on his destination, those images only grew more vivid. The last two miles were a winding, almost all-out climb on a narrow, poorly laid road. There was no town here. He hadn't passed through one of any note since he'd left Canton. Every now and then there were signs of life, but the rickety single-story homes were generally little more than converted trailers, made permanent with awnings and lean-tos.

Peltworth. The name was right there on the GPS screen but Ryker soon passed over it, no indication of anything there at all before he came to a T-intersection. No signage to indicate what lay left or right, but he could see on the map that to the right he'd hit the I575 within a few miles.

He went left. He'd already climbed a substantial amount, his ears had even popped, but there was no view here as the narrow road was enclosed by thick forest, the mostly pine trees tall and thin, the tops swaying in the breeze way up above him. Not quite ominous out here, but something close to it.

Still nothing showed on the map, but Ryker came to a closed metal gate. He got out of his car and moved up to it. No lock. Beyond the gate the road turned to compacted dirt. He heard dogs barking in the near distance. Could smell wood smoke. He opened the gate and moved his car through, closed the gate behind him before carrying on. A bend in the road took him down into a dip. Finally signs of life in a clearing. Four trailers, arranged in a semi-circle. Several vehicles in various states of use and disrepair were parked. Piles of tires. Piles of broken or otherwise discarded furniture. Trash. All a bit of a mess, really.

Two dogs – mongrels – were chained to a large propane tank and had spotted Ryker's car and were already pulling the chains tight, their necks strained even though he'd not yet got out of the car.

No signs of people though.

Ryker swung his car around so he was nearly facing the way back out before he turned the engine off and stepped into the open. Now the dogs' barking ramped up, their teeth bared. Ryker looked around. The wood smoke twisted up from behind one of the trailers, swirling into the darkening sky as dusk approached.

He went that way, moving tentatively, his open hands by his sides, fingers outstretched to hopefully show anyone spying on him that he wasn't armed.

He continued to scan. Spotted not one, but three modern security cameras around the place. One attached to a trailer, two in the trees.

'Hello?' he finally called out as he approached the left of the four trailers.

No response. He moved around the side, closing in on the smoke. He poked his head around the back of the trailer. The smoke was coming from a fire pit, dug into the soil with a stone surround encircling it. The embers glowed a deep red. A roasting spit sat across the top, but nothing was cooking. Six camping chairs were there. All were empty.

'You snoopin' in the wrong place, mister.'

The voice from behind him was accompanied by something hard – a shotgun barrel, Ryker imagined – being pressed into the back of his neck. He'd actually heard the footsteps behind him as he'd edged around the trailer but had decided against any sudden move because he didn't yet know who or what he was up against here. He only took it on hope – and a lot of lived experience – that whatever kind of badasses might live out here, they wouldn't execute him on the spot.

'Must have taken a wrong turn,' Ryker said.

'Yeah. You did.'

'No. He dint.' A different voice this time. Ryker caught sight of the second man in his periphery as he came around toward Ryker's front. 'You stupid motherfucker.'

The first blow to the back of Ryker's head sent him to his knee. The second left him sprawled on the ground, fighting to keep his eyes open.

A feat he failed at only seconds later when the third strike sent him to oblivion.

11

Ryker hadn't been out long. Seconds. Yet he'd awoken groggy, head throbbing, and had done little – unable to, really – to stop the men dragging him into one of the trailers where they dumped him on a chair and stood guard, waiting for him to come around.

No cuffs, no ties or anything like that, but each of the two men in front of him in the grimy and filthy trailer were armed. The first man Ryker didn't recognize. He wasn't too old – probably late twenties – although his skin was mottled and blotchy, with floppy, unkempt hair, and he had a smattering of tattoos on his bare arms. Not particularly muscled arms, but the guy was tall and fit. The shotgun he held was pointed at Ryker's chest. The other man – the one with an AR15 assault rifle in his grip – was short, stocky with a bushy beard. Ryker recognized him from the bar. The guy Stanton had arrived with.

'How's the leg?' Ryker asked him, eyeing the way he tried to keep the weight off his right foot.

'You wanna find out what it's like to get shot?' he snapped back.

'You think I haven't been shot before?'

The guy huffed but his friend marched forward and Ryker ducked down as he swung the shotgun toward him. The barrel clattered into the side of his head. An already sore spot, and when Ryker lifted up again it took several seconds for his blurred vision to clear. He felt warm blood dribbling through his hairline onto his neck.

'We're doin' the askin' here,' shotgun guy said. 'Unless you want another smack?'

'You think I haven't been smacked before?' Ryker said, and the guy jolted as if to come forward, but his friend held him back.

'Who are you?' he asked. 'Found no ID on you, in your car. You undercover?'

'What? You think I'm police? GBI? FBI?'

'Not with that dumb accent. You a Brit?'

'Yes. The name's James Ryker.'

'So what the fuck you doin' out here?'

'Looking for answers.'

''Bout what?'

'You know me, right? From Roadhouse. You were with Wayne Stanton. I don't know how that all turned to shit, but we were only there to talk. Me and my friend, Meg, we're working on a story. About the White Lions.'

Neither of them responded to the name.

'You know what I'm talking about?' Ryker asked.

'Why you askin' 'bout that?' the bearded guy asked.

'Like I said, we're writing a story.'

'Bullshit. After what happened the other night? The way you were fightin'? You think we're gonna believe you're just a hack coming here to ask 'bout some story?'

Fair point.

'I'm a PI.'

No reaction.

'I'm investigating Abby Hannigan's disappearance. Trying to find her.'

No reaction still.

'Abby Hannigan. The governor's daughter.'

Now shotgun guy's eyes widened. The other one remained stony-faced.

'I heard she used to be involved with the White Lions,' Ryker continued. 'A guy named Craig Boswell. You heard of him?'

No response.

'He died a few years ago, apparently. But he and Abby were both part of the White Lions. Meg was given Stanton's name as someone who could help us. That's all I'm looking for here. People who can help me.'

'Then why'd you shoot me and my friends, asshole?'

'I wasn't even armed going into there. And I definitely didn't start that fight.'

The guy mumbled something under his breath.

'Why don't we just bury this fucker out here?' shotgun guy asked his friend. 'What are we even doin' talkin' to him?'

'How'd you get the leg treated?' Ryker asked, sensing that the guy he'd shot was the more relaxed of the two. The one who'd engage Ryker, rather than just wanting to beat or kill him straight off. Except he didn't answer the question.

'I'm guessing you and your friends didn't go to the hospital. Too many questions. And I know none of you ended up in jail. I did. Two nights.'

'What did you expect for shootin' people?'

'Fair point. But I at least expected everyone else who'd been shooting to be in there with me too. How do you explain that? You guys paying off the cops?'

Shotgun guy glared at his friend as though he really didn't like that accusation, even if he was considering it as truth.

'If you wanna know, I took the slugs out,' he said.

Ryker held his focus on that guy a moment. Looked more closely at his arms.

'You were in the army,' Ryker said, nodding to the tattoo on his right forearm. The men exchanged a glance.

'Yeah.'

'You too?' Ryker asked the other one. At first he just glared at Ryker in response, but then huffed and put the AR15 down on the ground by his foot. He yanked up the sleeve of his shirt, revealing a bulbous bicep featuring an elaborate tattoo made up of a mishmash of ink swirls that Ryker couldn't quite make out. What he could make out at the top was a banner that read—

'Ranger.'

'Yeah. That.' Beard guy picked up his AR again but held it lazily, the barrel pointed to the ground in front of Ryker.

'What are two vets doing living up here, like this?' Ryker asked.

'You gotta problem with how we livin'?'

'No offense, but it's not exactly a hip and happening area. I heard you guys cook meth here. Isn't that why Earl Haden got busted?'

They both looked angrier now.

'Like I said, no offense. I'm just trying to understand you guys, what's happened to you. I was army too, if you want to know. British Army.'

Not true – although he had worked alongside the Army plenty of times, mostly the SAS, who'd also had a big hand in training Ryker. Not exactly happy times, but it'd helped mold Ryker into who he was, both then and now.

'Seriously, guys, what's the deal?' he asked.

'The deal?' shotgun guy said. 'The deal is we got no deal. You think we're the only vets strugglin' around here? Around anywhere? This country's gone to shit. White boys from the mountains like us ain't gon' get no job in the city or whatever the fuck it is you think we should be gettin'. There's nothing for us. Not anywhere.'

'Young white men're the most marginalized group in this damn country,' the bearded guy said, in an obviously oft-repeated sentiment. 'And it's our friggin' country.'

Ryker had hit on something. But he wouldn't push it with these two right now, even though he knew what they'd said fit a much wider narrative. He'd been told the White Lions, in past times, were a fringe white supremacist group. Whatever they were or weren't now, there was no doubt that such groups gained followers – and power – from disgruntled, disenfran-chised young men like those in front of him. Most people didn't hate others – whether race, religion, culture, or whatever – just because. It was nearly always down to personal grievance, one way or another.

'Did you guys ever deploy?' Ryker asked.

'Course.'

'Where?'

'What's it to you?'

'I was in the Middle East, mostly,' Ryker said. 'A lot of time there. Iraq. Afghanis—'

'I don't give a fuck,' shotgun guy said. 'You ain't one of us.'

Silence for a few moments.

'You want to tell me your names?' Ryker said.

The guy with the shotgun redoubled his grip and raised his aim from Ryker's chest to his face as he took a half step forward.

'You think this is just some regular conversation we havin' here? You think this is a friendly chit-chat and we gonna crack open some beers and sit around the fire?'

'Sounds good to me.'

'Not gonna happen. So why don't you tell us what you were doin' snoopin' around our property?'

Ryker paused and considered the question before answering. 'I already said. I'm investigating—'

'We don't know her. Abby, you said? Never heard of her. And she sure as hell ain't here.'

'I can see that.'

'And let's say I don't believe a word that's come outta your mouth.'

'Then you'd be wrong. I am looking for Abby Hannigan. Just like I was two nights ago at Roadhouse.'

Shotgun guy didn't respond but was becoming more and more agitated. Yet his friend wasn't. His friend remained steadfast, little emotion on his face. Army Ranger. Perhaps he was just one cool customer. Or perhaps the names coming out of Ryker's mouth meant a lot more to him than they did to his friend.

'I came up here looking for Gabriella Stricken,' Ryker said to AR guy. 'Looking for your friend Wayne Stanton too. Looking for any other people who were at the Roadhouse bar two nights ago and who nearly killed me and my friend.'

'You think you some John Wick hero or somethin'?' shotgun guy asked.

'No. This isn't about revenge.' Well, he did want to make things even with the guy from the truck, but better not to mention that right now. 'I'm just looking for answers. About Abby Hannigan. That's the truth.'

Neither of them said anything to that.

'Who are we waiting on?' Ryker asked.

No answer.

'Is it the guy from Roadhouse, the one with that damn big truck?'

No answer or even indication of any recognition to Ryker's words.

'What's his name, anyway?'

Still nothing.

'But we are waiting on someone else, right?' Ryker said. 'I ask because this isn't much of anything right now. Certainly no interrogation, because actually I'm asking most of the questions, even if you two aren't giving me many answers. So my best guess is we're waiting on whoever you called out here. Whoever's in charge of you two.'

'Who the fuck says we're not in charge?' shotgun guy asked, his agitation clear in his tone and by the increased sneer on his face.

'I do.'

The guy went to come forward again, as if to swoosh the shotgun against Ryker's skull one more time, but his friend spoke out to stop him.

'Kyle, no.'

'Kyle?' Ryker said. 'OK, now we're finally getting somewhere. And you?'

No answer.

'Guys, come on. Look at the situation. It's not like a first name is going to cause much difference.'

'Mac.'

'And the guy in the truck who smashed into my friend?' Ryker asked.

Mac gritted his teeth rather than answer.

'But that's who's coming out here, right?'

'Who the fuck is he talking about?' Kyle asked Mac.

Mac said nothing, but the question itself was a big giveaway. Whatever the setup between these two, whatever they were doing out here, Kyle wasn't part of the bigger picture, but it looked like Mac perhaps was.

'Why don't you just tell me his name?' Ryker said to Mac. 'Point me in the right direction so I can go talk to him. I'll get out of here. I don't need to come back.'

'He ain't tellin' you shit,' Kyle said, although Ryker kept his eyes on Mac the whole time.

'So?' Ryker prompted.

'What he said.' Mac nodded to his friend without breaking eye contact with Ryker.

'So you always dance to Kyle's tune? Army Ranger? I thought you'd have more balls. Be the one in charge of some infantry runt like him.'

'You piece of—'

Kyle burst forward. Just as Ryker hoped he would. All along he'd been the more edgy, more jittery, more angry of the two. Yeah, Mac was a Ranger, an elite, trained to deal with pressure. With a hell of a lot of things, really. It looked like Kyle was not.

He arced the shotgun through the air, more power, venom in the intended shot than the last time. And, unlike the last time, Ryker didn't initially move. Not until right at the last second, which only seemed to add to Kyle's determination and the amount of effort – and intended damage – that he put into the blow.

So when Ryker finally did duck down and plant his weight on his feet to pull himself from the chair, Kyle not only swung through and hit nothing but air, but the swing carried on, pulling him off balance.

Ryker jumped up and around him, peeled the shotgun from his grip and yanked on Kyle's shoulder to continue his momentum. He plunged sideways and smacked into the side of the trailer, the whole thing rattling from the impact.

Mac moved quickly. He let rip with the AR15 and Ryker dove for cover behind a stinking, stained sofa, firing the shotgun as he fell. Not a hit, but enough to cause Mac to pause and to slide for cover himself behind the L-shaped kitchen counter. Ryker fired again from his position, the shotgun pellets obliterating kitchen items, food, crockery, whatever on the counter, and raining debris on Mac below.

'This doesn't have to end like this!' Ryker shouted out. 'I didn't come here for blood!'

'You—'

Mac was cut short, or perhaps Ryker just didn't hear the rest of his words over the battle cry from Kyle as he dove over the sofa, knife in hand, and on top of Ryker. The blade grazed his shoulder as the two of them twisted in a heap on the floor. Kyle tried to right his grip and stab down onto Ryker's chest...

Boom.

The shotgun blast directly into his chest sent Kyle flying back.

Ryker rolled over, saw Mac up and out in the open and Ryker rolled again as a volley of gunfire pelted down toward him. But Mac wasn't sticking around. He was rushing for the door.

Ryker jumped up and darted that way. He reached the exit only to hunker and cower from another wave of gunfire from

Mac. Then voices outside. Shouting. Not just Mac out there now. Ryker ducked again as more bullets thwacked into the trailer, from both sides.

Fire. He didn't know how, but the kitchen was on fire. Flames leaped up the far wall, across the ceiling toward him, the trailer going up like a tinder box.

He couldn't stick around inside.

Ryker poked the shotgun out of the door and fired before jumping out and rolling to the ground.

He spotted movement. Fired again. Missed Mac as the guy darted out of view toward the clearing at the front.

Ryker got to his feet and crept along the edge of the trailer as the roar of flames grew louder. He flinched when the window above him shattered. Not a gunshot. The heat of the rapidly building fire.

He reached the edge of the trailer and risked a look out. Spotted his car. A truck too which hadn't been there before. Headlights on, blaring in his direction. So much so that he could make out little else, no people.

'Mac! This doesn't have to end like this!' Ryker shouted out.

He got no response.

Next moment he made a dash for it, aiming to run to the next trailer, closer to his car. Except he had to get past the propane tank, the dogs too, to achieve that.

He only hoped Mac – plus whoever else – wouldn't be stupid enough to fire at that thing – the tank was big enough to obliterate the entire encampment.

Except bullets did follow Ryker's path. The dogs too bounded at him, only to be caught on their chains. Ryker reached the back corner of the next trailer, kept on going. At least until an explosion pulled him from his feet and tossed him two yards forward into a heap.

Dazed, it took him a couple of seconds to recover as he gazed up at the flames licking out of the trailer right by him.

The explosion... Not the propane tank. He could still hear the dogs there, yapping. The explosion had been from inside the trailer he was next to.

Cindy said the guys up here had been cooking meth. Perhaps Mac's wayward bullets had ignited the chemicals.

Wayward? Perhaps that was their intent, with Ryker running right for the trailer.

A secondary explosion sent a heatwave blasting across above Ryker. Still on the ground, under the level of the bottom of the trailer, he was at least a little protected. If he'd been on his feet at that moment the blast wave – the flames – would have gone right through him.

But he couldn't stay there and await the next explosion.

He bounced up and raced for the far end of the trailer. Came out into the open, gun raised up toward where the truck was.

Pulled the trigger. Nothing left.

But he did see the figures scurrying into the vehicle. A moment later and the truck's engine roared as it swung around and blasted away.

Another explosion from behind him sent Ryker tumbling toward his car. He jumped in. Fired up the engine. Tried not to look at the growing inferno. Mere seconds now until that tank went kaboom. He didn't want to be anywhere near it.

As he tugged on the wheel to turn the car around he jumped in shock when a dark figure leaped up at his window. Then another, teeth snarling.

The dogs. They'd got free somehow.

At least they wouldn't be roasted meat now.

Ryker hit the gas and the car sped off toward the exit, each of his mirrors glowing with orange and red. The car jumped around on the dirt road, the suspension being battered by the uneven surface. Ryker too.

Until he came to the gate. Left open by the fleeing truck. He hit blacktop, relative peace and quiet taking over in the cabin.

At least until the boom in the background and the blast wave which rattled every inch of the car and him.

He'd got away in time though.

Ryker soon came to the T-intersection. Right to take him on the rural roads back toward Atlanta metro, Canton and else-where. Straight on and he'd hit the interstate. No indication of which way Mac and the fleeing truck had gone in.

He went right. Tried to keep it steady on the twisting road, blackness on both sides of him hiding the rugged – deathly – terrain. He kept it steady. A mile. Two. Spotted a road coming up on his right, the entrance lit up in his headlights. Nothing coming out of there. He didn't think. Until it was too late. By the time he got sight of the glint of metal caught in the arc of his high-beams, the truck – its lights off now – was already gunning at speed. Ryker could do nothing.

The truck smashed into the side of his car, tossed the vehicle across the road, onto the shoulder the other side where it smacked to a stop.

Ryker shook himself to. The truck's lights flicked on. Blinded him. Creaking and hissing from his mangled car filled the air, soon overtaken by the roar of the truck's engine.

A shunt sent Ryker's car teetering. Teetering over what, he couldn't see, but he could feel the sway.

The truck backed off a couple of feet. Ryker wrestled with his seatbelt but struggled to unclasp it.

The truck came forward again.

'No!' Ryker shouted out.

Nothing he could do. The truck hit his car a third time. Whatever had stopped its momentum before – a tree stump, perhaps – could no longer hold it back. With nothing remaining in its path, his car tumbled over the edge. Tumbled. Into the black abyss below.

12

The noise rattled around inside his head, although at first he had no idea what it was, what it meant.

Screech. Screech.

Over and over, not a distressing sound nor even a particularly loud one, but it was the one that Ryker's confused brain focused on.

At least until another smashed through his consciousness – or semi-consciousness at least.

Buzz. Buzz.

That noise was accompanied by a light vibration. Coming from Ryker's leg.

He opened his eyes, skull pounding, blood pooling in his head as he lay twisted with his body suspended upside down.

The buzzing was his phone.

He reached into his pocket and drew it out. But the call – a number he didn't recognize – had already ended.

Screech. Screech.

He groaned in pain. Everything ached and he had blood dribbling across his face from somewhere at the side and back of his head. But he didn't think he was seriously injured. Just battered and bruised and disorientated.

Ryker reached to his side and pushed the button to unclasp his belt and his body slumped down, smacking into the roof of the car.

Screech. Screech.

The windshield wipers. Going like mad across the cracked glass.

Ryker dragged himself out of the obliterated driver's window. Blackness surrounded him, though the scent of pine trees fought to overpower that of the gas running out of the smashed-up car.

Buzz. Buzz.

The phone again.

'Y... yeah.'

'Ryker. It's Cindy Valentino. Is now a good time?'

'Er... de... define "good time".'

'Is... something wrong?'

'You could say that.'

'Where are you?'

'I have... absolutely no idea.'

'Ryker, seriously, what's going on?'

So he briefly explained. As best he could.

'Fuck. That discreet setting in your head is more messed up than you told me.'

'Yeah... looks that way.'

'OK. Give me some time. I'll get someone out to you.'

* * *

About an hour later and Ryker was finally on the roadside up above. At the spot where he'd earlier been shoved over the edge.

Cindy had gone the extra mile for him. Had a mountain rescue chopper come and pick him up from the ridge he was stuck on. Lucky, really. At nighttime, out in the wilds, Ryker hadn't been able to see much of the terrain at all. Not until the searchlights of the chopper had come over.

The road itself was on the mountainside, the shoulder he was pushed off of falling some two thousand feet into a gorge below. Through nothing but luck, and the naturally tree-dense terrain, the car had tumbled only a hundred or so feet before it'd become wedged on thick trunks, teetering on a small ledge right by a near sheer drop that would, without doubt, have seen the end of him.

The medic on the helicopter had insisted Ryker needed to go to the hospital – protocol. With a bit of help from Cindy, he'd got them to drop him off on the road instead, where Cindy was already waiting for him.

Not just Cindy. An ambulance too. A couple of police cars, blue lights flashing. Even more had already headed past, going up to Peltworth and the mess that was now there.

The medics had tended to Ryker's head wounds right there by the road. Stitches to the back of his head from being hit with the shotgun, and a few more to the side of his head from the crash. Everything else was cuts and bruises that he'd deal with himself.

'You know, I only called to tell you Meg's awake,' Cindy said as Ryker stood staring over the dark edge. 'To see if you wanted to go see her.'

Ryker, deep in thought, didn't answer.

'What are we gonna find up there?' Cindy asked him, nodding north toward Peltworth.

'A good question,' Ryker said. 'At least one dead body. Kyle was his name. That's all I know.'

'You killed him?'

He looked over at her, a little unsure about her question. Whether she was asking because she was just after the facts of what had gone down, or whether she was looking for evidence against him.

'I shot him. With his gun. As he tried to stab me through the heart with a hunting knife. While his friend, Mac, tried to get a shot at me with an AR15.'

'James Ryker the victim.'

He didn't like the way she said that, but didn't bite back.

'That's twice I've heard this story now,' she said. 'About how it's others starting the fight with you. It's twice that story doesn't quite fit with what my eyes and my experience tells me.'

'I came here unarmed,' Ryker said. 'I left this place unarmed. I was happy to be on my way until they forced me off the road. Their intent was to kill me. That's pretty obvious when you look at what's down there.' He pointed to the dark valley. 'Unless you're telling me I'm making that part up too.'

Which she'd have a real hard time convincing anyone else, given the broken plastic and smashed headlight casings on the shoulder, right where they were standing.

'Do you know what vehicle it was?' she asked Ryker.

'No. Some sort of truck.'

'And you didn't see who was driving?'

'No. The lights were too bright, and I was concentrating more on not getting shot or blown up.'

Her phone rang and she turned and walked away from Ryker to take the call. He looked out over the dark edge again as his brain whirred with thoughts.

He couldn't hear much of Cindy's conversation but he knew she wasn't happy about whatever she was being told. When she finished she stormed back over to him, her creased-over face not hiding any of her agitation.

'Everything OK?' he asked.

'No, Ryker, everything is not goddamn OK.' She opened her mouth to say something else but then caught herself and took a couple of moments to calm down. 'Why don't I get you away from here.'

'OK?'

She drove them both back toward life. Neither of them spoke. They headed on through Canton, moving closer to Atlanta.

'Where are we going?' Ryker eventually asked.

'You know, I'd only called you to tell you that Meg is awake.'

'Yeah,' Ryker said. 'You said.'

'I thought you might want to go see her. Under supervision. Now... I'm not so sure I want you anywhere near her. Ever.'

Ryker didn't bother to contend that. He didn't even know which hospital Meg was in. It looked like for now Cindy was trying to keep it that way.

She unexpectedly braked hard, sending them both shooting forward in their seats.

'Why don't we get a coffee. I feel like this is gonna be a long night.'

Waffle House. Cindy got coffee. Ryker decided to get a little more. Waffles, bacon, sausage, egg.

'Don't worry, I'll pay,' he said to her when he saw the look of irritation on her face. As if she needed much encouragement to be irritated by him.

'Do you have any idea how much work I've put into the investigation into those guys up in Peltworth?'

'No,' Ryker said. 'I don't. And I'm sorry if I jeopardized anything.'

'Are you?'

Ryker chewed a mouthful of sausage rather than try to convince her.

'I heard you'd arrested Earl Haden,' he said when he'd swallowed. 'He was Gabriella Stricken's boyfriend. She was the woman who recognized Meg at Roadhouse.'

'Yeah, Ryker, I know.'

'That's why I went up there. To find Stricken, the others from Roadhouse.'

'I don't need you acting all vigilante, trying to avenge my sister.'

'That's not what I'm doing at all.'

Although he really did want to find that guy in the truck...

'I did find one of the others,' he said. 'A guy called Mac.'

He'd mentioned that name to her earlier as well. Both times now she'd kind of squirmed.

'You know him, don't you?'

'Yes! Yes, Ryker, I know him. He's a key player in the investigation into the meth labs in that area. It didn't start and stop with Haden.'

'But you didn't know he was at Roadhouse?'

'No. No, I didn't know that.'

'Look, Cindy, I get why you're pissed off with me. And please, believe me, I've not set out to harm your work in any way, but... there's something bigger happening here.'

'What do you mean?'

'I'm not after some drug dealers or whatever they are.'

'No, you're looking for Abby Hannigan, who it seems has got mixed up with—'

'Some very bad people. But I'm not talking about meth cookers.'

'Then what are you talking about?'

'The people Abby are with... I think they're responsible for the bombing at KDD Tech.'

He gave her a moment to think that one over. He could tell she needed it by her frozen features.

'Meg knew this too,' Ryker added. 'She may not have told you, but she was looking into the bombing already. It's how our paths crossed.'

Now she shook her head in disgust as though annoyed at her sister-in-law as much as she was at Ryker.

'What the hell is going on?' she asked.

'That's exactly what I'm trying to find out. And I'm only telling you any of this because... I think I can trust you with it. And as a show of faith because I know to you it seems like I'm causing a mess in your arena.'

'You can say that again.'

'The thing is... that's two times now I've just simply gone to these people and tried to talk. Tried to find out about what's going on with the White Lions, or whatever it is these people are calling themselves now. Both times I've barely got anywhere before things have turned violent. Before they've turned violent on me.'

'That's because you're dealing with some real bad people here, Ryker.'

'Yeah. I get that. But it's more than that too.'

'In what way?'

'These people are edgy. Over the top edgy. And it's not because they're afraid of getting busted for drugs. It's because there's something bigger going on. And what I've realized now is that I've been going after the wrong people so far. I've started too low down. But that was only because Meg had the lead to follow with Stanton.'

'Ryker, you've lost me. What are you getting at?'

'I'm just saying, I'm done running around after these low-key gangsters. They're not going to tell me anything, and it's only going to get me in more fights and make more of a mess of your investigation. They probably don't even know much about the bigger picture, whatever that picture is. But think of it like this. That bombing... it wasn't some random act. It wasn't something put together in a few minutes. It took preparation and skill in execution. Probably wasn't cheap either.'

'And so?'

'And so whoever these people are, they have expertise, and they have money. Someone is financing them.'

'You've lost me.'

'Who's running the investigation into the bombing for the GBI?'

She pursed her lips.

'You don't know or you don't want to tell me?'

'More the second one.'

'If you could get me in—'

'Ryker... I don't know you. I don't know why you're here. I'm not about to put my neck on the line by pulling you over to my superiors, asking them to bring you in to one of the most sensitive investigations our agency has ever had to run!'

'Cindy, this group... I know little about them, but I know one thing. This isn't the work of a lone wolf. I think these people are organized for... something bigger. And that means there could be more attacks.'

'But... why? No group has claimed responsibility for KDD Tech. No one has made any further threats.'

'I know, but just... trust me a little here. My instincts are screaming that this is just the start, and the very fact I'm here, knowing who asked me to be here, suggests I'm not the only one thinking that way.'

'Then why has this group not already come forward?'

'It's a good question, and my first thought is that because this is just a warm-up, and they don't want their bigger plans derailed too soon. The idea of a lone wolf keeps the media and the authorities looking in the wrong place, to keep people from getting to the truth too soon. They want to strike again while everyone's still focused in the wrong place.'

'You don't know this. This is all just in your head.'

She tapped her temple as though indicating she thought it was a circus inside his skull.

'Let me put it this way,' he said. 'I'm not going anywhere. I'll find what I need, one way or another. I'll find this group, I'll find who's in charge, what their plans are. I'll dismantle them. I'll do what I can to stop them before they hit again. I'd like to do all that with as little mess, and as much legitimate help as I can.'

'I... I can't help you, Ryker.'

'I already know the likes of Stanton and Mac and Stricken are too low down. I need to aim higher with my next move. Cindy, tell me, truthfully, who was the man in the truck at Roadhouse? He could be the key for me here. And the truck that tried to ram me off the cliff? Who would Mac and Kyle have called to come help them?'

'I... honestly don't know.'

She finished her coffee and wiped her mouth. She got up from her seat.

'I need some time to think. This is... a lot to take in.'

'You have my number. I have yours. Let's stay in touch.'

She left without saying goodbye.

Ryker finished his food. Checked his watch. Nearly 10 p.m. After the day he'd had... he could do with a rest, a good sleep.

But not tonight. Because he knew exactly what his next move would be, and exactly where to go to make it.

13

I watched the news in bed, warm, comfortable, some way content with Aisha asleep next to me. At first I didn't pay much attention to the report – not because it wasn't interesting, but because it wasn't relevant to me, and my mind was already turning over what was to come for the day.

Until I heard more of the story. And started to put together the pieces.

A plane crash. A small private jet. Five people dead: the pilot, plus a man named Bob Ferrer, his wife and two sons. The family had attended an Atlanta Braves game last night and were flying back to their home on the coast in North Carolina. Except twenty minutes after takeoff from the airfield in Marietta, a few miles north of Atlanta, the plane had plummeted, eventually smashing into the Blue Ridge mountains. A crash scene investigation was underway, but the remote location of the site meant it could take longer than usual to recover the remains of the plane, and the family, and determine what had happened. For now, the banner headline called it out as a terrible accident.

I thought otherwise. I knew of Bob Ferrer. He was a billionaire businessman, had founded and was the CEO of Atlas Information Systems. AIS for short. A Fortune 500 company based out of Charlotte, North Carolina – although Ferrer was an Atlantan, which explained his and his family's trip to the baseball game here.

AIS. I had no interest in that company or in the man who'd led it, neither was it part of my plans. Still, I knew that, like with so many other billionaires, the man and his business were intrinsically linked. With Ferrer's shock death, the stock price of AIS had plummeted, just like his plane, trading suspended less than an hour into the day.

A lot of people had just lost a lot of money.

The knock on the door across from my bed in my modest little studio pulled me from my thoughts. I didn't really get visitors, so my first instinct was one of suspicion. Aisha stirred in the bed next to me and turned over and looked at me and kind of... squirmed. Like she'd woken from a peaceful dream and was disappointed to be back in reality.

'What time is it?' she asked.

'Ten thirty.'

She groaned and sat up in the bed and rubbed her head and then looked at the side table, the empty bottle of vodka, the near-empty bourbon. No evidence of the Molly but she'd had a couple of those too.

'And that's why my head hurts so bad.'

Three more knocks came on the door. I reached under the pillow and took out the handgun and noted the apprehension in Aisha's eyes. She pulled the sheets a little higher as I stood from the bed and made my way to the window. I parted the slats of the blind.

Not who I expected to see at all. Not that I'd expected

anyone in particular, but I really didn't expect to see Hailey standing there.

'Yeah?' I shouted out.

'Marshall, it's Hailey,' she said, directing her gaze to the window just as I pulled back.

I waited a second, but she gave no indication of what she wanted.

'Give me two minutes,' I shouted in response.

When I turned around, Aisha was already nearly dressed. Well, it didn't take much. She didn't have any underwear, only her tiny little dress and her jacket, her heels and her purse.

I put the gun back where it was and pulled on my jeans and a T-shirt as Aisha hovered.

'That your girlfriend?' she asked me.

'No,' I said. 'I don't have a girlfriend. Why do you think you're here?'

She smiled a fake smile – the only one I ever saw from her and women like her – and I took my wallet from my pocket and thumbed through the bills before I handed them over to Aisha.

She counted them, looking pleased with herself.

'Thanks,' she said, before stuffing the money into her purse.

I moved to the door and opened up and Hailey initially smiled at me until she spotted my company over my shoulder.

'Oh... I didn't know...'

She didn't finish the sentence before Aisha brushed past me. She paused in front of Hailey, smirked a pretty ugly smirk before she sauntered away toward the stairs, hips swaying.

'You want to come in?' I asked.

Hailey glanced beyond me and pretty much pulled a disgusted kind of face.

'No, I, er... I came over because Kielder wants you.'

'He sent you to tell me that?'

'It's a... new thing. No phones.'

'Something happened?'

'Yeah. That's what he wants you for.'

'Give me two minutes.'

'I'll see you at the car.'

She glanced again into my studio, to the unkempt bed, I thought, before she turned and moved away.

Less than two minutes later we were both in her car as we headed south on the 285 toward Newnan.

'I didn't mean to disturb you like that,' Hailey said. 'I just didn't realize... you'd have company.'

'Why would you?'

She tried to respond to that but couldn't find the words.

'Because I'm such a freak, you didn't think I'd be able to get any woman to bed with me. Is that what you're saying?'

'No, I... It's...'

She trailed off, looked uncomfortable for a couple of seconds before she relaxed and smiled. Hailey had some backbone. A lot of people tiptoed around me. Or just plain up disliked me – Reed being a prime example. Hailey, even if she was at times wary of me, generally seemed intrigued more than anything else. Like a young kid who saw wonder all around them.

'But you'd probably be right to think that,' I added. 'Most of the hookers won't even come near me. Aisha's one of the few who does, but she charges three times as much as any other guy she sleeps with, and'll only come near me if she's up to her eyeballs with liquor and whatever else.'

'Marshall, it's not what I meant. I didn't mean because of... you know—'

'How I look?'

'I meant...'

She trailed off again. I smiled but she didn't reciprocate now, and she looked more uncertain of herself.

'I think what you're trying to say is you didn't realize I can still fuck. Right?' I said.

She winced. 'It's just that I heard... you don't feel anything.'

I laughed. I could tell she didn't appreciate it.

'You want to know if I can still get this thing up?' I grabbed my crotch. 'Yeah. I can. Getting hard is a simple physiological process. The blood still flows through my veins same as any other person. And I do feel, Hailey. I can be happy, sad, angry. Excited. Maybe my emotions are more muted than for most people but that's only because of what I've been through.'

'But you don't feel pain,' Hailey said. 'That's what I heard. I just thought that meant you couldn't... I don't know. Couldn't feel nice things either.'

'You're kind of right. Among other things the chemical receptors in my brain are fried beyond repair. So no, I get no highs, no rush of endorphins, and yeah, my brain stem and cortex were so badly damaged that I feel no pain.'

She glanced over at me, almost in awe.

'Like, nothing at all? You're just... numb to everything?'

'No. Not numb. You ever wake up in the night and your arm's just dead? You've been sleeping on it and you can't feel it, move it, anything?'

'Yeah. Like it's a dead weight.'

'It's not like that. If my whole body was like that all the time then I'd be paralyzed, right? But I have full control of everything still. It's only those receptors, the messaging that's broken. I sense pressure... but... Give me your hand.'

She looked reluctant, perhaps partly because she was driving, but she took her right hand from the wheel and I brought it closer to me and gently unwrapped her fingers. I took her forefinger in my hand and pushed it to the skin on my left arm. Then I slowly brushed her finger over my skin, down toward my wrist. Tense at first, I soon felt her relax as her finger rose and fell over the scars and the undulations of my melted skin.

We reached a red light and she turned to me, her intrigue even more intense than ever, and something in her eyes which I couldn't quite read – a combination of fear and magnetism.

'I feel that,' I said. 'I know something's touching me. Rubbing on me. It's a pleasant feeling because of what my brain's telling me is happening.'

I moved her hand back to the top of my forearm and she stared at my skin as she gently rubbed downward again, this time on her own.

I let out a long, patient exhale.

'I feel your touch,' I said. 'But not your warmth. Your hand could be ice cold or burning hot and I wouldn't notice at all. And what I feel with you caressing like that—' yeah, I deliberately chose that word '—would be exactly the same, and I mean exactly the same, if you took a razor blade in your grip and slid it down my arm peeling my skin away.'

I grabbed her hand and swept it down my arm and she gulped and yanked herself out of my grip. I burst out laughing and after a moment of unease she smiled too.

'Green light,' I said.

She got us moving. We went silent a few moments. I knew she was deep in thought.

'You really wouldn't know the difference?' she asked. 'A simple touch versus being skinned?'

'I'd feel no pain at all. But if I saw what you were doing, I would be very unhappy about it, believe me.'

'I don't know if... I could bear that.'

'I wasn't given a choice.'

Several cars were in the lot when we arrived at the office, including Reed's ridiculous truck. We headed inside and toward the boardroom although before we got there Hailey trailed off behind me. I stopped at the door – could hear animated voices beyond – and turned to her.

'I'm gonna get back to the data. When you're finished with them, come and take a look. I think I may have found something.'

The data. By which she meant the data I'd stolen from KDD Tech. We still hadn't found everything we needed, deciphered it all, but I trusted that Hailey would, even if she was still working alone mostly, which hadn't been our initial plan. But she wasn't just here because Kielder was screwing her; she was actually an excellent coder, hacker, software engineer. I felt pretty confident in that arena myself, but she was a step or more up. Better than Christine even, which was why it hadn't killed our plans that she had disappeared, only slowed things down.

'Sounds good,' I said.

She turned and moved away before I knocked on the door and entered, and several sets of eyes turned to me. Kielder, propped on the desk. Meyers, standing near his master. Reed, his resting bitch face frozen in a sneer, a bloodied knuckle-duster clenched in his right fist.

The blood belonged to one, or perhaps all three of the people, on their knees in front of him. Two men, one woman. Each had their hands behind their backs, wrists tied together with rope. Tape covered the mouths of the woman and one of the men. The second man had his tape-gag hanging off his cheek. Perhaps it'd been his turn to talk when I'd arrived.

'Where the hell have you been?' Reed said to me.

'At home. In bed. I didn't know I was wanted.'

'Lazy motherfucker. We're all here, getting our hands dirty while you're sleeping.'

'I would have come sooner if you'd let me know. If you'd called or texted. Except Hailey said something about no phones.'

'Yes,' Kielder said, with only a little less irritation directed to me than Reed. 'Because we have a problem.'

'And that is?'

'The English guy,' Reed said. 'He's come back at us again.'

Ah, yes. Actually I did recognize one of the men on the floor. Wayne Stanton. He'd been one of the people Reed had hauled in here a couple of days ago after the previous mess at that bar in Canton. A mess which, from what I'd heard of the incident, had been caused by Reed storming in and initiating a confrontation, which had resulted in two people, Stanton included, being shot.

'So?' I prompted.

'We have a name,' Meyers said. 'James Ryker. After the shootout at Roadhouse he was held by Canton police, but they let him go last night without charge. I've not been able to find out much about him. Except only hours after his release, I got a call from Mac saying he'd turned up in Peltworth.'

Peltworth. I'd never been to the place. I only knew about it because Reed had lost his shit a few weeks ago when there'd been a raid up there. Some of his redneck brethren ran meth labs. It was how Reed made his money. Kielder didn't like it. Thought it was beneath him, although I knew he took some of the profits, so he obviously didn't care too much.

I looked over the three chumps again.

'Which one's Mac?' I asked Reed.

'Me,' the guy with the tape on his cheek said. He looked at me warily. Not scared as such. He'd never seen me before, perhaps didn't even know anything about me, but seeing me for the first time – mask on or off – wasn't like seeing any other stranger for the first time, and this guy was probably in a head-spin as to who I was and why I'd been brought over.

'James Ryker came to you?' I asked.

'Turned up outta the blue. Kyle and me caught him. I called Reed.'

'But I was too busy, so I sent Meyers up there,' Reed said. 'Except Mac and Kyle, the idiots, couldn't even keep Ryker tied up a few minutes. The guy fought them. Killed Kyle. Blew the whole damn place to smithereens.'

'It was already chaos when I arrived,' Meyers said. 'I grabbed Mac and got us both out of there.'

'And Ryker?'

'We waited for him. Rammed his car off the road, down a ravine.'

'So he's dead?'

Meyers grumbled something under his breath. A weak excuse, perhaps.

'We've seen nothing to confirm his death,' Kielder said. 'Which is the problem. For whatever reason, this guy is targeting us. And if he's still alive, he's a liability and it's only a matter of time before he resurfaces.'

I wanted to say something along the lines of clusterfuck or Keystone Kops, as both those phrases sprang to mind. But I didn't think anyone else in the room would appreciate it much.

'So we're assuming James Ryker is still alive,' I said. 'Any idea why he's causing trouble?'

'N... No,' Mac said. The other two on the floor both murmured and shook their heads too, although I hadn't been talking to either of them.

'Like I said, I haven't been able to find out much about him,'

Meyers said. 'Definitely nothing official. Which is why we wanted you here.'

'You want me to torture these three for you?' I asked, and the captives all moaned and squirmed.

'No. Because they don't know anything other than what they've already told us,' Reed said.

'Maybe you haven't asked them strongly enough yet.'

'They don't know anything more,' Kielder stressed. 'But you can use your skills, your contacts, whatever, to find out what you can about Ryker.'

'It'd be my pleasure,' I said with a bow. 'So that explains the no phones protocol? You think someone has eyes and ears on us?'

No one said anything to that.

'Or maybe Ryker and whoever he's working for isn't getting intel from snooping on us, but from an inside man. Or woman.'

Again the three captives moaned as though I was pointing a finger of suspicion at them. I wasn't.

'What are you talking about?' Reed said.

'That it's sensible to be extra careful right now. There've been two incidents in three days now where this Ryker has been too close for comfort. Both times it was people associated to... you?'

'You're accusing me of something?'

'Only pointing out the facts.'

'If I was working for the Feds or anyone else I'd hardly get them crawling around my people, would I?'

I shrugged, enjoying the fact that I'd so easily got under the guy's skin. Again.

'There's no rat here,' Kielder said. 'That isn't what we're looking at. We're looking at a rogue agent for God knows who. And you're gonna find out the who.'

'I'll do my best.'

'Get them out of here,' Kielder said, and moments later Reed was kicking the three toward the door. 'But if I have to get any of you back here again... next time you won't leave in one piece.'

Reed took them out. I studied Kielder and Meyers for a few moments.

'I know you don't like him,' Kielder said, 'but he was with us for the best part of the last forty-eight hours. The person who hasn't been with us, is you.'

'Or Christine,' I clarified. 'Unless you're about to tell me she showed up, finally, but then disappeared again.'

No answer. Which I assumed meant no one had seen or heard from her still. Definitely odd, but it really was nothing to do with me. Why would I make Christine disappear when she was supposed to be leading the data trawl with Hailey? Until that part of the plan was finalized, we couldn't move forward.

Who did stand to gain from Christine's disappearance?

I hadn't figured that one out yet.

Maybe Reed had buried her after she rebuffed his amorous moves.

'But you're right,' I said. 'I haven't been with you, have I? Because you didn't ask me to be with you. Even though you were putting together a plot against Atlas Information Systems.'

Both men went silent as they glared at me. Reed was back in the room before either of them responded.

'What?' he said, picking up on the change in mood.

'I was just asking about AIS,' I said. 'Bob Ferrer. I heard he had a nasty accident last night.'

Reed laughed. 'Oh shit, Melty, are you upset we didn't tell you about that?'

'No. I'm angry that, even at a time when we have this James

Ryker guy breathing down our necks, you're carrying out risky plots like that without even consulting me. And risky plots that don't directly assist my plans—'

'Your plans?' Reed said, coming over and standing by the other two. 'That's your problem. You've got this weird fantasy in your fucked-up head that this is all about you, and what you want.'

'We need you here,' Kielder said to me. 'Because what you're fighting for is the same thing we're fighting for. But don't kid yourself that this is about ideology and nothing but ideology.'

'No. I get it. It's about getting filthy, greedy rich too.'

No denial from the three.

'You shorted the stock?' I asked, already knowing the answer. 'Is that why you targeted him? Because I know AIS has nothing of value to us.'

'Yes. We did,' Meyers said.

'How much did you make?'

'Over three hundred million. And that isn't just to make us filthy rich. It's to fund everything you're involved in, and also whatever comes after.'

'Keep telling yourself that,' I said to him, patting him on the shoulder and he dragged back, away from my touch. 'Guys, I don't care if you want to profit from what we're doing. But I do want to at least know what you're planning. If you ask me, this was too risky. In Atlanta? So soon after KDD Tech? How confident are you that this'll remain as an accident? And if there's suspicion, how long before it's put together with KDD Tech?'

'We're confident,' Reed said.

'And Ferrer? Does he have any relationship with you or BTC?' I asked Kielder.

'No,' Kielder said. 'We've met but we've never had dealings. And I don't like how you're questioning my decisions. But you are right to talk about risks. We need to step things up and move more quickly. So you and Reed are moving out to Texas, ASAP.'

Texas. That wasn't supposed to be until next week, to give us time to comb through the data from KDD Tech first. But other than that, everything was in place, really – the new timeline wouldn't be a problem to me.

'Oh, lucky fucking me,' Reed said. 'This is gonna be the road trip from hell, spending that long in the car with this douche.'

'Believe me, it's not how I'd choose to spend my time either,' I responded.

'Yeah. Well, if your fucked-up face wasn't so recognizable we could have just flown there,' Reed said.

'Because wouldn't it be ideal to have both our names recorded on flight manifests?'

'OK, guys, we get you don't like each other,' Meyers said. 'At. All. But there's not going to be a problem here, is there?'

'No,' Reed said.

'No,' I concurred. 'I've been through much, much worse than sitting in a car with a jackass like this for a few hours.'

'Then you better get on the road,' Kielder said checking his watch. 'I'll be keeping my eye on the news.'

'But if you think we're taking that god-awful truck...' I said, 'you may as well just shoot me here and now.'

'Please?' Reed said. 'Can I?'

'No,' Kielder said. 'No shooting each other. And not that damn truck, keep things on the low. We'll see you in a couple of days.'

'Let's go, cowboy,' I said to Reed, before giving my best yeehaw. He snarled and thumped into my shoulder to head out, me only a step behind.

14

A trip which might have taken only a couple of hours by plane ended up taking us through the night. Ten hours, total, with a bit of speed on quiet nighttime interstates and only basic rest stops when we swapped driving to give the other a chance to sleep. Of course it would have been quicker to fly, but as I'd told the others back in Newnan, what'd be the point in us having our names recorded on flight manifests right before and after what we were about to do?

But it wasn't only that. I just hated flying. I'd got used to wearing my mask. When I looked in the mirror now with it on, I saw me. A version of me, at least. I felt naked, exposed, on show without my face covered and the idea of standing in a line at airport security with so many eyes on me, scrutinizing, assessing, judging...

I didn't need it.

All in all the drive was straightforward, really. And quiet. I was a little surprised by that as Reed rarely kept his mouth shut. This part of our plan – my plan – had been in the works for some time, and I knew Kielder had put Reed with me on this as a test of sorts. A test of my loyalty, mostly, as if Kielder wanted to make sure I could work with this guy despite our differences, and hell, if I came back from this with Reed satisfied with how I'd done and no gripes to report to his boss... Kielder could surely have no more doubts about my aims, my allegiances.

Which he did have, I knew. He'd told me so.

To me, this was all my plan. They literally wouldn't have known where to start without me. But that didn't mean I could accomplish what I wanted to accomplish on my own. The help of Kielder and others was invaluable to me, even if they saw it the other way around – that my help was invaluable to their aims. A quid pro quo, I guess you could say, all parties aware that they benefited from the mutual relationship, even if the reasons for our actions, and the end objectives weren't fully aligned.

My objectives were not apolitical, but they weren't overly political either, even if politics had drawn me to Kielder and his disenfranchised crew who wanted to hit back at the system.

Kielder was a political activist, in his eyes at least. He felt aggrieved that the country he'd been born into and brought up in was no longer the same country he remembered or wanted to be a part of. He believed his White American culture had been eroded and eroded to the point that within a generation or two it would simply be a thing of the past. He believed young white men were maligned, marginalized, overlooked, and he wanted to do what he could to stop that, to preserve the whiteness – and masculinity – of America. Some would say such an outlook was in itself racist, xenophobic, a calling-card of the far right. Others would say it was simply deluded and didn't hold up to even the mildest scrutiny. But Kielder believed it, and so did a lot of other people.

Kielder – already a prominent mouthpiece for the wider

political movement, particularly given his recent appearances with his loudspeaker at protests and rallies – envisaged coming out the other side of our actions as a white knight in shining armor.

Time would tell. But the point was, Kielder clamored for a change in the cultural landscape of his country, and ultimately, that would come through politics and not violence.

Although stunts like the killing of Bob Ferrer and his family showed Kielder was also unashamedly in this for personal enrichment, however he tried to play what he'd done there. And getting rich was definitely not my aim and never had been.

But back to the trip... Surprisingly quiet, even if the air between me and Reed remained hostile. No attempts at chit-chat, bonding, getting to know each other, our pasts, our outlooks to see if perhaps we shared some commonalities that we hadn't before realized.

Of course we didn't. Reed was an obnoxious moron.

Although he was a dangerous moron. One I had to watch my step around.

I'd never been to Houston before, but I'd heard the horror stories of the traffic, the gargantuan highways. Atlanta was bad enough in that respect, but what I'd heard of Houston turned out to be correct. If Kielder wanted to make himself rich, rather than killing CEOs and shorting the stocks he should get himself into road-laying in Texas, because someone was making billions from it. At least arriving on the outskirts of the city a little after 7 a.m. on a Saturday morning, the multi-lanes weren't gridlocked.

We didn't go into the city but into the suburbs. Surprisingly leafy suburbs given the quite barren landscape, with executive homes on big lots.

'You think they're in?' Reed said when I pulled the car to the side of the road outside 785 Lantern Grove.

'Unless something changed in the last ten hours.'

On a Saturday morning, my best bet was that we'd find husband and wife in bed still.

'Then let's get this done,' Reed said, a devilish glint in his eye before he pulled the mask over his face.

* * *

The inside of the house was equally nice, if not nicer than the outside. Marble tiles covered the expansive entrance hall, which also featured an elaborate crystal chandelier dangling from a double-height ceiling. The rest of the downstairs was finished with obviously expensive oak flooring. The kitchen was sleek and sublime. The primary suite upstairs was at least twice as big as the studio I was renting, with no expense spared in the fittings either. Not to mention I'd spotted the extravagant pool outside complete with tanning deck and spa, the water glistening in the early morning sunlight.

All in all a very nice way to live.

Until today.

'Is there anyone else in the house?' Reed shouted, before he pistol whipped the man across his face again. Reed let go of the scruff of his neck and the guy slumped to the marble in the hall, deep red blood spilling from a gash in his eye and onto the luxury tiles.

The man didn't answer with a yes or a no. He couldn't, with the tape over his mouth. But he did violently shake his head at the question.

The woman – the man's wife – on her knees in front of me, hands tied, mouth taped, exactly like those three chumps yesterday back in Newnan, whined and moaned at watching her husband getting pummeled.

The couple were Larry and Matilda Baumann. Fifty-somethings. Not native Texans. Matilda was a second-generation German immigrant who'd grown up in New York. Larry was a Bostonian, perhaps with Irish in his genes somewhere in the not-too-distant past. The draw of money had brought the family south.

Reed added a boot to Larry's stomach for good measure before he crouched down and ripped the tape from the man's mouth, the sticky industrial-strength glue tearing off hair and skin too, leaving an ugly red rectangular patchwork across his face.

'It's just you two?' Reed asked, sounding calmer now.

'Yes!' Larry shouted.

'Your kids—'

'College!'

Which we expected from our recon, but best to make sure neither of them had snuck home for the weekend for whatever reason.

'No cleaner coming today? Maintenance? Pool guy? Landscaper?'

'No!'

Reed looked up at me as if questioning whether I had anything to add.

'What do you want?' Larry shouted. 'If it's money... jewelry? Just take it and leave!'

I resisted the urge to roll my eyes. Why did these people always boil our motives down to money and items of value? Perhaps because those things drove their lives, but not mine.

'We don't want your stinking money,' Reed said.

'Then what!'

Reed turned to me before his gaze fell on Matilda.

'Her,' he said.

Larry screamed. Matilda tried to as well, I think, although it wasn't very effective with the tape on her mouth.

Reed stormed forward and pulled her to her feet and dragged her toward the stairs. Larry went to get up as though he had a chance of helping her, even with his hands tied behind his back. I cut him off rather than watch whatever he'd intended and kicked him in the back to send him face first down to the marble again.

'No!' he yelled again after a couple of moments of spitting out blood and teeth.

'Come on, honey, time to get dressed for work,' Reed said, laughing as he hauled Matilda ungracefully up the stairs.

He was enjoying himself. Enjoying inflicting pain and misery like the sadistic, simplistic idiot I knew he was. He needed to lay off a bit. If Matilda turned up at the security gates to her place of work all bruised and bloodied it'd hardly be a good start.

'Looks like it's just me and you,' I said to Larry, who turned himself over to glare at me as blood dribbled from his mouth, nose, the gash above his eye. 'He's not gonna hurt her. This isn't about you two. It's about her work.'

'You fucking piece of shit,' Larry said. 'Hiding your fucking face from me.'

I said nothing to that, mainly because his words were surprisingly stinging. Even though both me and Reed were wearing masks. Hockey masks, so my day-mask which I'd worn through our journey here was completely covered. This guy had no idea what lay beneath, yet I hated anyone drawing attention to the way I looked.

So I launched my foot under his chin and the crunching impact sent him sprawling, head rolling.

That'd keep him quiet for a while at least.

Banging and more shouting from upstairs. Five minutes later, I saw the feet emerge on the landing. Matilda hadn't made much of an effort, really. Jeans, a halter-neck top and jacket. Business casual, Texan-style. Not exactly what you'd think of for a pretty senior businesswoman, but it was Saturday, I supposed.

And at least she'd done a good job of tidying her hair, and her face looked injury-free, even if her eyes were scared shitless.

'Focus, Matilda,' I said to her. 'If anything goes wrong out there, I'll leave the pieces of Larry right here for when you get back.'

'And he's not joking,' Reed said as he maneuvered her down the stairs. 'This guy is a fucking sick psycho. You don't even wanna know what he's capable of.'

I couldn't tell if Reed's words were mocking, deliberately shocking, or if that's really what he thought of me. Nor did I know which of those options I preferred, to be honest.

'This'll all be over for both of you very soon, Matilda,' I added. 'Just do exactly what he says.'

'Yeah,' Reed said. 'I think she's got that by now.'

She whimpered in horror when her eyes found her husband slumped on the floor, bleeding, but moments later she was at the door with Reed and not long after that they were outside. I heard her powerful BMW fire up and then the house went heavenly quiet.

Time to get settled in.

* * *

The Baumanns had a very nice home office. Not ugly, old world, dark wood like a lot of home offices I'd seen on TV and in movies. This one was bright and sparse, in a pleasing way. In the middle sat a functional, clutter-free desk. A few shelves with ornaments lined the walls along with vibrant pop art. The room also had a nice view of the manicured lawn, and I could hear the waterfall at the pool gently trickling.

I propped Larry up against the wall and poked around. Found an iPad, a laptop, a couple of external hard drives. Thumb drives. I bagged them all.

Larry stirred so I went over and sat down on the floor next to him.

'Shouldn't be long now,' I said.

'Where... is she?' he asked me.

'She went to work.'

'W... Why?'

'Because it's her job.'

'I don't... understand.'

'You don't need to. You just need to sit there and wait. Once she's done what she needs to do for us, I'll leave.'

He didn't respond to that but glared at me for a good while, and I genuinely wanted to know what he was thinking about me.

'You coward,' he said eventually.

'Coward?' I said. 'No, Mr. Baumann, I am the very opposite of a coward.'

The glare he continued to direct at me suggested he didn't agree.

'You believe in God,' I said to him, a statement because I'd already found the Bible in the desk drawer and noted the Jesus on the cross on the wall in the hallway.

'I do,' he said. 'And you'll get your punishment, in this life or the next.'

'But what is a god?' I asked him.

He huffed but didn't respond.

'A creator?' I suggested. 'A force of nature? A source of moral authority?'

He still didn't answer; he probably hadn't expected this line of questioning.

'Every religion has a god or gods. My question to you is this. Why is your god the real god, and not that of other religions?'

Still, no answer.

'Something else to think about.' I shuffled a little closer to him, my face close to his. 'How sure are you that god, gods live up in the sky? What if gods really, truthfully roam the earth? They always have done, from time to time. It's why there are so many disparate ideas of god from all over the world, from all periods of time.'

He shook his head but still didn't say a word.

'They appear like any other being, mostly. Until they show their true power and make their mark on the world. Then comes generation after generation of reverence, of storytelling, of mythology, the truth long forgotten but the idea and power of the deity unstoppable. In time... perhaps my own actions will see me revered as a god. A superhuman being, holding power over nature and the fortunes of millions, if not billions of people.'

He snorted, looked at me like I was insane.

'Perhaps you don't see it... but in the future... in a hundred years, in a thousand years... We'll see. One thing is for sure: I'll be remembered. You? I don't know about that.'

I laughed. He didn't.

My phone rang. I lifted it and answered.

'We're inside,' Reed said. 'On our way to her office.'

'OK. Stay on the line.'

'I know that.'

Nothing more was said but I could hear his breathing, footsteps. A door opening. His muffled voice as he directed Matilda. Several minutes passed.

'Heading back down to the car now to verify,' Reed said.

More breathing. The ding of an elevator. A crackle as the line fought to hold as they descended into the basement.

The soft thunks of car doors closing.

'Are you ready?' Reed asked me.

I was. I'd taken out my laptop a few minutes ago, Larry watching me with renewed intrigue.

'Giving you access now,' Reed said.

I took charge of his machine. Headed straight into the connected external drive. Had to do a bit of digging before I found what I was looking for.

'And the access key?'

Matilda's shaky voice came on the line and I imagined her in the driver's seat, phone pressed to her ear, tears streaming down her face.

She read out the long mishmash of numbers and letters.

'That's it,' I said to Reed. 'We have what we need.'

Larry whimpered, and I wasn't sure if it was in distress or relief. Did he not trust our word?

'Stay exactly where you are,' Reed said to Matilda. 'I'll call you when I'm outside the grounds. Then you're free to go home to hubby. My friend will leave him the moment I tell him to. You understand.'

'Y-yes.'

'Speak soon,' Reed said to me before the call ended.

Larry had started shaking. Neither of us spoke. Several more minutes passed. My phone rang again. I answered without saying a word.

'You ready?' Reed asked me.

'Yes.'

'Then you're good to go.'

I hit the enter key on the laptop...

Nothing. I heard absolutely nothing.

Yet I knew that thirteen miles away the bomb in Matilda Baumann's BMW had just detonated in the basement of Industrial Control Logistics Inc. It'd be enough to tear one hell of a hole in the side of the glitzy glass-fronted office building.

'OK. Put that sucker out of his misery and come pick me up,' Reed instructed before ending the call.

And I think Larry heard because he was shaking even more violently now.

'Please!' he said.

'Your wife is dead,' I said to him.

He sobbed.

'And I'm supposed to put a bullet in your brain right about now.'

I pulled the gun from my waistband, cocked it and pointed it toward Larry's head.

'You don't have to.'

'You really want to carry on living, knowing what we did to your wife?'

'Please!'

'Do you know why we set it up like this?'

He didn't answer.

'To give some basic cover. She shot you dead and went off to work and blew herself up.' I laughed, a little theatrically. 'It's up to the Feds to figure a motive in that. Pretty dumb stuff really, but it'll buy us a bit of time while they fight through the mess.'

He shook his head but didn't say anything.

'And I'm not afraid to shoot you dead right here. You wouldn't be the first person whose life I've taken.'

I played with the gun and released the magazine and checked the chamber, then cocked it again.

'But... don't you see? Don't you see the power I have? I told you before. The power of a god. The power not just to take life, but to give life.'

I could tell he didn't quite get it yet.

'If I gave you the chance to live... what would you do?'

He mumbled incoherently.

'I'm serious, Larry. If I passed this gun to you right now... would you wish me well on my way for sparing you? Would you kill yourself out of grief for your wife? Or would you use the single bullet in this chamber to blow my brains out? Revenge, pure and simple. Or justice, perhaps, in your eyes.'

He didn't answer. I placed the gun on the floor and took my knife and shuffled toward him.

'Don't move,' I said as I reached behind him and cut through his ties. He didn't flinch. Good for him.

I picked the gun up again, held it out to him.

He didn't take it to start with, just stared at it as though he couldn't figure out what the hell was happening.

'It's your choice, Larry.'

He reached his hand out, slowly, as though testing if I was about to betray my word and turn on him.

I didn't. He took the gun in his grip. His sobbing was even worse now than before.

'Now you're the executioner,' I said to him. 'If that's what you want to be.'

The gun shook in his grip so much I worried he'd pull the trigger before he'd even aimed.

But he somehow managed to control it. Lifted the weapon. For a moment I thought he was about to push the barrel under his chin and blow his own brains out. It would be an obvious route for him given his trauma.

No. The barrel aimed at my head instead. Revenge was such a powerful force.

Click.

I sighed.

Click. Click.

He could pull the trigger all day long. It wouldn't make a difference.

I snatched the gun from him and he cowered. I stood up.

'I'm disappointed in you,' I said to him. 'You had the power to be something more.' I turned and walked out, ignoring his shouting and crying.

Half an hour later and Reed was back in the car with me.

'You took care of him?' was the first thing he asked me. As though he already had doubts about me following through.

I didn't answer.

'Fucking hell, Marshall, did you kill the guy? Did you follow through?'

'He didn't need to die,' I said.

'Of course he needed to die! That was the plan! You idiot! Stop the car. Stop the damn car! We're going back.'

'We're not going back. The police will be swarming there by now. There'll probably be patrols out looking for us already. We need to get out of Texas.'

He slammed the dashboard with his fist. Did it again. So hard that the plastic cracked.

'You've screwed us.'

'It makes no difference. The cover was never supposed to hold, only buy us time. We want the truth to come out eventually. How else do we gain the visibility, the notoriety we need?'

'This wasn't the plan. And when Kielder finds out...'

'I'll tell him the same thing.'

'You're not in charge here.'

Except I begged to differ. Could I have killed Larry Baumann in cold blood? Yes. Of course I could. I had no qualms in taking someone's life if it furthered my aims. But just like with the General and his family... I didn't need to take lives unnecessarily. I had the power to choose.

I had the power to give life, and the power to take it.

Even if others didn't yet see it, I was a supreme being on this earth. A god in all but name.

The General had seen it, Larry Baumann had seen it. Others had before them, and many, many more would soon enough.

In time, the whole world would know my name.

15

A day and a night of relative quiet had passed and Cindy had finally caved and told Ryker which hospital Meg was staying at. He was sure he could have found out on his own, but he wanted to build trust with her so had waited it out, been on his best behavior.

And his quiet time had actually been productive anyway, because he'd tracked down truck guy, knew his name and where he lived.

Brad Reed, Marietta.

Simple surveillance had initially led him to Reed's house. Ryker had started at Missy's Gentlemen's Club, the same night he and Cindy had been to Waffle House. He hadn't gone inside, instead scoping the exterior, waiting and watching. He spotted not only Gabriella Stricken but Wayne Stanton that night, the latter limping along on his wounded leg.

Ryker could have confronted one or both of them. Instead he'd done neither. He meant what he'd said to Cindy, not just about not wanting to cause her trouble, but also about needing to aim higher.

So instead of confrontation, he'd made the decision to follow Stanton, had soon found where he lived. The following day he'd gone back and waited for Stanton to emerge and had tailed him over to Woodstock where he'd headed into a diner. As Ryker sat outside in his car, that over-the-top truck – a heavily modified GMC Sierra – had rumbled into view, heads turning as it swept into the parking lot. Again, Ryker had held back – a little more reluctantly this time – as he watched the guy who'd very nearly killed Meg saunter into the diner and stuffed his mouth with whatever.

Ryker had then followed him to his home in Marietta. Had once again held back and left the guy there and called in the address and the license plate in to an old ally, who'd called another old ally, who'd found the name of the guy and the next morning passed all the information over to Ryker.

Brad Reed. Georgia native. Two misdemeanors for drug possession in his early twenties but otherwise no criminal record.

Ryker had received that information on his way over to the hospital. He'd be acting on it as soon as he was finished there.

He knocked on the door and pushed it open and peered inside. Meg was in the bed, propped up, her eyes open but groggy. One arm was in a sling, one leg was suspended awkwardly in the air, a heavy cast covering it from her ankle almost to her waist.

'Want some company?' he asked, and she twisted her head an inch toward him before grimacing and groaning in pain.

'You bet,' she said through gritted teeth.

He moved inside and closed the door behind him and took the seat next to the bed.

'I would have come sooner but... I think your sister-in-law was in two minds.'

'I know. She said. Actually, I think it was me who managed to convince her.'

'She tell you about what happened then?'

'Yeah.' She tried to smile but gave up, as though even that simple move caused too much pain somewhere. 'Sounds like you're good at finding trouble.'

'Seems that way.'

'Shame I didn't get to go there with you.' This time she did manage the smile.

'It is. But I get why Cindy's not too happy with me. She's got her job and all the rules that go with it to consider. It might have been helpful if you'd told me sooner that your sister-in-law – ex-sister-in-law – worked for the GBI though.'

She didn't respond to that.

'How are you feeling?' he asked.

'Like I'm not sure if this is better than being dead.'

He winced at those words, the deadpan delivery. He hadn't expected such melancholic thoughts from her.

'You were lucky,' he said.

'Lucky? I have fourteen cracked ribs. A punctured lung. They had to remove my spleen, my right kidney too, both were so badly damaged. The femur on my left leg is in so many pieces that I still don't know if I'll ever walk again. Right now I can't feel it at all as the nerves are badly damaged too. Maybe I'll never be able to.'

She looked down at her feet and Ryker saw the toes on her left foot wriggling under the covers. He looked to her right leg, suspended. Nothing from that.

'You're alive, Meg.'

She snorted but didn't say anything.

'I'm sorry,' he added.

'I guess... maybe it would have been even worse. If you

hadn't been there with me. Maybe they'd have taken me into the mountains and killed me and buried me out there.'

'You might be right. And you know what? The fact they've been so willing to attack – twice now – is because we've hit on something. Something big. You might be in here now, but you started this.'

He reached out and put his hand over hers to offer comfort and she didn't resist his touch. She looked over at him as a tear escaped her left eye. He studied her a few moments. The few bits of skin he could see were mostly covered in a maze of purple and black bruises. The darkened patches rose up from her neck toward her head, like a poison inside her slowly taking over.

'You're a fighter, Meg,' he said. 'I'd have you by my side anytime.'

'Please tell me you've made some progress? That me being in here isn't all for nothing?'

'Do you know the name Brad Reed?'

She shook her head.

'He's the man who smashed his truck into you.'

She balled her fist under his hand. Clenched her jaw tightly shut.

'I don't yet know the ins and outs, but it looks like he sits above the likes of Stanton and the others in whatever group these people are running.'

'The White Lions?'

'I don't know. Nobody seems to be using that name, but they all know of it. But Stanton... The men I confronted up in Pelt-worth, they're not who I'm looking for. Reed could be. You been watching the local news recently? About the protests?'

She huffed. 'I am so goddamn bored of watching the TV.'

'I get that. But... how about this? Two days before the

bombing at KDD Tech, Brad Reed was one of the speakers at a rally in Atlanta where all sorts of white nationalist groups were thought to have participated.'

She sat up in her bed a little, grimacing again. 'You serious?'

'Deadly serious.'

'But... You're saying you think this all has something to do with the bombing?'

He sighed. His gut told him yes, but really he had no evidence of that, because so far there was no evidence – that he had, at least – of why that bombing had been carried out, or by whom.

Well, the only evidence being his presence in America, which itself meant that someone thought there was a bigger story going on.

'I think it's connected. I just don't know how yet.'

'You probably heard about the explosion in Texas too,' Meg said.

Ryker had. Though all he knew so far was what had been reported on mainstream news. But the correlation to KDD Tech couldn't be overlooked. A bomb attack at a corporate office. The explosion coming from beneath the building.

'I heard about it.'

'But... Do you think it's connected too?'

He didn't answer because his mind was too busy playing over the possibilities.

'What are you going to do next?' she asked.

'I'm going to keep on top of Reed. Find out who he reports to. Keep working my way to the top.'

'But I mean...'

'Are you asking me if I'm going to force the truth out of him? Hurt him for hurting you?'

'I guess.'

'Because you want me to or because you don't?'

'I'd like nothing more than for that asshole to feel even a tiny bit of the pain and the misery that I'm feeling right now. But I also know it won't make my life any better. Not really.'

Ryker knew what she meant, although he didn't entirely agree. Reed didn't deserve to be let off for what he'd done, but Ryker knew better than to go charging after the guy like a bull being heckled in a ring.

'I'm not going to confront him if I don't have to. Because I don't need the unnecessary attention, either from the GBI or the police or his own people.'

She slumped a little, as though actually a bit disappointed, her thoughts and emotions conflicting and all over the place.

'I'll keep you in the loop,' Ryker said, pulling his hand back.

'I'm glad you came.'

'I'll be back.'

He got to his feet.

'And Cindy?' Meg asked.

'What about her?'

'Are you... working with her?'

'Not really. I don't think she likes me much.'

Meg smirked. 'I wouldn't be so sure about that. Let's just say... she's complicated. Very good at hiding what she really thinks. But she's also dang good at her job.'

'I don't doubt it.'

He headed on out. Back to his car. Not even a thirty-minute drive to the house on Woodbridge Road in Marietta. The houses here were modest, the lots quite tight. Some of the homes looked rundown, yards tatty, but others were neat and tidy, well-kept. Several of the houses in the area had large Stars and Stripes in the yards, fluttering in the wind. One Confederate flag too. But on the way here Ryker had also spotted several shops and signs in Spanish, to account for the obviously large population of Latinos in the area. An area of clashing cultures.

Last time Ryker was here he'd spotted Reed's truck on the outside. This time there were no cars on the driveway. He carried on going, several houses along, before he pulled over and shut down the engine and got out.

He kept his eyes busy as he moved back up the street to Reed's house. Nobody else out, although he could hear people in their backyards, hear leaf blowers and other garden equipment too.

He reached Reed's house and headed up the driveway without breaking stride. Carried on along the side of the house to the garage. He went past that too and to the five-foot-high fence to the back which he jumped over with a little skip.

The back yard was small, square, plain. Not much going on except for an unkempt lawn and a grill and a few outdoor chairs. Ryker moved to the back door, took out his tools as he went. The torsion wrench and picks saw him through the lock in a matter of seconds. There could be an alarm. Could be a bolt on the inside...

He pulled the handle down and pushed the door open...

Neither. No sounds came from inside the home, which smelled of stale cooking grease. Ryker entered and closed the door behind him. He waited a few moments to make sure all was still quiet.

It was.

So he started searching. Which didn't take long, because it really wasn't a very big home. Everything suggested Reed lived alone: no wife, girlfriend, or kids.

A lot of mess.

A laptop.

He settled in the kitchen where he had a view of both the front yard and the back door. Although if Reed came back in that truck of his... it wasn't like Ryker wouldn't hear it from half a mile off anyway.

The laptop required either a PIN code or a thumbprint. Just as well Ryker had come prepared. He could hack the PIN code, but often it was even easier to hack the thumbprint. Especially in a home like this where the owner obviously didn't put much effort into wiping down surfaces. Ryker pulled out the little pot of wood glue and starting scanning. The dark melamine finish on the kitchen worktop was a network of smears and finger-prints, and Ryker's first task was to determine which of the stains was from a thumb not a finger. He settled on one and poured a smidgen of wood glue over the top then waited a couple of minutes for it to harden while he kept scanning. He laid down a second splat not far away then went back to the first and carefully peeled it from the surface and looked at the underside. He could just about make out the faint outlines, the swirls of the thumbprint. He woke up the computer and gently placed the glue on the scanner and pressed down.

No luck. He tried again. No luck.

Back to the second lot of glue. He peeled that one back, placed it on the scanner.

Bingo.

Ryker allowed himself a wry smile. Many people assumed a thumb or fingerprint scanner was a decent bit of home security. Perhaps they'd seen movies where the obvious – although extreme – way around such a measure was to chop off some-one's digit.

It simply wasn't the case. Such security was, in reality, for convenience more than anything else, and convenience meant it had to work easily, multiple times a day, in a variety of different environments. Plus, such scanners had become so ubiquitous on modern everyday devices that manufacturers cut corners on the quality of the software and hardware. Cheaper meant even more vulnerable.

Very helpful to people like Ryker.

Reed's laptop had direct access to his phone's messages, his contacts, his emails. It only took Ryker a couple of minutes to pull all of that data on to a thumb drive so he could go over it in more detail later.

He took a quick browse through recent internet searches. Shook his head in disbelief at the number of times over the last few days that Reed had searched for news articles surrounding the bombing of KDD Tech. Not that there couldn't be an inno-cent explanation for a local being interested in the attack. Ryker just didn't believe that was the case with Reed.

Also of interest were the searches he'd made related to Industrial Control Logistics Inc, the company whose Texas headquarters had been bombed last night. Which kind of answered the questions from the earlier conversation with Meg, even if Ryker didn't know what it all meant. Something else that caught his attention were the articles Reed had read about a company called AIS. And a plane crash not even three days ago in the north of Georgia which had killed the AIS CEO – Bob Ferrer – and his family.

Ryker hadn't seen that news, but a nasty knot twisted inside his gut and his own conversation with Cindy from a few days ago came back to the fore.

I'll do what I can to stop them before they hit again.

Except, given both the plane crash in Georgia and the bombing in Texas, it increasingly felt like Ryker had already failed at that.

Noise outside.

That damn truck.

Ryker logged out of the laptop and closed the lid. He picked up the bits of glue, placed the laptop back where he'd found it on the sofa. He tiptoed toward the back door as the truck came to a stop on the driveway. He had his fingers on the handle when he heard the key in the door at the front. Had a rush of different ideas in his head.

He could stay. Rush the guy. Floor him. Tie him up. Make him talk.

Reed was on the phone, blathering away. His voice loud, coarse. Just hearing it sent Ryker back to Roadhouse. To the grim images of Meg as she lay lifeless in his hands.

Ryker unwrapped his fingers from the door handle. Looked over his shoulder...

If he didn't move then Reed would spot him any second.

Ryker tapped the thumb drive in his pocket.

No. For now, he had what he needed. It wasn't like he wouldn't be able to catch up with Reed again if he needed to.

Ryker pulled open the door, stepped out and closed it quietly behind him.

He ducked down to pass under the kitchen window, scaled the fence and dashed toward the driveway. He slowed there, not wanting to be obvious to anyone on the street.

He saw no one and walked casually back toward his car.

Except... over the road. That car. A Chrysler sedan. A man behind the wheel, though his face was mostly hidden in shadow. Ryker was sure the guy stared at him a little longer than necessary.

He looked over his shoulder as he passed the car, making a note of the license plate. Soon reached his own vehicle.

Another decision to make.

The man in the car. Could be a cop. Could be a Fed. Could be up to no good.

Could be absolutely nothing.

Ryker turned on his engine. The car remained in place. Ryker pulled out into the road, moved slowly for a few yards to see in his rearview what the car would do. The man stepped out. So whoever he was, he wasn't intent on following Ryker.

Could be absolutely nothing.

That seemed to be the case when the man headed up the driveway of the house outside which he'd been parked.

Ryker sighed. Patted the thumb drive again.

He'd got what he came for. Time to find out who Brad Reed answered to.

16

Neither of us was given the chance for respite on our return from Texas. We got the call from Kielder as we were traversing Alabama, only two and a half hours left on our journey. As with the trip to Texas, we'd talked little on the way back, although after the call from Kielder I'd sensed a certain snideness even in Reed's silence. As though he believed Kielder summoning us immediately was to reprimand only me.

I drove the last stint. Which didn't exactly help matters as it gave Reed the opportunity to play on his phone, either texting the crew or searching news articles or whatever he was doing. There'd been a development, that was all I could surmise, and so I'd have to wait until we reached our destination – Kielder's home this time – before I learned what kind of trouble I was in.

Not that I was scared. Apprehensive, perhaps. Intrigued too.

I'd been to Kielder's home twice before. He lived in the upmarket neighborhood of Buckhead, an area just north of central Atlanta consisting of undulating, twisting, tree-lined streets where there were hundreds of multimillion-dollar homes dotted around. Kielder's place was big but not gargantuan. Expensive but not overly excessive. Similar in size, stature, to the Baumanns' home in Houston, although nowhere near as high-end in finish. In fact, much of the interior was in need of updating, the wood-paneled and garishly brown – although kind of ornate – kitchen, for example, which looked at least thirty years old. I put that down to Kielder having shelled out for the most expensive property he could afford, one that was in reality above his station in life, probably funded with a punishing loan or two as well, leaving little room to finish it off to a modern, high standard. As though he was trying to fit into this crowd of elites, force his way in, even though he didn't truly belong.

I parked the car next to a bright green Lamborghini in the turning circle in front of the house. That wasn't Kielder's.

'BTC's here,' Reed said as he got out.

Bryan Tucker Crawford. Clawface himself. Kielder's much richer friend. Financier.

I knocked on the thick oak door and we waited, Reed a half step behind me, so I turned to make sure he never left my periphery as just a small part of me believed that this could be a setup. That any moment Reed – perhaps someone from beyond the door too – would pounce to subdue me.

Kielder opened the door.

Beyond him Meyers and BTC were in the hallway. BTC came forward and shook hands with Kielder and whispered something in his ear. As he stepped outside he caught my gaze and kind of paused, his eyes flickering with unease.

'Have a good day, gentlemen,' he said before carrying on past to his brash ride.

'Inside,' Kielder said, to me more than to Reed, before he turned and stomped off.

I went in first, glancing over my shoulder, hands in my

pockets as though being casual, but actually I was primed and ready.

I didn't need to be. We all headed through to the living room at the back of the house where Kielder stood by the window looking out at the garden and the pool, the tiles grimy, the water inside green and murky and in need of a good clean.

He turned, arms folded, his glare directed at me.

'What the fuck?' he said. Asked. If those words could be construed as a question.

I shrugged.

'Have you seen the goddamn news?' he asked, whipping out his phone.

'No,' I said. 'I drove the last three-hour stint without a break.'

He grumbled and typed away then read out whatever news article he'd found.

'Larry Baumann alerted police after his attacker left, but by that point the bomb at Industrial Control Logistics Inc had already detonated... Baumann told police two masked men had broken into his home, violently attacked both him and his wife before one of the men abducted his wife, Matilda Baumann, Chief Information Officer at Industrial Control Logistics... The FBI believes the same persons who perpetrated this crime were also responsible for the deadly bombing at KDD Tech in Atlanta... No group has claimed responsibility for these atrocities, and no motive has been identified, but authorities have designated them as terror attacks. The deadliest on US soil since 9/11.'

Everyone turned to stare at me as though awaiting my explanation.

'We got exactly what we needed,' I said.

'You dumb mother—'

Reed burst toward me and I decided against turning and gutting him right there and then with the knife in my pocket, and he thumped me in my kidney and wrapped an arm around my neck to choke me as he came up behind me.

'This is all on you,' he said to me. 'I told you to kill him!'

I writhed, trying to get enough slack on the arm around my neck to still breathe. I glanced from Kielder to Meyers, waiting for one of them to come forward to attack. A fist? A knife?

Neither. Yet.

'You messed up, Marshall,' Kielder said. 'My question is why? Are you trying to screw us?'

I couldn't really answer with my neck so tightly constricted and I think Kielder got that as I coughed and spluttered, and he nodded to Reed who loosened his grip. I whipped out from under his arm and had to try really hard to hold myself back.

'You know this only works if sooner or later people know who we are, and what we're doing,' I said.

'Except that's not what you did, is it?' Reed said. 'You didn't announce who we are, you left a living witness.'

'And now we're labelled terrorists,' Kielder said. 'No different to goddamn mujahideen ragheads.'

'We are terrorists!' I shouted. 'We're instilling terror in the public, in the government! That's the plan!'

'That's not my plan!' Kielder yelled back. 'I'm not a terrorist. I'm a patriot.'

And he truly believed his pathetic words.

'Patriotism is the last refuge of a scoundrel,' I said.

Reed snarled and looked like he was about to come at me again, but Kielder held up a hand to stop him.

'Samuel Johnson,' Kielder said. 'Right?'

'Yes.'

'Or how about, "the tree of liberty must be refreshed from time to time with the blood of patriots and tyrants".'

'Which would be Jefferson,' I said. 'And if you want to talk some more about patriotism, don't forget it was me who gave years of my life to this country.'

Kielder didn't respond to that, but he seemed to calm a little, his chest deflating, as though I'd done enough to appease him with my knowledge of history.

'We're on track,' I said. 'Houston was a success. Once we get the hardware we need, we'll be ready.'

'But this isn't how we planned it,' Kielder said. 'You know that. We didn't need the two events linked so soon. We didn't need the heat. Not while we're still preparing.'

'The link would have been made anyway. But if we're talking of plans... it also wasn't the plan to blow up Bob Ferrer's plane, was it? So it looks like I'm not the only one diverging.'

Kielder growled, looked like he was chewing wasps.

'I told you already why that had to happen,' he said.

'And I decided that Larry Baumann surviving didn't harm us. In fact, his story, the furor caused will give even more prominence to us when we finally come forward. And more sympathy. We spared an innocent life.'

'And what if the link is made as to why we really targeted KDD and ICL before we get to the end goal?'

'That was always possible,' I said. 'So we should move on Florida and get the hardware sooner rather than later.'

The room went silent. Everyone looked at Kielder to await his verdict.

'How long do you need?'

'I could do it within seventy-two hours if needed. In fact, we should aim for that.'

Kielder thought that one over.

'OK,' he said. 'But I don't like this, Marshall. Another deviation from you and—'

'I get it,' I said. 'You don't need to threaten me.'

'Are you serious?' Reed said to his boss. 'You're letting this asshole off the hook?'

'Yes. I am. Marshall, move on Florida as soon as you can.'

'You got it.'

'Now get the hell out of my house.'

* * *

As I drove down the streets I was reminded of my conversation with Hailey from a few days ago. Where I'd talked to her about how I still felt emotions like anyone else. Except more muted. Like right now. I may have left Kielder's home looking and sounding calm, but that wasn't the case. I was angry. Not seeing red, uncontrollable rage, angry. But definitely angry.

At Reed. At Kielder. At Meyers.

At the world, really, which ultimately explained why I was doing any of this.

But I'd learned to focus my anger, to cope and to deal with it. To not act rashly.

Revenge is a dish best served cold, after all.

Reed. Right now he was my focus.

Which was why I didn't go to my studio, or to eat or anything like that, even though I could really do with some downtime, rest. Instead, I hid not far away from where Reed had left his god-awful truck the previous day, waited for him, and then tailed him. He went for food. Some shitty-looking diner. Alone. Then he went to a liquor store. Finally he headed home.

I parked some way down the street from his house and watched him get out of his truck and head up to his door.

Which was when I got a seriously unexpected shock.

No sooner had Reed stepped inside than a man came walking around the side of Reed's house and down the drive. Casual, but alert.

At first I didn't think I knew him, but as he made his way on foot along the street toward me I realized I was wrong, even if it still took a few more seconds to figure where I'd seen his face...

James Ryker.

Among the other things I'd been tasked with, Kielder had asked me to find out as much about this guy as I could. I'd barely had time to do that yet, but I'd been sent images from the video cameras at the bar which showed the guy's face, and I also had his booking-in picture at the police station.

This was definitely James Ryker walking right toward me.

Stupidly, I initially kind of froze, not knowing what to do.

I had a big call to make. Follow him. Or not.

Actually, first was to make sure he wasn't about to attack me...

No, he went right on past. Got into a car fifteen yards behind mine. I still didn't know if he'd made me at all, so I decided to call his bluff. I got out of my car and went up the drive of the house right by me. I knocked on the door, but before anyone had answered I heard the engine rev behind me and Ryker's car swung out into the road and gently carried on away.

'Can I help you?' said the woman who'd opened the door.

'Yes, I was wondering if you were interested in—'

'Read the sign, idiot. No soliciting.'

She closed the door in my face.

Fair enough.

I retreated down the drive. Didn't go to my car. Instead I

went to Reed's place. I knocked on the door. He opened and did a double-take.

'Aren't you going to invite me in?' I asked.

He looked hesitant. 'What the fuck do you want?'

I looked over my shoulder, feigning the jitters. 'There's something... I really need to talk to you about. It's Kielder. Can... I trust you?'

He looked as mad that I was on his doorstep as he was suspicious of what I'd said, but he still stepped aside and beckoned me in. So I walked over the threshold. He closed the door. He hadn't quite turned around when I reached forward and grabbed the back of his head and slammed it into the door frame. I swept his legs from under him and he fell to the ground, the back of his head smacking off the corner of a side table as he went – an unexpected bonus for me.

He looked groggy, but not groggy enough so I kicked him in the face. His jaw crunched. I crouched down and grabbed his hair to yank his head back.

'You know James Ryker was just in your house?' I asked him.

His nose dribbled blood. One eye was already swelling up badly. He tried to form a response to my question but stuttered.

It didn't even matter much what he said to me. I didn't believe Reed had known Ryker was here. Reed wasn't smart enough to be in cahoots and to have kept it so quiet. There was no subterfuge or underhand play from him. Ryker had been here snooping.

But it still meant that Reed was compromised.

And that was unacceptable.

I took out the hunting knife.

'I'm sorry, friend. I don't have a choice,' I said to him, as if I gave a shit.

'No, no!'

I plunged the knife toward his chest, but he reached out and caught my wrist and only the tip of the blade pierced his skin. He squirmed and wrestled as I pushed down, harder and harder.

'P-p-please!' he shouted out, all in a panic.

I hauled my knee into his groin and then thrust forward again, and this time he couldn't hold me back. The blade slid three, four inches into his chest.

His body quivered and his hands fell from mine.

I leaned right in. Nose to nose, my eyes boring into his.

'I'm glad I got to do this to you,' I said.

He gave no response to that.

I pushed forward again and with a suck and a squelch the knife plunged further, right up to the handle, right through his heart.

No coming back for him.

Reed was dead.

'It was gonna happen sooner or later,' I said with a chuckle as I slapped his lifeless cheek.

Time to clear up and clear out.

* * *

An hour later I was heading north into the mountains, Reed in the trunk. Some supplies on the back seat.

James Ryker being at Reed's place worried me. Mainly because Reed was nowhere near as clever as he thought he was, probably hadn't done enough to cover his tracks, and I didn't yet know what intel Ryker would now have that he shouldn't.

I could confront Kielder about this, but that would mean I'd also have to admit to killing Reed.

So I opted for a different plan instead.

Reed's body would never be found.

But his legacy would live on.

As well as his bullshit claims of patriotism and activism, Reed had wanted notoriety from what we were doing.

And I was about to make him more famous than he'd ever imagined.

17

Ryker had kept his head low for a couple of days as he sifted through the data he'd taken from Brad Reed's home, and also as he watched the news play out of the latest terrorist attack on US soil – the car bomb which had detonated in the basement of the headquarters of Industrial Control Logistics Inc in Houston, Texas. The press had been quick to confirm Ryker's original hunch and link the attack in Houston to the bombing of KDD Tech in Atlanta. At least as far as they believed that the two attacks were carried out by the same group. However, there had been no information disclosed by the authorities or the government as to who they believed this group to be, or what their intentions were.

As well as digging through Reed's data, Ryker had been busy looking at the two attacks – three, if the plane crash involving the Ferrer family was included – from different angles and perspectives. He'd had some old acquaintances look into the backgrounds of the companies, the key people involved at each, to try and tease out any common linkages.

He'd found little.

But that didn't mean he'd found nothing. He had leads. Just none that properly explained the attacks.

Today was back to basics. First off, a call to Klein, which Ryker made on the way to pay Adam Hannigan a visit.

'If you're not calling me to give me some answers, then you shouldn't be calling me at all,' Klein said when he answered the phone. No pleasantries required, apparently.

Ryker toyed with the statement for a few seconds. 'I take it you've seen the developments.'

'Of course I've seen the damn developments, Ryker. Every news station in the US, across most of the world, is reporting on the same thing. We have an underground terror group in the US who are blowing up people and businesses!'

Ryker stayed silent this time, Klein's pissed off tone clear, and the fact that he was, at least partly, pointing the finger in Ryker's direction.

'You were sent out there to stop these bastards.'

'Technically I was sent out here to find Abby Hannigan.'

'That was your cover, you dumbass, and you haven't even managed to find her, have you?'

'Do the authorities have intel on who this group is that's not been revealed?' Ryker asked.

'I'm not involved at that level. I'm CIA, Ryker, it's not my jurisdiction. You know that.'

Except Klein's anger, dissatisfaction, suggested what was happening here was still personal to him, one way or another. So why was he pretending otherwise?

'I am making progress here—'

'Progress? By that do you mean the gunfight outside a dive bar in Canton, after which you spent two days in a cell? Or do you mean the explosion and the dead body at the meth-head commune up in the mountains?'

'You expected me to come here and keep out of trouble? I thought you said you knew about my background?'

Ryker said that lightheartedly. The grumbled, inarticulate response from Klein suggested he didn't get that, or at least didn't appreciate it.

'I'll ask again,' Ryker said. 'Is there anything you know about these attacks that you haven't told me? Any linkage between these companies, the people involved?'

Silence for a few seconds from Klein. 'No, Ryker. There is nothing.'

Ryker wanted to believe him, but he didn't.

'KDD Tech and Industrial Control Logistics both hold contracts with the Department of Defense,' Ryker said. 'Did you know that?'

'Why would I know anything about either of those companies? And do you have any idea how many tens of thousands of companies the Department of Defense contracts with?'

Ryker sighed. 'There must be a reason those two companies were targeted. I don't believe it was random.'

'It's like I said right at the start. If you're not calling to give me some answers, then you shouldn't be calling at all.'

Ryker didn't respond to that.

'Seems like we're done here then.'

'I guess so.'

Klein ended the call before Ryker could say anything more.

Ryker gripped the steering wheel a little more tightly for the next couple of miles as he worked out his agitation. Klein was the man who'd sent him over here in the first place, so why would he possibly want to hamper Ryker's work by not telling him everything he knew? Yet Ryker had no doubt the guy wasn't being straight with him about something.

Hannigan was home alone. No sign of his wife, either of his

sons, any domestic help. Ryker wondered whether that was deliberate on Hannigan's part, wanting to make sure that he could keep Ryker steered in the direction he – and Klein? – wanted, with no diverging inputs from his wife or members of his family.

The spring morning was warm and sunny, and Hannigan fixed them both a coffee before he showed Ryker out onto the back deck which overlooked the gardens and pool.

'You've been busy,' Hannigan said, and Ryker didn't bother to question what he meant by that. No doubt he and Klein had been in touch, so everything Klein knew of the scrapes Ryker had been in, Hannigan would also know. 'But have you found any information on my daughter?'

'No,' Ryker said as he propped himself against the deck railing, while Hannigan settled into an armchair in the sun. 'Which is partly why I'm here.'

Hannigan raised an eyebrow.

'Do you know where she is?' Ryker asked.

Hannigan remained expressionless. An odd response, really.

'If I knew where my daughter was, then what would be the point of you being here?' he asked.

'There could be several explanations. But the most obvious one is to protect yourself.'

Now he did look confused. But he was a politician so also a very well-rehearsed actor. 'Protect myself from what?'

'From the truth getting out. Say, for example, that you know where your daughter is, the group she's associated with. But you'd rather someone like me comes in and pulls them apart, as messy as it could get, and hope that the truth dies with it, than risk any official investigation by the FBI or whoever else revealing the truth.'

'You don't think much of me, do you? To think I'd stoop so

low? Risk countless lives? Because that's what's happening so far. Innocent people are being blown to pieces.'

'I don't know you that well. But I've met plenty of people who would stoop that low, or much, much lower, actually.'

'But you're not looking at that person now. And, quite frankly, I think you should get the hell off my property if you've only come to insult me and—'

'What do you know of KDD Tech and Industrial Logistics Control?'

Hannigan paused, staring at Ryker.

'What are you asking, exactly?'

'Seems logical that if the same group of people have now attacked both companies, that there's a reason for it.'

'Yeah. I guess so.'

'Do you know that reason?'

'No. I don't.'

'Both are related to the government, one way or another. At least, they both have contracts with the Department of Defense. What do you know about that?'

'Why would I know anything?'

'Because you were the last president's National Security Adviser.'

Hannigan didn't say anything more, mouth firmly shut.

'Look, I get that in your previous role you were privy to a lot of information that you and the rest of the government would never want to be made public, but anything you do know about these companies could not just help me figure out who this group is, but what their plan is, their next target.'

'I don't know anything that links them beyond their DoD contracts,' Hannigan said. 'And I don't know any details of the contracts, just that they exist.'

'What about Bob Ferrer? AIS? Did you know him?'

'Yeah, I knew him. What are you—'

'Have you considered that maybe his accident was no accident?'

The shocked look on his face suggested not.

'That would...'

'What? Make no sense? But it made sense when KDD was targeted? Then Industrial Control Logistics?'

'That's not what I was going to say.'

Yet even though Ryker gave him the opportunity, he didn't clarify what he'd been about to say.

'Can I ask you a question?' Hannigan said.

'Of course.'

'What's your explanation? Or even a working theory?'

'That all three of those attacks are a smoke screen for something else.'

'A smoke screen? For what?'

'That's what I need to find out.'

'But why do you think that? Because a lot of people are calling this terrorism, pure and simple.'

'Terrorism is rarely pure and simple.'

Hannigan scoffed. 'Jesus, is this the best you've got so far?'

'Have you ever heard the name Brad Reed?' Ryker asked.

'Should I have?' Hannigan answered, almost without time for thought.

'He was the scumbag from that fight in Canton. Who nearly killed an innocent woman.'

'I don't deal with low-life scumbags.'

'I went to his house. Stole a lot of electronic data from him which I've had a chance to go through in some detail now.'

'Ryker, if you're about to tell me this guy once called or emailed me or something... Have you any idea how many people in this area I deal with on a weekly basis?'

'No,' Ryker said. 'Actually I didn't find any link between the two of you, although I definitely looked. But it's interesting to me that you jumped on that line of defense without prompting.'

'Because you're putting me on the spot! Challenging me.'

Ryker wasn't really sure he was. Not strongly, at least. He let it slide. Kind of.

'I'm convinced Reed is part of this group behind the attacks. To most people he seems like just a regular, white working-class guy. Except when you look at what he reads, and the communications between him and his friends, the fact he's been directly involved in some of these recent white nationalist rallies... This is one pissed off, regular, white, working-class guy. Hates every race, religion, sex other than his own. I'm only surprised I didn't find the KKK outfit in his home. Maybe he took it with him.'

Ryker laughed. Hannigan didn't.

'It fits the narrative,' Ryker said. 'Given Abby's previous association to the White Lions.'

'Which I told you was years ago.'

'Yeah. You did. But back to Reed. He's involved, but he's certainly not in charge. Two names of people who might be closer to the top. Terrence Kielder. Bryan Tucker Crawford.'

A flicker of recognition in Hannigan's eyes.

'Kielder? I don't know him,' Hannigan said.

'He's another who's close to these groups. Quite prominently, actually. From what I've seen of him online, the things he's called for at the protests he's led... He'd probably be on an FBI watchlist already, if the FBI were properly geared to looking into these guys and stopping them.'

'You're saying the FBI is compromised?'

'I have no idea whether they are or aren't.'

'Then I'm not sure why you brought that up.'

'I was just asking if you knew him. Of him.'

'I told you. I don't know him.'

'But Crawford?'

'Yeah, I know Crawford.'

'A local businessman. Pretty wealthy, from what I can see. It's also been suggested, although not confirmed by him officially, that he might go up against you in the next race for governor.'

Hannigan looked irate at Ryker for bringing that up. 'I've heard the rumors. He wouldn't stand a chance. He's a nobody, with no history in politics.'

'A very rich nobody. Both Kielder and Crawford are people Reed has been in contact with.'

'Are you saying that piece of shit Crawford could be part of this group?' Hannigan asked.

'Could be. But right now I'm only saying he knows Reed, Kielder.'

'And you believe those two are involved?'

'Based on the communications I've seen... yeah, I'm certainly leaning very close to that.'

He gave Hannigan a moment to process, to offer up anything in response. But he didn't say anything more.

'From what you know of Crawford, does it fit that he'd be affiliated to a far-right group?' Ryker asked.

'Define far right. I told you before about using terms like that. You're in the south now. This is a hugely conservative region, always has been, always will be. It doesn't mean everyone here is a bad person. In the vast majority of cases, in fact, it's the opposite. Many people here are deeply religious, follow the highest morals. So when you spout far right and the like... What you think fits that term... for many people around here is just... them. Their culture. It doesn't make them extremists just because they have different views to you.'

'I'm not sure that answered my question.'

'OK, then no, it wouldn't surprise me that Crawford knew guys who were part of a group that promotes far-right views. Would it surprise me that he was involved in a group who were carrying out deadly terror attacks? Yes. I'd be shocked.'

Delighted, might have been an alternative word there, as Ryker sensed that Hannigan would revel in any dirt on his soon-to-be political rival.

'I'll ask you, nicely, not to jump the gun and tell anyone else about this, that Crawford knows these people,' Ryker said. 'It's too soon.'

'So why are you telling me at all? I already sense you don't trust me.'

'Because there's something you can do for me. To help.'

'And that is?'

'There's a charity convention this week in North Carolina. I've seen the invitee list. Quite a group of people. Politicians, billionaires. That kind of thing.'

'And?'

'And you're on the list. And so is Crawford.'

Hannigan kind of snarled at that. Perhaps he hadn't known.

'What about it?' he asked.

'I want you to get me an invite. Specifically to the awards dinner on the second night. Me and a plus one would be ideal, gives me better cover that way.'

'A plus one? You want to bring a date with you? You are something, Ryker.'

'Not a date. This is purely work,' Ryker said with a wry smile.

Hannigan didn't look convinced.

'Can you do it?' Ryker asked.

'Yeah. I'm sure I can.'

'Good answer,' Ryker said.

* * *

The area around Brasstown Bald – Georgia's highest peak, up in the Blue Ridge Mountains – was a vast and rugged wilderness. The terrain, the thick forest, was not dissimilar to Peltworth, but several steps of remoteness on from even there, and the landscape had already seriously hampered both rescue and investigation efforts into the downing of the Ferrers' plane several days ago.

Ryker had called Cindy early in the morning, before he'd gone to Hannigan's, to ask if she'd take him to the site and show him around. He hadn't explicitly told her his suspicions about the crash and had no clue if she had any involvement in the investigation at all, but the fact that she agreed to meet him there with very few questions asked told him a lot.

The last three miles of the drive, to a hiking trailhead, was a steep, twisting climb with several tight switchbacks. His gas-guzzling but underpowered rental car at times struggled, the engine screeching from effort, speed dropping to below twenty miles an hour on several occasions even when his foot was to the floor. He made it though, reached the parking lot in the dense forest where several vehicles had taken over the space: ambulances, police cruisers, two mobile command units among them.

Cindy's car was already there too and she was out and in the midst of a conversation with two plain-clothed men.

Ryker parked up and got out, noting a lot of suspicious eyes his way, as though weighing up whether he was a hiker who they'd have to disappoint, or perhaps a reporter coming for a scoop or to try to snap some pictures of the wreckage.

Before anyone came to check, Cindy spotted him and headed over.

'Quite a trek up here,' Ryker said.

'In your car? A piece of cake. So what are we doing here, Ryker?'

'Are they GBI too?' he asked, nodding toward the two men.

'No. It's only me here from the GBI.'

'Is the GBI involved here at all then? Officially?'

'I'm not sure I have to tell you anything about what we do, officially, or unofficially.'

'No. But the fact we're both standing here...'

'Means that, like you, I think this idea of an accident stinks.'

He smiled. She didn't.

'What do you know?' Ryker asked. 'About what they've found so far?'

'That they haven't found enough to figure what happened. The black box is still unattainable. They think they know where it is but it's proving difficult to reach. The crash site is spread over a five-square-mile area. They've found remains of three of the five people on board, but no one's expecting survivors now.'

'Five square miles?' Ryker said.

'Yeah.'

'That sounds unlikely if the plane fell intact.'

'Based on your experience as a crash scene investigator?'

'Based on logic.'

'Not if it smashed into a ridge on its way down then carried on out over a canyon before its final crash.'

'And that's what's being suggested?'

'No, actually. But I'm just saying not to jump to conclusions.'

'But let's say if the plane was already in pieces, or even badly damaged as it came down... it'd suggest something happened in the air. An explosion, for example.'

'Yes, that's possible. And it's also possible such an explosion could be explained not by anything nefarious, but by a serious engine malfunction.'

'Is that based on your experience as a crash scene investigator?' Ryker asked.

Cindy tried really hard to not smile but failed.

'Why don't we go speak to the experts?' Ryker suggested.

'I was hoping you wouldn't say that.'

Ryker soon understood why, because there was no easy way to get to see anything of note without an arduous trek down a ravine to where the main fuselage had been found. And that was the easiest site to reach, as explained by the team of investigators-cum-mountaineers who'd been put together to try to get answers.

Ryker and Cindy spent the best part of two hours with the team, lots of climbing, scrabbling down ravines, lots of talking, lots of hypothesizing, but no real outcomes given the sketchy evidence.

One thing the time spent certainly didn't do was to convince Ryker that the downing of the plane was an accident.

'What is it you were hoping to find here?' Cindy asked as they walked back toward their cars, tired, sweaty. 'If Ferrer was targeted, then why?'

'I don't know,' Ryker said. 'It doesn't fit where I'm headed at all.'

'Explain.'

'KDD Tech and Industrial Control Logistics. Both big, multinational companies who specialize in offering services to others. Big contracts with big entities over multiple industries. But both also have contracts with the US government. The Department of Defense, specifically.'

'Why would that make them targets for terrorist attacks?'

'There's a lot of reasons why. It's a connection that needs

exploring further. But Ferrer and his company, AIS? I see no connection to the others.'

'Want me to tell you something I probably shouldn't?'

He definitely did. Although he was a little surprised that she'd offer that.

'Absolutely.'

'I heard a rumor, and that's all this is so far, but there's a rumor of some pretty dodgy options trading on AIS stock over the last few weeks.'

'Short selling?'

'You got it. So when Ferrer died, and the AIS share price tanked, someone, somewhere made a lot of money.'

'It's a possible explanation. Any idea on who made the trades?'

'Like I said, it's just a rumor, probably come from top-level trading data. I don't even know who's investigating it. If anyone's investigating it at all. But my point is, the same thing happened to the stocks of the other two companies as well.'

'Not a surprise, given the impact of the attacks on the companies.'

'No, it's not. But you were talking about connections. This is a connection. It could be this is all just about money. Someone is doing this not to create terror, not for any kind of political aim, but just to make billions on the stock market.'

Ryker chewed on that explanation. It made more sense than he wanted it to.

'I just don't believe it's that simple,' he said.

Cindy shrugged. 'The simplest solution is almost always the best.'

'Occam's razor. Yeah, I get that. But perhaps we just haven't seen the simplest solution yet.'

Cindy sighed.

'But the point you're making is valid,' he said. 'About the short selling. It'd be interesting to see if the same trading patterns were seen in the stocks of the other companies too. And find out who made those trades.'

'Not my department at all. But I can have a word.'

'And what about the bombing in Houston? Do you know anything else about that?'

She sighed. 'No. I'm GBI. Even if I wanted to be involved there, I have zero jurisdiction.'

'But the connection has been made to KDD Tech. So there must be cross-agency work going on here.'

She glared at him rather than give a response.

'OK. I get it. You don't want to tell me what you know.'

'No, Ryker, I don't know anything else.'

He believed her.

'Now, can I get back to my day job?' She sighed and looked at her watch. 'Although by the time we've driven back south it'll nearly be the end of the day.'

'I appreciate you helping me,' he said.

'Yeah.'

'One last question though.'

She sighed again. 'Go on.'

'Do you know any of these names? Brad Reed. Terrence Kielder. Bryan Tucker Crawford.'

She took a moment, looked off into the distance. 'Only the last one.'

'From?'

'It's just a name people know. He's not a celebrity, but he's a big deal in Georgia. One of our richest businessmen.'

'But the other two?'

'Never heard of them. Why are you asking about Crawford?'

He ignored her question. 'The guy who nearly killed Meg is Brad Reed.'

Ryker stopped there, waiting for a reaction. He didn't get much of one.

'When did you find this out?' she asked.

'A couple of days ago.'

She shook her head, looked a bit angry, as though she'd have wanted to know immediately, as though perhaps she would have done something about it. He didn't bother to explain that he'd also broken into Reed's house.

'I know Reed's in contact with both Kielder and Crawford, one way or another.'

'How?'

'Just... It's what I've found.'

'And you think they're all... what? Involved in these attacks?'

'It's what I'm trying to figure out. But that's where I'm heading.'

'This is...'

'What?'

'I don't know. Big. A stretch. Dangerous. I really don't know.'

'Have you met Crawford before?' Ryker asked.

'No.'

'Do you want to meet him? And... before you answer that... Are you free two nights from now? For a quick trip up to North Carolina.'

'Why do I not like where this is headed?' she said.

'If not for me, or you even, then for Meg.'

She paused, a look of determination taking over.

'Yeah, OK,' she said. 'I'm in.'

18

It was only me and Hailey in the office in Newnan. I had no idea where Kielder and Meyers were, nor any of the other guys who occasionally hung around, cloying for Kielder's attention.

Only me and Hailey. I liked it that way.

She had three screens set up in front of her as her fingers danced on the keyboard, her brain likely whirring at the same speed, as she sifted through and deciphered the vast data haul from KDD Tech. I watched her work, helped direct her at times, gave her suggestions, but the reality was that she was a lot better at this than I was.

She slapped the enter key and sat back and sighed.

'My head is swimming with these freaking numbers,' she said, rubbing at her temples.

'Maybe you need a brain break.'

She swiveled her chair to face me. 'No doubt I'd have been finished by now if Christine were here to help.'

'No doubt. But it looks like that's not going to happen now, doesn't it?'

'Yeah. It does. But what do you think happened to her? I didn't know her that well, but...'

'What?'

'I dunno. Still doesn't seem right that she just vanished like that. At a critical time too? I went to her place. She had a condo not far from here. It's all locked up. I looked through the window and everything looked normal in there. Nothing ransacked or anything.'

'Perhaps she just got cold feet. What we're doing... it's big. It's dangerous. It involves sacrifice.'

Hailey gulped. Even though I hadn't explicitly said what I meant by sacrifice, I took her reaction to mean the loss of lives. Innocent lives, you could say. Perhaps that had just been too much for Christine.

Or perhaps something else...

She sighed again. 'Coffee?' she suggested.

'I'll get them,' I said.

'No, not the machine. I meant, why don't we go get a coffee some place? Starbucks. It's a five-minute walk. We can get something to eat too.'

'I don't really... I'd rather—'

'Stay inside all day like a vampire?'

I laughed. 'Yeah. That's me.'

'You don't want to be seen out?'

I shrugged. 'I go out all the time.'

'Yeah. When you have to. But I just... get the sense you're never comfortable. On view.'

'Would you be, if you looked like this?' I said.

'Like what?' Hailey replied. 'I've never even seen your real face.'

Was she suggesting she wanted to? Damn, she'd run a mile. Or more.

'What I don't get though...'

'Yeah?' I said.

'That mask you wear... is that what you used to look like?'

I touched the rubber with my finger, my eyes rested on a warped reflection of me in the screen which made me look even worse than reality. More like how I felt I looked.

'Kind of.'

'Have you got any pictures?' she asked. 'Of what you were like before?'

'No. But you can find me easily enough. Just search my name.'

I was kind of surprised she hadn't before.

'You don't mind?'

'Can't really stop you.'

She looked hesitant but then took out her phone and typed away, and obviously found something because she went still and silent as she stared. When she looked back up at me she was a lot less animated than before.

'Not a good picture?' I asked.

'It's not... the picture. It's reading about what happened.'

I said nothing and gave her the time to digest whatever grim details she was reading.

'But... you looked... really... normal,' she said, before bursting out laughing. 'Kinda geeky.'

'Shit. Thanks so much. Not what you expected?'

She slapped my knee. 'I'm teasing. You looked good. Rugged.'

She inspected my face a few moments. 'I kinda see it in the mask, but...'

'But what?'

'Don't be offended, but the technology they have these days, laser printing or whatever, I don't know, but surely you could get something that's exactly like how you used to look. More... life-like too.'

'Yeah,' I said. 'You can. I could get a mask so thin, the fit so good, the look so lifelike that when I put it on nobody would know the difference at first glance. Most people would never think anything of it unless they were up close, staring. The eyes, mouth, nostrils are the giveaways eventually.'

'So why don't you? The one you have...'

'Is like something from a bad horror movie?'

She laughed. 'Yeah.' Then caught herself. 'I mean, no, sorry. Not a bad horror movie. A really good one.'

'Thanks. So much better.'

'But it's just... a little obvious. You know?'

'It's a middle ground. I'm not the same man I was, so there's no point in pretending and trying to be him. But I also don't want to show my real face, so a mask is a must.'

'I guess... that makes some sense.'

Although it didn't sound like it did to her really.

'Can you show me, though? Please?' she asked.

I thought for a moment. I was torn. As ever, I liked Hailey's interest in me, but I also realized it was likely mostly borne of a morbid fascination rather than any kind of genuine connection, sexual or otherwise. In the same way that some people were obsessed with true crime documentaries and scoured the internet looking for real – and bloody, gory – crime scene photos.

'If you want the mask off, you have to do it yourself,' I said.

She looked really unsure for a few seconds but then a deter-mination took over and she rolled her chair forward, her legs intersecting mine so that she was right up against me. She leaned further in. I could smell her perfume even more strongly now, could smell her breath too, could feel it on my lips and there's no denying that I knew I was getting hard even if there really was so little to feel down there. She reached forward with one hand, tentatively, carefully.

'Where is it?' she asked. 'The seam?'

'Under my chin.'

I lifted my head only slightly, as I wanted to see her eyes the whole time. I flinched a little when she touched me. If I was still capable of it, and if I hadn't been wearing the mask, she would have seen me blush. An unexpectedly childish reaction from me, but a subconscious one.

Her fingers caressed under my chin as she tried to find the end. She gripped the seam and peeled back an inch or so before...

'Rah!' I roared and grabbed her hand, and she nearly jumped right out of her chair, eyes wide in shock.

'Damn it, Marshall! I nearly peed myself!' she yelled, before she realized I was only teasing and she relaxed and got back to work.

She pulled the latex up over my chin. My mouth was soon exposed.

I was exposed.

I'd never felt so naked and so on show, in fact.

I hated it.

I felt exhilarated by it.

I wanted to grab her and kiss her and tear off her clothes.

She paused a moment, inspecting, and I wondered whether she'd already seen enough, too much, and wanted to pull the mask back down. But then she carried on, lifting up, my mangled nostrils soon feeling cold, dry air.

We both jolted when the door at the main entrance opened with a clunk. Hailey paused. Then when we heard the door slam shut, and the animated voices, she quickly scooted back and I pulled the mask down and smoothed it back into place just as Meyers stuck his face around the door.

'What are you two doing?'

Kielder came right on through too.

'We were just... What the hell do you think we were doing?' Hailey said, a little too flustered. 'We're frying our brains trying to figure all this out.'

She pointed to the screens, which she'd just woken up on cue, as if to prove her point.

'And have you?' Kielder said. 'Figured it out?'

'Nearly there,' I assured him.

'Good. But don't forget the timeline. Once Florida is complete we need that data, otherwise what's the point in any of it?'

'I know that,' Hailey said.

'What's happened?' I asked Kielder. Not just to deflect but because I sensed the way the two had stormed in meant they were rattled.

'That's a damned good question,' he said, turning to head out. 'Boardroom. Now.'

* * *

Not just Kielder and Meyers in the boardroom, but two other grunts too. Wayne Stanton was one of them. I didn't know the other. Just another redneck type. Always plenty of them ready to crawl out of the woodwork.

'No news is good news,' Kielder said. 'Right?'

He directed the half-baked question to me.

'I guess.'

'Then news, news, fucking more news is what?'

'Not good?' I suggested.

'It's a goddamn disaster!' he yelled, slamming the wall with his fist.

'And this news is?' Hailey asked.

'Reed,' Meyers said. 'The FBI have linked Reed to Texas.'

'How?' she asked, face full of doubt.

'Now that's a good question, isn't it?' Kielder said. To me. Again. 'Apparently, his fingerprints were found in the Baumanns' home.'

'Didn't you both wear gloves?' Hailey asked me. 'Isn't that one of the most basic steps?'

'Of course it is,' I said.

'So did you see him take them off at any point?' Kielder asked.

'Why are you asking me and not Reed?' I said.

'Because he's missing,' Meyers chimed in. 'The authorities say he's on the run. There's a reward out for any information on his whereabouts.'

'Does anyone here know where he is?' Kielder asked. 'Has anyone heard from him?'

A lot of head shaking in response.

'I don't like this,' he added. 'I don't like this at—'

He stopped when the buzzer from the door cut through the air. Everyone froze. Tensed. Until Meyers opened the app on his phone to look at the camera.

'You gotta be kidding me,' he said before showing the screen to Kielder.

'James Ryker. This is...'

'Is he alone?' I asked.

'Alone,' Meyers said.

'So this isn't a raid.'

'It's a complete mess, is what it is,' Kielder said. 'Why is he here?'

'Get that piece of shit inside,' Stanton said, squirming a little on his still-injured leg. 'I'll put a bullet in his head. After I've beaten him half to death.'

'No,' Kielder said. 'You will not. Shit. Shit. Shit!'

A big fucking baby. Apparently that's what this 'leader' was when things got real.

'I'll go,' Meyers said. 'Everyone stay calm. But... Be. Ready.'

He didn't say for what. To fight? To run?

Meyers headed out. Stanton and his buddy both took out handguns. I edged right over to the door so I could hear the conversation that was about to take place at the entrance. Kielder was right by me too.

'Hi,' I heard Ryker say. 'I saw the lease sign. I was hoping to take a look around the place.'

I couldn't quite make out Meyers' muffled response. Perhaps because he was facing away.

'I did a quick google,' Ryker carried on in his jolly British accent. 'Looks like only one company is based here. BTC Capital?'

'We have the top floor,' Meyers said.

'So you work there? What's your name?'

Meyers gave a bogus one.

'BTC is Bryan Tucker Crawford, right?' Ryker asked.

'I mean... I think so.'

'Does he work here?'

'No. He doesn't. Never seen him even. Could I—'

'What about Terrence Kielder? Does he work here?'

'How the fuck does he know my name?' Kielder whispered to me.

'I don't know who that is,' Meyers said. 'Sorry, Mr....'

'Ryker.'

'I'm really busy. If you wanted to—'

'I only want to have a real quick scan,' Ryker said. 'See what type of space it is. You see, I'm looking to open up a unit in the area, but I'm really not sure of the scale yet. What people I'll be looking for even until I find the right place. Might just be a small bunch of misfits, you know?' He laughed, kind of cackled. 'But it could even end up being a well-organized, well-equipped mini army.' He laughed again. 'Although... that's probably pretty unlikely, given what I've seen so far. Do you know what I mean?'

'Not really. I'm sorry, but I do need to go. Perhaps call the leasing agent?'

The door closed.

The tension in the room dropped – a little – as Meyers came back inside.

'How the hell does he know my name?' Kielder said to Meyers.

But Meyers didn't answer as he was looking at his phone screen again.

'He hasn't gone yet,' he said, turning the phone around, and I caught a glimpse of the camera feed. I moved closer to the window. Close enough to see Ryker out there through the slats of the blinds, by his car, phone to his ear as he scanned the building.

'He's probably on to the agent,' I said.

'Then call the agent and get this shut down!' Kielder yelled. 'He is not coming inside here!'

'We need to move the equipment,' I said. 'Move everything.'

Kielder didn't answer. Meyers was on the phone. Ryker had now finished his call. Meyers gave the agent an earful. Mentioned BTC's name a couple of times, the involvement of the big dog enough for Meyers to force his way. No deal for the agent today.

Moments later, Ryker was back on the phone again to hear

the bad news. He stared right over at the window I was standing behind.

'It's not too late,' I said to Kielder. 'We can grab him. Bring him in here.'

'Or we can follow him,' Hailey suggested.

'Or we wait,' Meyers said. 'The least risky move is to wait. Then we get this place emptied. And we don't ever come back.'

Kielder said nothing about any of the options. Moments later Ryker was finished with his conversation and held his stare in my direction a moment longer before he got back into his car.

'Last chance,' I said.

But I got no response before Ryker was on his way.

Him coming over asking about a lease? Obviously bullshit. And everyone in the room knew it, Kielder included, even if he was too arrogant, stupid or scared to have taken affirmative action. I had a very good idea which one of those three options was most likely.

'Shit!' Stanton said, looking all disappointed that he hadn't got to do any beating or shooting. Except from what I'd heard of the incident at Roadhouse, I saw no reason why the outcome this time wouldn't have been more of the same for Stanton.

'So now what?' Meyers said to Kielder, whose face was red with rage.

But he also looked lost to me. He just wasn't in control anymore, even if he still believed he was.

I wouldn't point that fact out now. It didn't achieve anything. But he'd realize sooner or later.

'Do you think Reed did this?' Stanton asked. 'Have the police got him and he's snitching on us?'

'I just don't know,' Kielder said. 'But we can't stay here.'

Hands on hips, he swiveled as he looked over each of us.

'Clear up. Everything. Leave no trace.'

'You got it,' Meyers said.

'But he knew my name,' Kielder said. 'BTC too. This is not good. I have to let BTC know.'

'If you need, I can try and bring Florida further forward?' I suggested.

Kielder considered that a moment. 'No. Actually... given this development? We need to stay close to one another. To BTC too. I think... I'd rather have you all somewhere else before Florida.'

'Yeah?'

'I'll explain after. First, let's get the hell out of here.'

19

Ryker collected Cindy after lunch to take them up to Asheville in North Carolina for the charity dinner that Hannigan had handily procured them an invite to. She'd initially been reluctant to travel together – actually, she'd been reluctant to go with him at all when he'd explained the deal – but he'd wanted the time together for them to talk, swap ideas. Hopefully get her to trust him – his intentions – that little bit more, because he knew her help over the coming days could be invaluable.

'Any news from within your ranks?' Ryker asked.

'No,' she said, and he waited to see if she'd expand but she didn't.

'There's no news? Or there is but you don't want to tell me?'

'There's no news that concerns you, or what you're doing here.'

He toyed with that answer for a few moments. Her continued caginess wasn't a surprise to him given their respective positions, officially and unofficially, but he was starting to sense that she was privy to more than she was letting on.

'Yesterday I tracked down Kielder and his cohort to an office building in Newnan,' Ryker said. 'An office building that's partly leased to BTC Capital LLC. It's one of Bryan Tucker Crawford's companies. He's also the building owner, through a network of other LLCs. I've done some digging and the guy has his fingers everywhere.'

Cindy didn't say anything in return; she seemed apprehensive about where Ryker was headed.

'I turned up there yesterday afternoon, unannounced,' Ryker carried on. 'Just to see what I'd find. Who I'd find. What'd happen, as by now these people know me. My face.'

'Well, as I didn't read about any gunfights in Newnan yesterday, and you weren't in a jail cell this morning, I'm guessing that things went... quietly.'

'Something like that,' Ryker said.

'Meaning?'

'Meaning I got the cold shoulder there. The guy who answered the door told me his name was Eric something or other, but I know it was Danny Meyers because I've already pulled a profile on him.'

'From where?' Cindy said, sounding a mix of surprised and annoyed.

'Just... That's not relevant.'

'It kinda is to me. I follow laws. Rules. You know?'

'And that always gets you where you need to be?'

She didn't answer the question.

'The problem is, Cindy, we're dealing with people here who don't follow rules and laws. So if we're tied in knots trying not to step out of line, we'll always be several moves behind them. We don't want to only catch these people after the next attack. Or the one after that, or after that. We need to catch them now.'

'You don't need to tell me how to do my job.'

'I wasn't trying to. Just explaining why sometimes my approach is needed.'

'Your approach. We'll come back to that. Because I still don't know what your approach is. Who you are. What you do. But carry on with what you found yesterday.'

Ryker took a moment. He hadn't expected the divergence, or the animosity, and it caught him a little off guard. Her hostility toward him was still there in plain sight, even if she was on this trip with him to North Carolina, which he was damn sure was not in any way sanctioned by her bosses. So she already was outside her rules.

Like she said, they could come back to that discussion.

'Meyers tried to bullshit me, first with his name, then with some crap about how he worked for BTC Capital, which is just a small investment firm, half a dozen employees. A front, no doubt.'

'Front for what?'

'I don't know. Might not be important.'

'But you really think Crawford himself is involved in this group?'

'I don't know that either. I've not seen him yet, but his name and his money keep cropping up. But back to the point, I wanted to get inside that place to take a look around. And to put pressure on them, obviously. So I called the leasing agent, right there and then in the parking lot, knowing that Meyers and whoever else was inside was still watching me. I got the agent to agree to an appointment, but no sooner had I ended the conversation with them than I get a return call canceling it, saying there's no space to lease after all.'

'Oh-kay. This isn't sounding like the biggest gotcha so far?'

'No. It's not. But we have time to kill on the drive, so I'm telling you it all. I left there. Drove away. Thought maybe someone would follow me. They didn't. A bit of a disappointment, really.'

'Because it'd been too long since your last confrontation?'

'Because confronting these people is probably, ultimately, the best way to bring them down.'

She didn't respond to that but didn't look convinced.

'I went back around there during the night and—'

'Please don't tell me you broke in. What was I just saying about rules?'

Ryker stayed silent.

'You did, didn't you? You broke in?'

Ryker didn't answer.

'Ryker, tell me!'

'But you asked me not to tell you.'

She slapped his leg. Quite hard, actually. 'Damn it, that's not what I meant.'

'OK. Then yeah, I broke in.'

She tried hard to stay mad but – perhaps because of his lighthearted tone – she failed and a small smile broke free. Finally, a crack in her tough exterior.

'But I found nothing,' Ryker said, a little more dejected. 'They'd cleared that place out. BTC Capital is only on the top floor and that place is just a standard little office, a few desks, computers, blah blah. But the lower floor... that's where they'd been.'

'How do you know anyone had been there?'

'I could just tell. There was basic furniture still in place, the kind that'd probably been left there by the agent, trying to show people what the space was good for, but it was definitely a used space. In one room I could see scratch marks on the floor from the wheels of a desk chair. Dust patterns on the work surfaces where equipment had been dragged off. Trash cans in the kitchen area were half-filled.'

'So you spooked them and they fled?'

'That's what it looks like.'

'And now? Do you have any idea where they went?'

'Not yet.'

'Not such a great move by you, perhaps?'

'Except we know Crawford will be in North Carolina. Maybe some of these other guys too, if they're protecting him.'

'Right. So your master plan was to deliberately spook them, make them flee, knowing it'd increase the chances of a heightened presence in North Carolina?'

Ryker shrugged. 'We'll find out sooner or later.'

She sighed. 'But... what were they doing there? This is a group of people who we believe are responsible for two bomb attacks. Quite sophisticated bomb attacks in many ways. What are they doing all together in an office space in Newnan?'

'Where would you expect them to get together? To plot? Plan?'

'I don't know. It just seems... odd.'

'Maybe. Maybe not. But I do have a theory.'

'Yeah?'

'Computers.'

'Sorry?'

'They wanted an office space like that because this is a group of people who need to get together somewhere quiet, discreet, but it needs to be functional too, so meeting in a dingy alley or a derelict warehouse isn't for them. They need functionality, equipment to run, access to Wi-Fi, whatever.'

'But why?'

'It comes back to the two attacks. KDD Tech. Industrial Control Logistics. These companies were chosen specifically.

What if the attacks were carried out in the way they were to conceal their true purpose?'

'A smoke screen?'

Ryker smiled. The exact way he'd described things to Hannigan. 'Exactly. Those companies are connected. Say our group attacked them not just to cause chaos and destruction, but to steal. Information. Data. Data which they could then work on from that office.'

'Data? What data? Like... government secrets or something? What are we talking about here?'

'It's what we need to figure out.' Ryker thought then sighed. 'Is there any way you can dig into this quietly, from your side, figure out what these companies—?'

'Ryker, I'm already stepping way out of line here for you, and I only agreed this time because I'll be hundreds of miles away from my bosses. You think me going around asking questions, digging my nose in, is—'

'But it doesn't need to be secret. It only needs to not be public. You can tell your colleagues about this, what we think, and figure it out the right way, with as much help from the GBI, the FBI, Homeland Security, whoever. Because somebody must know the answers as to what those two companies could have that this group wanted.'

'You don't think those agencies aren't already all over this?'

'Maybe they are. I hope they are. And that's why I need you to ask. To find out what they know. But if you don't want to start ruffling feathers at work... there is another way.'

'Another way to what?'

'To find out what that data is.'

'I hope you're not suggesting what I think you're suggesting?'

'I'm suggesting we go and take a look for ourselves.'

'We. You actually said we.'

'Because you could help get me in there. For KDD Tech, at least.'

'So now you want me to help you sneak on to the scene of an active investigation of national importance so you can steal private data? You really don't think I value my job much, do you?'

'Actually, the opposite. I think you're entirely invested in your job. In getting answers. It's why you're sitting in the car with me at all. It's why you helped me out in Canton. It's why you helped me out in Peltworth. You might not like my methods, but you can see I'm the good guy here, and you're willing to step outside your normal comfort zone because you sense I'm going to get things done. And that's what you care most about too.'

She didn't say anything to that. Nothing at all. In fact, they both went silent for several minutes and Ryker sensed a turmoil in her, that something he'd said had triggered.

'You OK?' he prompted.

'You just got me thinking, that's all.'

'About what?'

'Me. My life. You know... my parents never wanted me to join the GBI. In fact, my dad was so dead against it. He pretty much disowned me. Didn't speak to me properly for a long time.'

'Why?'

'Because it's... dangerous. Because it's pretty damn all-consuming. And, basically, it's not what my family saw as a traditional female role. They were happy for me to work, maybe, I dunno, as a shop assistant or something like that, but all they really wanted was grandkids. For me to settle down and farm some offspring for them to spend their twilight years with. The perfect homemaker while my husband went out earning.'

'What about your husband? What did he want?'

'And that was the problem. My husband, Meg's brother, Harvey, he was cut from the same cloth as my parents. Was brought up in a traditional conservative home. Church every Sunday morning, the works. We met in high school. And we really were in love. For a long time. And to start with, I think he liked that I was a rebel, intent on breaking the mold. Hell, his sister did too. You've seen Meg. Maybe you sensed what she's like.'

'Yeah. I definitely did.'

'It's why I love her so much. Why we get along so well. But it wore off with Harvey pretty quickly. Because he was happy for me to be that rebel as long as it didn't impact his plans. And his plans were to go out to work, get on the corporate ladder and have no distractions. To come home and have a tidied home and a meal ready for him every night. To have a... ah, dang, you get it. Right?'

'I can imagine.'

'I don't think people change. Not really. Just... sometimes they're good at hiding who they really are. Or maybe it's sometimes you just read people wrong, for too long. And he isn't a bad person, and neither are my parents. But... that's where I'm at. I couldn't do it any longer. And neither could he. Now I'm childless, divorced and all I have is my job. And my dad's whispered words, I told you so, every time I try to go to sleep.'

'When I said you're invested in your job—'

'You didn't mean to upset me? You didn't. I am invested in my job. One hundred percent. All of the time. Because right now this job is my life. And I want to keep it that way, Ryker. So yeah, I'll help you, because I know you're on the right side here. Even if I know pretty much damn near nothing about you.'

'You didn't try to find out about my past?' he asked.

'Of course I did. But all I found was that you have a record that's so sanitized it... points in one direction only.'

He didn't bother to ask what direction that was. He understood what she meant.

'My background couldn't be more different to yours,' Ryker said after a short silence. 'I was picked up by the intelligence services in the UK as a runaway teenager. Turned into the operative they needed. For a long, long time I didn't have any life outside of it. No friends, no partner. Just like you... that job defined me. I only realized too late that what I had wasn't really a life at all.'

'What made you realize?'

'You really want to know?'

'Yeah.'

'My epiphany was the day a sadistic terrorist had me beaten and pinned to the floor as he tried to saw my head off.'

Her eyes widened in shock, horror, although also confusion as though she wasn't sure if he was being serious or not.

'Obviously he didn't succeed.' Ryker laughed. She didn't. He pulled his shirt collar down a little to show one of many ugly scars he had. 'I was saved by others that day. If it hadn't been for them... I was finished. I truly thought I was done. But it wasn't the violence of that moment that changed me... it was more... the realization that if it'd all ended there and then... it wouldn't have even mattered that much. Nothing in the wider world would have changed and no one would have been saddened that I didn't make it. Yeah, they'd have been an agent down, but they always had plenty more.'

She was staring at his neck still.

'That scar—'

'One of many.'

'It looks old.'

'It is. This was years ago now.'

'And since your... awakening?'

'I've lived. I've lost. I was married too, believe it or not. To an FBI agent.'

Cindy laughed. 'Yeah? How the hell did that come about?'

'Funny story?' he said. 'Kind of like this. One day we found ourselves chasing the same thing. The same people. Spent a bit of time together. The rest is history.'

She blushed and looked away.

'Unlike you, we both really just wanted a quiet life. We both left our old jobs behind. Our old lives. Except my past... was never far enough behind. I got dragged back in. She... became a target. They went after her to get at me.'

'She died?'

'She was murdered.'

'I'm sorry.'

'Yeah. Me too. Because I did that to her. Because of the man I used to be. Although... it's like you said. People don't really change. I tried so hard to get away from who I was, from the man I didn't want to be anymore and look how it turned out. Really, I am still that man. All I know is this.'

'You're not painting a bright future for me here. Aren't you supposed to say something like, there's still hope for you yet, Cindy. Still someone out there for you.'

Ryker laughed at her gruff voice and accent – a poor, but funny, impersonation of him. 'I've no doubt that there is. If that's what you want.'

She sniffed and then sighed. 'Right now... no, it's not. Not so soon after being burned.'

'And I know better than to believe there's a better, quieter, happier life in my future.'

'Damn, was this supposed to be a pep talk? Because it's really heading south.'

'Just trying to show that we're on the same page here. We both understand the sacrifices that we've made, sacrifices to our own lives, but it does mean something.'

'The greater good? Is that what you're saying?'

'Yeah, why not.'

'Is this your way of convincing me to sneak you into KDD Tech once we're back in Georgia, so you can rummage through their servers for classified data?'

'Has it worked?'

'Ask me again in the morning.'

'Well, at least that wasn't a no,' Ryker said with a smile and a wink.

* * *

Ryker knocked on the hotel room door, stood back and waited. Cindy opened up a few moments later. Most of her hair was pulled back and tied up, except for a wave at the front left side that dangled across her cheek. Her makeup was tidy, tasteful, and she wore a pendant necklace that plunged toward the chest of her figure-hugging black below-the-knee dress.

'You look amazing,' he said, and she glanced down a little coyly. 'Like you've been hanging around billionaires your whole life.'

'You know, I could say the same thing about you,' she responded, looking him over. She stepped up to him and reached forward and smoothed down the lapel of his dinner jacket. 'You actually scrub up pretty good. Takes a few years off, you know. Wait... did you put on eyeliner?'

She burst out laughing when he didn't.

'Sorry. I'm just deflecting. You know I haven't worn anything like this since I was a ditsy prom queen wannabe.'

'I don't believe you were ever ditsy.'

'I wasn't prom queen either.'

She pulled at the ends of the dress as though trying to untwist it or make it more comfortable.

'You couldn't find anywhere to put your sidearm?' Ryker asked. Teasing her. Although the serious look on her face suggested she didn't get it.

'You think we should be carrying?' she asked.

'It was a joke,' he said. 'No. You don't need anything on you. There're scanners at the entrance anyway. But...' He tapped his side. 'I do have something. Just in case. I'll leave it in the car.'

She looked unsure but didn't say anything more before she closed her door and they made their way down the elevator and to the car. The drive was short. Under three miles. Most of the guests – certainly the most prominent ones – were staying on site, but as late additions Ryker and Cindy had to make do with a cheap hotel not far away. Still, they soon reached the gate-house to Biltmore Estate and sat in a queue of other waiting – mostly luxury – cars.

'Have you been here before?' Ryker asked.

'As a kid,' Cindy said, sounding a bit nervy now. A fish out of water. 'When I was younger I thought of this place as a fairy-tale castle. Like, somewhere a princess would live, waiting for her handsome prince to come and whisk her away.'

And Ryker soon saw what she meant by that. He'd read up on the history of the place before coming, but in the flesh it was even more impressive. Set on a huge and largely manicured estate the main residence, Biltmore House, was a Châteauesque-style mansion built for the wealthy George Washington Vanderbilt II in the late nineteenth century. It was still owned by Vanderbilt's descendants, and with nearly 200,000 square feet of floor space, was the largest privately owned residence in the country. Yes, the family still owned it, and technically people lived here. But the house also acted as a museum, was a huge draw to tourists, and had a large wing devoted to high-end events, conferences, and dinners like tonight's, which saw the most wealthy and most prominent people from across the South come to mingle.

Plus Ryker and Cindy.

'Jesus, Ryker, this really isn't me at all,' she said as Ryker parked on the gravel outside the main entrance where a flurry of eager valets waited.

'Just relax.'

A young, suited man with white gloves went to open Ryker's door, but Ryker held the handle.

'Be you,' he said to Cindy.

'What are we doing here though?' she asked. 'I don't even—'

'We'll fit in. You're my wife. I'm a hedge fund manager from England. That alone and my accent will get most people relaxed around me. But we don't even need to do much talking. We mooch. We watch. Find out who Crawford is friendly with. Keep on the lookout for Kielder, Reed, Meyers, Abby Hannigan... Perhaps that's a long shot, but look for anyone else who doesn't belong here.'

'Like us, you mean?'

He sighed. 'Yeah. Like us. Except we'll blend in more than I imagine those guys would. But still... stay vigilant. Stay close if you can. But if you can't, stay wired.'

Not technically wired, just a figure of speech in more modern times, but they both had subtle earpieces, and tiny microphones on their clothing so they'd be in constant communication with one another.

Of course, he and Cindy had discussed all this numerous times already. She'd clued herself up on the parties Ryker was interested in, knew what they all looked like, et cetera, et cetera. But it was good to go through it one more time, eke out last-minute nerves.

'You ready?' Ryker asked.

'And you think it's a good idea to use your real name?' she asked.

'Absolutely. I've not met Crawford but the people in this group have seen my face more than once, and given the fact I was locked up in jail in Canton... there's a good chance they already know my real name. Have probably tried to dig into my past just like you did.'

'Which won't help them much.'

'Probably not. The point is, I'm not here to hide. I want to see what happens when they're under pressure. When they know I'm on to them.'

'Like in Newnan.'

'Exactly like that.'

She held his eye a moment then sighed.

'OK,' she said. 'Then let's do this.'

Ryker nodded, then stepped out of the car.

20

Ryker handed the key to the valet and dug back in his pocket.

'We might need to leave early. Could you make sure you put it close by, easy access?' He slipped the young man a fifty and his eyes lit up.

'You got it, sir. You can go with the VIPs.' He nodded over Ryker's shoulder to the cluster of mostly supercars, parked close to the entrance to show them off. 'Give me a shout and it'll be right back here for you.'

Ryker thanked him and he and Cindy made their way to the entrance and inside where they both took a glass of champagne from the tray held out to them by a white-gloved waitress.

'Cheers,' he said to Cindy, and they clinked glasses before taking a sip.

Ryker looked around. More than 400 guests were expected tonight. The awards dinner didn't start for more than an hour. He wanted to make as much progress before that as possible. He and Cindy completed a couple of circuits together, greeting anyone who looked their way, but not otherwise engaging. The reception spilled out across three first-floor spaces, including the grand entrance hallway which came with an ornate split staircase, a landing area above it also for use by the guests.

The more prominent lookout spot of the landing was where he and Cindy ended up, by which point they both had their second glass of champagne.

'What do you think?' he asked her as they propped against the wrought iron balustrade, looking down below.

'I've recognized maybe a dozen or more faces so far.'

'Same.'

'But not Crawford. Or Hannigan. Not Reed or Kielder or Meyers or Abby either.'

'I'd be surprised if any of the latter would be here as guests. Maybe as security or something like that, if they've come to look out for Crawford.'

'Maybe. Although Abby Hannigan? However she's involved, I highly doubt she'd be here, given her father is.'

'True,' Ryker said.

'You know, I really don't know how she still fits into all this.'

'No. Neither do I.'

And every time he came back to that point, it made him feel like he was missing something big.

'But there's her father,' Cindy said, nodding across the way.

Indeed it was. Adam Hannigan and his wife Brenda. Talking to two other couples that Ryker didn't know.

It seemed Hannigan knew Ryker was there because he gave a couple of sly and nervy glances.

'Should we go speak to him?' Cindy asked.

Ryker didn't answer, because he already had his eyes elsewhere. Bryan Tucker Crawford, to be precise. The diminutive man, thick gray hair, portly belly, bulbous nose on a pockmarked face was strolling with a model-type woman half his age, bright red dress, nearly six feet tall on her heels. Not his wife – estranged wife, apparently – but certainly his plus one here. Quite a few eyes followed them both until they came to a stop with a small group. Four men, two women.

'You know any of them?' Ryker asked Cindy.

'No.'

'Let's get some pictures.'

Ryker took out his phone and Cindy posed as Ryker snapped away, as subtly as possible. A couple of selfies for them both too, Ryker with his arm wrapped around Cindy's shoulder, pulling her close, cheek to cheek, so there was still enough room in the frame.

'Enjoy the squeeze?' Cindy asked him when he let go.

'What? I... I didn't...'

She laughed. A couple of people looked over.

'Shall we mingle?' Ryker suggested.

'Let's do it.'

Ryker took the lead in breaking into the group, pretending to need to split them to get past before he stopped to fabricate some bullshit.

'Didn't we meet last year at the UN Convention in Brussels?' he said to a random man in the group. A bit grandiose. A bit altruistic. With his best version of the King's English – much more polished than his real accent – it was enough to get a conversation started.

Crawford looked a little unsure to start with, Cindy too, but soon the group were all talking and laughing together. Ryker took in as much as he could as people introduced themselves.

A CEO here, a private attorney there. A congresswoman from Alabama.

'So you're a hedge fund manager?' the congresswoman –

Mary Aspen – said to Ryker. 'What brings you to our part of the world?'

'I work with a lot of charities,' Ryker said. 'But naturally, I always like to keep a business hat on too. I'm actually looking to expand my business into the US. Perhaps open a fund, an office, out here. Actually, Mr. Crawford—'

'Bryan, please.'

'Bryan. I believe you have your own investment operations in Georgia, don't you? BTC Capital?'

An unsure flicker in his eyes, while everyone else was still all fake smiles.

'Yeah, but it's not that big, and it's not something I'm really involved in day-to-day. Probably not really what you're—'

'Funny story, us meeting like this tonight, because I was actually in Newnan the other day, scoping out some properties. I'm only just putting the pieces together now, but I'm pretty sure I was at your company's office.'

'Oh, you were? Right. I—'

'BTC Capital? Newnan? There's some space to lease right there. What about that? My company right under yours.'

Ryker knocked Crawford's shoulder ever so slightly. The guy didn't like that at all and now a few of the smiles around the group were fading.

'I'll need to go back there again, though. Maybe next time you might be around too? We could catch up again.'

'Honestly? I have little involvement in that company. It's my name but I have a lot of bigger enterprises, obligations, that take priority.'

'Yeah. I got that sense when I was there. Is it Terrence Kielder you have running it? Danny Meyers? I spoke with him last time. There's Brad Reed too?'

'Brad Reed?' said Aspen's husband. 'Isn't he the guy the FBI are chasing about those bombings?'

'Oh, is it?' Ryker answered. 'Maybe I got the name wrong. Or maybe not.'

He fixed his attention back on Crawford. So did most of the other people there.

'I'm sorry, Mr. Ryker, but you've really lost me. I don't know any of those names, and I have no idea why you'd think I do.' He looked at his watch. 'It was nice meeting you.' He tugged on his girlfriend's arm. 'We must go and say hi to the Blumsteins.'

And just like that he waltzed off. Ryker watched him a few moments, before he and Cindy excused themselves from the group too. They headed for the stairs, passed Hannigan on the way. The guy made sure not to even glance at Ryker now. Had he seen any of the exchange with Crawford?

'Can we get some air?' Cindy suggested, sounding a little flustered.

So they went outside. Not through the main entrance, but a side one which opened out into a courtyard, lit up tastefully with string lights. A few other stragglers were out enjoying the warm evening too.

'Is it really best to antagonize the man like that?' Cindy said as they sat down on a bench in a quiet corner.

'As opposed to what?'

'As opposed to... acting with a bit more discretion.'

'You saw his face when I started talking about BTC Capital. When I mentioned those three names. Whatever's happening... he knows something. Whether he's the ringmaster or not.'

'Yeah, he knows something, just like Mary Aspen's husband knew the name Brad Reed, because it's a name that's been plastered all over the news the last two days. Anyone'd be put on the spot if you suggested they knew that guy.'

Fair point, but Ryker didn't really believe that explained Crawford's reaction.

'So what now?' Cindy asked.

Ryker glanced behind them, back to the mansion. 'We should go back inside. Do another circuit, see where both Hannigan and Crawford have ended up. We could split up if you want.'

She didn't look convinced. About either of his suggestions.

'Or we could just chill out here for a while,' she said. 'Be a bit more subtle. The dinner starts soon. Probably most folk'll stick around for the reception after too. If you're looking to catch these people out, wait until later when they're up to their eyeballs in free alcohol.'

She had a point.

'Did you look at the seating plan?' she asked. 'We have quite a mix with us.'

'Yeah,' Ryker said. 'I saw.'

Quite a mix, if he was really interested in networking. He wasn't.

'I'm getting more drinks,' she said, and was out of her seat in a flash.

Back in another flash, two champagnes with her, filled right to the top this time rather than the measly measures they'd had before.

She handed Ryker a glass and the two of them sat and sipped, relaxed, talked, although Ryker always had at least one eye on the guests roaming around them.

'You want another?' Cindy said, holding up her empty glass.

'Perhaps we should take it inside?'

She shrugged.

'You'd rather just sit out here getting wasted with me?' he asked.

'Yeah. I really would. Although... maybe not here. Just a local dive bar'd work much better.'

'Probably not dressed like this though.'

'Definitely not dressed like this.' She sighed. 'But we came here for a reason. So let's get back to it.'

Except when she went to get up her heel slipped and she tumbled back down to the bench, right into him. Pretty much onto his lap. She looked into his eyes and laughed.

'Good catch,' she said.

But then her smile dropped and they both moved forward at the same time, planting their lips on one another's. A lingering, mouths-closed kiss, Ryker with his arm around her shoulder, her hands on his thighs.

She sighed and pulled away.

'I guess we're married, though, so it's allowed,' she said.

'Yeah,' Ryker said.

She pulled back further, her playfulness on the wane.

'You know what, Ryker?'

'What?'

'That was nice. I mean that. I like you. I think we... click. Don't we?'

'I think so,' Ryker said.

'But I think we click at this,' she said, waving an arm around the courtyard. 'I'm not saying I wouldn't want to do that again, but... I mean, you literally told me that you've done this sort of thing before. Fallen for an FBI agent. Who was murdered. I mean...'

'I didn't sell myself very well?'

She stared at him for a few moments.

'Whether you did or didn't, tonight is definitely not the right time,' she said. She got to her feet. 'You get the champagne. I need the restroom.'

She sauntered off. Ryker stood up, his head spinning just a little from the three drinks. Time to slow down.

He moved inside behind Cindy, but she was soon out of sight as he sought out a waiter. It didn't take long. He wondered how many hundreds of bottles of champagne would be consumed tonight. So far the supply seemed never-ending.

'Ryker, remember what you said about watching the staff?' came Cindy's voice in his ear a few moments later as he stood waiting for her.

'Yeah?'

'Meyers. I'm pretty damn sure he's here. In a waiter's uniform. But he's standing, scoping, not serving.'

'Where?'

'Near the restroom.'

Ryker turned. Spotted the sign indicating off to the right. He made his way through the crowd of people, much thicker now than before.

'You still see him?' Ryker asked, keeping his voice low, trying to be discreet so the other guests wouldn't think him a fool, or just be alerted to the fact he was wired up.

'Yeah. I didn't make it to the restroom. He spotted me so I kept going.'

'He doesn't know you.'

'He definitely does. He's following me.'

Just the first hints of nerves in her voice now.

'Where are you?' Ryker asked.

'There's more than one. They're trying to be subtle but they're definitely on me.'

'Cindy, where are you?'

'I went p... the restroom... back outside.' The line was crackling.

'Come back inside. To the staircase.'

'It's OK. They've gone,' she said. Clearer now.

'Meet me at the staircase,' Ryker said, who was already there, standing with his back to the wall, scanning.

'OK. Give me a minute... Wait. I see Meyers again. Talking to someone I don't know. Different man to before. They're outside. Main entrance.'

'Wait for me,' Ryker said.

'They've gone past the VIP cars. They're not stopping. I need pictures. My phone. It's in the car.'

The next moment he heard her talking to the valet, taking the key from him. Ryker put both glasses down and moved quickly for the exit. He made it outside, eyes falling on the parked cars.

'Cindy?'

No answer.

'Shit,' he said under his breath, as he strode down the steps and across the gravel.

'Cindy?'

'Ryker, I'm on to them.' Whispering now. 'Around the east side. There's... Ryker!'

'Cindy?'

'No. Get... off me! Ryker!'

He broke into a jog, zigzagging through the parked supercars, his rental coming up on the right.

'Cindy?'

Nothing from her now.

He tried the handle. Unlocked. So she'd made it here. The gun? He flicked open the glove compartment.

'Damn it.'

She'd already taken the gun out. That's why she'd wanted to go to the car.

He straightened up and turned around and froze. Found

himself face-to-face with a man. And the reason he froze and didn't immediately fight back, was because the man had already pushed the syringe he was holding into Ryker's upper arm, his thumb hovering over the plunger.

'Want to know what's inside this?' the man asked, his face mostly in shadow with the lights from the mansion behind him.

'Where is she?' Ryker said.

'We'll keep her alive. As long as you do exactly as I say. Understand?'

Ryker nodded.

'Let's get you settled in. Walk around to the driver's side.'

Ryker did, the syringe in his skin pinching with each step.

'Open the door.'

Again, Ryker complied.

'Sit down.'

This time Ryker paused.

'Unless you want her to get a bullet in the head right now, then sit down.'

'Cindy?' Ryker said. 'Do you hear me?'

'No, she doesn't hear you. We took the comms off of her.'

'Then how do I know she's OK?'

'If you sit down, I'll let you speak to her.' He wiggled the syringe a little as if for emphasis. 'Down.'

Ryker did so, the man coming down onto his haunches.

'Put your hands on the wheel.'

Ryker complied.

'I'm gonna cuff you there. Then I'll get in beside you so we can talk.'

No chance, even though Ryker nodded again to show his apparent compliance.

The man went to reach into his pocket with his free hand and Ryker saw his chance. He swiveled, sent a fist to man's head,

jumped out the car. He swiped the man's feet from the ground...
or tried to, at least, but the guy quickly regained his footing,
dodged another of Ryker's fists before sending an uppercut
under his chin. Ryker wobbled on his feet but forced through
the disorientation and lurched forward again. He landed a solid
kidney strike, an elbow to the man's head, before they were
grappling, close quarters, faces only inches apart, each of them
trying to gain the upper hand.

No, Ryker had the upper hand. The man had relaxed, no
longer fighting back.

Except the next moment a smile broke out on his face, and it
was only when Ryker felt the pinch in his side that he realized
why.

A hefty headbutt caused Ryker's vision and focus to waver.
The man pulled from Ryker's grip, sliding the syringe from
Ryker's flesh as he stepped back. He thudded a fist into Ryker's
gut before pushing him back down into the seat. He slipped the
cuffs on and locked them in place.

The door slammed shut. Moments later the man sat down
in the seat beside him.

Ryker looked over as his vision cleared. For the first time he
could see the man's face properly... or not. Because it wasn't his
face, but a latex mask. A prosthetic. An OK one, but definitely a
mask, given away by the quite crude eyeholes, mouth, the too-
perfectly symmetrical nostril holes.

'Want to know what's running through your blood now?' he
asked.

Ryker didn't answer.

'Painkiller. Just a boring old painkiller.' He laughed. It
looked so strange because parts of the face that should have
moved didn't. 'You wanted to speak to her?'

Ryker still didn't answer.

The guy sighed and took out his phone and called and put it on speaker.

'Put her on the line,' the man said.

'Ryker, there's three of them!' Cindy shouted, distressed, talking quickly. 'The man with you is called Marshall—'

Thud.

'Stupid fucking bitch.'

Thud.

Then quiet. Ryker channeled his anger as best he could. Nothing he could do to unleash it right now.

'Do we have things under control?' the man – Marshall? – said to his buddies.

'Yeah. We do. She's learning.'

'Good. If I don't call back in ten minutes, kill her.'

'Gladly.'

The call ended.

'Marshall, huh?' Ryker said. 'That you?'

He sighed. 'Yes, James Ryker, my name is Caleb Marshall. I'm not sure how they let that slip to your friend, but don't think that's some big revelation for you, even if you didn't know it before now.'

'So what are we doing here?' Ryker asked.

'You're looking for me, I think. And you found me.'

'I don't know you.'

'No. You don't. Not yet. Because you've been looking in the wrong place. Or, more specifically, at the wrong people. But that's really by design, my design, more than anything else.'

'Crawford?'

'BTC. It's what his friends call him.' He smirked. 'Can you believe that? The arrogance to have people call you by your three initials. As though those three letters couldn't mean anything else.'

'Bats Talking Chinese?'

The man huffed. 'Funny.'

'So BTC's your friend?' Ryker asked.

'No. Not my friend.'

'Boss?'

Marshall laughed. 'I stopped answering to bosses a long, long time ago.'

'What do you want?'

'From you? Or from life?'

Ryker decided not to clarify. The tone of the conversation, the confidence in the man's voice... Marshall was enjoying this. The power. Being in control.

'What's with the mask?' Ryker asked. 'I know your name, so what's the point? Wait... you're scared to show me your face? Are you really ugly or something?'

Smash.

The fist to Ryker's side was powerful, targeted, and he'd had no way to protect himself other than to tense his muscles. It didn't do much. Pain emanated from the spot. Didn't subside. He imagined his kidney burst open, pieces floating through him.

'OK. So... I shouldn't mention your face?' Ryker said through gritted teeth. 'Got it. What now? You're going to kill me?'

'If I wanted to kill you, you'd already be dead.'

'Why wouldn't you kill me? Given how close I am.'

'Close?' Marshall said with a chuckle. 'Close to what?'

'To stopping you.'

'Stopping me? You don't even know what I'm doing. What I'm planning.'

'I know that you and the group you're with rigged those explosives at KDD Tech. Industrial Control Logistics too. Probably were responsible for the plane crash that killed Bob Ferrer and his family.'

Marshall said nothing but held Ryker's eye, as though waiting for more.

'I know Crawford... BTC is involved. Perhaps funding you. Terrence Kielder—'

'No, no, no, no, no. Stop. Stop. Please, just stop. James Ryker, what are you doing?'

Ryker clenched his jaw shut.

'You're just listing out events you've heard about on CNN. You have no clue what is going on around you. Nobody does. Except for me. It's so much more beautiful, dramatic that way. But...' He leaned further toward Ryker, then whispered, 'Can I tell you a secret?'

Ryker didn't answer.

'We came here tonight to protect BTC. Because, yes, we knew you were watching us. And what we were supposed to do was to get you, torture you to find out who you are, what you know, who you work for, blah, blah. Then kill you. That GBI agent too. And I'm sorry to say, that if I don't call my friends back in a few minutes, she's dead anyway. But you know what?'

Ryker again said nothing.

'I'm looking forward to this. Aren't you?'

Marshall fumbled in his pocket and drew out another syringe. Then he reached forward with his free arm and rolled Ryker's sleeve up above his wrist. He pincered Ryker's skin with his gloved fingers.

'Feel that?' he asked.

Ryker did, although the sensation was definitely dulled from what he knew it should be because of the painkiller he had in him.

'Let me give you another, much stronger dose. You'll be amazed at the difference.'

Ryker tensed as Marshall pushed the needle into his thigh and watched as the liquid was pushed into his body.

'It should only take a few minutes,' Marshall said. 'So we don't have long. Tell me again, about my plans. About me.' He said that with a callous smirk. 'Impress me.'

'KDD Tech and Industrial Control Logistics,' Ryker said. 'Both have contracts with the Department of Defense. Your group... the White Lions, or an offshoot of it, is a rebel white supremacist group. My best guess... you're hitting out at the government.'

Marshall gave no reaction.

'Or... you're just doing it for money. Short selling so that after each attack, when the stock of the company you targeted plummets, you get stinking rich.'

Marshall sighed but didn't say anything.

'Or... you're doing this because you enjoy it. Because you want to cause chaos. Mayhem. Misery.'

Marshall smiled. It looked grotesque the way the cut-out mouth moved, straining the eyeholes, the cheeks frozen.

'Close, Ryker. You got real, real close with that last one. Yet you're still so far away. But the best part... you'll get to watch what comes next like everyone else. Soon you'll see. Everyone will see.'

'OK... so how about this?' Ryker said. 'The bombs were a deflection. You stole something of value from both those companies. Right? Data?'

Marshall laughed again. 'Ryker, Ryker, you really are so far behind the curve. It seems almost a shame to have to do this to you now, before you've even made any progress.'

He reached forward again. Pincered Ryker's skin again. This time Ryker could feel next to nothing.

'Do you like that?' Marshall asked.

He took out a knife. Ryker jostled but with his hands cuffed to the wheel he could do little to defend himself. When the tip of the blade was pressed to the skin on his neck he relaxed. Or, at least, stopped moving.

'You have no idea of the power it gives, to feel no pain.' Marshall tilted the knife and gently drew the blade across Ryker's skin, a line opening up behind it which dribbled blood. 'Amazing, isn't it? What the human body can do? How it can be so easily fooled.'

Marshall leaned further in and pushed the knife against Ryker's side now, to the tender spot where he'd early delivered that vicious blow. Ryker felt nothing there at all now.

'But the damage is still real, Ryker. I could take your kidney right out of you. You wouldn't feel it, but the damage I inflict with this knife...'

He trailed off but left the knife where it was.

'You have three minutes,' Marshall said. 'Then she's dead. And—' he took out yet another syringe and, no playtime on this occasion, he sank the needle and the liquid into Ryker's thigh '—that gives you about enough time before the tranquilizer knocks you out. Because I'm not killing you. Only... changing. Disfiguring, you could say.'

He pulled the knife from Ryker's side and to his cuffed hands. His hands which now felt so distant. Almost detached. If he was going to fight back here, he didn't have long. His only option was likely to break his own hands to free them from the cuffs. A desperate move. But he was desperate.

'Pinky first?' Marshall said, taking the digit in one hand, the knife there, ready to slash. 'Who sent you here? To America.'

'No one. I'm... looking for someone.' He maneuvered his hands, pulling them back, putting more and more pressure on his thumb's knuckles. A quick, sharp tug would hopefully be enough... If he could find the strength.

'Who, Ryker? Who are you looking for?'

'Some asshole who wears a stupid mask all the time because he's so damn butt-ugly.'

Marshall growled in anger and Ryker grimaced as the knife sank into the flesh of his finger... but then he paused. Had he heard too?

'Ryker... Ryker... I'm coming for you.' A soft voice coming through Ryker's earpiece.

Cindy.

'In... the car,' Ryker replied, only then realizing how out of it he already was. He pulled on his hands. As much as he could muster. Nothing happened. He could do nothing.

Marshall sighed and sat back in his seat. Several security guards rushed out of the mansion entrance, shouting, searching.

'It's a shame,' he said. 'We didn't get to finish this conversation as I'd intended.' He slashed at Ryker's arm with the knife. A show of pettiness, more than anything. Ryker's flesh opened up. He felt nothing. Marshall grabbed Ryker's head and pulled it down toward him and whispered into his ear. 'Soon, you'll see me for what I truly am. Not a man in a mask... something much, much greater and more powerful than a mouse of a man like you could ever imagine.'

When Marshall let go, Ryker barely had the strength to hold his head upright. He heard the faint clunk as the car door closed. A grainy voice in his ear.

'Ryker, are you OK? Ryker?'

He didn't have the focus to answer. His weary gaze rested on his arm. On the gash there, skin parted, blood oozing, dribbling out and down his skin.

'Ryker. Ryker!'

The voice was closer now. Not in his ear. All around him.

Closer. But even more distant and he only drifted further away.

After that he saw nothing but a wall of black.

21

The old factory in Douglasville had no doubt once been a hub of machinery, of dirt, sweat, and noise. Now the redbrick structure was decrepit and on its very last legs. The main roof had long since caved in, not much up there but a few rafters. Windows were mostly shattered or missing altogether and on the lower level there was a gaping hole in the structure through which it was possible to drive vehicles in and out.

Which is exactly what I did when I arrived, to see several other vehicles already there.

This place had always been on our list of safe spaces. It had good access to the I285 highway, was close to the airport and to the city of Atlanta, but it was also on an entirely deserted street of other old warehouses and buildings, nothing inhabited for more than half a mile.

It was also a dump. The worst of the worst. Not somewhere any of us would want to spend much time. Especially on a night when the heavens had opened and torrential rain poured down on and into the structure.

I stepped out of the car, my feet landing in a two-inch-deep pool of water that I hadn't seen in the darkness. Clean water at least – I hoped – given the concrete floor beneath my feet. But as I walked on there were patches of thick mud too where the concrete had eroded to nothing but the underlying soil.

The thick brick walls of the interior were at least still partly intact, which meant that we'd managed to create a 'dry' space to work in. To be specific, after we'd fled the office in Newnan, Hailey and I had set up a space, with the help of a few wooden boards and plastic sheeting, for her to work in, while the 'top dogs' and I headed to North Carolina. All very grim though, really.

Especially tonight.

'Where the fuck have you been?' Kielder said when I entered said space.

Hailey, Kielder, Meyers were inside. The other grunts who'd gone up to North Carolina with us had been sent on their way for now or maybe were hiding somewhere. Or maybe had been captured by the police already.

'I stopped for food. For all of five minutes.'

'They've only been here for about fifteen,' Hailey said from her desk chair.

'Did you tell her what happened?' I asked Kielder.

'They didn't need to tell me much,' she said. 'It's all over the news.'

'All of our names,' Kielder said. 'All of our faces. Except yours.'

'Wanted in connection with the bombs in Atlanta, Houston and for the downing of the Ferrers' jet,' Meyers said.

'Yeah, but that wasn't me,' I said, smiling. 'So I'm glad my name isn't associated with it.'

Kielder walked up to me. Put his face right up to mine.

'Your who gives a fuck attitude is really starting to grate on me.'

'You think I don't care? Then you've really not understood anything about me at all. Where's BTC?'

Kielder stepped back, shaking his head and grumbling.

'He got out,' Meyers said.

'Out of the country?'

'Yes.'

'Money really can get you anything.'

'And he made it just in time,' Meyers said. 'Because since we left Asheville the FBI sent a raid squad to his home. To his place on the Florida Keys too. To the office in Newnan.'

'To my house,' Kielder said. 'Danny's.'

Meyers nodded in acknowledgment.

'Not to mine,' Hailey added, a little wryly, and Kielder sent her a scathing look. 'I guess I should be glad that you didn't invite me to the dinner after all.'

'And we could have fled like BTC too,' Kielder said. 'Except we stayed because we still have a job to do. Hailey, please tell me—'

'I'm done,' she said.

Silence in the room. Expectant silence.

A wide smile spread across her face.

'Yeah,' she said. 'I'm done. Really.'

Kielder rushed up to her and wrapped his arms around her and lifted her from her feet, kissing her cheek and her neck over and over. Anger bubbled away in my gut, but I didn't let it show.

I realized Meyers was staring at me, a callous smirk on his face.

'I knew you could do it. Christine or no Christine. You're a star.'

Hailey looked a little bewildered by his unusual show of

appreciation, of affection. She glanced at me and then quickly away, just enough to gauge my reaction. Or lack of it.

'Just tell me again,' Kielder said to her. 'You've cracked both sets of data now? Exodus and Orion? And they're compatible?'

'Both,' she said. 'And yes, I've run some tests and it seems like they're interacting exactly as needed, although without the hardware I can't perform an actual dry run.'

'So all we need now is the hardware,' Kielder said.

Again, eyes on me.

'And I don't mean to spoil this mini moment of jubilation here,' I said, 'but I could have had the hardware by now, we would have been a hundred percent ready, if I'd gone straight to Florida and not up to North Carolina.'

'Yet it's just as well we did go there, don't you think?' Kielder said. 'Except... you had James Ryker in your hands... and you let him slip away.'

'The way I recall events is that you had his friend, a GBI agent, and she escaped handcuffs and fought three of you off before raising the alarm and leaving me no choice but to run. Like you.'

'No choice?' Meyers said. 'The choice was simple. Kill him. Eliminate the risk.'

'I was tasked with finding out everything I could about that man. Remember, Terrence?'

'That's not what I meant, and you know it,' Kielder said. 'But since we're on that subject... what did you find out from your nice little conversation with him?'

'Nothing that we didn't already know,' I said.

Kielder's face soured even further. 'You don't even know who he's working for?'

'No. But other than that GBI agent, I've a feeling he's alone here.'

'A feeling?' Kielder said. 'Out of the mouth of the man who feels nothing.'

I balled my fists rather than bite back. 'It makes sense. Otherwise there would have been a swarm of other agents in Asheville ready to take us down.'

'There certainly will be now.'

'You want to know what I think?' Meyers said, setting his beady eyes on me. 'I'm starting to get pretty damn suspicious now of all these little... inconveniences. Inconveniences that all revolve around you. Christine going missing. Reed going missing. The attacks being linked so soon, our names and faces all over the news. This James Ryker guy breathing down our necks, who you had a private conversation with before letting him go.'

'You think I want heat on us? That I want our plans to fail?' I said, unable to stifle a chuckle at the ludicrous proposition, although apparently no one else saw the funny side.

'No. But I'm starting to think that you are playing us all somehow. That you're not really in this with us.'

'You want to talk about Christine and Reed, I—'

'No,' Meyers said. 'How about we talk about General Pettier instead.'

'Who?' Kielder asked.

'Exactly,' Meyers said. 'Pettier. A three-star general with the US Army. A constant presence in the Middle East for more than two decades. Ran some of the most dangerous and secretive missions there, a lot of them involving special forces.'

Meyers paused, as though waiting for my reaction, or waiting for the others to react. He smiled. Nodded his head.

'Yeah, you know Pettier. I might not be able to see your face behind that stupid mask, Marshall, but I can see the look in your eyes. The hatred at that name.'

Or maybe the hatred for you.

Meyers turned to his boss. 'Pettier was murdered a few days ago. Right after KDD Tech. During those two days when Marshall went missing.'

'Did you do that?' Kielder asked.

'Yes.'

Kielder winced at my answer, but what the hell did it matter to him? He knew nothing about Pettier, the monstrous things he'd had others do, that he'd caused. And his death had no impact on Kielder. 'What else, Marshall? What else have you been doing without telling us?'

'A lot, actually. Both before and after we ever met. Did you think the information about Exodus and Orion just fell into my lap one day?'

Meyers and Kielder said nothing as they glared. Hailey looked bewildered. A little worried.

'If anyone's still wondering why we have the police and the Feds breathing down our necks...' Meyers said.

'Who else have you killed?' Kielder asked. 'How many?'

'You don't need to know.'

I went to walk away, bored of this line of conversation, but Kielder grabbed my arm. Hard. Not that I could feel the strength of his grip, but I could tell by the scrunched fabric of my jacket and his bone-white knuckles.

'Let's say I do need to know,' he said.

He left his hand there, awaiting my response.

'OK,' I said with a sigh. 'How about I start with the software engineer in Illinois who oversaw most of the original coding for Orion. Or the general in Kentucky who signed off the contract to KDD Tech. How about the chief information officer at Jeston Solutions in California, whose company acts as a key supplier to Industrial Control—'

'You killed them all?' Hailey asked, a horrified look on her face.

I didn't answer. Because, unusually for me, seeing her expression, her disappointment... I felt... something close to shame. But I pushed it aside just as quickly as it had built.

'None of you is stupid,' I said, even if I didn't believe that wholeheartedly. 'What we know about Exodus and Orion isn't information that just sits there, intact, on the internet waiting for someone to come across it. Very few people – and we're talking about people you can count on one hand – have as much detailed knowledge of the systems and where they're controlled as we do. So I'm sorry if you've taken for granted the information that I first presented to you.'

'Nobody took anything for granted,' Meyers said. 'It's just curious that you chose to never tell us any of this before.'

'You never asked before. You just took what I had with your tongues hanging out of your mouths like a couple of desperate yokels ogling a teenage silicone-enhanced stripper.'

Meyers went for me, but Kielder whipped around to hold him back.

'You should be thanking me for doing the dirty work for you,' I said.

Kielder turned back to me. Seething, just like Meyers. He flung his arms in the air a couple of times. Slapped them back down to his side. His face was red with rage. 'And what about Pettier? What did you get from him?'

'Satisfaction,' I said. 'Going after him was simply something I had to do. For me. It has no impact on what we're doing.'

'You think going after a decorated general, murdering him, at a time when we already have God knows who breathing down our necks has no impact? How do you know you killing him isn't why the FBI, this James Ryker are on to us in the first place?'

'It's not,' I said.

'You don't know that.'

'And what about Christine?' Meyers said. 'You were the last person to see her. Then Reed... We know you messed up in Houston. Didn't follow the rules. Then the next day we have the FBI pinning Reed's name at the top of their most wanted list, and no one's seen him since.'

I shrugged. 'He was always a coward.'

'No. I'm starting to think you killed him. Why? No reason, other than you didn't like him and because you could and because you're totally fucking insane. And Christine? Maybe because you tried to screw her and she wouldn't let you because you're such a goddamn freak.'

Despite thinking I retained the upper hand here I grimaced at that last comment. Tried not to look at Hailey, but I couldn't. And it made me even more sad, mad, to see the growing disappointment, the concern in her eyes.

'Marshall... I'll ask you this one time only,' Kielder said. 'Did you kill them? Either of them?'

'No,' I said without a thought. 'I gain nothing from killing them. And you want to know about Christine? What I found out about her?'

No one answered the question. I took that as a yes.

'A few minutes before I set those bombs off at KDD Tech, she made a call to the FBI. Warning them.'

Silence. I let that sink in. Kielder spoke up first. 'And how the hell would you know that?'

'Don't forget who I am. Who I was. I have sources, contacts, allies. I don't have to kill people to find information.'

'If this is true,' Meyers said, 'you're only implicating yourself even more.'

'Except I didn't do it,' I said. 'I only found this out a couple of days ago. And why would I have killed her knowing it'd jeopardize perhaps the most important step of our work? Getting Exodus and Orion up and running.'

Kielder opened his mouth to speak but then his phone vibrated in his pocket and he lifted it and turned away to answer.

Meyers took another step closer to me.

'I'm not afraid of you, freak,' he said.

'Perhaps you should be.'

'Danny,' Kielder said, off the phone already. 'We're going. Marshall... I don't like this. I don't like any of what's happened tonight. What you've just told me. But we're too far in to stop now. And we're so close. Agreed?'

'Agreed.'

He turned to Meyers.

'Agreed,' Meyers said, teeth bared.

'Get to Florida and get the hardware,' Kielder said to me. 'As soon as you have it, I'm making the announcement.'

He and Meyers left just like that.

Hailey remained. She didn't look happy. With me.

'What?' I said.

'I really hope you didn't do anything to her,' she said.

'But you don't mind if I did to Reed?'

'That's not what I said. But... please tell me you didn't hurt Christine.'

'The fact you need me to tell you that...'

I turned and left, feeling more wounded than she knew.

22

Ryker awoke quite peacefully. Relaxed, in fact.

The room was bland. But old. Small. A few tables and chairs, although Ryker was sunken in a couch.

Biltmore Estate. He was still at Biltmore Estate. A room for the service staff, perhaps?

He wasn't alone. Cindy was there. A suited man too. Not a dinner guest. An agent, Ryker knew, even before the guy turned to face him, realizing that Ryker was now awake.

'Ryker!' Cindy said, rushing over to him, but then she kind of just hovered, as if not really knowing what else to say or do.

'How long was I out?' Ryker asked, shuffling up in the seat. Agonizing pain stabbed in his side where Marshall had punched him. Pain too from the slash on his forearm which now had a neat white bandage covering it.

'A few... hours,' she said.

'You didn't think to try to rouse me?' he asked. 'A shot of adrenaline or something?'

She looked a little hesitant. Glanced at the agent.

'We thought it better to use the time to figure out what the hell is happening here,' he said.

'Ryker, I—'

'Are you OK?' he asked Cindy, reaching out and gently taking her hand in his. Her left eye was swollen. Her lip bulging and cut. She'd changed out of her dress and into jeans and a sweatshirt, although she'd rolled the sleeves up and he could see bruising on her right arm and ugly red lines ringed both of her wrists.

'No worse than you,' she said, glancing at his now heavily bandaged arm. Certainly not pain-free now. It stung like hell.

'How did you do it?' he asked. 'You got away from them.'

She shrugged. 'I did what I had to do,' she said a little sheepishly, almost like she was embarrassed.

'You probably saved me,' he said. 'Again. Thank you.'

'OK, OK, I think we're done with the reunion,' the agent cut in, a little blunt in Ryker's opinion. 'James Ryker, I'm Field Agent Gerard Bowry with the FBI.'

'Figures,' Ryker said.

The door opened and another agent walked in. Female. Same height and stature as Cindy but a bit older, a lined and stern face.

'And this is my partner, Agent Lennox.'

'Ah, he's awake,' Lennox said, sipping from a paper coffee cup. 'Are you up to speed?' she asked Ryker.

'Not even close.'

'They got away,' Cindy said. 'Crawford, Kielder, Meyers, Marshall.'

'We have an APB out for all of them,' Bowry said. 'And every port and airport across the country is on alert.'

'Not Reed?' Ryker asked.

'We don't think he was here. Still on the run, most likely.'

'Or already dead,' Ryker said. Lennox's eyes narrowed at the comment, as though suspicious of why Ryker would say that, what it meant.

'But how about you tell us your side of the story,' Lennox said. 'From the horse's mouth.'

Ryker didn't straightaway. He held Cindy's eye a moment, a silent question to her, asking what she'd already told the FBI.

'I told them everything,' she said, catching on. 'The truth.'

'I'm a private investigator,' Ryker said. Bowry stifled a laugh. Lennox remained with her stern, uncaring look. 'I was tasked with tracking down Abby Hannigan. Governor Hannigan's missing daughter.'

'You thought she was here?' Bowry asked.

'A group she's working with. Involved with.'

'And this group... is the group you believe is responsible for the bomb attacks in Atlanta and Houston.'

'Yes.'

'Because...?'

'Because that's what I think.'

'Based on what evidence?' Lennox asked. 'Hard evidence?'

'These people are all associated with Brad Reed for one,' Ryker said. 'It's your agency that already publicly announced he was a prime suspect in the attacks, right?'

'But Brad Reed wasn't here tonight,' Lennox said. 'We already established that. And as far as I know there is no evidence that Reed is working with or even linked to these other people. Unless you're telling me otherwise?'

Ryker didn't answer. Yes, he had evidence of the link in the data he'd taken from Reed's house. He also assumed that by now the FBI had the same, perhaps even more data than that. The very fact the FBI were here, in Asheville, suggested they'd linked whatever had happened tonight with those attacks.

'And you think Bryan Tucker Crawford is leading this group?' Lennox said. 'The attacks? He's a very prominent man. What's he gaining here?'

'You'd have to ask him.'

Lennox sniffed, glanced at her colleague who folded his arms and glared at Ryker.

'Can I ask you two a question?' Ryker said.

The FBI agents exchanged another look before Lennox said, 'You can.'

'Who is Caleb Marshall?'

Bowry fidgeted uneasily. Lennox sucked in air through her nostrils as though deciding how to answer.

'He was the one in the car with me,' Ryker continued. 'He was set on torturing me. Cutting me to pieces, if he'd had the time. Except Agent Valentino saved me.'

'How do you know it was Caleb Marshall?' Lennox asked, ignoring all the other stuff. 'Because I assume from your initial question you don't know him personally.'

Ryker said nothing.

'Did you see his face to ID him?' Bowry asked.

Ryker didn't answer.

'Did you?' Lennox seconded.

'No. He was wearing a mask.'

Lennox sighed. 'Then we really don't know who that man was, do we? But I'm telling you it wasn't Caleb Marshall. Because Caleb Marshall is dead.'

* * *

There were still a few stragglers from the canceled dinner hanging around both inside and outside Biltmore mansion as Ryker and Cindy made their way back to the car. All of the

Lamborghinis and Ferraris were now gone. The rich and famous had fled at the first opportunity, likely not wanting to get caught up in any media furor. But a few of the 'lesser' attendees had remained to watch the excitement unfold.

Not that much excitement was taking place now, several hours later, even if quite a few police cars, a couple of ambulances remained.

Ryker and Cindy weren't hanging around. After a quick stop at the hotel to pick up their things, and for Ryker to change, they were on their way back south to Atlanta.

'You called the police?' Ryker asked as he drove. The first thing of note either of them had said to one another since leaving Biltmore.

'You wouldn't have wanted me to?'

'That's not what I meant.'

'But the FBI showing was nothing to do with me. Not directly, anyway.'

'So they were already looking at some or all of the same people we are.'

'Certainly seems that way. But they never said. As you'd expect.'

'And what about your bosses? I assume they now know you were there.'

'I've been suspended. I didn't contact them but... just like the FBI turning up... these things get around quickly. The call came from my boss while you were still out of it. No discussion, no explanation, no questions asked as to why I was there. Just... I'm suspended. Pending further investigation.'

'I'm sorry,' Ryker said.

She didn't answer.

'Not just for you getting suspended,' he added. 'But for... what happened to you too.'

'I handled it, didn't I?'

She had. But she also seemed dejected, rattled by the experience. Which was only to be expected.

'You're angry at me?' she asked.

'For telling the FBI everything? No. Actually I'm not. I wouldn't expect you to lie to federal agents for me. And it wouldn't really help our aim anyway. We want to stop this group. The more resources out there looking for them, the better.'

'I know you say that, but I get the sense you don't really want it, either.'

'From my perspective? No. Because it's like I already said, I work best when I'm not constrained by the rules of agencies like the FBI, GBI, whoever.'

'What did you make of Bowry and Lennox?'

'Not a lot.'

'But did you think they were straight up?'

'Do I think they, the FBI in general, are hiding something?'

'Yeah.'

'Possibly. But not as part of some big conspiracy. Just because they see us as outsiders. We are outsiders to them.'

'They didn't believe you about Caleb Marshall.'

'Actually, I think they probably did. They just wanted me not to believe it.'

'I didn't recognize the name at first. But... I looked into him. I kinda remember his story. He was in the Army. Delta Force, according to rumors. He and a team were on a secret mission in the Middle East, aiming to locate and extract a high-value asset. But they were ambushed. Pinned down. The story goes that in the chaos two different special forces teams ended up fighting against each other, believing they were fighting the enemy. It ended when army commanders sent in an airstrike to obliterate everything. Better to destroy all evidence than have their men, the asset, captured. Except Marshall survived. Badly injured, his body burned horribly from the fire caused by the airstrike. A local militia pulled him out of the rubble before we could get any more feet on the ground. They treated him in a makeshift hospital, kept him alive at least, but didn't have the tools or the skills to treat his injuries properly. So his scars were... horrific. He was passed from group to group as a pawn. Eventually he broke free from his captors, wound up back at a US air base. When they brought him home he was treated as a hero.'

'The Burning Man. I vaguely remember the story.'

'The media turned him into a martyr, a hero, but it seems he only ever wanted to disappear. You know, other than a couple of written snippets, he never made any public appearances, never gave any interviews. Then came the headline that his body had been found in his rented apartment in Florida. Single gunshot wound to the head. His PTSD was blamed.'

Ryker said nothing as he took the information in.

'You really think Caleb Marshall was in the car with you?' Cindy asked. 'I mean... I knew the guys who had me called him Marshall, but at the time I really didn't think much of it. But now... Caleb Marshall?'

'Why else would he say so?'

'Why fake his own death?'

'You said yourself, he didn't want the attention. And he was suffering from PTSD.'

'Then why come back now? Why is he doing what he's doing with this group? Revenge? We know BTC, Kielder and the others aren't veterans out for payback.'

'But maybe Marshall's aims align with theirs still. At least surface level. Getting back at the government that tried to kill him, left him for dead.'

'So this really could all boil down to revenge?'

'It's about the most powerful force of human nature.'

'But the others? Crawford, Kielder, how do they—'

'Maybe they're just using Marshall. His hate. But maybe... it's the other way around.'

They both went silent, Ryker toying with those two scenarios, what each would mean. He tried to call Klein. The CIA man would likely know Marshall's story. Might know more than the publicly available spiel even. Would know if there was any evidence of him still being alive, a threat.

But Klein didn't answer any of Ryker's calls over the next couple of hours.

So he resorted to a more trusted source: Peter Winter, Ryker's long-term ally – boss – who now sat at the very heart of the UK's intelligence services. Even if Winter had nothing to do with Ryker's current mission, he remained a solid sounding board. And an even more solid source of information. The initial conversation was brief. Winter knew not to ask too many questions about a job that had nothing to do with him, because he knew Ryker wouldn't give him any clear answers.

Winter went away to gather what he could on Marshall.

Cindy too spent time on her phone. Quiet one-sided conversations, as though she didn't want Ryker to hear exactly what she was talking about, or to whom.

After her latest call, she turned to Ryker, face ashen.

'Crawford's gone,' she said.

'Gone? We already knew he and his friends had run.'

'No. Not just run. He's out of the country. He must have had options nearby. The notice from the FBI didn't get out quickly enough. Crawford boarded a private jet in North Carolina not even an hour after I alerted the police. It landed in Cuba. I'm still waiting on confirmation of what happened when he got there but... it's believed he took another flight already, some-where else. Somewhere we can't directly trace him.'

'At least this all confirms he's definitely involved.'

'But involved in what, Ryker? We still don't know anything about—'

They were interrupted by their phones ringing. She turned away as she answered. Ryker took the call from Winter.

'I have something, but it's not much,' Winter said. 'Mar-shall's records are about as heavily restricted, ops details-redacted as yours would be.'

'Which means what?'

'Which means most likely he wasn't Delta Force. Something much more clandestine.'

'Not CIA either?'

'Not mainstream, no. You know how it is, Ryker. These groups get formed here, there, and everywhere to slip under the radar. Usually just for a few specific missions before they're disbanded so there's never too much of a trail left behind, not many questions asked.'

'Plausible deniability.'

'Exactly. It's the world you've operated in for years. Marshall... If this really is Caleb Marshall, you're up against someone as skilled, as deadly as you are. And I don't want you to be flattered by that. I mean that as a warning.'

'I got it.'

'This man... the profile SIS have of him... He was never our asset, never worked on anything cross-agency with us, but we knew of him and he was categorized as a level seven operative.' On a seven tier rating. The level designating a combination of factors but ultimately denoting how much of a risk the asset was to the organization, based on a combination of their abili-ties, their perceived allegiances, and their mental state. 'Even you never made it past level five. We're talking about a man who, even when he was a protected asset for the US government, was considered borderline sociopathic and a major security risk.'

'Based on my interaction with him, he's well and truly moved past that border now.'

'Don't take this man lightly, Ryker.'

'I won't.'

Ryker ended the call. He knew Cindy was staring at him.

'What did you find out?' she asked, when he didn't say anything.

'Nothing that I didn't already know. Marshall is dangerous. Very dangerous. Cindy... if you want to step aside now... you should. You're already suspended, and—'

'I just spoke to Meg.'

That made Ryker pause.

'And?'

'And she has something to show us. Something big.'

* * *

Ryker hadn't seen Meg for a few days, and even if she remained bedbound in hospital she was definitely brighter, more with it, than the last time he'd been there. Even despite the look of concern on her face when Ryker and Cindy walked into the room.

'Couldn't keep away from work, huh?' Ryker said, indicating the laptop by her bedside.

'You think I'd just let these people carry on after what they did to me?' she replied. 'After what they've done to you two?'

Cindy hugged her ex-sister-in-law and the two of them

exchanged a couple of whispers before Cindy and Ryker took a seat.

'It works both ways,' Cindy said to Ryker, as if he needed an explanation of what they were doing here. 'I've always been willing to act as a source to Meg, reveal what I can about investigations at the GBI. In return...'

'I have quite a bank of sources myself,' Meg said. 'From all over, really. Police, FBI, government and business insiders. Just straight-up snitches sometimes.'

'I get it,' Ryker said. 'While we've been away you've been busy digging into dark corners wherever you can. Why don't you just tell us what you've found.'

But Meg didn't make a move for her laptop, where Ryker sensed the answers she was about to reveal lay, instead holding his eye, studying him.

'I heard about what happened in Asheville,' she said.

'Of course you did.'

'And that it was Caleb Marshall who...'

'Nearly killed me. You know of Marshall?'

'I've heard of him. Didn't know much. Now I know a bit more. You know... they say he doesn't feel any pain. That his nervous system was so badly damaged in the fire that he literally feels nothing. The one interview snippet I've read about him, a quote attributed to him, although maybe it was out of context or something, I really don't know for sure, but...'

'What?'

'I was never like everyone else. Now I'm even further from normal. I didn't ask for this, I definitely didn't want it. You could say I have a superpower now. It's too early to know what it means for me. Maybe in time I'll be thought of as a superhero. But so far... I feel anything but accepted. By anyone. Anywhere. So maybe... it'll go the opposite way for me.'

Ryker said nothing in return to the memorized statement. Cindy picked up the laptop and handed it to Meg.

'Show us what you found,' she said.

'It's about Crawford,' Meg said, as she typed away. 'Cindy mentioned there were questions over the attacks, about suspicious trading patterns for the companies involved. Bob Ferrer's company too.'

'Actually, it was data related to Bob Ferrer's company that initiated this lead,' Cindy said. 'Short selling of the company stock.'

'But it definitely looks like the same thing happened with KDD Tech and Industrial Control Logistics. I have a source at the SEC who has access to all kinds of trading data, and I got him to look back over the last twelve months at all big stock movements across major indices, to see if there were any other spikes in activity like this. And there were. Eight companies in total where short sellers took up massive positions in the weeks before big drops in the company stock prices.'

She turned the screen for Ryker to see. He moved closer, stared at the numbers, but it didn't mean much without context.

'Trades on this scale leave a paper trail, and there's nothing definitive yet because that paper trail is so complex, and from what I've been told no one is yet investigating this as a singularity, but... I can tell you one thing. In every single case, there are entities involved, offshore LLCs, that my source believes are connected to Bryan Tucker Crawford.'

'It's what you said, Ryker,' Cindy added. 'Crawford isn't just involved here. He's profiting from it all.'

'You said these entities are linked to him?'

'It's a minefield of data,' Meg said, 'so the links are there, but right now it's hard to say for sure exactly how much of the gains would directly benefit him because he has such a complex and secretive corporate structure, a lot of it in offshore tax havens. But... from the calculations I've seen, if you assumed the total gains from these transactions were for Crawford's benefit? You're talking about nearly five hundred billion dollars.'

Cindy, wide-eyed, looked at Ryker for a response. He didn't give one.

'Crawford hasn't just benefited from the attacks,' she said to him. 'Right now, he's potentially one of the richest and most powerful men on this planet.'

Ryker still said nothing.

'You look angry,' Meg said. 'I thought you'd be... more impressed.'

'I am impressed. I am angry. We had him in our sights. Now... who knows where he's fled to.'

'What are you thinking, though?' Cindy said. 'You were saying before that you thought those attacks were just to conceal something bigger. Stealing data, right? But maybe this really is only about money, and the power that that money gives him.'

'No,' Ryker said. 'Actually, this only takes me even further the other way. He's not done this to make himself the richest man in the world. He's done it to make him, and his group, more powerful. More unstoppable.'

'Powerful enough to do what?'

'Powerful enough to do whatever the hell he wants.'

'Did you hear about the riots last night in Ohio? Kentucky too?' Meg asked.

Yeah, Ryker had seen the news headlines. The protests that had started in the south were spreading, becoming larger, angrier. Tens of thousands of far-right protesters had taken to the streets in two new cities, the culmination of several months of heightening tensions across the country, as angry rhetoric became the norm, particularly across social media. Both those protests had turned violent, hundreds injured, when confronted by a combination of police and counter-protestors. The more blood was shed, the more impetus it gave the groups spurring on the anti-government, white nationalist movement.

'You think this is linked?' Cindy asked Ryker. 'Given that we were looking at these people in the first place because of their links to the White Lions?'

'I've no doubt at all that it's linked,' Ryker said. 'Just look at how well-funded they are now.'

'But what are they aiming for here?' Meg asked, sounding frustrated with his lack of elaboration. 'A coup? Could that really be possible?'

'For the richest man in the world? It's possible,' Ryker said. 'But I still don't believe this is just about funding a rebellion. There's more to KDD Tech and Industrial Control Logistics than just raising money to support protests, an armed insurrection even.'

'But you're still only basing that on a hunch,' Cindy said.

'A hunch. Experience. And based off having met Caleb Marshall in person. Whatever the end goal for these people, with someone like him in the ranks... there are no boundaries.'

'Then what do we do?'

'We find them. No more playing nice. We find them my way, and we figure out what they're planning. And... I've got a pretty good idea of where to start.'

23

Most people in the country had probably heard of Elgin Air Force Base, located on the Florida Panhandle. A lot of people might not have realized the base itself was right on the Gulf Coast, and close to many of the Panhandle's most renowned tourist spots. The airfields themselves covered a relatively small area on Choctawhatchee Bay, the commercial Destin-Fort Walton Beach Airport right next to it, and tourist hotels and condos within earshot of the often ferocious-sounding jets.

What many people who'd never been to the area didn't realize was that the base itself wasn't just contained within the airfields on the coast but comprised over 300,000 acres of land that the War Department had taken control of from the US Forest Service in 1940. Ride along some of the more scenic routes out of the area, such as the FL-20, and for mile after mile there were warning signs on the roadside informing hikers and others to not stray from designated paths because of nearby live-fire ranges that took up swaths of the Choctawhatchee National Forest. But it wasn't just live-fire ranges among the dense trees. In more modern times some of the most advanced research and testing centers in the entire world were based within this stretch of land, from the 96th Test Wing, responsible for test and evaluation of air-delivered weapons, navigation and guidance systems, and command and control systems, to centers responsible for research and development of advanced technologies, cyber-security, and biochemical weapons.

The US Special Operations Command also had a large presence in the area, which is how I'd come to know the place so well in the past.

I knew the long, straight roads here well, and even hidden in the back of the armored personnel carrier I could imagine the terrain outside. The tree-lined road. The signs at the sporadic entrances indicating what military site lay hidden beyond but which often really told little, usually just a bland collection of letters and numbers to hide the true significance.

I'd been in the back of the truck for nearly an hour before we came to a stop at what I knew was the entrance to Gate 4B of the Air Force Research Laboratory Munitions Directorate.

Up front in the truck were two US Army staff. Corporal Alessi and Lieutenant Damsgard. I knew Alessi, in the passenger seat, better than Damsgard. Well, actually I'd known his father even better. We'd worked a couple of missions together in Central Asia and in the Middle East. In fact, I'd worked alongside him on his very last mission, in northern Pakistan. A group of seven of us, a mixed bag from various special forces detachments, had been tasked with infiltrating a bunker network in the unforgiving and deathly Hindu Kush mountains to retrieve – dead or alive – a senior Al-Qaeda leader who'd been responsible for several massacres.

We found him. Alessi Sr. killed him. Possibly an unavoidable death, if truth be told, but in the heat of a fierce battle it had turned out to be easier that way. What wasn't so easy was our retreat from the bunkers and to the extraction point some five miles away.

I was the only one of the seven to make it back alive.

Three of the team never even made it out of the bunkers and were buried in there when booby-trap explosives detonated during our escape. The rest of us trekked across the rocky terrain to the extraction point but we were ambushed at various points before we got there. With less than half a mile to go it was only me and Alessi remaining.

He fought bravely, but we were simply overwhelmed.

I got out of there alive. Alessi Sr. was captured. His naked, mutilated body was put on display in a local town three days later while I ate comforting meals and drank beer back at an Army base in Kabul.

Alessi Jr. was only ten years old then. I made a point of meeting with him when I returned to the States. I told him how much of a hero his dad was. Told him there was simply nothing more I could have done to save him...

I couldn't exactly say otherwise.

Over the years, I kept in touch with him. He joined the Army as soon as he could. It was all he'd ever wanted to do. To make his dad proud.

But he'd been burned like many soldiers. Metaphorically speaking, that is. More recently he'd become a cynic. Not only because of what had happened to me, but because of what he'd seen happen to so many of his colleagues over the years. Friends sent on suicide missions overseas for what benefit to people on US soil, injured colleagues kicked out and forgotten about. And then came the post-army troubles. Unemployment and bankruptcy. Failed marriages. PTSD left untreated. Alcoholism, drug abuse and even suicide of people he'd fought side-by-side with.

He didn't know exactly why he was helping me today. But he was helping me still.

As for Damsgard... She was technically Alessi's senior. A commissioned officer. I don't think the two of them had ever served anywhere overseas together, but the quite simple reason they were in this together today was because they were having an affair.

Damsgard was married to a chef in New Jersey, but the beefy Alessi Jr.'s brawn was apparently too much to say no to. They'd been screwing for nearly a year and even though she should have held sway over Alessi given her rank, I knew that she'd been easily persuaded into this today because she was simply madly in love with him. I hadn't even needed to threaten to expose her secret, which likely would have cost her both her job and her marriage.

Perhaps she just knew that anyway.

I couldn't make out the full conversation that took place at the driver's window as we waited at the gate, but I knew how it'd go. The guard would be checking Alessi and Damsgard's credentials and scrutinizing the paperwork they'd brought with them. But the paperwork was irrefutable, signed off by General Pettier himself. It didn't matter that the General was dead. The paperwork pre-dated that incident, and most likely the guy on the gate wouldn't even know of the death of a general who'd lived hundreds of miles away and probably hadn't been here for years. But he would obey the command. A basic command, really. Alessi and Damsgard had been sent to collect a package. Simple as that.

Soon the engine rumbled, and we were moving once more. A minute passed, two, as we traveled along the long entrance road, designed specifically to ensure that any and all of the buildings ahead of us remained unseen from the public road.

Satellite images of these sites were scrubbed clean too, showing nothing but fields and forests. Quite different to the extensive structures that existed in reality.

The engine shut down. I heard two doors open and close. Then the double doors at the back of the truck opened. The wood panel directly above me popped off and light barreled in and I was staring up at Alessi who looked pretty damn pleased with himself.

'Simple,' he said.

'Just like I said it would be.'

I got out of the hole and moved to the back of the truck and jumped down onto the dirt ground. People roamed here and there, the thrum of engines and machinery filled the air, but I didn't feel nervous here at all, not like I was an imposter.

Damsgard stood, hands on hips, big aviators covering most of her face.

'So what now?' she asked.

'Alessi, wait here,' I said to him. 'Only two soldiers came in on this truck. Only two should go inside.'

'But we're not taking this truck back, you said,' Alessi countered.

'No, we're not,' I replied with a grin.

'Then what are we taking back?' Damsgard asked.

'You'll see.' I winked at her before moving for the warehouse in front of us.

* * *

Twenty-five minutes later and we'd navigated past two guard posts, broken in through another door to take us from D-wing to C-wing, and used the keycard I'd 'arranged' before today to gain access to the warehouse designated as F1B.

There we found the personnel carrier I'd come for. At least, from the outside it looked like a personnel carrier. Pretty much the same as the one we'd arrived in, except the back of this one had been kitted out into a sophisticated mobile command center with screens and gizmos that'd make a technology geek drool.

'Jesus fucking Christ,' Damsgard said as she stared at the inside. 'What is this?'

'If you don't already know, probably best that you don't.'

'And you're... stealing this thing?' she asked.

'We are.'

She huffed, obviously not liking the answer, but she was in too deep now to turn back.

I heaved open the warehouse doors enough to slide the vehicle inside. I closed the doors behind us and drove on to the truck where Alessi, looking more nervy than before, jumped into the back.

He whistled as he looked around at the equipment that he likely had no clue how to operate.

'Shit,' was all he said.

'Yeah,' Damsgard responded, turning to give him a scathing look, as though pissed off that he hadn't told her something.

'Swap the plates over, then let's get out of here,' I said to them.

It didn't take long.

I moved into the back, out of sight. Damsgard took over. I directed her to access gate 2D a few miles away so we wouldn't have to pass by the same guard again on the way out.

We had no problem exiting.

'And what the hell do we do with this thing now?' Damsgard asked as we returned to the public road.

'I take it with me. Head back to where we left your car

earlier, I'll leave you both there. Your money too. You've done your part.'

Damsgard didn't question that and didn't need any help from me in retracing steps to the secluded spot on the edge of the forest.

Each of us got out of the vehicle. I moved around to the front to find Damsgard whispering something into her screw-boy's ear.

'Everything OK?' I asked.

She moved her hand to her hip as she turned to me.

'It's just that—' Alessi started.

But didn't finish. Because I'd already pulled the handgun from my side. I shot Damsgard first. A single pull of the trigger. The bullet splatted through her face, just below her right eye.

As her body fell Alessi had just enough time to cower and throw an arm up, and it did save him at first because my initial shot in his direction caught him on the shoulder and sent him stumbling back.

'No, no! Wait!' he shouted.

The second bullet hit him under the chin as he tried to duck or twist away or something.

He ended up on his back in the dirt, blood gushing out of the hole in his neck.

He gargled as I stood over him, trying but unable to speak.

'Thank you for your service,' I said to him with a salute, before putting him out of his misery.

I stood a moment and sighed in quiet contemplation.

I knew as soon as Damsgard got a whiff of what we were taking that she'd get jittery.

Despite what I'd told the boy years ago, Alessi Sr. had been no hero. He'd been an idiot who I blamed for the deaths of the other people on our mission in Hindu Kush. If it hadn't been for his mistakes that day, I may have tried harder to save his life.

His son... Not even a chip off the old block. Nowhere near as talented as his father and that was saying something. Alessi Jr. was just a nobody who hadn't been able to hack the pressure of the job, so came up with grievances and excuses about everyone else. The Army was better off without him.

As for Damsgard...

I didn't know much about her really, in all honesty. Perhaps she was a good person, a good soldier. Except she'd been cheating on her husband for the best part of a year, so I couldn't fathom how the former could be true.

Really it'd only been a question of when I would have to dispatch them both, not if.

The trauma, the guilt of Damsgard's affair, may just explain why her and her lover ended up dead in her car in a forest in Florida. A murder suicide, perhaps. Or the husband getting revenge on them both.

I placed both bodies in the car, placed the gun in Damsgard's grip before firing a shot out into the woods to put some gunpowder residue on her skin.

Then I left the lovers there as I drove away.

Perhaps the scene would fool someone, perhaps their deaths would somehow immediately be linked to me, despite all the work I'd put into the planning.

Honestly, it didn't matter that much to me now, as I finally had everything I needed.

With a wide smile on my face – so wide that it tugged awkwardly at the seams of my mask, pinching the eyeholes and hampering my vision – I took out my phone to call Kielder.

24

More than one car was on the driveway when Ryker and Cindy arrived at the Hannigan residence. Ryker recognized the truck there as the same one Kyle Hannigan had arrived in on Ryker's first visit to the property. And it was Kyle who greeted them both at the door, before they'd even knocked.

Greeted being a very optimistic way of describing his introduction.

'What the fuck are you doing here?' he asked, basically blocking the doorway, arms folded, chest puffed out.

'Looking for your father.'

Kyle shook his head. 'There's been a lot of shit happening around here since you turned up.'

'Tell me about it. That's why I need to speak to your dad. Remember, he's the one who's paying me to be here.'

'You think? You're still going down that path?'

'Then what do you think's happening here?' Ryker asked. 'Because it seems to me maybe you know a lot more than someone in your position should about what's going on with your sister, about people like Bryan Tucker Crawford? Caleb Marshall?'

'My position?' was Kyle's pathetic response – signaling his offense, rather than any kind of question over the two names Ryker had just dropped.

'OK, OK,' came a voice from inside, and a sheepish-looking Adam Hannigan wandered up beside his son who remained in the doorway. 'If you'd called ahead—'

'Then you would have had time to prepare a more welcoming welcome?' Ryker suggested.

Hannigan slapped his hand onto his son's shoulder. 'Yeah. I may have had a chance to pull this one down from his high horse.'

He tugged on Kyle's shoulder and the kid soon backed down, but not without a huff.

'Come in,' Hannigan said. 'Kyle, go and... take a swim or something.'

'I want to hear what he's got to say.'

'And I told you to give us some space for a few minutes.'

There was only a brief stand-off between the two men before the younger saw sense and disappeared off out the back of the house, slamming the door as he went.

'Your wife home?' Ryker asked.

'She's upstairs. When I saw it was you... I think it's better we speak alone. Given the sensitivities.'

He looked at Cindy as he said that.

'This is Cindy Valentino,' Ryker said. 'You probably saw her with me in Asheville.'

No 'probably' about it really, because Hannigan definitely had, and no doubt knew exactly who she was by now, so Ryker didn't bother to expand on the introduction. The two shook hands briefly, both looking more than a little uncomfortable, but no words were shared. Hannigan showed them through to the kitchen where Cindy and Ryker sat at the breakfast bar while Hannigan messed with his coffee machine.

'You haven't asked how we're getting on,' Ryker said. 'In finding your daughter.'

Hannigan glanced over his shoulder but continued to use his fake busyness as a means to delay engaging.

'I assumed you'd come here to tell me about that.'

'Unfortunately, we've nothing to tell. You also haven't asked me anything about what happened in Asheville. How your party was spoiled.'

'My party?'

'Do you want me to tell you what happened there? Or do you already know all the details?'

Hannigan turned around properly now to face Ryker, a more hostile and confident air about him.

'Every news outlet across the country has covered the story in some detail,' Hannigan said. 'Every douche with a TV knows about it.'

'They know what's been reported, yeah.'

'Why would I know any details over and above what's been reported?'

'Indeed. So let me fill you in. We went there to observe Crawford, which I think you know anyway based on our last conversation. And it's just as well we chose to do that, because he brought a few of his crew for protection. Protection from me, I think. Anyway, it didn't quite go to plan, as both Cindy and I were ambushed. She was tied up by three men and beaten and threatened with a bullet to the head. I was attacked and cuffed in my car and drugged, and was on the cusp of being cut into pieces by a madman. Until Cindy managed to fight off her captors and come to my aid. At which point said madman fled, along with his accomplices, who included Crawford, Kielder, Meyers. The names you've probably seen in the news. The name you probably didn't see in the news was that of the madman himself. Caleb Marshall.'

Ryker finished his little monologue and studied Hannigan's reaction. The biggest tell of all was that he basically gave no reaction.

'You know who Marshall is, don't you?' Ryker asked.

'Yes.'

'And you'd also already heard he was with the others in Asheville?'

'Yes.'

'Did you know before then that he was part of this group?'

'Yes. But—'

'Have you spoken to Klein recently?'

No answer to that.

'I haven't,' Ryker said. 'I've tried, but he's not taking my calls anymore. And I think it's most likely because the cat is out of the bag, so to speak.'

'You've lost me,' Hannigan said.

'No. I haven't. Was I brought here to find your daughter? Or to stop Caleb Marshall?'

A pause this time before he answered. 'To find Abby. To stop more attacks like the one in Atlanta.'

'To stop more attacks orchestrated by Caleb Marshall, you mean.'

Hannigan kind of winced at the comment.

'You know, I could just get on a flight today,' Ryker said. 'Get out of the country and go take a break on a lake in Italy or something. I don't like being misled. I'm not an asset who has to follow cloaked orders. I can help, if that's what you want. But let's not pretend anymore. I want to know why I'm really here, who Caleb Marshall is, what he's planning. I want to know everything you know.'

Hannigan sighed and huffed and gave a pretty cheap theatrical performance as he determined whether he'd reveal his hand or not. Ryker didn't bother to put any real pressure on. He didn't need to. If these people wanted his help they'd only get it now by telling him the truth.

'Let me just explain what I do and don't know,' Hannigan said. 'There was no big deceit here, certainly not from me. You've seen what's happening on the streets in this country. We're at a tipping point. People voted in this new government in the hope it'd bring back something they thought they'd lost. Whiteness, American culture, whatever that is. The opposite has happened. Many people are suffering, certainly financially, now more than ever, and hostilities are growing all the time. Not just to immigrants and non-whites anymore, but directly toward the current government.'

'Hannigan, spare me your next campaign speech, please.'

Hannigan huffed, looked pissed off by Ryker's interruption, and took a couple of moments to recompose himself.

'Under the last president I was in the inner circle. I think I probably knew as much as he did about... everything. It's not the same now. Even if the same party is in charge, my day-to-day life isn't national security anymore. But that doesn't mean I don't... get to hear things. If I ask the right questions, I still have ways of getting answers.'

'You're blathering,' Ryker said. 'Just tell me about Marshall.'

'I had no idea Marshall was involved in anything until a few days ago, when you were already here. And that's the truth.'

'But others knew? Klein?'

'I can't speak for others. But I do know who Marshall is. And not just from the story of what happened to him. I knew him from my role as National Security Adviser. I sanctioned some of his missions. This man...'

'What?'

'Let's just say it makes more sense to me now that someone like you was brought here to help. And I don't mean that as a compliment.'

'You're saying Klein always knew about Marshall?'

'I already said, you'd have to ask him.'

'And how does Abby, her disappearance, fit into all this?'

A short pause. 'If I knew that, I wouldn't need you here, would I?'

Ryker mulled the lackluster response. Decided against pushing back on it. He felt there were greater concerns right now.

'Who's in charge of this group?' he asked. 'Crawford or Marshall?'

'I've no clue. Until you came to me the other day, I didn't know Crawford was involved either. This is as fluid for me as it is for you, Ryker. I've never lied to you.'

'But I'm sensing you have withheld.'

'Did you know that Crawford has been raking in billions from his involvement in the attacks?' Cindy asked.

'What?' Hannigan said, face all twisted – disgust more than anything else.

'It's true,' Ryker said. 'But I have no doubt that this doesn't boil down to money. Not for Marshall, at least. And it's not only about growing the protest movement. It boils down to whatever he stole from KDD Tech, and Industrial Control Logistics.'

Hannigan sighed and slumped, losing a couple of inches in the process. Again, it was such an obvious tell, like he'd been found out and just didn't have the energy to hold out anymore.

'Ryker, I didn't know what was going on. Please believe me, I really didn't know.'

'Didn't know what? What is Marshall after?'

'It's no longer a question of what is he after,' Hannigan said. 'It's much worse than that. It's what does he already have.'

'And the answer is?'

'Everything. Control over everything.'

The way Hannigan said that, the distress... A sickly feeling bubbled in Ryker's stomach.

'You'll have to explain that one to me,' Ryker said.

'The US military has been the most advanced in the world for decades, right?'

'Right.'

'And we always strive to stay several steps ahead. It won't surprise someone like you to know we do that both organically through our own research and... less organically.'

'Spying. Stealing intel, you mean?' Cindy asked. Ryker hadn't bothered because the answer seemed pretty obvious. And Hannigan didn't directly respond either.

'A few years ago,' he said, 'we got intel on a digital-based, highly secure system for controlling military hardware that the Russians were developing. Much more advanced than what we were using. In essence, it'd allow for near total remote control of all modern warheads, from missile silos here and overseas, to munitions on jets, warships, submarines. Like one giant goddamn computer game. But it's not just as simple as putting a chip in every explosive and having it all hooked up to the World Wide Web. It needs careful, precise, detailed planning, programing, security. We... couldn't allow the Russians to get a head start on something so advanced... and so...'

'You sent in Marshall to sabotage it?' Ryker suggested.

'Not just Marshall. This wasn't just one mission, one person, but he was involved. Heavily. We... removed a lot of the know-how from the Russian side, brought what we could over here. And... for the last several years we've developed it, made it fit for purpose. Tested it. Started to roll it out.'

'What exactly are we talking about here?' Cindy asked. 'What has Marshall got?'

'Two... programs, is the best way to describe them. Exodus is... a giant safety net. Next-generation encryption to make sure the system can't be tampered with from outside. I'm no expert, but I've been told there's no technology that exists that could decipher it because it works on an ever-changing cycle. Think of it like... During World War II, you heard of Enigma?'

'The German encryption machine,' Ryker said.

'Revolutionary for its time. Quite simple to us now, but it was a cipher that used a constantly changing key. Exodus works off a similar principle but on another scale entirely. There's simply no way to break through it. At least... not without having the coding itself.'

'KDD Tech,' Ryker said, putting some of the pieces together. 'They were responsible for developing Exodus.'

'It's not quite as simple as that. No single company, no single set of people developed or controlled it, because the whole point about this system is that it needed to be so secretive. But...'

'But Marshall has it,' Ryker said. 'Marshall has the Exodus program now? Or at least a copy of it.'

'Apparently so.'

'But you said Exodus was just a safety net?' Cindy said.

Hannigan sighed. 'I'm sorry, I'm trying to explain as best I can. Exodus... Yes, it's the safety net. It's also the pathway. Exodus includes the launch codes for every single weapon attached to the system.'

Cindy gasped. Ryker remained more steadfast, even if the

ramifications of what he was learning were abundantly clear. 'So right now Marshall can launch any weapon linked to the system?' Cindy asked. 'Is that what you're saying.'

'No. Thankfully, no,' Hannigan said. 'It's more complex than that. That's where Orion comes in.'

'Which I'm hoping you're not going to tell me is what he stole from Industrial Control Logistics.'

Hannigan didn't answer. Ryker sat back and sighed. He felt exasperated more than anything.

'Orion is the software that encapsulates Exodus and allows it to run. It connects the launch codes and the encryption keys with the physical items through the most sophisticated satellite technology we have. It—'

'But Marshall has that too,' Cindy said. 'So he has everything he needs—'

'Not quite everything.'

'Go on,' Ryker said.

'Like I said before, this doesn't just work off a laptop connected to the World Wide Web. There still needs to be compatible hardware to run the two systems together, in a live environment. Hardware that's specifically built for purpose. And that hardware only exists in a few select locations.'

'Are you going to tell me those locations?' Ryker asked.

'I honestly don't know them all. Only the current National Security Council would have access to that information, and even within that group it'd be a very select group of people who'd know the full details. But think of the obvious.'

'The White House? Air Force One?'

'Yes. And select military bases. Those places among others. Anywhere we could get the president, or at the very least a senior chain of command, in the event of an emergency.'

Ryker shook his head, lost for words.

'I didn't know this was happening, Ryker,' Hannigan said. 'When KDD Tech was attacked, I don't believe anyone knew where we were headed. Perhaps Klein, others always knew about Marshall's involvement, but... this isn't your average new piece of technology here. The secrecy that went into development... until the pieces started to be put together over the last couple of days, probably not a single person anywhere, not even the president himself, knew all the details of which companies did what and why, and how they all fitted in.'

'It seems like Marshall knew,' Ryker said.

Hannigan winced at that. 'As I already explained, he has quite a head start on most of us. Given his prior work. But believe me, I didn't know what KDD Tech did. I didn't know what Industrial Control Logistics did—'

'You don't need to keep trying to convince me,' Ryker said. 'You need to tell me what can be done.'

'We have to find Marshall. Find the rest of them. It's the only way. Find them before they get the hardware they need. Behind the scenes we're already on high alert, but I imagine it'll take time for the seriousness to filter through from the top without setting about a widespread panic, and without revealing too much about the system to people who don't need to know about it.'

'Are you serious?' Cindy asked. 'This is being kept under wraps to... what? Save face?'

'That's not what I said. I'm saying, from what I've heard from the White House, things are happening behind the scenes to try to minimize risk. Every warhead that's attached to the system can be removed from it, for example. But it's a manual, physical on-site process for every single item, and we're talking about tens of thousands of warheads, spread all across the world.'

'And until then... what?' Cindy asked. 'Everyone in the country, in the world, just carries on as normal? No warnings from the government that at any moment a nuclear warhead could be launched against one of our own cities?'

She was angry. She had every right to be.

'You think widespread panic is going to help this situation?' Hannigan said.

'I think firmer action, a lot sooner, would have helped,' Ryker said.

'Perhaps,' Hannigan said. 'But you're talking to the wrong person about that. I'm Governor of Georgia now. You want to complain about the current process? Take it up with my successor and the rest of them in DC. I already explained, no one knew this was where we were heading. Not until it was too late. But... I know Marshall... Whatever his next step is, I highly doubt that widespread death and destruction is his primary intention.'

Ryker stood up. Cindy did too.

'Unfortunately, Hannigan, right now, I think you haven't got a fucking clue what his primary intention is. And that should scare the shit out of you. Because it certainly does for me.'

25

Cindy and Ryker didn't talk for a long while as he drove them north, a destination in his mind, even if he felt that whatever he did next was perhaps too little too late.

'I can't believe this is real,' Cindy said, scrolling across her phone screen. 'There's just... nothing about this anywhere, not even rumors or conspiracy theories. Nothing except for the hunt for Crawford and Kielder, but even that is eclipsed in the news by all the ridiculous riots everywhere.'

'It makes some sense,' Ryker said.

'Does it?'

'Some. But not a lot. We have to believe that widespread destruction with no other purpose isn't the intent here.'

'Hope,' Cindy said. 'We have to hope that.'

'So these people... despite the power at their hands. They still must want something else.'

'What, Ryker? What the hell do they want?'

'It's almost irrelevant now. The point is it gives us time. Gives everyone, every police officer and agent who's out there looking for them time.'

'Goddamn it!' Cindy said, slapping the dash with her palm.

'What?'

'We had them! We had them in Asheville and if we'd just had... more help. More information, even. It would have all been over now.'

Ryker had thought the same thing. The opportunities had been there all along. If only he'd known the stakes sooner, he may have acted differently himself. If only agencies had been more connected... But that was an age-old story in his world.

'I should call my boss,' Cindy said. 'I need to know—'

'There's no point,' Ryker said. 'You're suspended. They're not bringing you back in now. And they may not even know the full story—'

'Then they need to!'

'You want my opinion? Trust the process. Trust that the people who know the truth are doing what they need to do, even if we can't see it.'

'Trust? You're actually telling me you think anyone has this under control right now?'

He thought about that before answering. 'No. Perhaps not. But calling your boss, asking for information, asking to be involved in whatever, isn't going to alter the landscape either. Right now, let's just keep moving forward.'

'But where are we even going?' Cindy asked.

'The key players are all on the run. But perhaps not everyone. We need to work our way from the bottom, back up again.'

A seemingly simple task, but a frustrating couple of hours followed as Ryker and Cindy worked their way across the north Atlanta metro area. Ryker had several addresses to check in on, from Gabriella Stricken to Wayne Stanton. But they didn't find any of those people, and as time wore on, the nervousness in the car only ramped up.

'We're achieving nothing here,' Cindy said, as Ryker took them through Canton, past the Roadhouse bar where he initially slowed, weighing whether to go inside, before moving on. 'Are you listening to me?'

'I'm listening, but right now I'm not sure what else to do. We'll find one of them. I'm confident of that.'

'One of the low-key hangers-on, perhaps. But it was only a couple of days ago you wanted to move away from these people because they were too far removed.'

'I know that.'

And he felt her reservations too, but he'd exhaust this route first before they moved on. Because they really had nothing else to go on.

After the next junction he again slowed the car, allowed a small smile to spread.

'See,' he said, nodding over at the parking lot to Missy's Gentlemen's Bar.

'You want to go see a strip show?'

'No. But I do want to see who's inside. Because that Toyota Corolla belongs to Gabriella Stricken. And the Ram truck? Wayne Stanton.'

'Shit.'

'Yep.'

He parked and they got out and both scoped out the area as they walked toward the closed doors at the front.

'Doesn't open until nine,' Cindy said.

'Probably a good thing. Less chance of members of the public becoming involved.'

'Involved in what?'

Ryker didn't answer. They reached the doors. He tried the handle. Locked. He looked up at the roofline where a camera pointed down at him. He looked back at the door...

Then he took out his gun and pulled the trigger. The lock obliterated and he thudded his shoulder into the door to push it open before charging in.

Shock on the faces of the three people inside the brightly lit space. A woman behind the bar. Stricken at a table playing on her phone. Stanton on his knees on a stage messing with wiring...

Ryker locked eyes with Stanton. The guy hesitated for only a moment before he shot up and bolted away.

'Ryker!' Cindy shouted in warning, but he already knew why.

Even if the barwoman remained frozen, Stricken was making a move, reaching into her purse. Ryker ducked and swiveled his gun that way but—

Bang.

Cindy shot first. Stricken screamed as the bullet tore through her hand.

'Get him!' she shouted, and Ryker set off after Stanton.

He jumped up onto the stage. Nearly lost his footing on the slippery surface. He slammed through the partly open door at the back that Stanton had run through...

A corridor. No sign of Stanton. Several doors off of it. An exit at the back.

'Don't make this harder!' Ryker shouted, slowing and reaffirming his grip on his gun. 'I'm not here to hurt you. You just need to take me to Kielder. To Marshall.'

A bellowing roar came as Ryker neared the open doorway on his left. He ducked and the baseball bat smashed into the wall by him, a ferocious shot that sent drywall debris and wood splinters into the air. A shot which also resulted in the bat becoming wedged in a crevice of its own making.

Ryker stooped and drove forward and took Stanton from his

feet and thumped him onto the ground. He reached down and hammered his fist where he knew Stanton's previous gunshot wound would still be tender and healing.

Stanton yelled in pain until Ryker dropped forward to smother his mouth. He put pressure on his neck too. Not so much as to choke him completely, but enough to let him know he was in serious trouble.

'You want to die right here?' Ryker said into his ear.

Stanton merely squirmed and writhed, trying to get Ryker off him. Although he couldn't really talk anyway, given Ryker's position.

'Do you want to die?' Ryker asked again, and this time he uncovered Stanton's mouth just a little, but he didn't get the response he was after.

'Fuck y—!' Stanton yelled.

A fist to his side stopped him completing the insult.

'I'll ask you one more time—'

'No!' Stanton shouted. 'No. I don't want to die.'

Ryker lifted off him and hauled Stanton up and pushed him up against the wall, twisting his right arm behind him into a hammerlock. Ryker patted him down. No weapons. Probably left those in his truck.

'Tell me where I can find them,' Ryker said.

'I don't know!' Stanton said, grimacing from the pain of his arm, pushed to bursting point.

'Are we good here?' Cindy said from behind. Ryker turned to see her with Stricken. Blood dribbled from Stricken's lip, her hands were clasped – cuffed – behind her. Blood from the gunshot wound in her hand dripped onto the floor. She looked mad but defeated.

'We're good. Wayne's about to tell us what we need to—'

'Fuck you!' the guy shouted out instead.

So Ryker let go of his arm and grabbed a finger and pulled back until it snapped.

Stanton yelled some more but didn't have much resistance now as Ryker retook him in a hammerlock.

'Tell us—'

'I know!' Stricken shouted out before whimpering, perhaps at the sight of Stanton's pain. 'At least... I know where they were. Just... Please don't hurt us.'

'That all depends on you,' Ryker said. 'You're both coming with us.'

* * *

The car was cramped with the four of them inside. Edgy, in many different ways. Quiet, really. Ryker only wanted one thing: to find Marshall and the others. He didn't care to know what else these two did or didn't know about what was happening.

'You're sure this is where they went after Newnan?' Ryker asked Stanton, who was in the passenger seat next to him.

'Yes.'

'You've been there with them?'

'No. But I know it's where they went.'

'And they're still there now?'

He didn't say anything.

'Hey, idiot – answer the question,' Cindy said, thumping the back of Stanton's seat.

'I have no idea.'

'I guess we'll soon find out,' Ryker added.

The old factory building in Douglasville looked seriously decrepit. Very quiet. Certainly no mini army here unless they'd all arrived on foot and were adept at hiding.

'I don't like this,' Cindy said, as Ryker rolled the car over the huge potholes in what was once a parking lot.

He knew what she meant but said nothing.

'You two stay here,' he said to her and Stricken, once he'd shut the engine down. 'Stanton, with me.'

Although Stanton hadn't moved by the time Ryker walked around the outside, and he dragged the guy out by the scruff of his neck and then shoved him forward, gun in hand, as they headed toward a large hole in the outer wall of the building.

'Doesn't exactly look the epicenter of anything,' Ryker said.

'I'm telling you, this is the place.'

'If you've wasted my time...'

They moved on through the hole in the wall. The inside of the building didn't look in any better shape than the outside. Perhaps worse even. Large pools of water lay on the ground in several places from last night's heavy rainfall. Drips echoed around the expanse as leftover water cascaded down the stricken structure from the failed roof.

'This is bullshit,' Ryker said, looking about the place. 'They'd need space for computers. This is—'

'I'm telling you, this is the place!' Stanton shouted, still cradling his broken finger.

Ryker was about to counter but spotted something in the corner of the space. Not much really, but signs of life at least where an interior wall had a somewhat shoddy looking structure – plastic sheeting, wooden boards – draped over the top.

He glared at Stanton who gave an I told you so look.

'Quiet,' Ryker said to him. 'Or I won't just shoot you dead. I'll break every other finger first.'

Stanton took the threat seriously and Ryker prodded him forward. They moved slowly, silently through the puddles and the debris to the corner. To a partially open door.

Ryker motioned for Stanton to step aside. Ryker used the barrel of the gun to push the door open several more inches to reveal the space beyond. The empty space beyond. At least, empty of people. The space was filled with computing equipment, hardware towers, screens, wires trailing all over, the hum of the machines filling the otherwise silent room.

'Shit,' Ryker said.

'Look, mister, I don't know—'

'Shh.' Stanton flinched, but Ryker had only held up a finger to quieten him down. His focus wasn't on Stanton. Not even on what he could see in the room he was standing in.

But on the noise outside.

Vehicles.

More than one and approaching quickly.

'Ryker!' Cindy said, running into the building.

Alone.

'Where's—'

'Screw Gabriella!' Cindy said. 'We need to get the hell out of here!'

The sound of the vehicles grew louder. Louder. No stopping.

Cindy raced toward Ryker. He spotted the beams of the headlights outside, bouncing, jostling, then blinding him as the first of the vehicles came into view through the hole in the wall. The vehicle didn't stop on the outside but raced on through.

'Cindy!'

She realized too and dove out of the way as the truck blasted past her.

'Get him!' Stanton shouted out. Not to the truck, but to behind Ryker.

He swiveled and spotted the figure launching toward him. He ducked and twisted and grabbed the shoulders of the person to slingshot them away from him. Stanton threw an elbow out that caught Ryker on the side of his head. Ryker bent down then exploded with an uppercut that caught Stanton under the chin and sent him flying, smacking down into a muddy puddle.

Ryker turned and was about to dive down onto the other attacker – a woman – but she pulled on his leg and he lost balance. He thought about trying to correct himself but instead dropped down with a thud and rolled over and smashed his elbow into soft tissue. Stomach. A big blow that knocked the wind out of her.

Ryker stared at the young woman's twisted face. Had half-expected... Actually, no, not quite. He'd fully hoped to see Abby Hannigan. But he didn't recognize this woman.

Gunshots filled the air, bullets tearing into the walls by Ryker.

He took a knee to the groin from the woman before he scrambled up, dragging the woman to cover behind a brick wall. She wrestled with him, trying to get out of his grip until he launched a fist into her side.

'You're not going anywhere.'

He checked his gun over. He had a few bullets left but no new magazine. He heard another vehicle come to a stop on the inside. Doors opened. He risked a peak, spotted Cindy. Her head, at least. She was out the other side of the building now, racing past a blown-out window toward his end. A hail of bullets was fired Ryker's way and he ducked down as brick fragments and dust filled the air around him.

The barrage was relentless, only momentary pauses every now and then. He stole another glimpse. No sign of Stanton now, he scurried back behind enemy lines. And the attackers weren't letting up, they were moving forward. Closer and closer.

Gunfire blasted from outside, toward the swath of shooters. Cindy, now at the far end of the building, a few yards past

Ryker. Her shooting provided the momentary distraction he needed.

He jumped up and dragged the woman with him into the open, firing at the attackers as he went, but moving in the opposite direction for the doorway at the very back of the building. His shooting, together with the woman trailing behind him would give him the cover he needed. He hoped. But then gunfire came his way once more. Bullets whizzed past him. One nicked his tricep, another was so close to his head that he felt the rush of air. He slung the woman forward through the opening and dove for the outside just as Cindy appeared there, firing back into the building to give him the last bit of cover he needed.

All three of them scrabbled to safety behind the wall, panting. The gunfire continued for a couple of seconds then paused.

'You OK?' Ryker asked Cindy.

'Who the hell is she?'

Neither the woman nor Ryker attempted to answer.

'You're shot,' Cindy said, nodding to the blood on Ryker's sleeve.

He shook his head. 'It's OK.'

'You think? There are four vehicles. Maybe a dozen shooters. How the hell did they know we were here?'

Despite the melee, Ryker had already asked himself the same question.

'She did it?' Cindy said, catching on to Ryker's thought.

The woman said nothing as she glared daggers at Cindy.

'Looks like your friends ain't so friendly with you,' Cindy said to her.

The woman still said nothing before another spray of gunfire came their way, but other than sending more dust onto them they were fine.

Cindy checked over her gun. 'I'm already out,' she said.

'Same.'

'Shit. Then what do we do?'

Another pause in the gunfire. A little longer this time. Engines grumbled to life and Ryker went to look around the doorway, but before he could see a thing more rounds of fire were sent his way.

'They're clearing out!' he shouted.

And when the next pause in gunfire came and he heard the engines fading away, he sensed they were already too late. He jumped up. Stuck his head out... A half-hearted volley of gunfire this time, from the far side of the building. A single shooter hanging out of the open window of a reversing truck. The bullets went harmlessly high and wide, and soon the shooter decided he'd had enough. The truck left the building, swung around and shot off out of sight.

'They're gone,' Cindy said, coming up to his side.

He didn't bother to ask who was gone. All of the shooters, yes. Stricken. Stanton. Yes. They were all gone.

He strode toward the makeshift room. The contents of which were gone too.

'They didn't come to kill us,' Ryker said. 'They came to protect their assets.'

He looked around at the woman who stood sheepishly between him and Cindy.

'Apparently you're not worth as much to them as those computers.'

The woman said nothing but her eyes diverted to the corner of the room, by the side of the one of the computer desks. A large handbag.

'Yours?' he asked her.

She didn't respond, but Ryker stepped over and kneeled and opened the bag to gaze inside. A load of... stuff. A laptop too.

Maybe not all was lost after all.

'We can still stop them,' Cindy said.

She rushed off. Ryker grabbed the bag and the woman's arm and went out after Cindy, knowing what she was planning, even though he felt it was already too late.

Outside, she slammed to a stop ten yards from their car.

Definitely too late. All four tires were slashed.

'I'll call it in,' she said, taking out her phone. 'We can get roadblocks. There were four vehicles in a convoy, someone'll pick them up... stop... them.'

She slumped as the last few words rolled out. She didn't make the call. Ryker wasn't sure it would have made a difference anyway, but he was curious what had caused her to stop.

'What is it?'

'It's...' She didn't finish as her finger swiped up the screen. 'A news alert.'

'What?'

'It's Kielder,' she said. Shouted, really. At him. Exasperation. Quite a lot of anger. 'It's Kielder. His group... They've made contact. They've finally announced what they want.'

'And?'

'And I think we're fucked.'

26

The office in nearby Newnan seemed as good a place as any to lay low in while they figured out what next. The GBI had already raided the place and likely found absolutely nothing, and probably wouldn't have any reason to come back anytime soon. It looked like BTC Capital on the top floor had been cleared out too, either by Crawford and his associates or by the authorities.

Quiet, empty. Until Ryker slung the young woman through the breached window and she rolled into a heap on the floor. He and Cindy followed in as the woman scuttled across the laminate and propped herself up against the wall.

Ryker studied her a few moments.

'What's your name?' he asked her.

No response.

'I'm James Ryker. This is Cindy Valentino with the GBI.'

A flicker of unease in the woman's eyes at the mention of the GBI.

'We're looking for Caleb Marshall. Terrence Kielder. Danny

Meyers. Brad Reed. Bryan Tucker Crawford. You know them, right?'

She didn't say anything.

Ryker looked around the room. 'I mean, this office building belongs to Crawford. You and your crew were based here until a few days ago.'

Still no answer.

'What's your name?' Cindy asked.

Nothing in response.

'Can we cut the bullshit?' Cindy said. 'Let's just jump several steps ahead here. We know what you've been up to. We know about Exodus, Orion—' a snide smile crept up the woman's face – pride, kind of '—and as of about an hour ago, the whole fucking world knows what your people are planning on doing with what they have.'

By which Cindy was referring to the video of Kielder that had been posted across social media sites not so long ago. A video in which Kielder had professed his love for his country, although a country and a culture he claimed was in decline. A video in which he'd called on every patriot in the country to rise up in support of his movement. A video in which he'd demanded the resignation of the president and his current administration. A video in which he'd given twelve hours for confirmation of that, before a direct attack on Washington DC and other major cities.

Even as they'd made their way from the factory in Douglasville to the office in Newnan, the ultimatum – fueled on the ground by others most likely being funded by the group – had led to an explosion of panic and protests in urban centers across the country.

'You have a little under eleven hours,' Ryker said. 'You can help stop this. Help stop more mindless violence.'

'Who says I want to stop anything?'

Cindy stomped over and slammed her foot down onto the woman's hand. She ground across the knuckles, several cracks erupting as the woman writhed and cried out in pain.

'Listen, bitch, we can do this the easy way or the hard way.'

Cindy's quick morph into badass surprised Ryker, but he did nothing to stop it.

'My... hand!' the woman screamed and Cindy lifted off. The woman pulled her mangled fingers close to her chest as tears rolled.

'Why don't we start with the basics,' Ryker said. 'Because you just saw what can happen in a few seconds. Imagine what we can do to you in eleven hours. And we will do what's needed. No one's coming to help you. And no one's coming to stop us.'

'Hailey!' the woman shouted. 'My name's Hailey Matthews.'

'That's a good start,' Ryker said. 'And the computer equipment in the factory... you were in charge of it?'

'Yes.'

'Can you expand on that?'

'You already know! Exodus, Orion. I was the one... who pulled it all together for them.'

'You and you alone?' Cindy asked.

Hailey didn't answer that.

But a thought struck Ryker.

He flitted through his phone, found the picture and showed it to Hailey.

'This is Abby Hannigan,' he said. 'She was helping you too?'

'Abby? That's... She's not called... That's Christine.'

Ryker and Cindy shared a look.

'Christine, Abby, whoever,' Ryker said. 'She was working on the programs with you?'

'She was supposed to be. But no one's seen her for days.'

'Because?'

'Because she disappeared! I've no idea what happened to her.'

Cindy went to move forward and Hailey cowered back. 'I'm not lying!' Hailey screamed in panic.

'Without you... Can they still run the programs?' Ryker asked.

Hailey slumped. 'Yes. Marshall pretty much knew anyway. I don't know how. He knows everything. But I set up our system that way. To give them direct control.'

'More like, they set you up,' Cindy said. 'And now you're worthless to them.'

And the defeated look in Hailey's eyes suggested she realized that too.

Ryker's phone buzzed. It had done so multiple times over the last hour. This time he decided to answer.

Klein.

'It's been a while,' Ryker said.

'Excuse me?' Klein answered, sounding pretty pissy already. 'You think I have time to explain to you how busy I am right now?'

'I—'

'Ryker, you better tell me you're closing in on these psychos?'

'I wish I could.'

A sigh. 'Where are you?'

'Newnan, Georgia. I have one of their accomplices. A woman who was working on Exodus and Orion for them.'

Silence for a few moments. 'Is she talking?'

'She's talking a little,' Ryker said, holding Hailey's worried gaze. 'I think she's got more to give up still.'

Hailey whimpered at that.

'Then do what you need to do. You've seen the news—'

'You think the threat is credible?' Ryker asked.

'One hundred percent.'

'I was under the impression the group needed hardware to make this work. That the hardware they needed was only—'

'Yes, Ryker. You're right. But they got it. They slipped into a military base in Florida right under our noses and took it. It's a prototype mobile command center, looks like nothing more than a regular military personnel carrier.'

'How would they even know about that?'

'Exactly. They've been so far ahead of us the whole time, probably with help, support from a lot of different people that we have no idea about.'

'I thought every military base was on alert.'

'What can I say? Maybe they had help there too. The point is, now they have everything they need.'

'So what's happening? What am I not seeing?'

'You know I'm not the man on the inside, but I know there's a war room set up outside of DC, which is where the president is headed to, his whole cabinet. The president will be making a public announcement shortly—'

'And is he going to give in to the demands?'

'I honestly don't know. What I do know is two things. One, there's a manhunt on the go that's bigger than anything you or I have ever seen. And two, it's likely that any and all official action will be at least partly thwarted.'

'By who?'

'By people who want this. You already asked how they were able to so easily get that hardware? And—'

'And how, even after the second bombing in Houston, the response to put the pieces together was so slow,' Ryker said, thinking back to his conversation with Hannigan. The excuses

Hannigan had given as to why no one had figured sooner that Exodus and Orion were the targets. Not that he believed Hannigan had lied, but perhaps someone, somewhere had tried to cover the truth.

'Obviously some people feared the worst as soon as KDD Tech was hit,' Klein said. 'It's why you're there at all, Ryker. Not just because of the significance but because it's hard to know who to trust.'

'From the start there's been a cover up,' Ryker said.

'This man Terrence Kielder, he's just a mouthpiece. We know this is much bigger than him. And I know right now there are senior figures in the military, in the government, who are siding with these terrorists, whether they publicly admit it right now or not. And that's why everyone's been so slow to react. And that's why we're still up against it as the next few hours count down.'

'This isn't terrorism,' Ryker said. 'This is a coup.'

'I fear you're right about that.'

'And what are you doing?' Ryker asked.

'There's not a lot more I can do. Like I said, there's a war room, there's a nationwide manhunt. But... there's also you. You said you have one of them?'

'Yes.'

'Then do whatever you can. I've already briefed my bosses on your presence there. It doesn't mean every authority will see you as a friend but take it from me that until this is over, you've got carte blanche. Do what you need to do.'

The call ended.

Ryker thought for a few moments, aware that both Cindy and Hailey were staring at him.

'Anything?' Cindy said.

'How do we stop them?' Ryker asked Hailey.

She shook her head.

'You want me to mangle your other hand?' Cindy said to her.

'There is no way to stop them!' Hailey said. 'I can't get access to the system remotely. No one can. That's the whole point.'

'We don't need to get access remotely,' Ryker said. 'We just need to find out where they are.'

'I don't know!'

'And I don't believe you,' Cindy said.

'They picked up the hardware in Florida,' Ryker said, thinking out loud.

'I know they...' Hailey started but then paused as though debating whether to carry on or not. Whether she wanted to withhold, suffer more. 'I know they were talking about Louisiana.'

'Where in Louisiana?'

'I don't know!'

'They left you in that factory,' Ryker said.

'Y-yes?'

'Why?'

'Because... they were supposed to pick me up. Me and the equipment.'

Cindy laughed. 'Yeah, like I said before, guess we know now which of those was more important.'

'But you had a way of contacting them?' Ryker said. 'Which is why they raided that place after you raised the alarm.'

No answer. Just a bit more squirming.

'Who?' Cindy asked. 'Who did you tell?'

'Terrence,' she said.

'So you still have a way of contacting him?' Ryker asked.

'Answer the goddamn question,' Cindy said, lurching forward with threat once more.

'Yes!' Hailey said. 'I do.'

'How?'

'Dark web. A message site.'

'Traceable?' Ryker asked.

'There's a reason we use sites like that,' Hailey said.

'And there's a reason they picked someone like you to decode and make the data for Exodus and Orion ready to deploy. I'm guessing you're pretty good with computers.'

She didn't exactly smile, but she certainly looked a little flattered by the words.

'So... if we get them to respond to a message from you...' Cindy said, obviously thinking as she spoke, 'we could trace their location?'

'In theory,' Hailey said. 'But it's not as simple as that. There'll be layers to unpeel.'

'But it's possible,' Ryker said.

'Yes. It's possible. If they replied at all.'

'Let's find out,' Ryker said.

Hailey cowered as Ryker moved to her and pulled her to her feet.

'W-where are we going?'

'You said Louisiana, right?'

A nod.

'Then that's where we're going.'

'And you'd better pray that they come to your rescue,' Cindy said.

27

The barn on the western edge of the De Soto National Forest in Mississippi was about as isolated as a place could get with not a single other inhabited building within perhaps ten miles. Despite its remoteness it was also strategically placed for our next move in a few hours' time. I watched the gaggle of workers as they strategically took apart the prototype command center I'd stolen from Florida. Well, take apart insofar as they worked on disconnecting the epicenter from the truck-bed. The equipment itself would – and needed to – remain intact.

Kielder stormed back inside, phone in hand, Meyers not far behind.

'News?' I asked him.

'He's not backing down.'

'You really expected the president to cave, just like that?' I said with a snap of my fingers.

'We'll tear every city apart if we have to,' Meyers said.

'Or you could just send a preemptive strike now,' I said. 'Which is what I suggested several hours ago.'

'Yes. We know you did,' Meyers replied. 'Except we were still waiting on the goods from Georgia.'

'A strike where?' Kielder asked. 'Washington? They're still barely evacuating. We'd kill tens of thousands.'

'You don't need to strike a population center. You only need to demonstrate that we really do have control. You have to make it so our demands can't be refused.'

'You think I need your advice on strategy?'

I didn't answer the dumb question.

'Don't worry,' Meyers said, before he slapped Kielder on the back. 'The freak's only pissed because you left Hailey behind. You know he was crazy in love with her.'

I held my nerve at the jibe. The fact was, Meyers was right. I was pissed. Kielder had sent a crew to get her and the equipment to bring both here. Had run into that damn James Ryker in the process. They'd retrieved the computers, but they'd left Hailey behind.

Kielder didn't seem torn up about that.

'But you can work the system,' Kielder said to me. 'You don't need Hailey?'

'I can do it,' I said.

Meyers grumbled under his breath. Basic jealousy on his part, because he knew I remained far more valuable in this venture than he was.

They both moved away. I took out my phone. Navigated to the message from Hailey that I'd received more than two hours ago now. I knew she'd reached out to Kielder too. And I knew exactly why. James Ryker. He was trying to coerce us into a response. A response which, with a fair amount of deciphering, most likely by Hailey, would reveal our location. Which is why I hadn't typed a thing in return, and I knew Kielder wouldn't have either.

But on his part... I knew it was because he really didn't care about her after all...

She didn't deserve to be left behind, to be left out in the cold after all the hard work and dedication she'd shown while these idiots in front of me, Kielder and Meyers, stood to gain so much.

My finger hovered over the screen a few seconds, but I didn't type anything before I put the phone away. It didn't mean I'd abandoned her, though. It only meant I was still thinking how to win her back.

* * *

Two hours later and the command center was fully disconnected from the truck bed and everything was up and running, Orion and Exodus were live and I sat back and sighed as I stared at the screens and the controls that now held sway over the future of the world as we knew it.

'It's ready?' Kielder asked, hovering over my shoulder.

'It's ready.'

'Then let me call BTC. It's time for him to make his move. We need to push these bastards to breaking.'

'Hold on,' I said, raising a hand to stop him from leaving.

Kielder paused. Meyers came in behind him. Good timing.

'Let's just a wait a few minutes to see what happens first.'

'To see what happens with what?' Kielder asked.

'This,' I said before I dropped my hand and pressed my finger on the enter key.

I turned around, broad smile on my face. Not that they'd see the full effect with the mask on.

Kielder looked panicked. Meyers looked mad.

'What did you do?' Kielder asked as he looked from me to the screens behind. 'What the fuck did you do!'

He lurched as if to come forward to attack me, but he didn't move anywhere near as quickly as Meyers did. The younger guy launched himself for me, but he really should have thought it through more, dealt with his anger and his animosity a bit more cleverly.

I was on my feet before he reached me, and I kicked the chair out toward him. The back hit him in the midriff, causing him to bend forward. I grabbed his head and pulled it down and hauled my knee up into his face then tossed him to the ground. I stomped on his chest as I pulled out the knife from my side and outstretched my arm to place the blade upon Kielder's neck as he wrestled for his holstered gun.

'Are we cool?' I said to Kielder, who did the right thing of pausing.

'What the hell are you doing?'

'Everything I can to get the outcome we want. And it was Meyers who went to attack me just now. You saw that.'

Meyers, just about conscious, mumbled something but didn't bother to try to fight back.

'I didn't mean about Meyers. I mean about that,' Kielder said, nodding at the screen.

I smiled and pulled back the knife and put it back in its sheath.

'I told you, we needed a preemptive strike.'

'And I told you that wasn't the damn plan!'

'But I disagreed.'

'What have you done?' Meyers asked, pulling himself away from me but staying down.

I laughed at that. I didn't mean to really, but their panic had amused me.

'Let's wait and see,' I said, turning back to the screen. I pointed to the little blinking light. 'This is the warhead. It's a

modified BGM-109C Tomahawk fired from a Long-Range Fires
Launcher located at the training academy in West Point.'

'But what the fuck is the target?' Meyers asked as he pulled
himself to his feet.

'Wait,' I said, sitting back down in the chair. 'First, I need to
do what I can to make sure it hits.'

It took only a few seconds to make sure that the layers of
defense embedded in the system I controlled would all turn a
blind eye to the warhead. Not a hard task for this level of muni-
tion. Fired from a relatively short distance, and traveling low,
the most advanced layers of the system wouldn't – couldn't – be
engaged at all, as they were developed to intercept long-range
missiles at high-altitude.

'Ten seconds to impact,' I said, watching the blip on the
screen, fingers crossed hoping that it kept on going. By this
point the only defense left was men on the ground firing from
outdated mobile surface-to-air missile systems like the MIM-104
Patriot, or even a man portable system like the Stinger. In those
last few seconds, I jovially imagined a couple of army rats with
Stingers on their shoulders, pointed up to the sky to launch
their last-ditch efforts...

Whether they did or they didn't, it made no difference. The
Tomahawk landed exactly as intended.

Silence.

'Is that... Is that it?' Kielder asked.

'That's it,' I said. 'It worked. It landed – exploded – in a field
in Virginia. Close enough to DC, to the Pentagon, to cause quite
a few guys in suits to shit their pants. Not so close as to hit any
urban center.'

Although I certainly couldn't guarantee no deaths. We'd
have to await the reports from the ground for that.

'You piece of shit,' Meyers said to me.

'I moved this damn thing along,' I said to him. 'You want us to be taken seriously? Now we'll be taken seriously. Not only should they fully believe we will launch when the deadline is up, but they also should now know that whatever defenses they were hoping to rely on will be more or less useless.'

Neither of them said a thing. I'd never seen these two men look so small, insignificant, and that was saying something.

Perhaps finally they understood the true pecking order here.

'Probably a good time to get BTC to make his announcement, don't you think?' I said, unable to hide my glee.

28

Ryker and Cindy restocked on supplies and ammo before heading west with Hailey – Louisiana their final destination even if they still didn't know where in the state. Although Ryker had an inkling.

'Any response?' Ryker asked, looking at Hailey in the rearview mirror. Both she and Cindy were in the back as Ryker drove the latest stint.

'No, nothing,' was Hailey's simple, dejected response.

Both he and Cindy had overseen the process of her sending the two messages, one to Kielder, one to Marshall, and had dictated the messages too, ensuring that Hailey didn't use any kind of code words to alert them. Although really the messages were something of a long shot. Of course Kielder and Marshall would have heard that Ryker and Cindy had been at the factory, that Hailey had been left behind with them. The simple ruse in her messages that she had got away from them and wanted to reconnect with her team was about the best they could do right now.

But it seemed like Kielder and Marshall hadn't bought it. Or, even if they had, they still hadn't bothered to reply to Hailey. They'd cut her off. And as the journey went on, Ryker sensed a growing malaise in her demeanor as the ramifications of being abandoned became increasingly real.

She felt betrayed. Ryker wanted her to feel that. It could help.

'Is there any other way to contact them?' Ryker asked. 'Anything at all that you can think of to help find them?'

A head shake from Hailey.

'Did they plan to stay in the country?' Cindy asked.

'I already said, I don't know. I only know Louisiana was a destination. I don't know if that means it was the final one or not.'

'Seems like they were never intending to take you along then,' Cindy responded. 'Whether or not we'd turned up at the factory, they were keeping you in the dark.'

Hailey didn't respond but Ryker could tell the comment annoyed her.

'Tell us about them,' Ryker said. 'Who's in charge? Crawford? Kielder? Marshall?'

'Marshall?' Hailey scoffed.

'What?'

'He's not in charge. The others think he's a freak. Literally call him that to his face.'

'Freak? Because of his... The way he looks?'

'Yes,' Hailey said, sending a glare Ryker's way. Another interesting tell from her about the dynamic between the people in the group. 'I've never even met Crawford,' she added.

'But the others are taking orders from him?' Cindy asked.

'I don't know for sure, just that... he's definitely involved.'

'But he's funding it all,' Cindy said. 'Using his power and his money right across the country to sow unrest.'

'I... think so,' Hailey said.

'So it's Kielder that's running the show?' Ryker asked. 'Is that what you're telling me?'

'He certainly likes to think he is.'

'You don't like him much?' Cindy asked.

Hailey huffed. 'He's my boyfriend.'

Although she said it in such a way that suggested she wasn't at all happy about that.

'What about Marshall?' Cindy asked.

'What about him?'

'Did you get along with him?'

'Yes, actually. I think... if you knew what he'd been through... I understand why he hates this country and the people running it as much as he does.'

A shiver ran through Ryker. The way she'd said those words... The more he saw and heard, the more he thought a lot of people had perhaps underestimated Caleb Marshall and his role.

'What is Kielder's end goal?' Cindy asked.

'Exactly what he said on the video. He wants the president gone. The entire government. He wants the country run by... white men, basically. He's a traditionalist. America is a white, Christian country, and we need to get back to that before our whole culture goes down the toilet.'

Strong words, in a sense, although there was no real feeling in them, and Ryker didn't bother to counter any of the ideals she was espousing, nor the contradictions in them. Now wasn't the time.

'Do you think he'll actually attack?' Cindy asked. 'I mean, do you really think he's capable of attacking our cities? Killing thousands, millions, to get what he wants?'

Hailey just stared out of her window. And the question was

soon forgotten because Ryker could tell Cindy was distracted by the pings on her phone, a deep frown settling on her face.

'Turn on the radio,' she said without looking up.

Ryker did so, flicking through a couple of music stations until he found a news bulletin.

'...have confirmed the projectile was a US-made Tomahawk missile, fired from West Point Military Academy in New York. It's not yet clear if the missile hit its intended target, if there was a malfunction, or if last-ditch defenses sent it off course. But there's no doubt that this is a worrying escalation, and the proximity to both the White House and the Pentagon cannot be overlooked. We're still awaiting news on casualties, but there're thankfully expected to be minimal given the rural location. The White Lions terrorist group believed to be behind this attack are yet to provide comment, though it's expected that the president will be making an address to the country shortly. We've already heard from senior officials within the administration that this attack should not be taken lightly. More could be coming, and large population centers are likely targets. Rumors that martial law will be declared across the country is growing. There were celebrations from far-right factions in the streets in some cities, along with counter protests, threatening to boil over into violence, particularly across the red states in the south. Despite a growing support across social media for the White Lions and their cause, millions of others are holding their breath as they await the next stage in this terrifying and mounting catastrophe.'

Ryker turned it off. He pulled the car over to the side of the road.

'West Point,' he said.

'What about it?' Cindy asked.

'It's an academy, not an active base.'

'So?'

'They know the military is working around the clock to deactivate as many warheads as possible, probably starting with the most lethal first. Probably no one thought about how much firepower sits elsewhere.'

'Just because these assholes likely won't have nukes, doesn't mean this won't turn real ugly, real soon.'

'I agree,' Ryker said. 'And I didn't say they won't have nukes, just that I'm sure that's exactly the type of weapon that those in charge will be scrambling to disconnect from the system first. Either way, this was a test. A show of power too. It's proof not only that these people have access to the system and that the military is defenseless to stop them, but that they're willing to use the system to fire on US soil.'

He turned around to stare at Hailey who was refusing to meet his eye.

'What?' she eventually said.

'Is this what you wanted?' he asked her. 'Missiles fired at US cities?'

'Kielder already made it clear what we want.'

'And if he doesn't get it? What then? How far is he willing to go?'

'I don't know what bullshit radio station that was... but what we're doing... People want what we want. We have support. Didn't the reporter even say that? That people are celebrating this? And people like us... They no longer need to be scared to say how they really feel. We're the majority. I have no doubt about that. And you know it too. It's why you're all scared shit-less right now. The sooner we take our country back, the better.'

'You think it's a good sign that people are celebrating a missile attack on US soil?' Cindy asked her.

Even if Hailey didn't say anything, Ryker knew the answer.

Hailey didn't think it was a good sign at all. Despite her statement, he could tell she was the one scared shitless at the thought of what might be to come.

'Hailey, get your goddamn head out of your ass!' Cindy shouted. 'People will die! Thousands, millions? You think if you send a nuke into any US city you're only going to kill the people you hate? Bombs don't discriminate like you do. This will be a tragedy like nothing you could imagine.'

Hailey didn't say anything but her dejection was growing. Her hands were shaking and she tried to stop it by clasping them together on her lap.

'This won't get your country back,' Cindy said. 'This could destroy it. Forever.'

'You can help stop this,' Ryker said.

Hailey still didn't respond.

'Send another message,' Cindy said, holding Hailey's phone out toward her. 'To both Kielder and Marshall. You have to try again. We must find them before this goes too far.'

'You don't want this blood on your hands,' Ryker added, although he sensed it probably wasn't necessary.

Hailey took the phone. 'OK,' she said. 'Just tell me what you want me to say.'

29

I was outside the barn, in the Mississippi sunshine, listening to the birdsong and getting some air when the phone pinged in my pocket. I lifted it to look at the latest message from Hailey.

Please, Marshall, I'm really scared. I don't know what's happened to you. I need to know what to do.

I read the words in her voice, imagined her distress, even though my head told me to ignore it.

My head won. I slipped the phone away when Kielder and Meyers came out of the barn, followed by their gaggle of minions. Except the gaggle of minions kept on going to their vehicles. We're leaving soon. Only the three of us remaining now.

'BTC's recorded his piece,' Kielder said to me. 'You want to see?'

'Not really.'

Because I knew what he'd be saying. The whole plan to this point was to ensure BTC kept a distance from us and our actions. Even if he'd been fanning the flames of discontent indirectly with his money up until now, our small crew here was soon to be seen as rogue. So that at the eleventh hour, BTC could ride in, the white knight in shining armor, claiming to be the savior of our nation. His address would be pointed in three directions: firstly, directly at the current president, appealing for him to stand down for the good of the country and its citizens; secondly, to those citizens themselves, to appeal for calm and togetherness; and thirdly, to us, calling on a halt to our attacks to give diplomacy a chance, stating that while he agreed with much of our aims, he didn't agree with our methods.

Total bullshit on every single front.

'Less than an hour to go,' Kielder said, checking his watch.

'And, surprise, surprise, the president hasn't caved,' I said.

'There's still time,' Meyers chimed in.

I shrugged. 'Yeah. There is. But it's just as well that another warning shot is—' my turn to check the time '—gonna hit in thirty seconds or so.'

'What the hell, Marshall?' Kielder said. 'You're serious? This same shit again?'

'You don't think we need to ramp up the pressure now that time's a ticking?'

'I don't believe this,' Meyers said, storming back inside.

I followed. Kielder too. Back to the screens. Not that either of them really had a clue what they were looking at without me, and even less idea how to change it.

'We should never have left him in control,' Meyers said.

'If only you'd had Christine and Hailey here, right?' I said.

Neither responded to that, though I remained angry at Kielder for having so readily cast Hailey from his life.

'Please tell me this is another near miss?' Kielder asked. 'You risk screwing with everything we've planned!'

'Miss?' Meyers said. 'The last report I heard stated there're already more than twenty casualties from the Tomahawk.'

'This one won't be that much worse,' I said. 'We're still in the original twelve-hour window. We don't need to do anything more extreme. Yet. But what I suggest you do is to use the remaining time to make a final push.'

'Listen to this guy,' Meyers said. 'He really thinks he's got everything figured out. That we should all be jumping to his tune.'

Kielder said nothing to either of our statements.

'Wait a few minutes,' I said to him. 'But that's all you have. Then make one final plea to the president to do the right thing. You have to make them believe the threat is real. That the next strike will be the biggest ever detonation on this continent, by far the biggest loss of life. They've tried so hard to take every nuke offline, but there's still enough non-nuclear warheads at our hands that could level any American city in minutes.'

Meyers stared at his boss, waiting for a response. I sensed the turmoil in Kielder. I'd long had doubts about whether he was up to the job, about how far he'd go when it came to this time... Those doubts were growing still. But perhaps he only needed my guiding hand.

He rubbed at his face for a few seconds, as though refreshing himself with cold water. Except without the freaking water.

It left his skin red and mottled when he looked up at me.

'OK,' he said. 'You're right. Let's get this done.'

30

'They've hit again,' Cindy said. Ryker checked the clock on the dash. They were into the final hour now. 'Another Tomahawk. This one landed in the Hudson. It wasn't even a mile from Manhattan.'

'These aren't misses,' Ryker said. 'These are direct warnings.'

'There must be something we can do?'

Hailey was looking out of her window, as though not hearing us.

Cindy grabbed Hailey's shoulder. 'Is this what you want? You really want Americans blown to pieces through your work?'

But Hailey didn't say anything.

Cindy growled and let go and went back to her phone. Even though she didn't say anything more, Ryker could tell she was looking at another development.

'What is it?' he asked.

'The president. He's spoken again. Confirmed that he has no intention of stepping down. That he'll bring the perpetrators to justice. That... martial law is in effect in every town and city with a population of more than a half million people. But that...' She took a moment as if trying to calculate in her head. 'But how do you even do that? Most major cities are made up of multiple municipalities. Just look at where we're from – Atlanta. Which parts do you include? And... even on the most basic level... every city greater than half a million? This report says there's around forty centers that meet the criteria. But you're talking about probably not even 20 percent of the country's population. So what the fuck about everyone else?'

'Because the Army, the National Guard, can only do so much,' Hailey said, her interjection a surprise to Ryker. 'So they're concentrating on the areas of most significance. It's the only thing they can do now.'

'You have family?' Ryker asked her.

Hailey held his eye a few beats in the mirror before answering. 'Yes.'

'Parents? Grandparents? Siblings?'

'Yes to all.'

'Are they worth sacrificing for getting what you want?'

'You have no idea what I want.' Her eyes welled with tears.

'That didn't answer my question.'

'It's all fun and games, right?' Cindy said. 'The idea of a few thousand undocumented migrants getting blown to pieces. But when you realize it's just as likely that moms and pops will be obliterated? That kinda touches a nerve with you.'

Cindy spoke with a quiet snide look on her face. Though Ryker felt it was warranted in this instance, because it was clear that the more they pressed Hailey, and the more they highlighted the flaws in what she'd done, the more frightened she became.

'I think we have to accept that at this stage, they're not biting on those messages,' Ryker said to her. 'Wouldn't you agree?'

Hailey nodded in response.

'And you literally have minutes left now to stop this. Please, Hailey, is there anything else we can do to find them? To stop them.'

Hailey took a big gulp. 'I... I... Yes. Maybe there is.'

'Go on.'

'It's the system itself. They've launched two warheads now. Even if they were in close proximity to the launches, there'd be ten, twenty, maybe even a hundred satellites that... participated. That were part of fulfilling the command. Even if the system is impenetrable, it means... they've left a trace showing where the command originated from. At least in theory.'

'A signal where?' Ryker asked. 'In the system itself? On the satellites used to control it?'

'Both,' she said.

'But you'd need access to the system, wouldn't you? And the system isn't hackable.'

'Yes. And no.'

'No?'

'The system can't be hacked. But... Do you still have the laptop?'

They did. The laptop being the one that she'd had at the factory. Hailey's personal device that she'd had in her bag which the others had inadvertently left behind.

'I was trying to find different ways to test the system. To test parts of it, to make sure it'd all come together and...'

'And what?'

'Put simply... perhaps I can find those traces. Which satellites were activated.'

'And from that you can see the location the commands came from.'

'I... really don't know for sure. But it's possible.'

'Then do it, Hailey,' Cindy said, handing her the machine. 'And do it quickly.'

31

We watched the final countdown in the barn, clustered around the computer terminals. No one had spoken for more than five minutes. Lots of checking of phones and watches. Meyers was shaking as he stood by my side. Kielder had a more resolute stance. But I knew inside he was in turmoil.

'One minute to go,' I said.

Meyers quickly checked his phone for the ten millionth time.

'Do you think they've been in contact with BTC directly?' he asked to no response. 'How will we even know if the president caved? He's not going to call us, right?'

Again he got no response to his dumb questions. Of course the president wasn't going to call any one of us. Nor BTC. Nor was he going to suddenly appear before the nation to officially hand in his resignation.

'We have to be ready to—'

'Just wait,' Kielder cut in, having the audacity to raise a finger like I was a petulant child.

Wait. Yeah, he wanted to wait. Because now we were in the

crunch time, his doubts were growing and growing and were becoming so big he'd soon be overwhelmed.

'Ten seconds,' I said, then watched our countdown wind down, down, down to zero.

Absolute silence from all of us. I'll admit, in that moment my heart was racing, a hundred fifty, sixty, thudding against my ribs, adrenaline surging, anticipation skyrocketing. We all just stood there, as though expecting something, the end of the world, air raid sirens or what I don't know.

'It's done,' I said, breaking the unease. 'Which means we have to make the move.'

'Let me... Let me speak to BTC first,' Kielder said.

He disappeared leaving me with Meyers. I stared at the guy, trying to read his thoughts.

'Have you ever wondered what it feels like to have the power of a god at your fingertips?' I said to him.

He looked at me but didn't answer.

'That's the power we have, Danny. In every sense, right now we are gods of this world. We sit above every single other person, creature. We're so much more powerful. More vengeful. We have the ability to shape the future of this planet in our image.'

He said nothing to me at all.

'That's what we're doing this for, isn't it? That's what you've wanted all along?'

He still didn't answer but looked over my shoulder as Kielder returned.

'I can't get hold of him.'

'Does that mean... Is he comprised?' Meyers asked.

'I don't know.'

'OK, gentlemen,' I said. 'We hit. We hit now. New York was the plan. Are you ready?'

The command was already programed. All I had to do was press the button.

'They only started the evac a few hours ago,' Meyers said. 'There could still be hundreds of thousands of people on Manhattan Island. The other boroughs? Probably the same. We should wait. Just a while longer until we know the position from all parties.'

I turned to Kielder who stared at the screens as though the answers lay there. He hadn't responded before his phone vibrated and he turned his back to take the call. It didn't last long.

'BTC?' Meyers asked.

'He says we should wait too. Another hour. He's trying to get hold of the president as we speak.'

'So that's it?' I asked.

'For now, yes. We wait.'

I held Kielder's eye. Did he have any idea what I was thinking?

'Marshall, you piece of shit,' he said. So perhaps he did know. 'I said we wait! And that's a goddamn order.'

I laughed. 'The problem is, I stopped taking orders from anyone a long, long time ago.'

I slapped my hand down, pushing my finger on the button to execute the command.

The next moment I felt the pressure against my skull. A gun barrel.

'What the hell did you do?' Meyers said.

'What we set out to do,' I responded.

'No, no, no, no!' Kielder shouted. 'Stop it! You have to stop it!'

'That's not possible.'

The next moment Meyers swiped the gun across the back of

my head. Even though I felt no pain, my head twisted beyond my control. He grabbed me and tossed me to the ground and his ferocity, his speed of movement, genuinely caught me by surprise. He launched a boot into my stomach. Another to my face which sent my mask askew so I was only looking out of one eyehole. He hit me again, again, again until I was on the brink of unconsciousness.

He crouched down, lifted my head up. Peeled my mask off. That was better. I could see him properly again, even if my vision was a little blurred from the pummeling.

He hesitated as he took in my face. The first time he'd seen me like this.

'I should have done this a long time ago,' he said, before he swiped the barrel of his gun against my jaw. I heard a crack. Ended up with a couple of teeth in my mouth which I spat out before he hit me again.

'Danny!' Kielder shouted, but that was all he did to offer me any aid.

Meyers let go and my head slumped to the floor.

'I thought you were supposed to be indestructible?' Meyers said. 'You don't feel pain?'

He pointed the gun at my thigh and fired.

I felt the impact. Like someone tapping their finger on my skin. But that was it. I laughed, blood dribbling from my mouth.

'You like that?' Meyers said.

'Sure,' I said to him, the word a little more garbled than I thought it'd be.

'Screw this. You're done.'

He pointed the gun at my face.

Shouldn't have hesitated.

I twisted the knee of my good leg, pulled my heel toward me and hooked it around his leg to pull him off balance. He fired the gun. The bullet whizzed above my head. I reached up and grabbed his arm and dragged him toward me and sank my teeth into his neck. I clamped down hard then yanked back, tearing off a huge chunk of flesh, and in his panic he let go of the gun to clasp both hands to the wound as he fell to his knees, his eyes bulging in shock.

Kielder whipped his own gun out, but I already had my knife in my hand and I tossed it toward him, the blade rotating through the air until it smacked home in his gut, sending him stumbling back. I launched a spin kick his way to knock the gun from his grip. He clattered into the wall and slumped down, gazing at the handle protruding from his belly.

I looked into Meyers' eyes. Shuffled closer to him.

'I bit right through your carotid artery,' I said to him. 'Whether you keep your hands there or not, you're bleeding to death.'

He didn't say anything.

'You were never good enough,' I whispered. 'It just took a really, really long time for you to realize it.'

I threw my fist forward. Power, precision. The knuckles caught him on his Adam's apple. Probably not enough damage to have killed him outright, but enough to cause him added panic as he choked for air. He flopped, spluttering a few breaths, his hands soon falling free from his neck as the last of his life pulsed out of him.

I got up and moved to Kielder on the floor, limping badly now, given the bullet in my thigh. He cowered from me as I approached. I lowered myself down and yanked the knife from him, causing his eyes to bulge even more.

'Out of everyone... you disappointed me the most,' I said. 'At the start... I really thought you had it in you to become a hero. Sadly... no one will remember you.'

I made it quick for him. Used his own gun. A single bullet to the forehead.

Finally, I was on my own. Able to make my own decisions without interference or second guessing.

I turned and stared at the screens with a smile.

It was time to achieve my destiny.

The whole world would know my name.

Not just now, but forever.

32

'I can't believe this is happening,' Cindy said, glued to her phone like she had been for much of the journey.

Hailey continued to work at speed on her laptop, although with the fingers on one hand broken, no doubt she was going slower than she otherwise would have done. Ryker had turned the radio off a while back. He didn't want to hear anymore.

Cindy though... She couldn't stop.

'Fourteen missiles were launched at New York,' she said. 'Tomahawk BGM 109. An... AGM 84E...' She read the names out in a robotic manner, the letters and numbers meaning nothing to her. 'They're even saying there was a... Common-Hypersonic Glide Body missile. A hypersonic weapon fired from one of our own ships. But... that one failed. In fact... it looks like only two of them actually hit as intended because what's left of the Army is scrabbling to make use of several anti-quated missile defense platforms that sit outside the Exodus system. But it's still a goddamn fucking disaster.'

About that, she was absolutely right.

'I got it,' Hailey said, almost so quietly that it took Ryker a couple of seconds to decipher the words. She looked up into the rearview mirror. 'I found them. At least... where the commands came from.'

She sounded more apprehensive about that than anything else.

'And?' Ryker prompted.

'Mississippi.' She turned the screen around and Ryker kept his eyes on the road as he reached behind and took the laptop from her. He looked at the coordinates. Plugged them into the GPS.

'We need to tell everyone,' Cindy said, already on her phone. 'Get every single agent, officer nearby to that position right now.'

Ryker sensed perhaps they already had the upper hand in that sense. Almost every police precinct, FBI office, Army station would be using all its manpower to enact evacuations, the martial law directive.

And already traveling through Mississippi en-route to Louisiana... Ryker, Cindy, and Hailey were already so close...

* * *

They'd left the blacktop road a mile and a half back, traveling along a twisty dirt track with neat rows of newly planted cotton stretching away in the fields either side. A large barn came into view in the near distance, a couple of hundred yards away, the structure fenced off from the surrounding fields indicating it didn't belong.

Intact but derelict-looking, Ryker saw no signs of life, no vehicles. As he'd suspected, they were the first to arrive, despite assurances given to Cindy that available units from both the police and FBI would be there as soon as possible. Perhaps those were hollow assurances, the authorities not believing that a suspended GBI agent and a foreigner not officially working on US soil could be so close to tracking down the most wanted men in the world. Or perhaps resources really were spread so thin right now given the chaos taking place in every major city across the country.

'Is this really it?' Cindy asked, leaning forward between the front seats, to look out of the windshield.

Ryker double-checked the destination marker on the GPS screen. 'It has to be,' he said. 'There's nothing else around here.'

He slowed the car down to a crawl. No one spoke a word. In fact, everyone held their breath for the final approach, until Ryker put the car into park and turned off the engine.

'Come on,' he said. 'We're all getting out.'

Because he wanted Cindy there as backup, and he couldn't leave Hailey on her own in the car. Ryker went first, Hailey in the middle, Cindy at the rear.

Ryker's eyes darted over the scene as he moved. He paused briefly to turn to Cindy and indicated the ground.

'Recent tire tracks,' he said, and Cindy nodded in agreement. The rain that had swept across the region over the last few days would have washed them away otherwise.

He reached the large double doors at the front of the barn. The left hand one was a few inches ajar, and Ryker pulled up alongside the frame and stole a look into the darkened interior.

'Kielder!' Ryker shouted out. 'Marshall!'

'Ryker, what the hell?' Cindy hissed at him.

'What? If they're inside they'll already know we're here.'

Although he'd already scoped out the outside of the building and on the approach road that there were no cameras. And he got no response to his call, just as he'd expected. So he lifted his weapon and flung the door open as he moved inside. Then paused, staring at the scene.

'Terry!' Hailey screamed, rushing forward.

'Ryker, grab her!'

But he didn't. He didn't see the point. No one was alive in here. Hailey scrambled past him and kind of tripped, kind of slid to the floor where she crumpled onto her knees, gazing up at the two bodies.

Kielder. Meyers. Both were swinging from the rafters, a noose around each of their necks. But it didn't look like the nooses had killed them. Among other injuries, Meyers had a hole in his neck the size of a golf ball. Kielder had a bullet hole in his face and a stab wound in his side. The fact they'd been hung was simply an indignity inflicted by Caleb Marshall.

Hailey turned around to Ryker and Cindy, tears streaming.

'Marshall did this!' she shouted. 'He killed them! That fucking animal!'

Neither Ryker nor Cindy said a word. At least on Ryker's part, it wasn't because he felt any sympathy for the two dead men in front of him, but because he was busy trying to figure out what had happened here.

'That's the mobile command center they stole,' Ryker said, pointing to the carcass of an armored personnel carrier, parts of it scattered around the space.

'Meaning... what?' Cindy said.

'Meaning Marshall has already taken what he needed off that thing.'

'But... why? I don't understand the point.'

'Because every law enforcement agency across the country is looking for this vehicle.'

'Ryker, have you seen the size of that thing? It's not like he could have fitted the back of it onto a Ford F-150. So what are you saying?'

He thought a moment. Dragged Hailey back up onto her feet. She shrugged him off angrily, as though he were in some way to blame for the deaths of her boyfriend and his ally.

'Why would he do this?' she asked to no response.

'You said Louisiana,' Ryker prompted her.

'Louisiana? Who gives a fuck about Louisiana! Look what he did!'

Cindy grabbed her arm. Hard enough to make Hailey wince and writhe. 'Oh, so now you care about people dying. Screw the millions at risk of being blown to pieces by this psycho, but it's all so heartbreaking that Marshall turned on these guys? Get a fucking grip.'

Hailey pulled out of Cindy's grasp, her shock, sadness turned to anger in that instant.

'Hailey, focus,' Ryker said. 'You mentioned Louisiana—'

'Because that's what Terry said.'

'To you?'

A pause. 'Yes.'

'And it was definitely him and not Marshall?'

'Yes!'

'What are you thinking?' Cindy asked him.

'What would be big enough to fit all of the equipment in it, but still be intact, mobile?'

'A shipping container?'

'Exactly.'

'You think they planned to leave the country?'

'Crawford already has. I think that was the plan for all of them. Louisiana? You have some of the biggest ports in the whole country right there.'

'Shit. Then that's where we need to go.'

She went to turn around, but Ryker held her back.

'No. Because that was Kielder's plan. Crawford's too, whatever. It wasn't Marshall's plan. This—' he pointed to the bodies '—was Marshall's plan. To kill them when he could, take over. Just him against everyone else.'

'So what are you saying? You don't think Marshall is leaving the country?'

'Not quite. There's been no more attacks, right?'

'Not that I've heard.'

'Which most likely means he's on the move. That's a good thing. He's on his own now. As long as he's moving he's not sending out missiles. But we have to stop him before he gets the chance to fire again. He won't want to have too much downtime. So I don't think he's traveling all the way down to New Orleans or any of the big ports in that direction.'

'Actually, he can pre-program attacks,' Hailey said.

Ryker thought about that. 'OK. Fair enough. But I still think I'm right. Whether he can pre-program or not, he'll want to be at the controls as much as possible, to move on the fly if some attacks don't go as planned.'

'Then where would he go?' Cindy asked, already scrolling on her phone. 'The two largest ports near here are... Gulfport. Pascagoula—'

'Which is the largest?' Ryker said.

Cindy took a few moments. 'Pascagoula is the largest seaport in Miss—'

'Then not that one,' Ryker said, his own phone out now. 'Gulfport. It's smaller. It's also a lot closer to where we are right now. I think Marshall always intended to go there.'

'I really hope you're right about that.'

'Only one way to find out.'

33

I'd watched from a safe distance as the looming crane lifted the container from the truck and swung it around to place it onto the ship. Thirty minutes until cruise time. I'd be on the vessel too but would wait a few minutes more before I emerged from my position behind the warehouse.

I checked my watch. I'd pre-programed several barrages in this downtime. I'd soon find out how those went, but my biggest, most destructive actions were still to come. Before that I needed to get clear of here. And I also wanted to make my own announcement to the nation, much like Kielder and Crawford already had. Mine would be different. Not begging the current president to do anything. I didn't need to ask for power. I had no intention of becoming leader of this or any other nation. I only wanted to send this country to its knees so that a better one could be born from the ashes.

Not long to go. Once clear of the coast I'd sneak into the container and record my message, and by the time we reached our destination in the Caribbean, the United States of America would never be the same again.

I checked my watch once more.

I'd waited long enough. I initially crept out of my position, looking all around me across the vast open space. The port was quiet. Only two vessels here today. It's why I'd chosen this particular dock, at a time when every law enforcement agency was focused on heavily populated areas.

But not everyone out there was preoccupied and looking in the wrong direction, and I'd made it halfway across the concrete platform when I heard the car engine behind me. I could have carried on to the ship but instead decided to divert to the stack of containers nearby where I hid to get a view of the approaching vehicle.

Except... it didn't drive by. It'd already stopped, out of sight because of the angle. Yet this wasn't an all-guns-blazing take down. No sirens. No flashing lights. No heavy-booted feet stomping or anything like that.

'Marshall!' came the shout moments later. I recognized the voice. James goddamn Ryker. Inevitable, really. 'I have Hailey. Why don't we do a swap? Her for the hardware.'

I had to laugh at that. He'd done well to track me down, so he wasn't stupid, but was that really the best he had?

'Marshall, please!' Hailey screeched out.

I growled at the pleading in her voice. It shouldn't have mattered to me now, but... I'd spent so long being maligned by everyone, my own family included. Hailey... Whether through true sincerity or something else, she'd treated me differently. Normal, almost.

And I'd let her down. I'd left her behind. I regretted it. But not so much as to let her get in the way of my plans now.

'You've got ten seconds,' Ryker shouted out. 'Then I'll put in a bullet in her head. Then I'll come and do the same to you.'

I didn't respond.

'Don't doubt me, Marshall.'

I glanced around the side of the container stack. Spotted Ryker and Hailey fifteen yards away, both looking over in my direction. Ryker had an arm around Hailey's throat. A handgun pointed at her head.

'It's not too late, Marshall!' Ryker shouted.

'Actually, it's been too late for a long, long time!' I shouted in response, before I rolled out into the open, gun in hand. I fired two shots. Both hit Hailey. I think I was kind to her, really. I could have quite easily put both bullets into her chest, into her head. So the leg shots were my way of saying thank you to her. Or something like that.

She went limp in Ryker's grip as she screamed in pain and he turned his gun on me. Her movement gave me just enough of an aim to sink the next bullet into his brain.

Except I hadn't pulled the trigger before a gunshot hole erupted from my side.

'Fuck!' I yelled. Anger, more than anything, because of course, other than the dull thud, I didn't really notice the bullet tearing through my shoulder, even though I knew it had.

I spun to fire back that way. Caught a glimpse of the woman darting for safety behind the metal containers. Ryker fired on me but missed and I rolled away and adjusted my aim. Pointed the gun up. Fired. Three shots. Damn good ones, and sufficient to bust through all but one of the four chains holding the container above us. There was a huge crunch as it swept downward, still one chain keeping it from splatting to the ground. For a few seconds, at least.

A few seconds which gave me a chance to rush for the ship.

I flinched at the huge crash behind me as the last chain gave way and the container smashed into the concrete.

I dodged left and right when the gunshots came my way. I

tried to pump my arms and my legs faster but it felt like running through treacle, the bullet wound in my thigh from Meyers still fresh, and now the new wound in my shoulder slowing me down.

I reached the gangway leading up and turned to fire off what remained in the magazine. Both Ryker and Valentino were on me. Both cowered out of the way. No sign of Hailey now. Perhaps she'd done her bit for them already.

I reached the top of the gangway and darted right. I knew exactly where my container was because I'd been watching it closely ever since I left it.

My plans had rapidly changed. I no longer cared about my message, about waiting for the ship to be clear before I rained hell. I was going to hit now, hit hard, with everything I had at my disposal.

An orange-jacketed worker, oblivious, stepped out of a cabin into my path.

'Move!' I screamed.

The idiot froze instead and I stumbled into him, but his hefty weight meant I didn't quite run through him. He realized something was off when he spotted the gun in my hand. Was perhaps about to try to fight me for it before I bent down and grabbed him below his waist. I lifted him from the floor and tossed him over the railing.

Crack.

His body landed in a twisted heap on the dock below.

Bang.

A gunshot from behind me. The bullet clanked into metal, sending sparks flying into my face.

I retreated inside through the doorway the worker had come from. As I looked back out I saw flashing lights in the distance on the coastal road. Soon heard the sirens too.

'Marshall, it's over!' Ryker shouted out. 'You've got nowhere to go! This ship will never leave this port with you on board.'

I said nothing in return. I had to get to the container before they got to it or me. I didn't mind going down in a hail of bullets. If that was my fate... so be it. But it wouldn't be before I'd destroyed this country.

I turned and raced away inside. Took a right. Machinery hummed and whirred. I heard voices, footsteps of workers in the rooms beyond the corridor but no one else was yet on alert.

At least until I reached the doorway to lead me back outside. As I lifted my fingers to the handle, a pulsing alarm blared. Red lights flashed. I pulled the handle and shoved open the door and rushed outside and from around the corner in front of me... Valentino.

I slammed into her. Took her from her feet. I roared with effort as I carried her several yards through the air and slammed her into the side of a container. I let go and she crumpled to the deck.

Bang.

Another gunshot from behind me. Another near miss as the bullet clanked into metal only a few inches away from my head.

I ran around the corner. Took a left, then a right through the maze of containers.

Found mine.

I heaved open the doors and raced for the controls. As quickly as I could I typed out the commands.

'Marshall, stop.'

A surreally calm command from behind me.

I paused, glanced over my shoulder.

'It's done,' Ryker said.

The most curious thing was that he hadn't just put a bullet through my head, even if he had his gun pointed at me.

I turned to face him.

'You're out,' I said.

He smirked.

'Am I?' he said.

'So is this the part where you beg me not to hit the enter key?'

He glanced behind me.

'Or would you like me to explain to you why I did all this or something?'

'No,' Ryker said. 'You can save that for someone who cares. This is the part where you—'

He didn't finish because I grabbed the wrench from the worktop and tossed it toward him. He cowered from the spinning projectile and I whipped around to finish sending the command...

I slammed the key with my finger just before the same wrench came back into my view. Not spinning this time. Plummeting. Down. Down. Onto the top of my hand with a crunch that told me near every bone in my hand was pulverized in that moment.

Ryker grabbed me by my neck and hauled me away from the controls, tossing me to the floor of the container. As I righted myself, my right hand hanging uselessly, he came toward me again, an animal in his eyes that I so rarely saw in other humans.

It reminded me of... me.

Perhaps he'd have recognized the same look on my face were it not for the mask.

His intention had been to stomp on my head. With his boot raised I burst up and grabbed his leg and hauled him back.

'No!'

Valentino. Again. She fired her gun. Again. I turned and

crashed into her. Taking her back from the container entrance onto the deck of the ship. Then I jumped up and rushed to the next container and climbed the side to the top. A little more clumsily than I intended but even if I felt no pain, the injuries still impeded me. I raced – as best I could – across and climbed again. On the dock below police cars gathered. Three, four, already there, with more arriving. I climbed again then jumped across onto a container suspended above the others, the onboard crane holding it in place, a chain in each corner meeting the middle where the winch above would lift and lower the hulk. The ladder for the crane was a few yards beyond. I could leap for it, then—

The whole thing rocked as another body thudded down behind me.

Ryker, of course.

I kept my balance as the container swayed. Ryker moved into a fighting stance, knees bent, arms outstretched in front of him, stooped and ready to either defend or attack.

'I told you it's over,' Ryker said. 'I don't care if you get off this thing dead or alive. Either way you're finished.'

I didn't respond. Just kept thinking through my next moves.

'Hailey's in there right now,' Ryker said. 'All those rockets you just let loose? Not a single one will hit where you wanted.'

Even if that was a bluff, I wanted to race for him and gouge his eyes out.

'I get that you were screwed over,' Ryker said. 'I've been screwed over plenty.'

'You think?' I said. 'You really believe you have any idea how I suffered?'

'Maybe you had it worse. Fine, I won't argue that. But what you've done? It's beyond getting your own back. You've already destroyed so many innocent lives. For what?'

'Someone like you would never understand.'

'Someone like me?'

'I'm a god among men. In centuries to come, people will still know my name. You're... nothing.'

Ryker actually laughed at that. A big, hearty, patronizing laugh. He really still didn't get it.

'You're a fucking spineless loser,' he said. 'That's all. Scared to show your own face. You probably always were a loser. And that's certainly how you'll be remembered.'

OK. So that comment ground my gears, it's true.

I roared as I went for him. He'd soon see how wrong he was. A loser? I'd tear him to pieces. He thought he was a match for me, but I was so far above him we shouldn't even have been on the same planet.

I was flying through the air when the gunfire burst from the dock below. Rapid fire, from several weapons. I bundled into Ryker but hadn't delivered a blow before, just like earlier, down on the dock, at least one of the bullets caught the chains holding the container in the air. With a snap one of them broke, the container shunting before another gave way from the pressure and the container swung widely ninety degrees through the air, throwing me off Ryker, and throwing us both toward the edge.

'Stop firing!' came a yell from below. Valentino on the ship's deck.

The firing did stop.

With one hand already badly injured I scraped and scrabbled to stop myself from falling and I clambered to the doors that sat at the top of the now vertical container. Ryker was there too.

'Close one,' he said to me as we squared off again on the smaller space, his arrogant smirk igniting rage inside me.

But then I noticed him distracted by something to his left. I looked that way too. Valentino. Climbing the ladder to the controls a few yards above us.

'I did it!' came another shout from the deck. Hailey, hobbling and bleeding. Gutsy. That fucking bitch. 'I stopped them all!'

I only saw Ryker coming for me at the last second. My focus on Hailey's betrayal, I couldn't do enough to defend myself... Actually, that wasn't true. I did defend myself initially. I just had misread Ryker's intentions. I thought he'd been set on tackling me. Punishing me. But actually he blasted past me and I only realized too late that he'd wrapped a thick fabric cord around my neck. A cord that before had been clipped to the chain in one corner. He kicked my legs out before he leaped for the ladder and I was left swinging just like the container. I pulled at the cord around my neck but with my weight pulling me down there was nothing I could do to loosen it, and my feet flailed uselessly in midair. I looked up. He'd wrapped the other end of the cord to the central chain holding the container.

'Now!' Ryker shouted out, and up above me the crane started to reel in the chain, pulled the container, and me, higher and higher. I looked across at Ryker, holding on to the ladder still, facing me. So close... but no way for me to reach him now.

'I told you it was over,' he said to me.

The machinery clunked and whined as the cord, wrapped up in the metal, was chewed up by the reel mechanism. I swung, twisted, did everything I could to free myself, but the cord only went tighter, tighter around my neck. And in my movements my hair got dragged into the knotted metal chain too, my head pulled back.

I couldn't breathe. Not at all. My neck was simply too

constricted. My whole body quivered, my hands dropped down to my side. I tried to fight it but had nothing left.

My eyes dropped down. I saw my body hanging, swinging above the ship's bow and I already dreaded that this was the end.

An end I truly didn't deserve.

But I was wrong.

Because the next moment I felt a jolt as the cord pulled tighter still with a final, ghastly pinch. My head stuck in position, held in place by my hair mangled into the mechanism, I watched as my body came free, my torso, arms, legs, cascading down and away as blood poured from my severed head.

My decapitated body splatted down below in a broken, bloody mess.

'Try coming back from that one, Burning Man,' came Ryker's faint, taunting voice before I drifted into nothingness.

34

Ryker had kept his head down for the three days that followed the ugly death of Caleb Marshall. It was by far the best course of action for him to take given the huge media furor that continued, not in the least helped by the fact that grim footage of Marshall's final moments had been caught on camera by eager dockyard workers and quickly uploaded and distributed across the internet. In the short time that had followed, despite the best efforts of authorities to pull the material, and despite threats of legal action on those promoting the video and images in any way that supported further violence or unrest, anyone who'd wanted to watch the shocking footage would have.

Ryker certainly didn't.

Although it had at least been confirmed to him that the poor, shaky quality of the videos meant that his own face was obscured. His presence there, his role, couldn't be hidden, but his identity had. While Cindy had been lauded by the press, by the president himself actually, and had been subject to interview after interview for every major news station that mattered, Ryker's identity remained a secret, him only referred to by varying descriptions from the real life Jason Bourne to the grim reaper, to the undercover hero, and even to the savior of the free world.

He hated that last one the most.

He wondered how much effort, if any, the likes of Klein had gone to in ensuring Ryker's name and identity were kept anonymous. He'd had the briefest of brief calls with the guy only a few hours after Marshall had met his end. Klein had thanked him, had actually apologized for not being in touch more regularly, but he'd said little else and the call had lasted all of thirty seconds as though to emphasize that he was still too tied up to give Ryker any more of his time, or any other explanations of what was happening now or next.

Ryker got it. He'd worked with people like Klein plenty of times in the past.

And anyway, Klein's parting words said it all, really.

I'll be in touch when I need you next.

A hint both to Klein's satisfaction with Ryker's work and to the fact Ryker was now on Klein's list of assets for the future.

No harm in that.

No mention had been made of Ryker needing to do anything more for Klein on this assignment, but that didn't mean he didn't still have his own loose ends to tie up here before he left the country. He'd been to see Meg already the day he'd returned from Mississippi, and on a grim morning of torrential rain and howling winds he decided to make one last stop off to the hospital.

As the last time he'd seen her, she was ever more alert and bright, was even managing to maneuver about the room unaided now, even if she had to cling to furniture with each step she took, given the heavy plaster on her leg, the bones still some way off being healed.

'He's back,' she said with a broad smile when he came into the room. 'And he brings food. Must be my lucky day.'

He put the brown paper bag down on the nightstand and she delved in, taking out one of the two filled bagels.

'Thought you might be getting sick of the food in here.'

She didn't say either way as she chomped through nearly half of the bagel and its bulging filling in a few quick bites.

'You seen Cindy's latest endeavor this morning on Fox?'

'No. I've been trying to keep out of it.'

Meg laughed. 'Yeah. Talk about opposites. It's like she's been waiting her whole life for this moment.'

Ryker detected just the slightest jealousy in her words, as though she was angered at the attention her ex-sister-in-law was now getting.

'Apparently, the FBI have offered her a job,' Meg said.

'Yeah, she told me that too.'

Meg didn't say anything more as she carried on with her bagel.

'Don't forget you still helped to start this,' Ryker told her. 'What Cindy's doing… it's only rhetorical surface stuff. You can go deeper, do the piece that this story really deserves.'

She didn't respond.

'If you needed anything from me at all, I'd give it to you.'

She still didn't say anything.

'And there is the other angle to this too,' Ryker said.

'The other angle?'

'Right now, everyone's still concentrating on the heroics. On the outcome, that we avoided widespread death and destruction.'

'A hundred and thirty-four people lost their lives in the attacks three days ago.'

'Yes. That's true. But—'

'Not to mention the deaths in the earlier bomb attacks. The other people that they're now alleging Marshall killed even before that, the General and others who were responsible for his operations.'

All good points. Some people in the FBI had been quick to delve into Marshall's recent past to come up with all of that.

'But isn't that the point?' Ryker asked.

'What is?'

'This was never just about Marshall, Crawford, Kielder. What put those people where they were was something more than that. The divisions in this country have been growing for years. So who and what is driving it? And for what purpose?'

'Do you know the answers to that?'

'I have ideas. Certainly we know for sure that some people – Crawford, for example – benefited financially from this—'

'For all of a few days, before a Delta squad picked him up in Venezuela and brought him back here.'

Ryker smiled. He wished he'd been part of that team. To see the look on Crawford's face when he realized his game was up.

'But there'll be others too,' Ryker said. 'Investors, members of the government, the media, in the military, people all over who either benefited or aided them, one way or another, or at least turned a blind eye to what was going on.'

'You're saying you don't think this is over?'

'This? Define this. But no, the circumstances that led to this group forming didn't start and end with them, so I don't think we're now on the way to all-out peace and happiness and prosperity among all three hundred and fifty million people in this nation. It's never happened before, and I don't see why it would now.'

'That's pretty cynical. Particularly for someone not even from this country.'

'This country is no different to any other. It's not the USA I'm cynical of. It's people in general.'

She humphed. He wasn't sure what she meant by that. Disappointed by his attitude? Or perhaps just by the reality of his words. 'And your point was?'

'My point is that there's a huge story still to be told here.'

'And you think I should tell it?'

'I think you will.'

'And so will everyone else. I hear Hailey Matthews is squawking like a demented parrot.'

'I heard so too.'

'But...'

'But what?'

'She did come through in the end.'

'You think she doesn't deserve life in prison for what she did?'

'It's not for me to decide. But there are definitely mitigating factors.'

Meg scoffed. 'The way I see it, she only turned good in the end because she felt jilted.'

'Perhaps. Like I said, not for me to decide.'

'And what about you?' she asked.

'What about me?'

'What do you do now?'

'I'll probably be leaving in a day or two.'

'For where?'

'I haven't decided yet.'

'Does Cindy know?'

'No. But, she's not stupid. She probably suspects.'

'Did you two ever... you know.'

Ryker laughed. 'No. I think we were a bit tied up for that.'

'But you're not anymore.'

'No.'

'So why not?'

'Are you her matchmaker now?'

'I just... know her. Would you... stay longer if she asked you to?'

Ryker didn't answer, because he was too busy thinking about how to answer.

'Her problem is that she'd probably never ask,' Meg said. 'Even if she really wanted to.'

'And what about you?' Ryker asked. 'Would you want me to stay?'

'For work or for pleasure?' she asked with a cheeky glint in her eye.

'I meant work.'

'Good. Because even if I think you're kinda good-looking in a... brutish way, I guess... I just don't think... me and you...'

Ryker laughed. 'You don't need to explain.'

Even though she bowed her head to finish the rest of her food, Ryker noticed her reddened cheeks.

'If you did stay a while... you could help me get this story started, at least.'

'About that,' Ryker said.

'What?'

'I think I have a pretty good starting point for you.'

'Yeah?' She sat up in the bed, enthusiasm taking over.

'Grab a pen and a notepad. Or your laptop. Or whatever. You'll want to write this one down. It's about the White Lions. And... you'll probably need to swap notes with Cindy later today.'

'What the hell are you talking about?'

'That's what you're about to find out.'

* * *

The rain hadn't let up as Ryker followed the truck across Marietta. The heavy downpour probably made it harder for the driver to see him, but it also made it harder for him. Still, he hadn't needed to tail for long before the truck pulled into the parking lot of a strip mall.

Ryker put his foot down a little to make sure he got there in time and he slipped into the spot next to the truck just as the driver was opening the door.

'Good morning,' Ryker said to Kyle Hannigan.

'You? What the hell do you want?'

'How about I buy you a coffee.' Ryker looked around. Pointed to the diner nearby.

'Why would you do that?'

'I thought you'd want to talk to me. About what happened.'

'What are you—'

'Come on, we're getting soaked,' Ryker said, tugging on the guy's sleeve. 'I'm buying.'

* * *

Kyle remained grumpy, skeptical, as they sat in the booth, a waitress pouring them both a coffee from her ever-filled pot.

'My dad said he's not heard a word from you. Even though he's been trying to reach you for three days.'

'I know,' Ryker said. 'I'll speak to him soon and apologize. I've been pretty tied up. And I wanted to speak to you first anyway.'

'Yeah? About what?'

'About Abby.'

Kyle chose to take a sip from his cup in response.

'You're probably wondering how my investigation is going?' Ryker said. 'Because, don't forget, it's why I came here in the first place. To help track her down.'

'OK? So have you?'

'No. Not precisely. But there is quite a picture now emerging.'

Ryker paused, waiting to see if Kyle would say or ask anything more. No.

Not really the actions of a concerned brother.

'So here's what I know. Abby was definitely part of the group known as the White Lions. The same group she was associated with years ago, but in most recent times was known as the terrorist group that tried to undertake a coup right here, tried to overthrow the government and threatened death to millions of Americans.'

Again no response from Kyle, though he did look a lot more jittery now.

'Only, it seems that at some point she tried to change her identity. At least her name, probably because being Abby Hannigan, daughter of the Governor of Georgia, just made her too recognizable. Particularly as your dad wanted nothing to do with a group like that, or its views.'

Kyle finished his drink and motioned to the waitress for a refill. When he'd lifted his hand from the table an outline of his sweaty palm and fingers was left for a few seconds. Nerves.

'Christine was her new name. Do you know what she was doing for the White Lions?'

'I have no idea.'

'She was one of two expert programers. Responsible for making the Orion and Exodus systems work on the stolen platform. You probably know by now about what those programs are.'

'I've heard.'

The waitress refilled both of their cups. Ryker gave Kyle a few seconds more to stew.

'In any other circumstance, a brother would likely be hugely proud of his sister for her talents.'

OK. Not nerves now. Kyle was getting angrier. Ryker could tell by the tight grip on the coffee cup. His clenched jaw.

'But she's missing,' Ryker said. 'And that's the simple fact that I've found. It's been at least two weeks since anyone in that group last saw her.'

Ryker let that comment sit there. Thirty seconds. A minute.

'What are you expecting me to say?' Kyle asked. 'You think she ran away?'

'No. I think someone killed her. And so, given why I was asked to come here, I thought it only right, even though I've already stopped these terrorists from inflicting carnage, I thought it only right I look into her last movements a little more. Do you know who the last person to see her was?'

A headshake.

'Caleb Marshall. I didn't hear that from him, because he's lost his head recently, but I've got some friends in the right places and I've trawled through a lot of security tapes the last few days, and I've found footage of Marshall with your sister in the hours that followed the bombing at KDD Tech.'

Kyle brightened a little.

'So... you're saying... Marshall killed her?'

'No. I'm saying he saw her then. After that, she traveled back to Newnan, probably dropping off the data dump that was stolen from KDD Tech. That night she went back to her condo. The next day...' Ryker looked around the room. Then outside. Kept his gaze out there several seconds until Kyle looked that way too.

'Holy crap,' Ryker said.

'What?'

'This is the strip mall she came to! No way. What a coincidence. Because it's also a regular stop off for you, isn't it?'

Kyle went to get up but Ryker grabbed his wrist. Pushed his fingertips in the bundle of nerves there until Kyle winced in pain and eased himself back down again.

'She came to meet you, didn't she?'

No answer.

'I know she did. Because I've already traced the call you made to her. And I've seen the footage of your truck arriving here. And leaving. I've tracked your truck heading west past Kennesaw. And you didn't head back this way for several hours that day. Is that a normal trip for you to make on a Wednesday afternoon during work hours?'

Nothing from Kyle now.

'When did you find out about her?'

Nothing.

'You killed your own sister,' Ryker said. 'Why?'

No answer.

'Does your father know? Did he ask you to do it? Because unless you say otherwise, that's exactly where this investigation is headed. He'll be finished if—'

'No!' Kyle said. 'He didn't know. He thought the sun shone out of her fucking ass, even after all the misery she'd put our family through.'

'Kyle, you killed your sister.'

'It wasn't like that!'

'Then what was it?'

'All I ever did was protect my family.'

'Like when you rammed Craig Boswell off the road, all those years ago?'

Kyle growled at that but didn't deny it.

'I gave her the choice,' he said. 'Told her she needed to finish it. I had no idea what she was doing for them, what they were planning. How could I?'

'And?'

'And she flat-out refused. She hated me. Hated all of us, even though we'd only ever wanted the best for her. She was a terrible, spoiled brat.'

'So you taught her a lesson? One final, deadly lesson.'

'Actually, no. She tried to attack me.'

'But you killed her.'

'I didn't want to! I didn't... mean to.'

'And then you drove the body out into the wilds.'

'Yes!' he shouted. 'Yes.' He was trembling now. Fear, but also some sort of relief, as though he'd been burdened by what he'd done. He wasn't a natural born killer. He was in way over his head. 'Given what she was doing... perhaps she didn't deserve any better. You killed to stop the White Lions, didn't you?'

A fair point. He stood up from the table when he spotted the flashing blue and red outside. Kyle didn't budge. Just stared at his coffee.

Ryker had no parting words before he headed out into the rain as the gaggle of GBI officers rode in, guns raised. Cindy met him outside. At least the rain had temporarily stopped, although the wind seemed even more vicious now, swirling around, debris flying, traffic lights bouncing.

'Just like you said,' she shouted.

'Yeah.'

'Don't look so disappointed,' she added. 'He murdered his sister. Probably Boswell too.'

Ryker got that. Kyle Hannigan had done two terrible things. But in a way... hadn't he done them for the right reasons? And his parting comment to Ryker... it had hit home. Because Ryker had killed a lot more people than Kyle Hannigan. Yes, he'd had orders that had allowed him to do that, and his own moral guidance meant he felt justified. But Kyle had justification too. He'd been against the White Lions and their aims all along. Perhaps if more people had taken such a strong stance—

Ryker was pulled from his thoughts when Kyle emerged from the diner, cuffed, his head down in shame as four GBI officers marched him away.

'Thank you,' Cindy said to him.

'Yep.'

Her face fell into a frown. Like she knew what he was thinking.

'I'll be tied up for a few hours,' she said. 'But... we could meet up later. Get a drink, maybe? We've got a lot to catch up on.'

'Yeah. Yeah, why not.'

'Unless... you have... Oh. You're done here, right? Is that it? You're leaving?'

He didn't answer. She spent a couple of seconds trying to keep her flapping hair out of her face.

'It's... a shame,' she said. 'I was hoping you'd stick around longer. We never really got to just... I don't know. Talk without the weight of the world on our shoulders.'

Ryker laughed. 'It's true. But... I think a lot of the time people like you and I put that weight there ourselves. I'm not sure I've ever lived any other way.'

'No. Me neither. But still... I'd really like you to stay.'

'You don't need me, Cindy. You've got this.'

He leaned over and pecked her on the cheek but before he could pull back she grabbed him and wrapped her arms around him and squeezed hard and he hugged her back. She broke off first, her eyes welling, although it could easily have been from the biting wind as from emotion.

'If you change your mind...'

He only nodded to her before she strode off after her colleagues. Seconds later Ryker was in his car driving away. Several minutes later he hit the junction for the freeway.

Right to go south to the airport.

Left to... not go there. Spend some more time here. With Cindy.

He sat at the lights for several seconds. Had noticed them go green but still didn't move until a cacophony of honks erupted from behind.

Decision finally made, he tugged on the wheel and headed on his way.

* * *

MORE FROM ROB SINCLAIR

Another book from Rob Sinclair, is available to order now here:
https://mybook.to/James15BackAd

ABOUT THE AUTHOR

Rob Sinclair is the million copy bestseller of over twenty thrillers, including the James Ryker series. Rob previously studied Biochemistry at Nottingham University. He also worked for a global accounting firm for 13 years, specialising in global fraud investigations.

Download your exclusive bonus content from Rob Sinclair here:

Visit Rob's website: www.robsinclairauthor.com

Follow Rob on social media here:

facebook.com/robsinclairauthor

x.com/rsinclairauthor

bookbub.com/authors/rob-sinclair

goodreads.com/robsinclair

ALSO BY ROB SINCLAIR

The Simon Peake Thrillers

Dead Reckoning
Deadly Mistake

Standalone Novels

Rogue Hero

Boldwood

Boldwood Books is an award-winning fiction publishing company seeking out the best stories from around the world.

Find out more at www.boldwoodbooks.com

Join our reader community for brilliant books, competitions and offers!

Follow us
@BoldwoodBooks
@TheBoldBookClub

Sign up to our weekly deals newsletter

https://bit.ly/BoldwoodBNewsletter

Printed in Dunstable, United Kingdom